SPEAKING TRUTHS

Dayna Hester

iUniverse, Inc.
Bloomington

iUniverse books may be ordered through booksellers or by contacting:

iUniverse
1663 Liberty Drive
Bloomington, IN 47403
www.iuniverse.com
1-800-Authors (1-800-288-4677)

Because of the dynamic nature of the Internet, any Web addresses or links contained in this book may have changed since publication and may no longer be valid. The views expressed in this work are solely those of the author and do not necessarily reflect the views of the publisher, and the publisher hereby disclaims any responsibility for them.

ISBN: 978-1-4502-1436-0 (sc)
ISBN: 978-1-4502-1437-7 (hc)
ISBN: 978-1-4502-1438-4 (ebook)

Library of Congress Control Number: 2010904692

Printed in the United States of America

iUniverse rev. date: 3/31/2011

dedicated to anyone who feels the pain …
and still knows how to love.

Acknowledgments

I want to thank *so many people* who have contributed to my sense of wholeness as a human being. I fear, though, that the longer the list, the larger the shadow becomes over the eight special souls who mean so much to me.

Bruce. You work hard to preserve our love, and you are successful in never letting my frustrations contaminate it. You are the smartest man I will *ever* meet.

Drew, Paige, and Whitney. Each of you has always been self-sufficient as I pursue my dreams but yet, without qualm, seeks dependence on me when you need a mother. I live in the best of two worlds wherein some say one must eclipse the other.

Mom, Dad, and Dad. You have given me the space to define, redefine, and define again our parent-child relationship. I see us as an evolution of beauty. I love all three of you.

Brittney. I like being your big sis. It makes me feel good.

Foreword

It always amazes me. You find great talent in the oddest of places.

I first met Dayna Hester socially - at a wedding, through a very dear friend. We spent the evening drinking and laughing. I never knew she was a writer. She mentioned she was working on something, and I'm sure I promised to look at it when she was finished, but it could have been anything. I assumed it was movie-related.

It wasn't until years later that she sent me a book to read. I was floored.

'Speaking Truths' is far more than a coming of age story. It is a lyrical and literate character study of Landon, a not-so-average high school junior who doesn't fit in. Constantly acting out in school, his incessant troublemaking provides a graphically effective foreshadowing that hints at much deeper levels of tragedy, especially when Landon is apprehended by the feds.

'Truths' sucks us in immediately. Hester does a superb job of placing the reader in the protagonist's shoes. When questioned by the FBI, Landon slowly pieces together the clues about his life, and soon we learn there are many types of truths. One truth is about the abusive man Landon lives with, Bob, who is very unfortunately not his father.

Author Hester now easily transforms Landon from problem child to sympathetic protagonist, one whose very sanity is on the line. When Landon's truths start to fully reveal themselves, we are completely engaged. And as Landon struggles to accept the truth about his life and attempts to transcend its tragic realities, 'Truths' has us by the throat.

It is marvelous to watch such a young writer so skillfully balance so many intriguing narrative tensions, and Bob's arrest by the FBI provides a startling pivot point. A later plot turn threatens to spin the story in a whole new direction, but not to worry, the author is in complete control, never forgetting what the soul of this piece is.

Shocking at times, but always imminently readable, 'Speaking Truths' is an authentic look into the pain and tribulation of what it is to be this troubled youth.

I simply could not put it down.

Nick Cassavetes
Los Angeles 2010

(1)

It had been three days since I showed up to English class. I hated school. I never fit in. Everyone stared at me like they're better than me. Maybe they were; I don't know. The kids were getting their folders out of their backpacks, which I forgot to bring. I leaned over to the cheerleader chick next to me to ask for a pencil, but that's when the teacher, Mr. Sanders, walked up with a slip of paper. "Landon, I'm sorry, but the office needs to see you." He put the paper in front of me on my desk. He was lying. It didn't say to go to the office. It was a hall pass to go see the guidance counselor.

"That's messed up. What the hell?" I bashed my fist against the desk.

Sanders leaned into me like what he had to say was just between us. "If you want to talk about it, let's go outside." There was a time when I thought he was cool. It was the first day of school. I learned on the second day that he was just another nerdy prick with leather loafers and khakis. That wasn't my style. My style was baggy jeans and a hoodie pulled down over my I-don't-give-a-fuck green eyes.

I looked around the class. Everyone was staring at me. Frozen. Mouths open with their jawbones unhinged. I had been in school with most of the kids since eighth grade because the hellhole village I lived in was so small that they crammed middle school and high school into the same building. I pulled my hoodie back to look Mr. Sanders in the eye. "No way. I came to class to fix things. You said I could make up my missed work."

"Go to the office and see if they'll help you, Landon. It's not up to me anymore." He was just looking for excuses. He wanted me out of his class.

The stupid, "Yes, Mommy and Daddy" kids just sat there with their blank faces like they'd never done anything wrong, especially the fat-ass slob who sat behind me. I turned my head to look at him. "What are *you* looking at?"

"Nothing." He jerked his head back so quick it made his double chin double again in size. I wanted to make a stupid joke, but then I got pissed off even more when I saw him look up, over my head, to Mr. Sanders. It was a coward move, like he needed a savior or something. That's what you found in Nebraska: cowards.

The more I looked around at everyone, the more I started thinking about how I knew they talked about me when I wasn't in class. I could tell I was gonna lose my cool, and I didn't care. I was sick of how they all thought they were so much better than me. When my eyes came back to the fat kid behind me, he was still looking up at the teacher. I leaned into him and dropped my voice. "Does your dad know what a coward you are?" That's when I felt Mr. Sanders's creepy pedophile hand grip my shoulder. "Landon, please. Don't disrupt the class."

I turned around. His bushy unibrow was right in my face. I jerked my shoulder away. "Get your hands off me. I'm done with this shit anyway." I tried to stand but my leg hit the desktop. It's not like I'm super-tall: barely six feet. I lost my balance and almost fell to the ground. That's when the pig-snout kid snickered like he's all that. My anger exploded. All I remember is flipping my desk over, grabbing a book, and ripping the pages out.

Why can't people understand me?

Next thing I knew, I was waiting for the guidance counselor's door to open. I stared at the crack at the bottom hoping to see when someone was walking toward the door to open it. The waiting thing was getting to me, though. It was giving me too much time to think. I started freaking myself out, thinking what Bob would do if he found out about my school screw-up. I had been unplugging the phone between six and eight o'clock every night when the school computer would call to say I had missed classes. Bob never asked about school or my grades, but if he found out I was in the guidance counselor's office …

My stomach started cramping. I couldn't stop pumping my foot up and down. I kept zipping and unzipping my hoodie, obsessing over how bad I needed to fix the mess I was in. The door opened. "Landon?"

I nodded. "Yeah," I murmured and threw in a smile. I'm sure it didn't look natural. I knew I was screwed.

"Come in." She held the door open like she was inviting a guest, and her I-want-to-help smile was as fake as her penciled-in eyebrows.

I stood. "Oh, thanks." I made my way past her.

Her room looked stupid, cluttered with "Teacher of the Year" fake apples and college pamphlet posters. The walls were plastered with thank-you cards from last year's graduating losers. I avoided the beat-up couch in the corner where I knew all the spoiled kids sat at lunchtime, talking about whose daddy would be spending the most on college tuition. I felt my anger creeping up, so I grabbed one of the wooden apples off her desk and started gripping it. I had to focus on getting my ass out of there without Bob finding out.

I saw her look down at my knuckles, turning white from squeezing the apple so hard. The red paint was chipping off onto my sweaty hands. She didn't say anything, though. I'm sure that's because my English teacher called in, telling her about how I threw my desk and shit. She probably didn't want me to blow up and start throwing stuff around in her little castle.

She cleared her throat. "Landon, do you know why you're here?"

I kinda wanted to have some fun and say, "To fill out my college applications?" but something told me sarcasm wasn't the right route. Instead, I lowered my voice and pulled back my hoodie. "Yeah. I've missed too many of my classes."

"You've missed twelve out of thirty school days, and your teachers are reporting that you haven't made any attempts to make up missed assignments."

"I don't know, I just—I mean, school's not for me, you know."

"But being in school is the law."

I came so close to telling tell her I don't give a fuck about the law—I never met an honest cop—but I bit my tongue. "Yeah, that's what my dad was saying."

"Your dad knows about your school situation?"

"I told him last night. I thought that when I got the note to come in here it was because my dad already talked to you." I was feeding her bullshit, but I knew it was what she wanted to hear. School people love to think you have parents who care.

"No, I haven't heard from your dad."

I shook my head. "Well, I know he's calling today to talk to you guys. He's pretty worried about my situation and stuff, you know." I had to choke back a laugh. Bob didn't give a damn about school. He only sent me because a truancy officer busted him for not having me enrolled.

"The only option for you to graduate with your class is if your father enrolls you in a continuation school. That will allow you to make up the credits that you need to graduate."

"So when can I come back to school?"

"If you make up the credits for the core classes—math, English, history—and then take summer school for the other credits, you can re-enroll in September for your senior year. You'll be able to graduate on stage and participate in the senior activities." She ended her speech with a smile, like she was offering an incentive to get my act together. I wanted to roll my eyes, but instead I said, "That's cool." She didn't know who she was talking to. I couldn't have cared less about the stupid senior stuff. They acted like that crap was for all the students, but I knew better than to think that I was really invited.

I don't belong.

I saw kids outside her window so I knew the final bell had rung. I realized then she had probably watched me walk by her window cutting class a thousand times yet had never bothered to come out and ask me what was going on. Of course now that her paycheck was on the line and she had to do the job she's paid for, she acted like she cared about my future. The whole school thing was just such a load of bullshit. If it weren't for Bob, I would have been doing my own thing.

She continued. "Landon, does your dad pick you up from school or do you take the bus?"

I almost gagged on my spit. The thought of Bob driving up to the school in his junky van was hilarious. "No, I usually take the bus. But, you know, he might be picking me up because he wants to talk to you guys."

"Well, if he does, have him come see me. Meanwhile, I'll keep trying to get a hold of him over the phone."

"Yeah, okay. I'll tell him." I couldn't believe she could be that stupid. To her credit, though, she was used to dealing with the goody-goody kids, you know. That's just not how Bob and I rolled.

"I'm sorry about this, Landon, but these are the rules."

"Oh, no, it's cool. You got to do what you got to do, right?"

"I wish you luck, and hopefully, we'll see you next year."

"I'm sure you will."

As soon as I got the sign that it was okay to leave, I was out the door. My mind started spinning about what I had to do next. My plan was to unplug the phone in the bedroom. Then I'd let the battery drain on the cordless phone and put a piece of clear tape over the metal part so it wouldn't charge in the cradle. The next morning, I'd leave like I was going to school. But most importantly, I'd make sure Bob had a twelve-pack in the fridge when he got home from work.

I didn't go back to my locker. Didn't matter; I forgot the combination on the third day of school. Anyway, I wanted to leave everything about me behind. In a weird way, it was that thought that made me calm inside and brought me the confidence to know that I'd figure it all out.

(2)

It was my job to clean the trailer before Bob got home. Our trailer was small, like if you had to hitch it up to a truck and take off, you could do it in an hour or so. We couldn't do that, though, because Bob took the wheels off a couple of years earlier and jacked it up on cement blocks. And also, the trees around the trailer were overgrown so much that you couldn't see it when you first drove onto the property. We were stuck.

It usually only took me about fifteen minutes to clean out the ashtrays, pick up the beer cans, make our bed, and clear the counter in the bathroom. The kitchen trashcan, though, always filled up quick with the throwaway plastic trays from our microwave meals. Looking at the dried-up food scraps from the night before reminded that because I didn't have school, I'd have to figure out how I was gonna eat lunch. I didn't have to worry about that before because I was on the free-lunch program. Honestly, that's why I stayed at school most days: to eat.

I started obsessing about how the stupid-ass school pissed me off. I mean, I was there every day, and I always planned on going to my classes. It's just that I'd stop by the metal shop to smoke a bowl with Sam and the guys. I could've gone to class high, but I didn't think the teachers would find it cool. So instead, I'd wait for my buzz to wear off, get my free lunch, and go to afternoon classes. If the school didn't screw around and put the class schedules on rotation, starting every day with a different first period, I would have only been dropped from my first and second classes, and Sam said he had connections to get me enrolled in the double-period metal shop. That way, I could have kept up my credits. It all would have worked fine if the school hadn't ruined it. *God, I hate them.*

I also hated taking the trash out. I talked Bob into letting us get one of those big trashcans for the kitchen that you put in front of the house so I didn't have to empty it all the time. Of course there it was, spilling over with shit. *What else could go wrong?*

I looked at the clock. I knew Bob would be home in about an hour, so I clasped the lid on the trashcan, dragged it outta the kitchen, across our dirty living room carpet, out the trailer door, and down the plywood steps. Funny, it sounds like a long way, but it was really only like fifteen feet. What *was* a long-ass way, though, was that I had to haul the trashcan up to the main house on the property to empty it.

One time, when we first moved into the trailer, I tried balancing the trashcan on my skateboard and pushing it up to the main house, but it fell over on me. There were maggots crawling all over the food scraps. I puked inside the can before I got the courage to pick all the shit up. I learned from that mistake to just latch the lid and drag it.

The lady who owned the property, Evelyn Barker, let Bob and me move in when she hired Bob to be a ranch hand for her dairy farm. But then, like two years after that, I guess the dairy farm went bankrupt or something, and she got rid of all the cows and illegal workers. The place was deserted for a long time until she had someone plant corn. Bob still did some small repairs and stuff for her on the weekends if he didn't have a plumbing job. I'm sure that's why she let us stay in our shit-hole.

I got the trashcan emptied and put back in the kitchen. That's when I figured everything was ready for Bob, but I was never positive about that. I had this checklist in my mind of the stuff I had to do before he would get home, but even though I would run through the checklist in my mind, I would also have to actually go … look … and make sure I did it. *I'm stupid that way.* Sometimes I'll think I got everything done and then remember, "Oh, shit, I didn't do that." And I knew I couldn't afford to set Bob off with all the school crap going on.

When I was sure everything was done, I decided to kick back for a while, have a cigarette, and listen to this iPod that Sam gave me that morning. I was sure he had jacked it from this rich snob in fourth grade who had moved in down the street from him. He gave it to me without the charger and it had downloaded Disney Channel songs. I didn't care, though. I just thought it was cool to feel the headphones in my ears, like everyone else walking around with iPods.

I finished my cigarette and went to throw the butt outside. That's when I caught sight of Bob's headlights flashing through the tree openings. The driveway onto the property was about a quarter of a mile long. Just long enough to let my gut tighten and tangle up at the first sign of Bob's headlights. It was the suspense: you never knew what kind of mood he'd be in.

I decided to hide the iPod behind the television because Bob didn't always react too good to new stuff. I bent down to hide it, and when I stood up, my head knocked against the gun rack. The gun on the bottom almost fell out, but I caught it.

Bob had the biggest hunting rifle collection you ever saw. That's how he made extra cash, refurbishing rifles. Some were basic refurbs, like the wood needed to be sanded and re-stained. Or like one time some guy gave Bob a Burnside Breech-Loading rifle from the Civil War to restore. It was all rusty and dinged up when we picked it up from the post office. It took Bob three months to fully refurbish it; I got to help. On the weekends, we drove all over to get the parts. When it was done, the guy wanted Bob to send it back in the mail, but Bob said the gun was too special to do that. We drove twelve hours to hand-deliver it. It was a beauty. I always knew Bob was in a good mood when he started up a conversation with, "Remember the Burnside refurb, Landon?"

I heard the engine power down; the headlights dimmed to nothing. My eyes were glued to the gun rack, making sure I got everything back in place. I counted to three as I really stared at the rifles, making sure they were all in their place. *I needed our evening to go right.*

I could hear his footsteps. Bob wore these black work boots that crunched over the leaves as he walked up to the front door. That was actually my favorite thing about autumn: the leaves covering the ground made it so I could hear Bob coming. One thing you don't want is to have Bob sneak up on you. I've had it happen before—*not good.*

The metal trailer front door flew open. "Hey, kid."

"Hey, Dad."

"Grab me a beer."

"You got it." I bolted for the refrigerator.

He turned around in the doorway and sat on the threshold facing outside so he could take off his work boots. His hunched-over chest filled the space of the open door. Like, even if I wanted to, or had the courage to, I couldn't have stepped around him to get outside. And it wasn't that his chest was pumped up with muscles, either. It was more like he was a big guy and made bigger from his twelve-pack-a-day habit.

Once he got off his boots, he placed them on a paper grocery bag by the refrigerator just inside the front door. Bob always said his boots were too muddy to wear in our filthy house, which made me laugh to myself. *Nothing was too dirty for our trailer.*

I slammed the fridge door, popped the lid on his first beer, and held it out so it would be the first thing he grabbed when he shut the door behind him. The sound of his first gulp told me the evening would go smoothly.

(3)

I never went to sleep before Bob. I hated it, though, when Bob would fall asleep in his recliner, because I didn't know if he was asleep for good, or if he'd get up and make us go to bed. *Together*. It was always a toss-up—unless it was a heavy drinking night, which meant we would stay wherever he had his last drink.

Whenever we did sleep in the living room, I basically never fell into a heavy sleep. My dreams were always about regular life stuff. That's probably another reason I missed so many classes, but I would never try to tell Bob that. And it wasn't his fault, anyway, that I didn't sleep right. I was just too tall to fit on the small trailer couch.

That night was for sure a recliner chair night. Bob started in with shots of Jack Daniel's right after dinner, and soon he was laid out flat, snoring, with the television blaring. I started to settle in on the couch but remembered about the iPod I hid. I got up quietly to get it from behind the television, and that's when I saw my friend Sam standing outside our trailer. He was jumping up and down to get my attention.

Sam was the only person I'd ever had over to my house. The only reason I felt comfortable with him is because his home life was worse than mine. His mom had some kind of pain illness, so she popped Vicodin all day. She never knew where Sam was and stayed in bed except for when it was the first of the month. That's when her food stamps came, and she needed to sober up enough to sell them for cash so she could buy cigarettes and beer. Sam's dad was worse off. He was doing life in prison over in Lincoln. He had been gone since Sam was ten. The summer before, he wrote Sam and said that it would be better if Sam stopped having contact with him. Sam said it was no big deal because he only heard from him like twice a year. I didn't think it was cool, though. It made me so upset that I actually asked Bob how a dad could do that. He said, "Out of sight, out of mind." I didn't think that was the best explanation, but it made sense.

And I guess Sam's dad felt that what was best for his son was to force him to go find another father.

Sam wouldn't stop jumping up and down, waving his hands for me to come out. I figured he probably wanted to talk about the school thing. I looked over at Bob, dead asleep with the remote control half slipping out of his hand. I looked back at Sam and gave a nod.

In the spare room of the trailer, there was a hatch that you could exit from. The trailer was lifted up on the blocks high enough so that if you dropped down through the hatch you could crawl out to the front without getting dirty. There was no way I was going out the front door. You could shoot out every window in our trailer and if Bob's in a Jack Daniel's sleep, he won't budge—but the second a door lock clicks open, *Bob's there.*

When I got out front, Sam was pacing back and forth, pumping his fists like he had to take a piss. He didn't stop pacing when I said, "Hey, what's up? How did you get here?"

"Dude, are you seriously kicked out of school?"

I saw his bike leaned against the trailer. "Yeah, but I'm still riding into town on the school bus. My dad hasn't found out so I gotta act like I'm still going to school. What's up?"

"He's gonna kick your ass if he finds out, huh?" Sam had seen my black and blue bruises before, and he knew by my puffy eyes to never ask me on the bus what happened the night before. Of course he was right about Bob kicking my ass. But still, the good thing about bruises is that they fade … and so do the memories. "What's up, Sam? Why did you ride out here?"

"I was calling but you didn't answer."

"That's because of the school thing. I unplugged the phone. What's up?"

"Well, dude, get this. You know Craig, right, the guy my mom's been seeing? He got me a connection with his dealer over in Madison."

"That's cool."

"But the thing is, I gotta go see him tonight."

"How?"

"Can we take your dad's van?"

"Madison is way the hell out there. No way. We'd have to drive on the 91." Taking Bob's van out wasn't anything new, but we only drove over to see Sam's friend who lived in downtown Leigh, right on Finch Street.

"Landon, c'mon, you gotta come through for me. Craig hooked it up with the guy to sell me a half ounce, and he gets his shipment tonight."

"Man, whatever. You don't have any money."

"No, I know, but he's gonna let me trade him my mom's prescription for it."

"No way. You took her Vicodin?"

"Yeah. So, dude, I told him I'd come tonight. I gotta go tonight."

"Won't your mom know you took her pills?"

"Are you kidding? You've seen her. She's got like six different doctors writing the prescriptions. She only knows how many she has when she's close to running out. And if she sees they're missing, she'll just call the pharmacy and say she accidentally spilled them. But dude, listen, I already have half of the weed sold. I'll make enough to buy another twenty-sack, and I can keep half for myself—well, I mean I'll give you some, too. But Landon, c'mon. I need a ride. We gotta take the van."

"I don't know, Sam. We've never driven on the highway with the van."

"It'll be for only like four miles. What the hell? Don't pussy out."

"But I'll get the shit kicked out of me if my dad finds out."

Sam snorted. "How's he gonna find out, huh? And if he does, you can tell him about the school shit and get everything over with at once."

That was kinda funny. He was right, though. We had taken Bob's van out before. And I was sixteen, even though I hadn't started driver's education because you have to pay for it.

Sam was getting antsy. "Landon, dude, this isn't cool. I get you high all the time, and you don't pay for shit. C'mon. Craig's dealer says I gotta come tonight or forget it. I'll split my own stash with you, the half I'm keeping for myself. Please!"

The only reason I started thinking about doing it was because I wanted everything I'd gone through that day to leave my mind. Bob was out cold and, honestly, I really needed to relax. "I don't know, Sam. We'd have to push the van away from the trailer. Why can't Craig take you?"

"Then he'll want a cut. I came to you—I offered it to *you*, dude. If you go, you can meet Craig's dealer. That way he'll know that you're cool with everything. You owe me, don't you?"

"Yeah, but," I sighed, knowing I was probably gonna give in, "Bob better not find out."

"Go get the keys. C'mon." He was begging. "It's only gonna take thirty minutes there and back, Landon."

"All right, whatever." I didn't think about it. I just did it. And pushing the van down the dirt driveway really sucked. I still didn't have a handle on how the steering wheel goes the opposite way when the car goes backward, but whatever. I wanted to prove to Sam I was a good friend.

(4)

I'd never been that high. I couldn't keep myself on one thought. I wanted to keep thinking about meeting Craig's dealer. He called himself D-Dawg and was talking about how he just moved to Madison from Lincoln, and that he still mailed the kush to his smaller dealers back at his old place. He was expanding his business to our area, and he was super-cool with knowing that Sam would be selling at Clarkson High School. He was tripped out with skull tattoos and piercings at the back of his neck like he was a reptile. When my high started kicking in, I got really paranoid because I kept finding myself staring at him when he wasn't talking to me. He was paying Sam respect and telling him how the future deals would go down.

When Sam and I walked into his apartment—actually, it was a room in the back of this beat-up, old house—D-Dawg took the Vicodin pills from Sam right away and tested them somehow. It was like a cashier checking for fake money. He said half the kids that bring in their parents' meds tried to fool him with sugar pills. I knew Sam wouldn't do that; the deal meant too much to him.

As soon as we left D-Dawg's, all Sam could talk about was how he was gonna be on the map as the best weed supplier at school. I felt really happy for him. That's crazy to hear me even say that, you know, for me to be happy for someone. I don't know why, but I'm always around fucked-up people who hate their lives. But whatever, in that moment, sitting in Bob's van, I didn't want to start thinking about sad shit. Sam was driving really good, and I just wanted to kick back and relax riding shotgun.

I started to listen to this song that Sam's iPod was playing. He brought one of those cords that plugged into the radio so he could play his music on the van stereo. I started laughing to myself, comparing Sam to Bob behind the wheel. I could tell Sam was being really careful. He kept looking in the rearview mirror. Then he slowly reached over with his right hand and grabbed his backpack that had the weed in it. I remember thinking to myself, *I bet he feels like he's on top of the world.*

I sensed that my eyes were barely open, and I knew I couldn't make them open any wider even if I really tried. I started to laugh. "Dude, this shit is so good. You're gonna have a line out of the metal shop to buy blunts." Then my thoughts shifted again, but it was all good. "Oh man, I don't know what the hell I'm thinking about. I can't even fo—"

"Just shut up. All right?" Sam kept leaning forward, looking in the side mirror and readjusting the rearview. He turned off of Highway 91, onto one of the side streets near his friend's place in Leigh. For a second, I thought maybe he was going to make his first sale, but then that thought left my mind and the next one floated in. My words flowed out before I knew I was talking. "Dude, Sam, listen, can you believe we pushed this stupid van all the way down the driveway?"

"Landon, I'm serious. Dude, shut up. I gotta focus."

"What? Whazzat mean, you gotta focus? You're driving fine. You drive better than Bob." I started cracking up, thinking about how Bob gets pissed off at everyone on the road, starts cussing, and winds up tailgating. People flip him off left and right. I don't know how he got a license to begin with. The DMV should have kicked his ass out when he asked for one. Half the stuff I was thinking, I started wondering if I was talking out loud about. Then because I had to wonder that, I started laughing.

"Dude, shut up. Stop laughing." Sam was trying to be so serious. But I couldn't. The thought of not laughing made me laugh more.

"Fuckin' hell, Landon, get serious. We're gonna be screwed if you don't stop."

"What do you mean?"

And then it all happened so fast. Sam pulled over in front of some random house, left the engine running, hopped out with the backpack of weed, and acted like I was dropping him off at home.

"Sam, dude, what are you doing?" All he did was wave as he walked up to the house acting like he lived there. I was dazed. I started to yell out to him, but then I saw the cop car. It slowly cruised by. I thought about leaving the van and following Sam, but I knew that would look weird. The van was idling, its headlights illuminating the house that Sam was walking up to. The cop hit his brakes and slowed down. He didn't stop, though.

My heart was racing and my buzz disappeared. I hopped in the driver's seat so it would look like I was taking off. Then the cop turned the corner and was out of sight. I took a few breaths trying to calm down. I knew

Sam wasn't coming back. The dashboard clock said 1:28. I hit the steering wheel with my fist as hard as I could. I muttered aloud, furious at myself. "Damn it! Why the hell did I let Sam talk me into it?" I kept repeating over and over in my mind, *I hate myself. I'm so stupid.*

I started thinking about Bob waking up to go to the bathroom and seeing I wasn't on the couch asleep. I had been gone with the van for more than an hour and a half. I started to get jittery, overcome with a feeling like I just had to get home right that minute. Then I thought, *What if the cop was just going around the corner and would be back any second?* If I was still sitting in the van, he'd probably want to know what was up. I put the van into drive and took off.

I knew how to get back to the trailer by the side streets. I was close enough to home that I even thought about leaving the van and letting Bob think it was stolen, but then I relaxed. I was the one who drove us to D-Dawg's. I knew I could drive home. I just kept focused on the yellow line in the middle of the road. "It's cool," I kept breathing to myself. "I'm almost home."

I unplugged Sam's iPod cord from the lighter charger. I was going over in my mind everything I had to do to make sure Bob wouldn't know I had taken the van, and that's when the red lights came on. I tried to act like I didn't see the cop, but he came on the loud-speaker telling me to pull over.

My mind was spinning. I wasn't thinking about the stupid cop, though. I was thinking about Bob. I thought about gassing it, taking off, running the van into a ditch, and then trying to get away. Instead, the coward part of my brain slowly pulled the van to the side of the street. I just sat there in the driver's seat with my eyes closed and my forehead on the steering wheel. I couldn't believe what was happening.

"Step out of the car." The cop used his flashlight to knock at the window. The police lights were flashing like a red strobe and his spotlight blinded me when I turned my head toward the rear of the van. "Step out of the car. Let's go."

I started to roll down the window. "I didn't do anything wrong, officer. I just dropped my friend off, and I'm almost home."

I could tell he was getting irritated. "Get out of the car, son. Now."

I went to open the driver door and step out but the van rolled forward. I hadn't put it in park when I stopped because the cop lights scared the shit out of me. That pissed the cop off. I barely had enough time to throw it into park when he yanked me out of the van and threw me onto the cruiser's hood.

"What the hell? I can't drive around at night? I didn't do anything wrong." When I lifted my head off the hood, I could see into the cop car. I noticed someone sitting in the backseat. *He already busted Sam.* "Fuck!" That's all I could say.

"Are you sure you didn't do anything wrong, son?" He pushed my head back down onto the hood. The heat of the idling engine warmed my cheek. The cuffs went on. His hands searched all my pockets, around my waist, up my crotch. I couldn't stop my words. "What the hell? Don't be an asshole. I wasn't doing anything wrong."

A second cruiser showed up and stopped in the middle of the street. They acted like they were so cool, like they were going to hold up traffic or something, but the streets were dead. All the streets in Leigh are dead, even during the daylight hours.

The cop that had me pinned down leaned forward. "Your friend already told us everything. You have anything you want to add?"

"There's nothing to tell. Let me go already." The cops think they're so smart, but like I'm going to believe my friend could just rat me out like that. That's when the second cop got out of his car and walked over to the jerk who handcuffed me. He held up Sam's backpack that had the weed in it. "They stashed it in a trashcan."

I raised my voice. "What do you mean, 'they'? I didn't get out of the van with him. What the hell?" They just ignored me, though, and kept me slammed against the hood. I was yelling for Sam to tell them the truth when the second cop said, "Take a look at this," and he pulled out a small handgun from the front pouch of Sam's backpack.

"I didn't know anything about that. I swear!" I was yelling to Sam, "Tell them! Tell them it's not mine!"

The first cop slammed my head into the hood even harder, shutting me up. "We'll see what you have hidden in the van, son."

"No, dude, I swear. I was just giving him a ride. It's not even my van."

He yanked me off the hood, and I knew then he was gonna put me in the second cop car. I tried to fight, kicking and yelling. "You can't do this. It's illegal. I was just driving him home. I was giving him a ride. Ask him." It took both cops to get me in the back of the car. I was kicking like crazy. The seats and flooring were a big piece of plastic. I was still kicking when they shut the door. Then I fell on my side with the cuffs on and my hands behind my back. I couldn't get my balance to sit up and see what they were doing inside Bob's van. All I knew was that I was screwed, and it wasn't because I was going to the police station. It was because they weren't going to keep me there. The only thought running through my head was that maybe, just maybe, they wouldn't be able to get a hold of Bob. He didn't know I had unplugged the phone so he wouldn't plug it back in. And maybe, just maybe, they'd release me by morning so I could clear all the shit up before Bob found out.

(5)

I was still high when I thought that they might release me without Bob finding out—because that was a dumber-than-dumb idea. Of course it didn't happen. The registration in the van led them right to Evelyn Barker's property, and that led them to Bob.

I was released from the Schuler Police Department around five in the morning. Schuler was the village where all the holier-than-thou "educated" people lived. The cop at the front desk told me I was lucky, and that they did Bob a favor by not towing his van. I didn't say "thanks" because I hated giving the cops any credit, but honestly, he was right. Bob kept his plumbing kit in the back of the van, and the thought of him waking up and not being able to go to work twisted my gut into knots. I've seen Bob out of work and out of money before. It's basically impossible to please him at that point—might as well not even try.

The cop at the counter gave me my court date and buzzed me out into the lobby. When I walked toward Bob, he wouldn't look me in the eyes. That wasn't a good sign. He kept his head down so that long strands of silver hair fell over his face. Before I even reached him, he stood up, walked to the exit door and pushed it open. I followed silently.

When Bob's that mad, the best thing to do is walk two steps behind him, and if he decides to talk, take a big leap forward so you don't miss a word. I learned that lesson when I was younger and a lot shorter. I was trying to keep up with Bob's long strides and answered him with a "Huh?" because I wasn't sure if I heard him right. He responded with a backhanded swipe across my mouth and told me that would clean out my ears. It did— the message came through loud and clear: when Bob speaks, listen.

I stood at the passenger door of the van until Bob unlocked it for me. I knew better than to speak yet. Instead, I just got in and waited, staring straight ahead. Bob always said real men stand tall in the face of punishment. I wasn't that strong, though. There were so many times when the coward inside me wanted to cry out how bad I screwed up and let him know, *I'll never do it again. Please. Please believe me. I'm sorry. I'm really, really sorry.* But an attitude like that doubled the punishment with Bob. So I pulled my hoodie back, lifted my chin, sat up in the passenger seat, and waited for a sign that would indicate what was on Bob's mind.

Once we got out of Schuler and on the highway back toward Leigh, Bob turned on the radio. I wanted to sigh in relief; it meant he was going to handle my arrest better than I thought. That's also when I knew it was okay to talk, so I lit into it right away, talking shit about the cops. There was no response, but that doesn't mean anything with Bob. I knew I was saying the right thing. Hating the cops was one thing, maybe the only thing, Bob and I had in common. The whole way back to the trailer, I shot my mouth off as fast as I could, saying everything I could think of to prove to Bob how alike we were. He just kept his eyes on the road and let the music play.

We pulled up to the trailer. He turned off the van and continued looking straight ahead. I did exactly the same thing, keeping watch on him just out the corner of my eye. I sure as hell wasn't getting out of the van before him. We sat there in silence for a long time, long enough that I started to feel my heartbeat speed up. I'm not gonna lie; that's when things can get scary with Bob. I sometimes worried I might stop breathing and then pass out, but I just tried to keep my breathing steady and wait for him to gimme a sign.

Some motion caught my eye. Bob was turning his head toward me. I looked his way. He started to speak, and I swear it was like he was talking in slow motion. "Landon, I have something for you."

"What's that?"

He didn't answer me with words. Instead, he leaned forward, reached under the driver's seat and pulled out the nine millimeter handgun that sat on our nightstand. He cocked it and pressed it to my left temple. "You shouldn't have fuckin' let the cops catch you."

I always tried to nod just the tiniest bit when he put a gun to my temple. It's like you have to let him know you hear him, but at the same time, you're afraid that if you jerk your head too much his index finger might slip on the trigger. And to be honest, I knew what he was saying. Nothing good can come out of being around the cops. Some parents threaten to ground or spank their kids; this was Bob's way of getting my attention … and it did.

He pulled the gun away and let it rest on his lap. "I need to cut back on my drinking. This wouldn'ta happened if I was with it a little more. Things woulda gone differently. I've gotta fix stuff."

I shook my head, just once. "No, it's my fault. You're doing the best you can. I screwed up. I let Sam talk me into it. I need to be a leader, like you're always saying. I'm not gonna hang around him anymore. You watch, I promise." I tried not to let my voice sound panicked, but the thought of Bob not drinking was worse than being cuffed and slammed into that cop car.

I could see Bob's body relax a little. His shoulder blades hunched forward. "You remind me of myself when I was younger, kid."

I tried to smile. I couldn't look him in the eye, though. I mean, I tried to agree with some of the stuff that Bob said, but deep down I knew I wasn't anything like him. My eyes fell to the gun on his lap. I tried to pick the right words. "Just give me another chance. Let me show you I'm gonna change. I can prove it to you."

He popped the clip out of the gun, blew into the hollowed part where the clip fit, and jammed it back into place. That sound, the sound of the clip locking into place, automatically made every single muscle from the bottom of my spine all the way up to my neck tense up, no matter how many times I had heard it. I watched Bob's lips move. "I'm sorry that I'm the one to tell you this, kid, but you're not worth second chances. The one thing I tried to teach you is to get it straight the first time. But you don't listen, do you?" He spat on the dashboard, jumped out of the van, and slammed the driver-side door shut.

I released my breath as I slowly opened the van door to follow him inside. I wasn't sure if the loaded gun to my temple was the end of my punishment.

(6)

"Landon, go to bed." Bob was sitting in his recliner, trying to make good on his promise to cut back on drinking. It wasn't a promise I wanted.

"What? No, I'm awake." I wasn't, though. It was only nine o'clock, but between the police station bullshit the night before, and then trying to fake a school day when I didn't have one, I was exhausted. I readjusted myself on the couch and tried to keep my left eye open, the one on Bob's side, and let the other one shut.

"Landon, you're falling asleep. Go to bed." There was something kind of sad in Bob's voice. I figured it was because he didn't have the Jack Daniel's flowing through his veins. Bob and sobriety don't mix. He had this angry side to him, like the world was out to get him, and if something set him off, he was gonna take care of it—sober or drunk. But I learned early on that if he's drunk, I could get him sidetracked by agreeing with him and telling him I saw the world through his eyes.

And anyway, I wasn't too worried about his mood. I looked over to the half-filled bottle of Jack on the kitchen counter. I was sure it was only a matter of days until the top came off again. His "cutting back" on the drinking always followed the same pattern: something crazy would happen, like me getting arrested; he'd vow not to touch the hard stuff and only stock up on beer; a few days would pass; by the end of the week, he'd be back to shooting whiskey chasers during TV commercials.

When we first moved into the trailer, back when it was a dairy farm, Bob used to hang out with the workers. Most of them were from Mexico, and they left their families to come work in the United States. They lived on the property in what Bob called "the army barracks." I went inside them a couple of times. They were these half-circle metal buildings filled with bunk beds. They didn't have indoor bathrooms because there were only three places with running water on the property: up at the milking barn;

the main house, which was off limits; and our trailer. That's how I met Jandro, one of the workers. He knew enough English to tell Bob what the workers needed or what needed to be fixed, and to joke with me. I was his *el niño leche.*

Bob started taking Jandro and a couple of the guys into town on paydays to make a tequila run. When they'd get back, everyone would sit around on plastic milk crates in front of our trailer, and Bob would build a bonfire. One time, one of the workers got up to use our bathroom, which wasn't a big deal because everyone was kinda relaxed about going in and out of the trailer. I was twelve at the time and the memory plays in slow motion. Through the window, Bob saw the guy who was using our bathroom stop to touch one of his rifles on the gun rack above the television. In a split second, Bob lost it. I was standing at the front door, inside the trailer, looking at the guy holding the rifle. He was wobbling back and forth, so drunk that he couldn't hear what was going on outside.

Bob jumped to his feet, pulled out the nine millimeter that he kept tucked in his belt when he's home, and started pointing it at everyone around the fire. It's weird what a gun does to people. I saw one or two of the workers run away, not afraid of being shot in the back. The rest, though, put their hands up and shook their head, saying words in Spanish that Bob didn't understand—I could tell that was making him angrier. I saw the beads of sweat dripping from their foreheads. I wondered whether it was from the flames flaring up out of the fire pit or because of Bob's drunken index finger on the trigger.

I backed into the kitchen as I saw Bob wobbling his way toward the opened front door of the trailer. I was pinned against the refrigerator, my eyes frozen on the gun. Bob stumbled up the stairs into the trailer. I was positive that he'd trip over the last step and the gun would go off.

Bob yelled out to the worker, "Put my fuckin' gun down! Now!" only he was so drunk that his sentence slurred into one unidentifiable word. The worker turned around, not because he understood Bob, but because he heard the footsteps. His eyes widened and he started mumbling something in Spanish as he backed into the wall. I just prayed that he wasn't thinking about running away.

Then suddenly a hand grabbed mine, yanking me out of the trailer behind Bob's back. It was Jandro. He wrapped his arms around me to hold me still and put his hands over my ears. I could smell the tequila on his breath and felt the sweat through his T-shirt. My heart pounded in my ears. I tried with all my strength to break free, but Jandro kept holding onto me. From where I was, I could only see the back of Bob's feet standing inside the trailer. I couldn't scream for fear that Bob might turn around and think I was trying to run away. I knew Jandro didn't understand what he was doing, but he was holding me so tight, I could barely squirm. He was patting my back, thinking it would calm me down; it just made things worse. Tears started streaming down my face. I kept my eyes glued to Bob's heels, praying he wouldn't turn around, wondering where I was.

The gun went off.

I heard Bob's laugh, a belly-laugh from the bottom of his gut.

The worker holding the rifle bolted out of our trailer. Jandro's eyes followed the worker, confused. His grip loosened. I squeezed myself free and ran into the trailer. There was Bob on the couch, laughing hysterically, and a bullet hole in the wall about a foot away from where the worker's head had been.

I looked out the living room window and the workers were gone—all of them, even Jandro. The dairy farm closed about six months later, but even before that, there were no more tequila runs, no more bonfires, and Bob drank only beer for three days after.

"Landon, go to bed. You can have the bed to yourself."

"No, it's okay. I'm fine out here."

"I'm telling you to do something. *Go do it.*" I bolted up before he said any more. I didn't want any part of what happened that morning after the police station to repeat itself.

"Wait," Bob commanded.

I stopped in my tracks and turned around to face him. "Yeah?"

He leaned forward in his recliner, making sure his nine millimeter and remote control balanced on his lap. He shook his head side to side slowly and looked over at me through the corner of his eye. "I try to help you do things with your life but you never see it. You don't take my advice. You think you're better than me somehow, don't you?"

"No, that's not true." My eyes darted over to the counter. The half-filled Jack Daniel's bottle was still untouched. A sober comment about life wasn't a good sign from Bob. I felt my palms sweating. "I know you try to help me. I just do stupid things sometimes, but I want to learn from what you —"

He turned his head and looked me straight on. "You were a mistake. One big mistake."

"What do you —" I caught myself, looked again at the whiskey bottle. I let my hands rest at my side, dropped my head, and relaxed my body, wanting to give him all the signs that I wasn't there to resist. I tried to pick my words to express the right thought. "I'm sorry, Dad. Maybe you can help me fix myself."

"Too late. You're too old now. And you're not worth it anyway." He turned his head back to face the TV. I stood for a second, waiting for any last words, but he didn't utter a sound. He leaned back in his recliner and focused on watching his war movie while the TV reflection flickered off his face. I was positive he'd be waking me up in a couple of hours to work out his aggression. *Maybe I deserved it.*

I was dead asleep. The first sound I heard, I think my brain just said, *There's a weird noise outside,* but I didn't fully wake up. I was too tired. It was some kind of swishing sound against the outside wall of the trailer. My arms and legs felt heavy. I was going right back to sleep when I heard the noise again and realized I knew exactly what it was.

Leaves.

Leaves crunching on the ground.

I threw the covers to the side and sat bolt upright. I thought my ribcage would burst because my heart was pounding so hard. I looked left; Bob wasn't there. The blankets were untouched. The gun wasn't on the nightstand. I jumped up, moved the blinds away just enough to see outside. *Flashlights?* Then a huge crashing sound came from the living room. I went to run down the short hallway toward the front door but froze in my steps as our trailer started to rock back and forth.

"Get on your knees! FBI!"

I dropped to the ground. The first sign I saw of them were the small lights attached to their rifles. Beams of lights swirled and bounced all over the walls. Two men in all black, with their faces behind their rifles, came down the hallway and grabbed me.

I was dizzy, confused.

I didn't see Bob. Or his gun.

The television was off.

The remote control was on the ground.

They held me under my armpits and rushed me out of the trailer. When we got outside, I saw FBI agents everywhere, criss-crossing in front of me. Most were dressed in black with knit caps, and a couple had a big "FBI" in white letters on their backs. All of them were holding rifles in firing position, like they do at the shooting range. I saw at least two guard dogs, the ones that sniffed out drugs. Through the trees, I caught a glimpse of car headlights driving up the dirt road. The headlights from a car in the back illuminated a cloud of dust that the lead cars had kicked up. A helicopter swooped down and hovered around the area. Its spotlight created a frantic sun shining on the trailer.

The two guys that had a hold of me were nothing like the cops who busted Sam and me. There was something serious about them that filled me with fear. "In here." I could barely hear them over the hovering helicopter. The night was a riot of sound: dirt swirling through the air smacked into the cars; the overgrown tree branches whooshed and clanked in the wind. The agent opened the back door of a black car parked nearby and put his hand on top of my head, pushing me down lightly to make sure I didn't hit myself on the door jamb. He shut the door. I wasn't kicking or squirming. I didn't have words for what was going on. I just stared as a huge spotlight powered up. The whole scene looked like daylight, except in the background the moon hung—suspended and still in the night sky.

As if on cue, the helicopter began to rise and banked away. One of the guys hopped into the front seat, nodded to me, dropped it into drive, and we were out of there. I turned around to look through the back window. I could see cars driving up to the main house. In the far distance, over the cornfields that used to be cow pastures, the helicopter spotlight roamed, zigzagging from side to side. I tried to compose myself and gather whatever information I could. I stared out, scanning for Bob's van, but between the dust and the dimming lights, the world I left had all but disappeared.

When the agent made a right turn onto Highway 91, I faced forward and dropped my head. I was detaching from my life, like a balloon let go in the sky, floating farther away each second. I wasn't that kid who walked into English class two days ago. I was terrified. Whatever was going on, it was larger than me. Yet a part of me knew it wasn't larger than Bob.

(7)

The car ride was endless. I don't know how I did it, but I fell back to sleep. I was totally out of it but started to wake up when the car stopped and started at intersections. The unmarked cop car wasn't a sports car, but I could tell it had some horses under the hood. When the agent stepped on the gas, the car *moved*.

I sat up and realized we were in Omaha. I had been to a gun convention there with Bob, maybe like six months before. It's a huge city but it seemed deserted, and then I figured it had to be close to three in the morning. I knew better than to ask the driver what time it was. I had tried earlier to ask a question, but the only response I got was that it was going to be a long drive and everything would be explained to me later. When "later" was, he didn't say.

We pulled into an underground parking garage. The driver turned in so quickly, I figured he probably worked there every day. Two guards standing at the bottom of the ramp waved us in. He pulled off to the left into what looked like a loading area, where a group of people were just standing around. I knew they were waiting for us. The driver got out and opened my door. One of the guys in the group, a black guy, was wearing a jacket and tie. The way he stepped in front of everyone told me he was in charge. He leaned forward, toward me. "Landon Starker?"

I swung my feet out and onto the ground. I was in the sweats and T-shirt I had been sleeping in. Socks, no shoes. I was used to putting my hands in my jeans and pulling my hoodie down over my eyes. As I ducked my head under the car doorframe, I was sure my brown curls were tangled from the few hours of sleep I had. I felt awkward so I just nodded. I don't know why, but the first thing that popped into my mind was that pig-snout kid behind me in English. He would have been crying if this were happening to him.

"I'm Agent Drysdale—Leon Drysdale. Why don't we head this way?" *I hate people who phrase commands as questions.* He put the palm of his hand on my back, like introducing himself automatically made us friends. I jerked my shoulder away, more out of habit than anything else, but he got the hint and took the lead about three steps in front of me. The rest of the group followed behind.

A security guard or FBI agent—whatever he was—opened the glass door to the lobby of the building as we were walking up. No one talked, just nodded, which made the sound of footsteps against the marble flooring echo in my ears like gunshots. I could sense them looking at each other behind my back. It felt like I was walking into English class again, but this was about a hundred times weirder. To make matters worse, I was still trying to shake the groggy feeling from falling asleep in the car.

The Drysdale guy took his FBI badge and swiped it over a black box on the wall by the elevator. The doors immediately opened, and he put his hand on the rubber of the open elevator door so it wouldn't close on me. "Go ahead, Landon. We're going upstairs to a briefing room. Nothing to be alarmed about." I stepped in. Drysdale and the driver agent followed.

The rest of the group just stood there, outside the elevator, looking stupid, except for this woman who shouldered her way forward and joined us. She was thin, with dark red hair and big brown eyes. She was tall, at least compared to the women I had met—teachers, Sam's mom, and the old lady up at the main house.

Agent Drysdale pushed the "Door Close" button. For a quick second, I made eye contact with the woman. She gave me a tight smile. You know, no teeth, like the ones you get from people who don't really want to talk when you say "hello." I don't know if I smiled back.

I saw Drysdale press the button for the fourteenth floor, and then he looked over at me. "We have some questions to ask you, but again, I don't want you to be too alarmed. Everything is going to be just fine."

As soon as the elevator doors started closing, reality hit. I relived how they rushed me out of the trailer, holding me under my armpits. How the wind from the helicopter was swirling the dirt everywhere, and it seemed like it was right over my head. How the agents held their rifles as if they were extensions of their bodies, and how they had intense control over every movement. I looked around the elevator.

I had no control.

I was theirs.

The elevator started feeling smaller and smaller, closing in on me.

I kept going over the events in my mind, trying to figure out how everything changed so quickly. Five hours ago I was falling asleep, planning how I would meet up with Sam to find out what his mom did about the arrest. When my brain settled on Sam, everything clicked into place. It had to be the handgun in Sam's backpack. I figured Sam had jacked it from Craig. That prick had probably used it in a robbery or something, and now the FBI was involved—I knew they automatically dealt with bank robberies and stuff. All this crap over a stupid gun that wasn't mine. But figuring it out kind of calmed me down, because I felt like I was gonna be able to fix things. And maybe it was good news that I hadn't seen Bob. Maybe he hadn't stayed away from the Jack Daniel's like he said he would, and so he had to leave to go get another bottle. That was good because he wouldn't be hassled with all the FBI bullshit at the trailer. Then another thought occurred to me. Maybe Sam was already there in the building, and we'd have the same story, and then I could leave.

I turned to Drysdale. "I didn't even know Sam had the gun. It's cool. I'll tell you guys everything you need to know. But I don't think you guys should have taken me like that. That wasn't cool."

Drysdale looked at me and lifted his eyebrow. "Sam?" He said it like a question, as if the name caught him off-guard. That's when I started to heat up, pissed off that they were playing games with me—just like the cops the other night.

The memory of not seeing Bob's gun on the nightstand popped into my head. And the fact that the television was off was weird. *If Bob was just running to the store, he would have left it on.* I couldn't picture Bob surrendering and getting in the back of an FBI car, at least not without blowing up our trailer first.

My mind then jumped to the idea that Bob would have to pick me up at the FBI building. I pictured him driving all the way to Omaha in his van, hunched over the steering wheel, cussing at me under his breath. I would never survive the ride home. This fog of fear dropped over me. I felt like I needed to run away, to flee. I had to find Bob—*no, I had to let Bob find me.* "I can't be here. You guys shouldn't have taken me. You need to take me back. I have to go back to the trailer."

"What?" Drysdale leaned forward to look me in the eye.

I couldn't focus on anything; my heart was pounding too hard. "You guys can't keep me here. Don't call Bob to pick me up. Just let me go." I started pacing in the elevator. Bob's second-chance warning repeated over and over in my head. "You guys gotta let me go. Nothing's my fault. You can't keep me here. Please, let me go!" I couldn't get the clicking sound of Bob's gun to stop echoing in my ears, and his words in the van that morning kept getting louder and louder. "You guys don't know what it's like for Bob to be mad. I'll talk to you guys, I swear, but just let me go. Please." I was begging.

Drysdale kept his voice calm and low. "Tell us how Bob gets mad."

"No, man, don't fuckin' play games with me. I gotta go. Let me go!" I tried to pry the elevator doors open. I saw the agent reach over and hold down the "Door Close" button. I freaked out worse than I had in English class. "No! I can't stay here." I felt the agent's free arm wrap around me. I started kicking, screaming. "You guys don't get it! I can't be here!" I couldn't move. He pinned my arms to my sides. The elevator doors opened. Tears streamed down my face as the agent half-pushed, half-carried me out of the elevator. "No, come on. Please! You gotta let me out of here. Whatever you guys want from me, take it, but I can't be here! Please!" My chest was burning, my head spinning. The world that I had worked so hard to patch together was ending, crumbling, all in the time it took to reach the fourteenth floor.

(8)

Drysdale and the agent left me in a cold room, totally bare except for plastic chairs, a metal table, and linoleum tiles. No clock. No openings to the outside world. There was just a huge black glass window on the same wall where the door was. I'm sure it was a two-way mirror. I felt like a wasted specimen in an observation lab. I took three of the plastic chairs and lined them up so I could lie down. The only soft thing in the room was a thin, worn-out blanket that gave no warmth. I wasn't comfortable. I wasn't sleeping; I didn't even try. What I was trying to do, though, was confront death. But I knew I wasn't that courageous. *I'm the coward that Bob says I am.*

The door opened, and I sat bolt upright. Drysdale walked in first, saying, "Landon, I'm sorry that you've had to wait so long without knowing what's going on. First off, this has nothing to do with your friend, Sam Ricksen."

I narrowed my eyes. "How'd you know his last name, then?"

He took a folder from under his arm and lifted it up in the air, gesturing toward me. I took it as a sign that everything he needed to know was in there. My eyes followed the folder as he set it down on the table.

The tall woman from the elevator came in after Drysdale and shut the door behind her—softly and silently. Her gentleness irritated me. I dragged one of the three chairs over to the table and took a seat across from Drysdale. The woman walked behind me and sat at the end of the table. I assumed she was Drysdale's secretary or something.

Drysdale didn't have his suit jacket on anymore and his tie was loosened. He had a holster on the side of his waist with a gun in it. I could tell the safety was on; Bob would have laughed about that. Drysdale's FBI badge dangled from his shirt pocket. He was younger in the picture, no curly gray hairs around the ears like he had in person. He put his open hand on top of the file. Didn't open it. "Your full name is Landon Bernard Starker?"

"Yeah."

Drysdale looked over at the woman. She looked back.

That was weird.

"Good. My intent here is to make this meeting as short and painless as possible. So I'll jump right into a few topics I'd like to know about tonight, and then tomorrow, we'll pick up where we left off."

"Tomorrow?"

"Yes, tomorrow."

I wanted to make a run for the door, but I knew there was no chance. There were probably ten guys with guns behind the two-way mirror. I thought about reaching for Drysdale's gun. *Another stupid idea.*

"Landon, are you with me?"

I turned back to Drysdale. "Huh?"

"I'm going to try to make our meeting here quick and to the point, so stay with me. I'd like you to talk to me about the trailer."

"Our trailer?"

"Yes. Who lives there with you?"

"Just my dad."

"You mentioned a Bob. Is that—"

"Duh. I mean, yeah, Bob." My intestines started to spasm but the feeling went away. I was too exhausted for overreactions.

"So only the two of you?"

"What?"

"Was it only you and Bob living in the trailer?"

How many times was he going to ask? "Yeah. Who else would be there?" Drysdale and the woman exchanged looks again. I added, "Why am I here? I think maybe you guys have the wrong person. Are you asking about the lady that lives up at the main house?"

Drysdale responded right away. "No, I have the right person, Landon. But you bring up a good point. Let me confirm what I know about you. You're a junior at Clarkson High School. Or, actually, you were until they kicked you out for cutting too many classes." I shrank into myself, molding my back into the plastic chair as he continued. "You and Bob moved into the trailer about a month before eighth grade started, which would have been a little over four years ago. Is that right?"

"Yeah, I guess."

"Before the trailer in Leigh, where we found you tonight, is it true you lived in an apartment in Coleridge, Nebraska?"

I nodded.

"Is that a yes?"

"Well, I remember we used to live in Coleridge."

"Do you remember the apartment? I believe it's called a bungalow if that makes a difference."

I shrugged. When he said "Coleridge," a sidewalk leading up to a door flashed in my mind. "I just remember Coleridge, the town, you know."

"That's fine. And the lady at the main house that you just mentioned, you've met her before?"

"Yeah."

"Is her name is Evelyn Barker?"

"I guess."

"What does that mean?"

"Yeah, that's her name."

"And when you moved to Ms. Barker's property, who moved into the trailer with you?"

"No one. Just—you know, just—"

"Just you and Bob?"

"Yeah." I was trying to focus on Drysdale's questions, but for some reason, the boxes that we had in the spare room of the trailer popped into my head.

"What is it, Landon? What are you thinking about?"

"Your question. I mean, yeah, it was just us that moved into the trailer."

"To whom are you referring to when you use the word 'us'?"

"My dad and—I mean, Bob and me. It was the two—yeah, the two of us." I felt like I was babbling but couldn't stop. "We moved there, and my dad—well, Bob worked on the dairy farm—I mean, it was a dairy farm then and—"

Drysdale cut me off. "Let me ask you this: did anyone else live in the bungalow in Coleridge with you before Bob and you moved to the trailer in Leigh?"

"I just don't really remember being in Coleridge, you know. I was, like, only twelve then—yeah, maybe eleven." The boxes in the spare room of the trailer flashed in my mind again. They were cardboard moving boxes, and as long as I could remember being at the trailer, we always had them stacked in the spare room. I hadn't paid attention to them in so long that

I'd basically forgotten that they were there, even though I went into the spare room all the time to use the hatch or grab something for Bob, like his gun-cleaning supplies. It was weird that Drysdale's questions brought back thoughts about them. My muscles kept tensing up, and I couldn't relax. I hunched my shoulders and squinted, shaking my head like there was some kind of pain deep inside, and I wanted to shake it off—or, no, more like I wanted to keep it hidden.

"Landon, are you still with me?"

"Yeah, yeah. It's not that. I just … I don't know. Can't you tell me what's going on?"

"I will shortly. But first, going back to Coleridge, do you remember the Cordia Bungalows, the apartment that you lived in before the trailer?"

A feeling like the world was gonna end started coming over me. I saw Drysdale look over at the woman. She nodded in response. Drysdale then looked back at me. I shook my head again. The worried feeling wasn't leaving. "Why are you asking this stuff? This is weird."

Drysdale took a small breath and replied, "There were some items in the spare room of the trailer, and we want to know who they belonged to. So if you can, Landon, I'd like you stick with this line of questioning until we get that information."

I dropped my eyes and stared at the ground.

"Do you remember the Cordia Bungalows that you and Bob lived in before you made the move to the dairy farm in Leigh?"

I nodded. "I think so. Just a little bit. Like, I couldn't take you there." My eye started twitching, like it did when Bob's gun was at my temple. I knew the questions were going to start getting weirder. I hadn't thought about the bungalow in Coleridge or those boxes in the spare room for so long. I mean, I just never thought about why they were there, even though of course I couldn't help but see them when I went into the room.

Drysdale's voice broke in. "What are you remembering, Landon?"

"What? What do you want from me … I mean, jeez, that was a long time ago. Why …" I wanted Drysdale to stop causing me to think about the boxes or the bungalow in Coleridge. I tried to block out his voice by tightening the muscles in my ears. My body took control, rocking back and forth.

"Landon, are you with us here?" He leaned forward, moving closer to me. I couldn't look up. I tried to focus on a speck of dirt on the floor. I wanted to leave my body and get my mind out of the memories. "Landon, can you hear me?"

I slowly looked around the room. It was just us three. I nodded, slowly, and then the words came out. It was like I couldn't even control them. I knew Bob would make me pay for answering Drysdale's questions, but I just wanted everything to be over. I mumbled, "K.C. used to live with us at the bungalow. He wasn't there when I came home to the trailer." I lowered my voice to a whisper. Drysdale stopped the sound of his breathing so he could hear me. Tears welled up in my eyes, but I kept talking. "I didn't know what happened to K.C. I remember telling Bob I didn't know what happened to him."

Drysdale put a hand on the table. Calmly, he asked, "What did you think happened to him?"

I shrugged. I didn't want to think about that answer. I sat there, frozen.

"It's okay to talk about this, Landon."

But it wasn't ... it really wasn't. I knew at my very core that I had already said too much. I kept staring at the ground, trying to keep my face still so the tears wouldn't fall. If I couldn't stop myself from answering the questions, I could at least try not to be the coward Bob said I was.

The room fell silent. I tried to gather the strength to push my emotions back down, away from the surface. Sounding far away, Drysdale said, "Let's put the question about K.C. and Bob on hold until tomorrow. Okay?" I withheld a sigh of relief to prevent the tear resting on the edge of my eyelid from falling. Out of the corner of my eye I saw Drysdale give another nod to the woman.

She gently and slowly moved her chair closer to where I sat. "Hi, Landon. My name is Tracie Lodin. I specialize in helping children who have been through traumatic experiences. After this interview, I'll be taking you to our facility, which is about thirty minutes from here. I'm sure you'll be very comfortable there." She reached behind me, grabbed the thin blanket I had been lying on before, and covered my shoulders with it. What she did for a living didn't sound good, but even worse, she confirmed that I wasn't going back to the trailer, and I had nothing left in me to fight against that fact. I nodded ... and *my first tear fell.*

Agent Drysdale pulled a piece of paper out of the folder, but didn't look at it as he resumed speaking. He had one of those solid voices that make all the pronunciations sound the same. "Landon, I know it's been a long couple of hours, and I promise you, we're here to help." He flipped over the piece of paper. It was a picture. He inched it in front of me. My throat closed. My ears started ringing. A part of me left the room even though my body stayed. "Landon, you know who this is in the picture, don't you?"

I didn't have words.

"It's you, isn't it?"

I just stared at the picture of a little boy ... *of me.*

I knew that picture. I came back to my body. My mind jumped into the picture, into the moment when I first saw the picture. I was running across the playground yard. The grass had just been fertilized and my feet were muddy. My backpack pounded against my back in rhythm with my strides. I could hear the other kids laughing and playing. I looked down and in my hand was my school picture, the same picture Drysdale placed in front of me.

"Landon, can you remember where you were when this picture was taken?" Drysdale's voice sounded like it came from down a long tunnel. I jumped out of the chair and barely made it to the trashcan as the vomit rushed into my throat and my stomach turned inside out.

Tracie knelt at my side. "Hang in there," she murmured as her hand rubbed my back soothingly.

Drysdale's monotone drifted over from across the room. "Landon, we believe you were kidnapped four months after this picture was taken. You were playing basketball at the Arthur Black Rec Center. It was in the evening, and your basketball game was inside the building. You went into the restroom unsupervised. The rec center at the time had two access doors to the bathroom: one from inside the rec center and the other from the outside. When you entered the bathroom, we believe your abductor took you through the outside door. I have newspaper clippings if you—"

Tracie interrupted, "Leon, please. Give him some space."

I heard Drysdale sit back down in his seat, but my only reaction was to bring my knees into my stomach and hold my breath so my cries wouldn't make any noise. I felt the blood rush into my head and a thankful feeling of blackness swept over me.

I passed out.

(9)

Drysdale was wrong. He and his "we believe" assumptions pissed me off every time they entered my mind. I knew what my life had been about. I don't know if in the interview room I truly passed out or if I just kind of made myself stop listening and not seeing. I've done both before. When I came out of it, though, Drysdale tried to ask me more questions, but he had it wrong. I knew the truth. I lived it.

Before I left the FBI building, I had to go through a physical. They did the normal crap like listen to my heartbeat and check my ears and throat. But then the doctor started with weird shit, like looking for scars. He asked me to undress and put on a medical gown. I told him I'm not going down that road. He grabbed my arm when I hopped off the exam table and tried to convince me to go along with the examination so everyone could understand what I had gone through. I snorted and thought, *Scars don't tell a story, they only remind you, and strangers don't help you because you have a few marks.* I saw through his bullshit and jerked my arm away.

I stayed in my dirty sweats and T-shirt but threw away my socks, which were covered with crushed leaves and dirt dust. Looking down at them on my feet only reminded me of being dragged out of the trailer and put into the FBI car. I didn't want that memory. What I did want, though, was my hoodie. I wanted to hide behind it, to smell it when it covered my face … to feel my dampened hair against the back of my neck from wearing it.

The next doctor, Dr. Williams, was even worse. Tracie was in the room with us. He gave me a test with stupid questions on it, like, how often do I think about killing myself. A real no-brainer. I told him to divide the hour by four, and there you go. I was fine with all their crap until he wanted to know why I saw myself as such a bad person. You can't put into one sentence the feeling of how you stand next to someone and you just know that they're clean and you're dirty. Or how, when you feel that way, it makes you hate the world and sometimes even think about ruining it. I just sat there silently, and pretty soon he gave up on looking for an answer.

Then it was back into the unmarked car. They were taking me to Tracie's work, clinic, hospital, trauma center—whatever. They called it a hundred different names, but they didn't bother to mention why exactly I was going. The sun had already set. I had gotten to Drysdale's building just before sunrise, and now I was back in the car without having seen daylight. I told myself to get over it; it's the same sun that rises every day.

My mind went back to the day before, or whenever it was, when Bob and I drove home from the police station. Then I jumped to thinking about being in the trailer when the FBI busted in. That thought led to the Drysdale interview room. *I hate when my mind obsesses about things I don't want to think about.* But the first real favor of the last twenty-four hours was from Dr. Williams. He gave me a pill to lessen the thoughts, and I could feel it working. I let my head fall back against the headrest. The pill let me just sit there in the car and watch the world revolve around me. All I could manage to think about was a vague hope that someday soon I wouldn't have to be a part of this world.

When we got off the highway, I knew we had to be close. The driver was the same agent who had driven me away from the trailer and then later pinned me down in the elevator. Tracie was in the front seat with him. At a red traffic light, I quietly reached over to the door handle and pulled it to see if it was really one of those child-lock doors—you know, the ones where you can't open it from the inside. It was. I was going wherever they were going. I wanted to be pissed off, but the pill was working, and I just couldn't drum up the emotion.

We turned into a driveway, and I saw a sign: The Emily York Trauma Center. I didn't get a good look at the front of the place because Tracie pointed for the driver to pull around back. When we walked in, some people at the front desk with welcoming smiles stared at me. *You've got to be joking*, I thought. But by that point, the pill was so strong I couldn't focus on the expressions of their faces. There was little to no meaning attached to anything around me. The place looked deserted, but I guess that was because it was already night. You could sense, though, because of the scattered magazines and filled-up trashcans, that during the day there was a lot going on.

"Landon, I'll get you settled into your room, and tomorrow I'll have someone give you a tour of the facility." It was Tracie's voice. She was walking as she talked about the place. She had to use a code to open the first set of doors we went through. I was too zoned out to try to memorize the code so an escape would be an option later. As soon as we were behind the secured doors, the driver said goodbye and wished me luck. His job was to get me from one hell-hole to the next, apparently.

Tracie continued narrating our walk. "Our building is split in half. The area before we came through the secured doors is the outpatient therapy wing. This side, of course, is our inpatient center. You're free to move around in the secured areas, which includes the atrium in the center of the building. I should let you know as well that every inch of the facility is on video recording. We do that for your protection as well as that of our staff."

There were large windows looking out into a plant area. It looked cool, with all the little trees, lights, and benches. It wasn't the kind of landscape you saw back at the dairy farm. I felt almost mesmerized, but Tracie gently moved me along. She reached for the elevator button as she added, "There's also a sundeck on the rooftop. We have a handball and basketball court up there. I'm sure tomorrow you'll run into the other patients. We have two sisters, ages five and seven. The young man across from you is Joseph. He's fifteen and will be leaving us shortly. Nice guy. Do you have any questions so far, Landon?"

I shrugged. The only thing I was thinking about was what the elevator ride was going to be like. I knew there weren't fourteen floors to the place, so I was trying to be optimistic. The doors opened. I stepped in. Three floors. *Relief.*

"You'll have access to the first and third floor, where your room is, as well as the roof, but the second floor is off limits. It requires a security code to enter. My office is on the first floor." The elevator ride was quick, but Tracie just kept talking. I worried she would prattle on forever. "Your room is this way. They'll bring you up some dinner soon, and I'll bet you'd like to take a shower. There should be sweats and a T-shirt waiting for you tonight, and tomorrow I'll have some new clothes for you to wear. Try to make yourself as comfortable as possible. I have requested that your clothes be brought to you to make you feel more at home, but … well, I hate to say this, but you should know it's unlikely we'll get anything out of the trailer."

She opened the door to the room. It looked halfway between a hospital room and motel. It was carpeted, had a bed, a wall-mounted television, and a large fluffy chair facing the window. Off to the side was a bathroom. I didn't notice when we drove up, but the building was facing the Missouri River, which was cool.

"You met our staff psychiatrist, Dr. Williams, at Agent Drysdale's office. He'll be coming to your room shortly to check on the medication that he gave you and possibly to give you another pill. Are you sure you don't have any questions for me? You've been through quite a bit in the last twenty-four hours."

I looked around at the room, trying to take it all in. A pair of sweats and a T-shirt lay on the bed. I touched the drawstring on the sweats. *This was really happening.* I couldn't make a dream feel that weird. No one told me about Bob and where he was or might be. I was in a town where I didn't know any of the streets. I was in a random building that I didn't know existed before that day. I had none of my belongings, just my body. *What kind of question could I ask her that would help explain all this?* All I could say was, "No, I'm cool."

(10)

A shower helped. I hate tiled bathrooms, so I went to dry off in the bedroom, but then I got worried because I didn't close the curtains, plus Tracie said she would be back to see me before she left the office. It all worked out, though: I dried off, no one saw me, and the sweatpants fit. I sat on the bed, trying to clear up the confusion that was tumbling around in my head.

The memory that shot into my mind when Drysdale showed me the school picture was gone. I mean, I remembered having the memory, but it was flat. I couldn't get my body to move around in the memory like it did when Drysdale asked about the photo. It was more like fiction—you know, like when you read about a character in a book or when someone talks to you and you picture in your mind what they're saying: it's one step removed from your real world.

Drysdale gave me the third-grade picture to keep. He also explained what the "Ameritek ID" card paper-clipped to the photo was. It's got the same third-grade picture but it's a lot smaller. The whole thing is about the size of a business card and almost looks like a fake driver's license. Across the top in big letters it read "Ameritek ID." Typed next to the picture was a description of me, and my fingerprint from when I was seven years old.

Before I left his office, Drysdale showed me with a clear overlay how my fingerprint that they took when I got busted with Sam matched the one on the Ameritek ID card. There's an expert at his office who could go over it in detail if I wanted. What I really wanted, though, was to go back in time and tell Sam for real that we couldn't take Bob's van. I was doing fine with my life two days ago. Yeah, getting kicked out of school was messed up, but I had it under control.

A nurse brought me food. At least, I think she was a nurse. She wasn't wearing a nurse outfit, but it still felt like I was in a hospital or something.

41

The wall clock said it was almost midnight. They kept the room warm. It was weird that I noticed, but the heat came out of the vents in the walls. In our trailer, we had these plug-in heaters. You couldn't watch TV and have them on at the same time, or it would blow the fuse, and all our electricity would go out. In a weird way, I missed the trailer. Not because it was cold and the carpets were stained, but because I could walk around and not keep questioning who I am and what the next day would be like.

The picture Drysdale showed me didn't mean anything to me. I couldn't explain it. I left that kid alone. I left him to be a ghost walking around the world somewhere. The kid in the picture, it's not who I felt like inside at that moment, or two weeks before. I picked up the Ameritek ID card and read the description. "Brown hair. Green eyes. Weight: Forty-seven pounds. Height: Three feet eleven." I couldn't smile like I did in the picture without feeling stupid and fake. I took the picture and walked over to the bathroom. I don't like mirrors. I don't like looking straight on at myself … but, I wanted to see how I had changed.

I turned the light on and went to stand in front of the mirror, but the only thing I could focus on was green wall tiling, the metal frame around the mirror, and the bright light dangling above the sink. That elevator feeling came back over me: *something bad was gonna happen right then, right there.* The left side of my neck started to tighten and tense. My heart rate took off. I jumped out of the bathroom and slammed the door shut. I stared at the closed door like some mysterious force might open it and suck me in. After a minute, I shook it off. *I hate myself for being so stupid.*

I turned and went to stand by the window. The parking lot lights threw off enough illumination that I could see glimpses of the running water in the river. I caught sight of my reflection in the window. I was a lot older than the boy in the picture, but I could see some similarities. My freckles were lighter and my hair darker. I've always had the big curls. The big difference was my eyes. In the picture, my eyes were round, but as I studied my reflection, I noticed they weren't anymore. It was more like the corners drooped and pointed down. My eyelids seemed to rest halfway closed. With my long eyelashes, my eyes looked more closed than open. I tried to smile like I did in the picture, but the door to the room swept open and the incoming light took my reflection away. It was Tracie.

She smiled a little bit as she said, "How are you doing?"

I turned and put the Ameritek ID card on the small table by the fluffy chair. I felt embarrassed, like she caught me checking myself out.

"I'm sure the pills Dr. Williams gave you are helping you relax. You've been under a tremendous amount of stress. You appear to be handling it very well. Certainly better than I would."

I hate people who pretend to act like they know what you're going through when they really don't. As if she really knew what it was like to live life as a sixteen-year-old, just eighteen months away from being on your own in this screwed-up world, and then have Drysdale tell you that you're only fifteen and born in November, not March. Worst of all, when he said all that, I just stared at him like a stupid fuck, because in some weird way I knew all that about me but forgot it—wanted to forget it.

Tracie came and sat on the floor, her back leaning against the wall. I took a seat in the chair next to her. It never worked that way with Bob, though. If Bob entered a room, I'd watch his every step to see where he wanted to sit. Once he sat, I sat, and then I'd wait for signs that it was okay to relax. But she had this laidback feeling about her. *She wants information from me,* I thought.

She saw the Ameritek ID card lying on the table. "May I?" She started to reach for it.

"Sure."

She picked it up and studied it. "Wow, it's amazing how things connect up, isn't it?"

I shrugged. *What do you mean by "amazing"?* I didn't ask the question, though.

Her next words were, "Tyler Roberts."

"Huh?"

She clarified. "Your name. Tyler Roberts."

I snatched the card from her hand. She pointed to where it said the name. I could swear when I was reading the description earlier I didn't see the part that read, "Name: Tyler Roberts." Like, it wasn't there. I swore. I could feel Tracie's stare on me as I studied the card, stunned.

"Do you remember being called Tyler?"

"Huh?"

"When did you start using the name Landon?"

"I don't know … I mean, my name *is* Landon."

"You were never Tyler Roberts?"

"This is all so damn stupid. I hate these dumb-ass questions!" I started to jump out of the chair, but she put her hand on my knee to stop me. "I'm sorry. Please. The best thing right now is to let the medication you took relax your mind. You need a break from all this information. We've got a big couple of days ahead of us."

I felt like saying something sarcastic about her use of the word "we," but I let it go. The pill was working. Even though I got pissed, the anger left right away.

This huge gap of silence started separating us. She was looking around the room. "Maybe we could get them to bring in some DVDs, or a PlayStation for you."

I shrugged. "Whatever."

There was more silence.

"Landon …" She waited until I looked at her. "You haven't asked about your parents."

"What parents? They got rid of me."

She tilted her head to the side. "Do you remember that?"

"That's not something you forget. They didn't want me."

"But do you remember being with them and leaving them?"

"I don't have to remember it. It's something I know. That's why I ended up with Bob."

She leaned back. "I'm sorry. I didn't know. All I know is what Agent Drysdale has told me, and what the newspapers reported when the kidnapping occurred."

"Yeah, well, that's all bullshit, about me being kidnapped. Bob found me when I didn't have anywhere else to go. But whatever; you guys will find out soon enough." She wasn't the kind of person I'd normally cuss around right away. I mean, when I'm really pissed off, I don't care who I cuss around, but usually with women I'd try not to do it right off the bat. Right then, though, I wanted to show her how irritated I was with the kidnapping bullshit. I wanted them to lay off it.

"Our office here at the Emily York Center is not part of Drysdale's office. We're not part of the FBI. I don't want you to think I work for Drysdale. I'm here only to help you."

"With what?"

"Transitioning. You're going to be encountering a lot of changes, and I want to help you work through those. It's my job to try to assist you in understanding what you've been through in the last seven years, and ultimately help you feel control over your life."

I couldn't help but give her a sarcastic laugh. *How could I have control over my life when they had me in a secured building with cameras everywhere?* I wanted to hate her, but I couldn't stay angry enough—because of the pill.

I put my head back against the chair. My eyelids were getting heavy. The two of us sat there not saying anything. My eyes started to close.

"Landon, why don't you go to bed?" *Bob's voice.*

I jerked out of my sleep. My heart skipped a beat. Tracie leaned forward. "Are you okay?" She saw that *her* words scared me. I looked around the room. *No Bob.* The only sound was the hot air coming out of the vents.

"I'm sorry, Landon. I didn't mean to frighten you. I know that the pill is strong, and you just had the second one thirty minutes ago. I think maybe you should head to bed. The phone on the nightstand connects you with the operator, who can put you in contact with me immediately if you need anything. Anything at all."

I didn't hear everything she said but I knew a nod would answer her. The sound of Bob's voice was so clear, as vivid as that memory in the interview room. I looked out at the river. The moon lit up the treetops but the ground was pitch black. Bob was out there. It was like we were still linked together. I couldn't explain it. In some ways, it was good to be away from him, but at the same time, it terrified me.

(11)

Agent Drysdale was shorter than I remembered. Maybe it's because I felt so small in the FBI interview room. He had a clean look about him, too. I don't know if it was the soap-smelling cologne, his clean fingernails, or his soft hands. Bob always had something bad to say about black people. I never understood it but always agreed with him because disagreeing wasn't an option. So I was curious about Drysdale. He seemed to be on the up and up.

He tossed a file on the table and must have noticed that I was nervous about what was in it. He smiled reassuringly and said, "Don't worry. No more surprises. I promise." *Promises don't mean anything.* I wanted to tell him that, but I didn't want to give him attitude. After all, he owned a gun.

I imagined Bob and Drysdale walking toward each other on a narrow sidewalk. I was trying to picture who would step to the side to let the other go by. In the last year or so, Bob had grown a crazy beard that flared out from his chin, and his gray hair reached below his shoulders. He had a beer gut that he could barely keep covered with his T-shirts, and there was something about his walk that forced people to step out of his way. Even though both Drysdale and Bob owned guns, if Drysdale left home without his and didn't have a suit and tie on, I think he'd be scared to go face-to-face with Bob. But then, of course, maybe if he walked up to Bob with his FBI badge hanging out, it would be a different story. Bob might back down from someone for the first time.

Drysdale organized his stuff: pen, paper, file folders. He took off his jacket and swung it around the back of the chair. Then he looked over at me and started talking, which snapped me out of my daydream. It was his usual monotone voice. "I was caught up at my office this morning. I'm sorry if you were waiting for me. Did Tracie make sure you were given a tour of the facility? I hear through the grapevine they have a basketball court on the roof."

I shrugged. He didn't demand a response like the night before, but I knew that wouldn't last. You could tell by the way he asked his questions that he looked for the rhythm of truth that only comes when lies don't get in the way. His next question came on quick. "And did you sleep well?"

"I guess."

"You guess?"

"Yeah, I did."

"Good." He smiled at me as a reward, pulled the file on the table over, and flipped it open. I couldn't read the words of the handwritten note he was looking at. Without looking up, he began, "So let me tell you what to expect in our meeting here. First, I'm going to ask some basic questions about Bob. I'd like to learn a little more about K.C., but only if you feel up to it. I'm not asking you to wrack your brain, looking for memories to answer any of my questions. If you know the answers, great; if not, tell me you don't. Not knowing is never a problem between us. Do you understand?"

"Yeah, I got it."

"There was a press conference this morning regarding your abduction." He looked into my eyes, lifted his brows, and paused, studying my face. "We've disclosed where we found you, and notified the public that Bob is at large. We're asking for help to bring him in." He paused again. I returned his look with no expression. He continued. "After your session with Tracie, you'll be having the reunion with your parents, as you know."

When he said that, I looked away. I tried to block out his words, but I couldn't. I couldn't stop his voice from reaching my ears. "They arrived earlier this morning from Colorado Springs." I could tell he wanted to see beyond my eyes, wondering what the reaction inside me was. I offered a nod. His gaze bore into my temple, but I didn't meet his eyes. Finally, he dropped his head down to study his notes.

I was nervous to ask, but I had to. My throat was dry but I scratched out, "What's going to happen to Bob when you guys find him?"

Drysdale leaned back in his chair, crossed his legs. "I'm not going to start off our relationship by lying to you. At the same time, it's my intent to be open with you as much as I can as long as it doesn't compromise our investigation or cause you emotional harm. Because of that, I'm not going to answer that particular question." I could feel my face moving into a scowl, but I listened to his words. "It's important for you to understand that the information you give me here is only to confirm what we already suspect or know. In other words, what you say isn't going to get Bob into any more trouble. If anything, it will help us resolve everything more quickly and smoothly. Okay?"

This time, I didn't know how he wanted me to answer. I wanted to tell him he was an asshole, but I could tell it wouldn't faze him. He'd probably say something stupid, like, "You're entitled to your opinion, but let's move on." I knew he wasn't the kind of guy who got pissed off, lost control, and said stupid stuff. He had one more comment to add, though. "But let me also say that I understand your concern for Bob, and it's a natural reaction considering everything you've been through with him."

I shrugged. "Whatever. It's fine."

"To start with, I understand you feel more comfortable being called Landon, not Tyler. Is that correct?"

"Yeah, that's my name."

"And when you or I refer to Bob, we're talking about Robert Bernard Starker?"

"Yeah."

He pulled a picture out from behind his written notes. I could tell it was one of those jail pictures, a mug shot with the face turned sideways and then facing the camera. "Is this Bob?"

It was, but he was young and thin in the picture. His hair wasn't gray yet. It was more of a sandy blond color. He had a full mustache in the photo, where the sides grew all the way down to the chin. As I was looking at the picture, a thought popped into my head. I was under a dining room table, sitting on my ankles. I was short enough to be able to sit straight up and my head wouldn't touch the underneath of the table. There were no chairs. To my right, there were three phonebooks stacked up against the wall. It was dark in the room. I couldn't see the living-room furniture, if there were any. The only light coming into the area was peeking through these tall, long blinds that were pulled shut along a sliding glass door. When the blinds rubbed against each other, they made a soft clacking sound. I was staying as still as I could, staring at the front door.

"Landon, you drifted off there. Do you want to share with me what you're thinking about?"

"Yeah, that's Bob. I mean, he doesn't look that way now, though."

"Yes, of course. This picture was taken about fourteen years ago." He pushed the picture to the side. "Did you ever meet any of Bob's family members?"

"No. They all died when he was really young."

"How do you know that?"

Duh. "Bob told me."

"Did he ever talk about a sister?"

Weird question. "No."

"Do you know if Bob took any medications?"

"Does Jack Daniel's count?"

He smiled. Apparently, he liked my joke. "Aside from alcohol."

"I don't think so. I don't know. I never saw any. He doesn't believe in going to the doctor."

Drysdale's smile slipped away, and his questions continued. "I know what kind of work he did for Evelyn Barker, when it was a dairy farm, but I'm wondering if there is any other type of work that Bob does?"

"Yeah, he works as a fill-in plumber, like when the regular guys are sick or the company is really busy. And then he has his gun business."

"Guns?"

"Yeah, he makes them look new. You know, like old guns."

"Restoration?"

"Yeah, exactly."

The whole time, Drysdale kept taking notes. While he was writing, I got curious. "Well, I think when you guys get Bob, you know, he's gonna clear up how he found me and all that stuff. But can I ask a question?"

"Sure."

"Was Bob's van at the trailer when you guys got there?"

"Yes, we have the van in our possession." When he said it, I realized I wasn't expecting that answer. It didn't make sense to me. *If the van was there when the FBI busted in, where was Bob?*

Drysdale's next question attempted to change the subject. "Would you feel comfortable if I asked you about K.C.?" But the confusion in my mind about where Bob went wouldn't leave. I couldn't stop myself from asking, "How come Bob wasn't in the trailer?" *What a stupid question!* I thought in my mind. I wanted to take it back as soon as I asked it. Like, how would Drysdale know why Bob wasn't there.

But then when I saw the way Drysdale looked at me, I knew he had the answer, and in the brief second before he started to talk, for some reason I wondered whether he was a dad. "I do know why Bob wasn't in the trailer when we got there. Unfortunately, that's one of those answers that I can't disclose right now. I'm sorry. Okay?"

"Yeah, whatever. No biggee." *I wanted the answer, though.*

Drysdale cleared his throat. "Can I ask you about K.C. now?"

"Sure." And I was being serious. I wanted to think about K.C. I wanted to talk about K.C. but Bob never let me. When I woke up that morning, even though I was at the trauma center, I had tried really hard to remember exactly what K.C. looked like. I couldn't recall anything except his blue eyes, which made me feel weird because we were like brothers during the time that we lived together.

"Do you know how K.C. and Bob came to be living with each other?"

"They were living with each other when Bob found me."

"Right." He hesitated and then added, "I'm sorry. I have to ask you for a clarification. When you say Bob found you, what are you referring to?"

"This shelter place."

"What does that mean?"

"I remember the building—I mean, inside the building. There were wooden closets that stuck out from the wall. They weren't built in, like how in a house there's a door and you go into the closet. And I remember that there were beds just lined up along the wall. But I can't remember any people there."

"Do you remember the town?"

"No." I tried to think more about the place, tried to picture what it looked like, but the memory wouldn't move away from the wooden closets and the rough, splintery plywood walls. I couldn't picture clothes in the closets either; they were empty. Weirdly, my heart started racing when I thought about walking up to the closets. Drysdale said something and it shook me out of the memory. But then I cut him off midsentence to ask, "Can we go back to talking about K.C.?"

Drysdale was studying my face. "Of course we can. I was asking, did anyone ever tell you how K.C. came to be living with Bob?"

"K.C.'s mom was Bob's girlfriend for a while, and then she just took off and left K.C. with Bob."

"How did you learn about that?"

I shook my head. "I don't know how I knew it. I just did. I can't remember the conversation. But I know that's how it was. Bob was always talking about how K.C.'s mom left him and stuff, and that he was all that K.C. had. Like me, too."

"What do you mean like you, too?"

"Well, I mean, K.C. and I both knew, if it wasn't for Bob, we wouldn't be able to live. Like we'd end up on the streets, or in foster care, where they'd separate us, and we'd never see each other again."

"You and K.C. would be separated?"

"Yeah."

"How much older was K.C. than you?"

"I think about two years."

"And in our last meeting, you were telling me that you came home to the trailer and K.C. was gone. Did K.C. go to the same school as you?"

"No, he couldn't go to school."

"Why?"

"They wouldn't take him. Bob didn't get his papers from K.C.'s mom because she left in the middle of the night without telling anyone."

Drysdale kept talking as he wrote his notes. "And again, how do you know all this?"

"Someone told me, Bob or K.C. probably. I'm not sure. But Bob didn't want the foster people to find K.C., because if they found out his mom left him, they would take him away. And we didn't want that. We wanted to be together."

"Why weren't you worried that the foster care people would take you?"

"Bob knew that my parents didn't want me. Plus, he had the papers that he needed to get me into school. I wasn't at first—going to school, that is—but now I remember that the manager of the bungalow that you were talking about last night started asking Bob about why I wasn't in school."

"That's the manager of Cordia Bungalows in Coleridge?"

"Yeah, and then this truancy officer, one of those guys who makes sure kids are in school, he came out and talked to Bob." The memory of being under that dining room table popped into my head again. My heart was beating a little faster in the room with Drysdale, which made me feel like I was right back in the dining room with the table, waiting for the front door to open. The memory swirled away when Drysdale asked his next question. "What happened after the truancy officers came to talk to Bob?"

"Bob put me in school because he had the paperwork." I said it matter-of-factly because that's exactly how I remembered it.

"But, Landon, the paperwork that you are talking about to get you into school is a birth certificate. The one that Bob used to enroll you in school doesn't have the name that you were born with on it—it's not the name your parents gave you."

I shrugged again. There was a pause where we just stared at each other. Then I said, "I don't know what you want me to say. I wanted all of us to be together." And while I said it, I could hear the blinds clacking together in my memory of the dining room, sitting there, completely still, watching the front door.

"Let me ask you this," Drysdale said. "Before Bob got the paper to get you into school, the paper you were talking about just a second ago, what name did people call you?"

Drysdale's question forced another memory into my mind. K.C. and I were making a fort, with pillows for walls and sheets for a roof. We made a tunnel we had to climb through to get into the fort. We wanted to get inside the fort area without the tunnel collapsing. I saw myself crawling through the tunnel. I could hear our laughter. We finally made it into the fort, and K.C. leaned into my face and whispered in my ear, "Good job, Tyler." We giggled like we were sharing a secret. I could see K.C.'s face so clearly. It was the memory I was looking for earlier that morning when I woke up. Suddenly, in the memory, a door slammed. The laughter stopped. Bob was home. "Landon! K.C.!" Our rooftop sheets were torn away. I stopped the memory there, excited to have K.C.'s face in my mind once again, but too scared to remember the pain that came from Bob's fists.

"Landon, are you with me?"

"Bob always called me Landon. Everyone called me Landon." I went into my mind to replay the K.C. memory. I loved K.C. I watched Drysdale's lips move, but my mind was floating away from the interview room. Instead of reliving the fun that came from the tent memory, I felt my stomach sink as an undeniable sense of reality popped into my mind. I cut Drysdale off again to say, "K.C. is never coming back."

"How do you know that, Landon?"

My mind was back at the trailer. I was just coming home, not knowing where K.C. was. I couldn't figure out what happened to him. Bob answered my confusion by jamming the butt of a rifle into my ribcage. He tried to erase K.C. from my mind by giving me broken ribs. I knew I couldn't blame Bob for doing it, though. We were both in pain. We both wanted K.C. back. After that night, K.C.'s name never left my lips again, and day by day my memories of him as my brother started drifting away. I had been tricking myself into believing he just left, *which isn't the truth.* He was gone forever. I knew it before I walked up to the trailer that day. And then sitting in the room with Agent Drysdale, I realized I had been fooling myself ever since.

Drysdale's voice pulled me back. "I'm asking you a question, Landon. How do you know that? What makes you know that K.C. is never coming back?"

I shrugged, confused. A light fog blanketed my memories. I had no answer.

"I think we need to take a little break, maybe let you walk around a bit, okay? They've shown you the atrium where you can get some fresh air, right? Or you can go upstairs, and I'll come find you."

I took a deep breath, looked around the room. Now that I wasn't at the trailer, I wanted to think about K.C. again. I was so close to him, like a brother. It was exciting, in a weird way, that he could come to life in my mind. It's the closest that we could get to being together, to being brothers once again. I shook myself out of my thoughts long enough to answer Drysdale. "Yeah. Yeah, they showed me where everything is." *A break would be good,* I thought. I wanted some quiet time to sit and daydream about K.C. and our wrestling matches in the living room.

"I'm going to get some coffee." It was Drysdale's voice coming from the open interview room door.

"Okay." I wanted a cigarette really bad, but I couldn't imagine how I'd pull that off. The whole building knew who I was and how old I am.

"Landon?"

I turned around to face Drysdale. "Yeah, what?"

"You're a survivor. I meet people all the time who have gone through tragedies, and you can see in their eyes that their spirit is broken; yours isn't. Hang in there." He stood at the door, looking my way. I didn't know how to respond.

(12)

Finding a cigarette butt wasn't the problem. It was that I didn't have a lighter. That's me for you, a brilliant thought with no way to follow through on it. *No wonder I'm such a loser.*

In the atrium, I found this little area with a lot of overgrown plants and a couple of benches. It obviously was where the people who worked at the place hung out to smoke. Some of the cigarettes had barely been lit and were propped up on the side of the trashcan ashtray, waiting for their puffer to come back. I picked up one that had hardly been smoked. It had a little lipstick mark on the end, but whatever, just holding it started to calm my nerves. It's not like I smoked all day, every day. I'd have a couple with Sam and the metal shop guys after we'd smoke a bowl, maybe one after school, and then if I had time after cleaning up the trailer, I'd light up one of Bob's Camel non-filters.

I looked down at the shoes that Tracie had brought to my room that morning. Brand-new tennis shoes, like the ones they want you to wear in gym class for running. Bob would always say, "They can go fuck themselves before I spend fifty bucks so you can look like a fag." He always had comments like that. Some were funny; some were mean. I laughed at them all, though. You couldn't afford not to agree with Bob.

Everything I was wearing was new, even the socks and underwear. They weren't anything like the clothes that I had left behind. Actually, if I walked into English class looking like I did—khaki pants and a long-sleeve dress shirt—that unibrow-sporting prick of a teacher, Mr. Sanders, probably would have given me another chance. People care so damn much about what you wear. I used to try to dress like everyone else, but that never worked. Something was always wrong: my hair was out of place or my clothes fit me funny. I just stopped trying. And in a funny way, I started fitting in better as an outcast. I was just "the weird guy with a hoodie."

And anyway, I knew why my clothes were all messed up. Bob would drop me off at the Laundromat once a month, with twenty bucks to do our clothes. The only way to get some money for myself would be to overload the washers and dryers so I didn't use all the quarters. It was a fair trade-off: our T-shirts and jeans were wrinkly, but I was able to buy a soda with my free lunch at school. Bob never complained about the wrinkles, but the kids at school did. Not like they had to wear the clothes. Except Sam—he never ragged on me.

"Hey little man, what's up?" The raspy voice caught me off guard. It sounded like the speaker needed to cough up a gob. I slowly moved my hand over to the side of the bench and dropped the cigarette butt.

"Hey," I responded and looked up to see the janitor smiling at me. I'd seen him in the hallway by my room earlier, pushing his cart of mops, brooms, and cleaning crap. He was smiling then, too. He pulled out one of his music earplugs, which I thought was ridiculous; the dude was like a hundred years old. My iPod—the one Sam jacked for me that I hid behind the TV—flashed in my mind. Then that thought led to the realization that I didn't have *anything* anymore that belonged to me. *Whatever*, is all I could say to myself to keep calm.

The wire to his iPod was under his shirt, so if you looked really quick, it looked like he had a hearing aid in each ear. Still smiling, he rasped, "You need a light?" He jerked his head a little toward the cigarette butt I had dropped.

"No, no, I'm fine. I don't smoke."

"Oh, is that right?" I coulda sworn he winked at me. "Okay, okay, just asking." He started to gently lift off the ashtray top from the trashcan, making sure not to knock around the cigarette butts that the workers were saving. He pulled out the filled trash bag, put in a new one, and returned the ashtray to the top. Then he reached into his pocket and placed a book of matches on the rim of the ashtray, gave me another wink, and said, "I was a kid your age once." He put his earplug back in and waddled out of the smoking area on bowed legs, pushing his cart.

I looked down at the matches. I felt bad. When I had seen him earlier, the first thing I noticed about him was his smile, and that was the reason I decided to hate him. I'd avoided meeting his eyes and went right for the stairwell, thinking how pissed off it made me when people smiled like they cared but they didn't even know your name.

I grabbed the butt off the ground, lit a match … inhaled. I tried to figure out in my mind what day of the week it was. Starting with the Sam arrest, my nights were all messed up. I'd been at the FBI office from sunrise to sunset. And then the night before, with the pills Dr. Williams gave me, maybe I slept through a whole day, and it's really not the day I thought it was, but the next. To top everything off, there I was smoking a cigarette butt with lipstick on it.

The butt was almost down to the filter. I dropped it to the floor and put it out with a stomp and twist. I went to reach for the other butts resting in the ashtray. I was going to pocket them for later, but I stopped. It just didn't feel right. I mean, the people who put the butts there were coming back to finish them. Then this other part of my mind was telling me how stupid I was. Like, they had jobs, they could buy all the cigarettes that they wanted. It was hard to argue with myself about why I should leave them, but I pictured the workers coming to look for something that was theirs, and how it would be gone. Even though they wouldn't know that I took it ... I don't know, it just didn't feel right, especially after the janitor did something nice for me. And because he was so careful not to mess up the cigarette butts, it made their owners, in a weird way, come to life for me. I did take the book of matches that he left for me (or at least I thought he left them for me). And that's when Drysdale walked up. "There you are. I see you've found the local hang-out."

"What? Am I not supposed to be over here?"

He just stood there with his hands in his pockets, looking over every inch of me, and it felt like he was looking inside my brain, too. I kinda wanted to know about him. If he did have kids, was he their Little League coach? Was his wife mean? Had he met anyone like me before? I mean, not a kid that looked like me, but if he had ever gotten someone out of a trailer like they did me.

"You're absolutely fine sitting here, Landon. If not, I would have asked you to stay out of this area." He waved me toward the door, and I stood up right away. I wasn't sure why I did, but it probably was because I just didn't want to get any crap for smoking.

Drysdale and I walked out of the smoking area side by side, just like the first time I met him when I got out of the agent's car. I started to get a little tense, like he was gonna give me a pat on the back again. Instead, his hands went back into his pockets. "I'm going to have to cut short our interview time. Your parents are here, and they've already met with Tracie. It wouldn't be right keeping everyone apart any longer than is necessary."

My stomach tightened and this rush of heat filled my chest. I was sure I couldn't swallow. Drysdale was making it seem like such a wonderful thing was about to happen, but I wasn't so sure.

"Tracie's in her office waiting for you."

"With them?"

"No, you'll meet with her first to make sure you feel comfortable. She's better at explaining how everything will happen than I am." My chest started to relax a little. "Do you know where Tracie's office is?"

"Yeah, it's on this floor, down the hall by the elevator."

"Good. We'll talk soon, okay?" Drysdale held open the glass door, and as I passed him, that's when he gave me that damn pat on the back. But whatever, I felt dazed and empty inside. I turned down the carpeted hallway. I hated being told where to go, but really, what were my options, you know? I could feel Drysdale's eyes boring into my back as he stood there at the glass door. An hour ago, things were going pretty well, or at least better than before. I had K.C. back; not in person, of course, but in my mind. And it was the old K.C., too. The K.C. I used to wrestle with on the living room floor.

The carpeting in the hallway outside of Tracie's office had these big squares printed on it. Every time I stepped into the middle of one of the squares, I'd think to myself, *I didn't ask to leave the trailer.* I knew that was weird, feeling that way, because the trailer was so screwed up, but it made me stop obsessing over how bad I just wanted to be the person I was four days ago.

(13)

Tracie's office had a small waiting room. I walked in and put my ear to the door of her office. When I didn't hear any voices, I took a seat. I was wondering if *they* were in there. Drysdale said they wouldn't be. *But like his words really mean anything.*

I caught myself and yelled back in my mind, *Stop thinking that way. This is a different world.* I knew, deep down, that Drysdale wouldn't lie or trick me like that, at least not on purpose … but maybe he just didn't know.

I started jiggling my foot as I waited. I felt like I was reliving the day I got kicked out of class, waiting for the guidance counselor. *But, yeah, right, that was too good to be true.* I caught myself again. I wanted to believe, even though I knew differently, that this might be a good thing. And even if it wasn't, I didn't want my—I didn't want Dale and Cathy Roberts to see that asshole side of me, like the dick I was in English class.

Dale and Cathy Roberts. *My parents*—that's what I was trying to say, but the words were frozen, stuck right below my Adam's apple. All I could do is repeat it over and over in my mind. *My parents.* Then I finally got the nerve to whisper it: "My parents."

It felt better to just say Cathy and Dale Roberts. The word "parents" to me felt like a word from a foreign language. I was trying to remember the last time I had thought about them before the FBI stuff went down. No specific date or timeframe came to mind. I just knew it had been years. It's a weird feeling to grow up knowing that your parents don't want you. You want to be mad at them, but at the same time you understand. Even though you can't put it into words, deep down, you kind of know why.

The butterflies in my stomach were flying crazy loop-the-loops. I wondered if the Robertses would be like the parents I already knew. Like Sam's mom, always in her bathrobe and slippers, holding a Pabst beer mixed with orange juice. Or worse, maybe they'd be like the parents I had seen that one and only time Bob and I went to a Back to School Night in eighth grade. All those parents with "dry clean only" clothes and judgmental eyes, who didn't want Bob or me around their precious kids.

My mind jumped to thinking about Tracie grabbing the Ameritek ID card and saying my birth name: "Tyler Roberts." How weird it was that I didn't even see the name the first time I looked at the card.

Everything about me felt sped up. My foot jiggling. My heart pounding. The air rushing in and out of my lungs. I saw the doorknob twisting open before I heard any sound from the door hinges. It was Tracie, smiling. "Hi there, Landon. Come in."

I tried to look past her to see if anyone was in her office in case maybe they were whispering and that's why I didn't hear them when I put my ear to the door. I didn't want it to be obvious that I was looking around, so I kept my head down but still managed to see that her office was empty.

I was sad … but relieved.

It felt like when you see a rollercoaster from the road and you're really excited about riding it, but when you get your chance to do it, you just freeze up and puss out. As you walk away from the opportunity, you're relieved you didn't take the risk but you still wish it could've happened. That was me in the moment, there in Tracie's office.

Anyway, I kept telling myself that the longer I could hold off the meeting with Cathy and Dale, the better. I mean, I was fooling myself thinking that they wouldn't see the same outcast kid that the snobs at school saw. Or maybe that was it, you know. Maybe they saw that kid in me before anyone else in the world did.

"Landon, why don't you have a seat wherever you feel most comfortable? I have to take care of one quick e-mail that just came through." Tracie passed by me to head for her desk. *That was a dumb thing to say. How could I possibly feel comfortable with all this stuff going on?* I looked around the office. There was a couch and three chairs surrounding a large round, white marble coffee table. Two of the chairs were right next to each other, and the third one stood alone, opposite them. I picked the third one; it looked like a loner.

Tracie finished what she was doing and looked over at me. "Oh, you picked my chair." I went to get up, but she gestured for me to sit again. "No, please, stay. It's absolutely fine." I sat back down. Tracie slipped me a small smile. "So, how are you doing?"

"Fine." *Another stupid question.* Although … and I wasn't gonna say it out loud, but I had to admit that after my meeting with Drysdale—I knew I sounded stupid saying it, but it felt like the sun still shined. Bob cared for me in Bob's way. But K.C., he cared about *me … for* me. And I cared about him, no matter what Bob used to try to tell me. I tried to lighten up and tell myself that maybe with K.C. back in my mind I was doing fine after all.

Tracie took a seat in one of the two other chairs. "We'll have your parents join us shortly. While you were with Agent Drysdale, I was meeting with them, trying to help them understand what you've been through. And before we have them come in, I wanted to spend some time with you to answer any questions you may have. I'll also talk about how we'll be proceeding in the next month or so in order to make the transition back with your parents go as smoothly as possible. Okay?"

"What do you mean the next month or so?"

"Based on our clinical evaluation and the tests that were given to you at Drysdale's office, Dr. Williams and I are admitting you to the facility, and Agent Drysdale is supporting the recommendation."

"Can I leave at all?"

"Not initially. But yes, toward the end of your stay here, we encourage children to participate in community events and, in your case, research school options or learn about employment opportunities. These are all things that we'll discuss when the time comes." She just looked at me.

I didn't know what to say so I blurted, "I smoke."

"Have you been looking for an opportunity to quit?" She smiled again.

"Not really."

"I don't support teenage smoking. But there's no doubt you're a survivor, so I'm sure you'll work it out, won't you?"

I took that as a compliment.

"Do you feel comfortable with all this, Landon?"

I shrugged. My freedom to even answer questions felt like it was taken away from me the night they dragged me from the trailer.

"I'll discuss with you in more details what your stay will entail, but—"

"What did the Roberts say about this?" I interjected.

"I'm sorry, what's that?"

"Cathy and Dale, my so-called parents. What did they say about my staying here?"

"It was part of our discussion this morning. I'm hopeful that they understand how important it is to help you establish—"

"That figures," I cut in again.

"What does that mean, Landon?"

I looked away. "Nothing." She stared at me. I knew what the stare meant. I sighed and shifted in my chair. "It figures that they wouldn't fight to take me back to their home."

"I believe that they would, actually. I'd like for you to understand that your stay here is a decision that comes from our facility as well as from Agent Drysdale. Your parents have had no input into this. In fact, it may be that they petition the court for your release from the center. I've seen parents do that."

"Whatever."

"I think we may have jumped into this discussion a little early. Maybe if I could backpedal and give you some background on the facility, you'd see that if your parents do cooperate with your stay here, it should send the message that they care about you. Mind if I try that?"

"Knock yourself out."

"Great. So when I met you in the interview room for the first time, I introduced myself as a trauma specialist. I work for a federally funded program that's onsite here at the Emily York Center. One of the things we do is provide trauma support for children who have been kidnapped. When children come to us, such as you, we try to help them and their families move away from the traumatic experience."

The word "kidnapped" kind of set me off. I mean, I told her how my parents didn't want me, but it's like she can't leave that alone and let me try to forget about it. I must have made a face, because she said, "What is it, Landon? Did I say something that bothered you?"

"Nothing. I'm fine. Go ahead." I shrugged and leaned back in the chair. We locked eyes, but I had nothing to add. She finally continued on, "The majority of children I've worked with have been abducted by a parent; therefore, much of the research regarding missing children comes from those situations, and not from situations like yours where you were abducted by a stranger."

I couldn't bite my tongue this time and butted in, "I *told* you how I ended up with Bob."

"Yes, I know that's your belief, Landon, and I am not looking to challenge that belief today. I've explained to your parents as well that I don't think you're ready to challenge that belief."

"What's that supposed to mean?"

"It means that your mind and the way you have remembered things or not remembered things served to protect you, and right now that process works very well. When an individual is ripped away from the world he knows, such as you were, the natural reaction is to patch together a reality that helps you survive and make sense of the world. In other words, we remember or choose to believe things that help us function in our environment, however dysfunctional. Does that make sense?"

I was a little confused, but I mostly got it. "I guess."

"As an example, you have no recollection of the day when you left or were taken from your parents; is that right? That's what I understood you to be saying in your room last night. You didn't have to remember it, because, like you said, you *knew* it. I would venture to guess that Bob told you that, which is also typical behavior. Most abductors use that explanation to—"

"But I know deep down it's true. It's not just Bob telling me that."

She let out a sigh. "I have to be honest with you, Landon. There's no indication from your parents that they ever wanted to give you away. They care about you. And the police investigation surrounding your case shows no indication that your parents were involved in your disappearance."

Her bullshit didn't mean anything to me except to irritate me. Bob explained how if people give their kid away, the police automatically get involved if they find out. That's why when Bob found me, he explained that if we were to go to the police, my parents for sure wouldn't want me back because they would get in trouble, and it would be my fault. And if they *did* want me back but the police were involved, the police would put me into foster care before they'd ever let me go back with my parents—who got rid of me in the first place.

I saw Tracie's lips moving, but the words were fractured. "The memory of your abduction is lost right now … you can't remember it … but we can work on bringing …" I was trying to listen to her but her words kept fading in and out. The bathroom upstairs in my room flashed into my mind, and I got that worried feeling, like a weird force was approaching and would suck me right out of the room. I couldn't get the sight of the green tile out of my mind. That bright light above the sink swung back and forth, making it seem like the bathroom walls were breathing. I could hear Bob's voice, like he's on the brink of crying, whispering in my ear, "They don't want you, kid." It was replaying over and over, like he was right there with me in Tracie's office. My breathing sped up, faster and faster. Tracie's voice pulled me back a little bit. "What are you thinking about, Landon?"

"Nothing." The thought faded away.

"I'm here to help. If you're having any thoughts that are disturbing, it may help you to share them."

"Okay." *The thoughts weren't disturbing; they were stupid.* They were about a stupid bathroom that I had only been inside one time. She kept staring at me, though, and that's what made me feel weird. I shrugged. "What?"

"I'll continue with what I was saying, but again, if you're having disturbing thoughts, it's good if you can talk to me about them. I may be able to help."

"Yeah, I get it. Whatever."

There was another pause. Finally, she moved on. "Let me give you a general understanding of how repressed memories form. When someone experiences an event that is so out of the ordinary that it makes no sense and is perceived as being way beyond the person's control, it becomes too painful to play the event over in the mind. This is a form of trauma. After the trauma, the person's conscious mind, the part that reasons with you and gives you pictures to help you grasp the meaning of things, that part of the mind tries to protect the person by locking the memories away. It serves as a way to help you avoid reliving the trauma. Are you following me?"

"Mostly, except for what you mean by 'reliving' it."

"In fundamental terms, reliving means that the mind will replay the event through your memory, and each time you run through that memory in your mind, you run the risk of feeling the emotions of the event all over again. Let me try explaining it this way: have you ever had an experience that was a lot of fun, and then the next day you remember the fun event, and doing so brings with it a sense of happiness?"

"Yeah, I guess."

"Well, it's the same notion with trauma, but the mind attempts to protect the person from re-experiencing the pain that comes with the memory. It does this by blocking the memory from your conscious mind. You lose the ability to recall it. Does that makes sense?"

I nodded. I kinda knew what she was getting at. In a way, it was like how I woke up that morning and couldn't see K.C.'s face, but after talking to Drysdale, I could almost touch him in my mind.

"I don't want to recreate the interview room situation that you had at Agent Drysdale's office when you saw the picture, but Landon, you have to try to wrap your brain around the fact that you were kidnapped."

"But I don't remember that. That's not how Bob found me. Bob told me how he found me. I know how Bob found me." The closets in the shelter popped into my mind.

"That's what I was trying to explain, how the mind works in that regard. I know this is a strange way to explain it, but you don't have to have a real memory to know what reality is—the mind is so powerful that it can create, essentially, a reality for you without any memory attached. You confirmed this yourself the other night, when I asked you if you remember being with your parents and then leaving. Your response was that you didn't have to remember it, you just knew it. Right?"

"Yeah, but I didn't force myself to believe that. I knew it already."

"Could you have been programmed to believe that? Is it possible you were *tricked* into believing it?"

It felt like the air in the room thickened and the temperature dropped. "This is getting too strange." I felt the chair sides closing in on me, about to trap me.

"Are you feeling panicked, Landon?" Her eyes focused on my hands as they gripped the arms of the chair.

"No, you're just saying weird things."

"Do you think you could try to accept your abduction as a fact?"

"Why are you asking me this?"

"It may be difficult to initiate a reunion with your parents if all of us are not in agreement that a kidnapping took place."

"Then I don't want a reunion." I was getting irritated. The collar on my shirt was scratching my neck. The stupid bathroom upstairs flashed into my mind, alternating with visions of the closets in the shelter where Bob found me. When I tried to loosen my collar, the button flew off. I wanted to stand up. I needed to go.

I felt trapped.

I was worried that I was getting dizzy.

"I can see that you're getting upset, Landon. Can you share with me what you're feeling right now? I'd like to help you learn how to deal with these emotions."

"How?" Without meaning to, I started yelling. "What do you want from me? You guys have taken everything from me! I'm not even wearing my own clothes. I don't have my home anymore—even though it was all fucked up, it was my home! You guys won't tell me what's going to happen to Bob. I didn't want to stay in that world with him, but it saved me. It was the only world I knew. I didn't ask to leave! You guys say you want to give me something, give me my parents, give me back my family, but to do that you have take away a part of me? I don't get it. What the hell do you *want?*"

Tracie met my eyes calmly as she responded, "You said it. We do want to see you back with your family, if that's possible. Sadly, it is not as easy as many would think for the reasons we're talking about right now. But more than anything, I want you to feel in control over your life, over your thoughts, over your emotions and memories. Please know that you can share with me whatever is going through your mind."

"Fine, you want to know what I think? I think this is all stupid! Feel in control? How do I do that when you guys are the ones rewriting my history? You're telling me what I should think, what my memories are supposed to be."

"That's not our goal here. Can you try to take a few deep breaths? Can I show you a breathing technique to help you calm down?"

"No! Shut up. I don't want help." I dropped my head into my hands and gripped my hair, hoping I could pull it out. "I don't want anyone's help. I wasn't asking for help when all this shit went down."

I didn't see Tracie do it, but she moved her chair next to mine. "Landon, most importantly, I just want you to learn how to help yourself; that's all. Can you breathe in? Just take a deep, slow breath." I don't know why, but I did what she said. *I hate myself when I get that weak.*

"That's it. Breathe in. Hold it for a second. Breathe out slowly." It was helping. I let my chest relax. I still didn't want to be there, though. I let Tracie's words enter my mind: "All I wanted to do, by talking to you, is to get you to understand that your parents want you. I'm hoping that, starting today, you can be open to thinking that they love you, and they have always loved you. They want their son back."

My voice was lower and calmer. "I was trying to believe that before you said all this to me. Now I don't know what I want to believe." I looked around her room, trying to make sense of everything around me. *This would be so much easier if I knew my parents hated me,* I thought. That would have been the easiest truth to believe in.

(14)

I knew their faces … *I was so relieved.* A minute before the door opened, I was sure I wouldn't recognize them. I know that about me; when I'm not around someone for a while, I can't remember their face. Like Evelyn, the old lady up at the main house. It had only been a couple of days since I saw her when I took the trash out, but all I could remember about her was messy black curls and straight gray hairs popping out everywhere. Nothing about her face.

Before Tracie left her office to go get my parents, she offered to show me a picture of Cathy and Dale, but I was done with pictures. She also offered to show me the newspaper clippings about my kidnapping, but that would just be more of hearing other people's versions of my history, and I was done with that.

Tracie walked in first.

I stood, which was surprising because my knees felt too weak to hold me up.

Dale walked in behind Tracie.

It really was them.

That was the other thing. I didn't know if I cared enough or had the courage to call them "Mom" and "Dad." In fact, the only question I had for Tracie before she went to go get them was, "What do I have to call them?"

She put her hand on my arm gently and said, "Call them whatever you want. It's certainly understandable to feel uncomfortable calling them 'Mom' and 'Dad.'" The strangest part of all, though, was that I called Bob "Dad" and never thought twice about it. Tracie said that wasn't weird at all. She said maybe I felt uncomfortable calling Cathy and Dale by those names because it would show them I wanted a close relationship, which involved trusting them to offer it back to me, and that was scary. Because if they did offer it back, the fear of losing them again would always exist.

66

That seemed too complicated to understand without having her repeat it like five times, so I just nodded. I figured, I didn't know what to call them, so I would try not to call them anything.

When Dale walked up to me, I felt like a wimp, a straw man with no guts. He was about Drysdale's height, with thick arms and legs. Not like a bodybuilder or anything, but every part of him was hard and strong. He had on khakis, a short-sleeve dress shirt, and brown leather shoes like the science teachers wear. He put out his hand for a shake. It took me at least seven seconds to lift my arm. His grip was tight. I tried to match it; Bob taught me that. I could tell Dale was happy with the handshake pressure—it's a guy thing, you know. That's when he smiled, and with the other hand, he reached up and cupped my elbow.

We locked eyes. I could see tears welling right above his bottom eyelashes. I didn't have any of my own to give back, but you could tell by the way he stood and his solid stature that he wasn't usually a man for tears. He gave me a tight smile, the kind where you tighten the mouth but you still manage to turn the ends of the lips up. Our hands fell apart, and he backed away with a wink, no words.

That one went smoothly.

Cathy started to step forward. The silence in the room got louder, if that makes sense. I felt Dale and Tracie staring at us from the side as Cathy inched her way toward me. It's like they wanted to compare whether we still looked like mother and son. When Cathy moved, her jewelry jingled. *I didn't remember that about her.* It seemed like eternity—however long that is—for her to take three steps my way. All of a sudden this jittery feeling came over me. I didn't want it to happen. I didn't want to meet her. I didn't want to hear her voice. I promised myself I'd run if she tried to give me a hug. She was too close. It didn't feel right. I wanted to yell, "Please, just stop! Don't come any closer." But even if I summoned every bit of asshole attitude that I had, I couldn't find the courage to stop her.

She came to rest one step away.

I calmed down.

That's when I saw a mascara smudge under her left eye. For the first time I kind of believed what Tracie had told me. Maybe they didn't ever give me away. I could see in Cathy's expression that she wanted me to call her Mom. I tried to ignore the sad frown lines on her forehead. I looked away.

These stupid questions kept popping into my mind. *What were the last twenty-four hours like for them? What does their home look like? Do they have a dog? Where were they when they got the call from Drysdale?*

When I looked back at Cathy, I saw a tear gently drip from her eye and slowly make its way down her cheek. What if what Tracie said was true—what if they *did* love me? It made me wonder … an image flashed into my head of Cathy wiping away tears, so many tears, every single day for the last seven years. I could see her looking in the mirror to see the mascara streaks that told the world of her pain. There was a part of me that wanted to relieve her suffering by saying, "I'm back, Mom." But the other part of me wanted to save myself by running away. I compromised. I just stood there, frozen.

With her open hand, she rubbed the side of my cheek. "You are such a handsome young man. You always looked like your Grandpa John when he was young." She looked over at Dale, "Oh God, can you believe he's here with us?"

Dale didn't respond.

I could see her throat twitch, like she was gulping down her emotions. Then that uncomfortable jittery feeling started to swell up in me again. I looked around at the doors in Tracie's office, wondering which would be the best for a quick exit. I looked back at Cathy. She tucked one of my dangling curls behind my ear and her fifty thin silver bracelets clanked in my ear like a prison guard's keys rattling as he walks.

She was thick in the waist. She looked squishy. Like, you could squeeze her really hard but never quite reach her bones. And she was shorter than me, which was the strangest part. Just then, I had a quick memory of hugging her somewhere, a grocery store or something, and my cheek getting scratched by her belt buckle. The reality of our relationship flooded my mind for just a blink. *I was her little shadow. Her belt-loop tag-along.*

The jittery feeling intensified, getting stronger than I was. I almost felt like calling out for help to Tracie, telling her that I might lose control. Tracie's office was getting smaller, which meant we would all be getting closer. Cathy kept trying to lock eyes with me, but I couldn't do it. I kept my eyes darting back and forth, from corner to corner. Her hand inched back over to cup my cheek. She smiled and whispered, "Oh honey, you need a haircut. I'm so excited to see you still have all your curls. They're just as I remembered them. And the long eyelashes. Oh, heaven, I bet the girls just love you, don't they?"

I hate you for asking that question, I thought. The jittery feeling subsided, leaving me feeling weak and queasy. For a second I thought I might vomit all over her, because who she was hoping I would be and who I really was … well, those things were never going to be found in one person. I felt a sliver of anger starting to expand within me. Its familiarity brought a sort of relief. I just had to work on controlling it, and then I knew I'd be fine.

"Tyler—" Her voice cracked a little and came to a halt. I knew why. Tracie told me that they were going to try to call me "Landon," even though it was weird for them. Cathy caught herself, looked Tracie's way and cleared her throat. I'm pretty sure Tracie gave her a little, almost-imperceptible nod. Cathy looked me up and down again and said, "My God, you just haven't changed one bit."

You shouldn't have said that, I yelled in my mind. I started chanting in my head, *Don't lose it. Don't lose it.* I looked around the room to see where everyone was. Dale was blowing his nose. Tracie was indicating for him to take a seat on the couch. His tears had dried up and his handkerchief was going back in his pocket. I brought my eyes back to Cathy just in time to hear, "Your father and I have missed you so much. You have no idea." And before I could finish the thought of how I hate people who tell me what I may or may not know, she came in for a hug.

It hurt.

Where was my anger when I really needed it?

"Your father and I never gave up on believing that you were alive. You have to know that, honey. We have always been here for you." Her arms around me tightened and her voice in my ear was deafening. "You need your mother now more than ever." Her palms opened on my back, squeezing me, pulling me in. I tried to dig my tennis shoes into the carpet so she couldn't bring me closer. I could feel a part of me backing out of my body. I tried to make my chest concave … to keep her away from my heart.

"Let's all have a seat." Tracie's voice rescued me.

I took a deep breath as Cathy's arms fell away. She was silent. Disappointed in my emptiness, I'm sure. I felt satisfied, though. Maybe now she would see that I had changed.

(15)

"Landon, I know you like this chair, where you sat earlier in our meeting. Why don't you have a seat?" I plopped down in the loner chair. I saw that Cathy and Dale had sat on the couch with enough distance between them that it was clear they were hoping I would squeeze in. When Tracie took her seat in one of the chairs, they closed the gap, and Dale reached for Cathy's hand. I could see he was giving it a little squeeze. I knew what that felt like from his handshake with me. Their eyes met as they exchanged a little smile and nod. It's like they mirrored one another. It was nice to watch, I guess, but I was glad I wasn't sitting between them, where I would have to feel their love pass over me.

"Dale, Cathy, I want to thank you for cooperating with our care of Landon. As I was telling Landon earlier, the first meeting in these situations doesn't always go as smoothly as many would think. I know you both were prepared to board the plane as soon as you got Agent Drysdale's call that they had found your son, but when you have parents separated from their child for years, that instant celebration can be more awkward than easy. Successful reunions involve a lot of work from both the parents and child."

I could still hear the emotions in Cathy's voice. "Oh, well, there's no question about that. Dale and I want to do what's best for our son." Hearing her use the word "son" and knowing she was referring to me sent a dagger of fear through my body. The world sped up. Things were going to move too fast.

Deep breath.

I calmed down.

I looked over to Tracie to hear a response. "Yes, that's clearly the case. In my few talks with you both, it's apparent that you care very deeply for Landon. And your support will definitely help move the process along much faster. I have to say, the hardest aspect for most parents is understanding that at this stage the child is in the throes of trauma. And especially in Landon's case, because Bob has not been brought in yet, the perception of threat hovers over the traumatized mind."

I turned my eyes away. I didn't want to see how they reacted to hearing Bob's name. I wish they had never been told about Bob. I knew that was idiotic, but just in the ten minutes of being around Dale and Cathy, I knew Bob's world wasn't anything Cathy and Dale could imagine. They were clean people, they were … they were everything Bob wasn't.

I exhaled a deep breath as Tracie pressed on, saying, "Trauma research shows that the mind and body have a difficult time being convinced that the threat of harm has retreated, that it no longer exists." Her words went in one ear and out the other because I was watching Dale. I could tell he wasn't listening. His eyes wandered over Tracie's framed college degrees, how her desk was organized. Tracie continued, not paying attention to his distracted eyes. "I hope that out of this meeting, one thing we can agree on is how we should move forward with Landon's care."

Cathy leaned forward. "Well, after our meeting earlier with you, Dale and I called a psychologist who we found through our church. Dale talked to him about, you know … about what you were saying earlier. Is this okay to … um, well, to talk about this in front of Ty—oh, God, sorry, in front of Landon?"

"Of course it is." Tracie didn't hesitate, didn't look my way for a response. She answered with authority, like she was confident I could handle whatever was said about me. It felt good that she believed in me like that.

"Okay," Cathy said hesitantly. She looked over to me. "I'm sorry, honey, I just don't want us to … well, you know …" She trailed off.

Tracie took control. "I think it's important that we all try to be as open as possible with each other. What I don't want is for Landon—" She looked my way. "I'm sorry to speak about you like you're not in the room by referring to you as a third person, but it's just that I'm trying to address everyone."

I shrugged.

Dale gave me a weird look.

Tracie turned back to Dale and Cathy. "It's very important that we ask Landon to participate in his well-being so that he develops a sense of control over his life. And to do this, he needs to be educated on his choices. So yes, I think we should speak as openly as possible. But I appreciate your concern, Cathy." Tracie looked each of us in the eyes, one by one, and turned her palms to the open position. "Does that make sense to everyone?"

I shrugged again.

Dale's eyes glanced over Tracie and landed back on me. I dropped my gaze.

Cathy was the first to speak. "Dale, shouldn't we tell her?"

He cleared his throat. "Ms. Lodin, what Cathy is getting at is we've also spoken to an attorney to know our rights in this process. It just seems absurd that you could be telling us that we can't assert our parental rights."

I wasn't sure if Dale was done speaking because Cathy jumped on the end of his sentence so quickly. "And the psychologist that Dale spoke to, he's local, in our area, the Colorado Springs area, and he told Dale he's not a specialist with trauma, but … well, it's that we finally have our son back. It seems like by keeping him here at the York center, you're making him so close, yet so far away. We don't understand how that could help. And how do we tell our friends that he didn't come home with us? There were thousands of people involved in searching for him. His rescue is on the front page of the paper today." She looked over at me and added, "We just want you back, honey."

I got the courage to look up at Dale, but his eyes had moved to focus on Tracie. In a low voice, he stated, "When I spoke to the psychologist, he was vaguely familiar with Tyler's situation because of the news, and he said he'd be happy to help us. Of course, he'd have to do his own evaluation."

A memory flashed into my mind. *Dale is an engineer.* I remembered driving by his work but never going in. I was young, barely able to see over the dashboard.

Tracie's tone commanded our attention. "I'm not the individual to speak to regarding the legality of Landon's stay. I can direct you to the appropriate department here at Emily York after our meeting concludes. And as far as the psychologist whom you contacted, he may be a good resource for the two of you to understand Landon's circumstances. And if that's a route you both choose to take advantage of, I would be more than happy to keep the psychologist apprised of Landon's progress here. Separate counseling for the family is highly recommended." There was a pause in the room, with everyone's eyes darting in different directions. Tracie continued. "But I'm sorry, Cathy, Dale, I have to stand firm, and I know Agent Drysdale is behind me on this. Landon is currently in a state of transition. If the next few months are not handled properly, catering to his psychological state, he will not have the resources he needs to cope with the past and deal with the future. Our unit at this location alone deals with hundreds of children each year. Even in those situations, when the child's abductor was his or her own parent, the child needs assistance transitioning back, forming new identities, finding ways of incorporating the old self with what he or she sees as the new self." Her last syllable stopped with a strong look to Dale. He didn't meet her eyes. Instead, he picked a piece of lint from the crease on his pants and flicked it away.

Tracie leaned back in her chair, her shoulders relaxed. "Mr. and Mrs. Roberts, it would be a great disservice to Landon if, at the very minimum, we didn't help him learn to recognize his own trust issues, which are the link to healthy relationships."

Dale finally spoke up. "Like Cathy said, we want what's best for our son. We're simply in the process of exploring our options. It's been a painful seven years, and to think we're being asked to prolong the separation is preposterous. We want our son home."

It kind of made me feel good to hear that Cathy and Dale wanted me home. I mean, I couldn't say that out loud. It felt way too stupid to even suggest that that's what was going through my mind, so I sat there just hoping my facial expression was blank. Even so, there was a small stream of excitement running through my body, down my spine, and out into my legs and arms. It made me shiver to think maybe, possibly, this could all work out.

I didn't really get what Tracie was talking about, but I think she was saying the right stuff about what I needed. I mean, even though I hated almost all the kids at school, and I had reasons for it, there was a part of me that wanted to know why it was always like that. I'd seen new kids start at my school and not end up like me. They fit in somehow. It was like there was some kind of bridge inside me that had been broken so I couldn't link up and understand people. I liked hearing that it might be fixable.

And I wasn't being stupid thinking that Tracie and Dr. Williams were going to help me just because I'm me. It wasn't personal. It was because they thought that what was going on with me was larger than me, like some of the other kids Tracie was telling me about. And I liked it when she talked about the other kids. It told me I wasn't alone in how I saw the world. Or at least that's what I was hoping it meant.

Tracie's voice brought me back to the moment. "Here at Emily York, we'll be working to give Landon an awareness of his trauma symptoms so he can learn to implement coping skills. Having coping skills helps alleviate the psychological pain. We are prescribing antidepressants and an anti-anxiety medication as needed. We'll continue with the family visits like today as well as arrange for Landon to go home for a visit."

"A teenager on antidepressants? How can you think that's safe? I've heard about the stories." Cathy jerked her head toward Dale in a state of panic. "Dale, am I right? Say something. This isn't right. You remember the Kinsley family, the boy, their teenager, he was on antidepressants, and it made him worse. He ended up committing—"

Dale stopped her in midsentence. "Cathy, let's hear her out. We need to make informed decisions. Let's not get too worked up about this. Tyler—" He cleared his throat, shaking his head a little. "Er, Landon, excuse me, doesn't need the added stressor of hearing us argue about issues that we haven't yet been educated on."

I liked his words. I was staring at his profile as he was talking. This weird thought occurred to me that I needed some kind of wink, some eye contact from him, just to prove he really meant what he was saying. But it didn't come. His focus returned to Tracie while my mind drifted off, chasing recollections of what I remembered about Dale. They were blurry memories about playing sports, knowing he wasn't there to watch. The clearest memory was his home office. It popped into my mind in vivid detail. I could remember standing at the door, looking at his drafting table, the pens and pencils, his books lined up along the walls, a lamp, the turned-off television. Everything was so still, organized, and neatly resting in its place.

I wanted to picture what he looked like in his office. What he would look like leaning over his drafting table, reaching to turn on the lamp, grabbing a book from one of the shelves. But the only way I could picture him physically in his office was with him standing with his back to me. Like, I knew every inch of his office, but I didn't know what it was like to be in his office when he was there.

"Landon, are you with us?" Tracie's voice caught me off guard.

I looked their way. They were staring at me. "Yeah, sorry. Go ahead."

Tracie turned her attention back to them. "I understand the parental concern of a child being on antidepressants, but needless suffering cannot be a choice. While Landon is with us at the unit, he will be under twenty-four hour surveillance. In my professional opinion, these are not options, Mr. and Mrs. Roberts."

"Forty-five days. My Lord." Cathy wasn't throwing as much emotion behind her words as before, but I could still hear it. "It's just that we've been waiting for this moment for so long. Our church has been so supportive, you know, with all their prayers and thoughts. It seems like our whole town is waiting for a celebration. And our family—gosh, we have family members who want to see and meet Landon."

There was a pause. The women broke out in light laughter. Dale smiled and looked at Tracie. I hadn't caught it at first, but then realized Cathy called me "Landon" without thinking about it.

Cathy's next words came out more calmly. "Dale is right, Ms. Lodin. We need to make informed decisions. We want to do what's best for everyone. So we'll just take it day by day, and I guess see where we go from there."

I wanted to give back and join in the conversation. You know, like try to call them Mom and Dad. My plan was to say some random comment, and then stick a Mom or Dad at the end of the sentence. But when I went to open my mouth, I wasn't sure if my vocal cords were frozen or what—nothing came out.

I took a deep breath.

I almost started the sentence.

I exhaled.

Then words came out, but I wanted to hit myself. They sounded so retarded. "I just, um, wanted to say that I was nervous but, um, I mean, I'm glad I saw you guys, and I think that—"

Cathy jumped on my words. And worse, she was talking to Dale. "Oh darn it, Dale. We forgot the gift from Becca that she sent for Tyler." *Maybe she saved me from being a fool; who knows.* Cathy looked over at me. "Do you remember your Aunt Becca?"

I shrugged. "I don't know."

Dale responded, "That seems to be every teenager's answer these days." He wasn't smiling, but his voice sounded like it had a smile in it. He crossed his arms and looked over at Tracie to ask, "So what do we do from here?"

"I think what we should do is have the three of you visit alone. Landon can show you our cafeteria. You can catch up on a few things, like we discussed earlier, and then we'll meet back here. Sound good?"

Cathy got the last word in. "Yeah, that'll be great. And I'm sorry I got so worked up. I just sometimes get ahead of myself as Dale knows. And maybe Tyler remembers." She giggled.

I kept my head down and my irritation under control. I tried to tell myself it was no big deal that they didn't want to hear what I was gonna say. That's what life was like for me. It was that way yesterday, the day before ... always. *Why think today is special? Just deal with it, dumb-ass.*

Dale stood up, tucked his shirt in, and headed my way. I jumped to my feet when I saw him look at me. He reminded me of Bob. They're both the kind of guys you need to take note of when they move. Know where they are and what they're doing. I knew in my gut that things would go better if I followed Dale's lead. He nodded toward the exit. Without thinking, I turned and headed for the door. He took his open hand and gave me a Drysdale pat on the back. I clenched my fists inside my pant pockets but didn't flinch.

"I see we dress alike, son." He was referring to the nerdy khakis that Tracie had brought me that morning. I went to say, "No, these aren't my clothes," but I bit my tongue and let him assume he knew something about me.

(16)

Dale pulled away from Cathy and me and walked a few steps ahead. We made our first turn toward the cafeteria when Cathy went pull out her cell. "You know what, honey, I should check my messages before we visit, okay? Everyone back at home is sitting on pins and needles waiting to get an update." She unzipped her purse, or maybe it was a piece of luggage, I didn't know, and then stopped like she'd hit a wall. She looked at me, inhaled, exhaled. Smiled. "Oh, dear Lord, aren't you just absolutely adorable?"

Who the hell was she asking? Like I would agree to a question like that about myself? *Dumb.* I clenched and unclenched my fists, which were still buried in my pockets. My green eyes and long eyelashes must have come from her side of the family. That's what she liked about me, I'm sure. I smiled back, though. I was trying to look at the positive side. If she only focused on those parts of me that reminded her of herself, maybe she'd never see the real me, the jerk that everyone else saw.

"Checking her messages" turned out to involve a major search for her phone. Her purse was gigantic. She was throwing crap around inside looking for it, making her bracelets clink like crazy. "Oh, would you look at this? I'll be darned. Where is the silly thing? Just hang tight, honey."

Dale turned around and walked back our way. "What? You probably left it at the hotel, Cathy. Or on the airplane. Did you take it on the airplane?"

"Yes, Dale. You saw me this morning talking to Becca when we were waiting for our luggage at the airport."

"Well, I don't know. Maybe you were using my cell phone."

"No, it was mine. I have Gene and Ronnie on speed dial. I remember dialing them with my own phone. Remember on the drive to the hotel I showed you Evan's cute text message that came from Becca's phone?"

"Yeah, yeah. Just keep looking."

At first, hearing them talk was kind of funny. It sounded like an old married couple who knew yelling words back and forth wouldn't lead to a divorce. Then it hit me: they were supposed to be my parents, and I didn't know any of the names they were mentioning. I couldn't picture in my mind a Gene, a Ronnie, a Becca, or an Evan. They were talking about their family circle, and I wasn't in it.

Dale took another pace back and forth. "Jesus, Cathy, you lose everything."

"Dale, please. That's not helping." Her head actually went inside her purse to look around. The stupid luggage thing was that big. She pulled her lipstick out and palmed it. Then this gigantic, bulging wallet came out with papers sticking out everywhere, and she tucked that under her arm. A calendar-like thing fell out and hit the ground; Dale grabbed it. Then her keys came out, which were weird looking and made twice as much noise as her bracelets. It actually wasn't the keys themselves, but the fact that she had close to fifty of those decoration things that people put on their key rings.

I leaned my back against the wall, looking straight ahead and trying to give them their space. The janitor came waddling down the hallway toward us. He didn't see me at first. His attention was on my parents. His eyes widened, entertained by their chaos. When he passed by, he smiled at me, rolled his eyes with a jerk of his head at my parents, and winked. I gave him a nod back, the same head movement and … I smiled.

I was sure about the smile. It was a normal smile, like I'd give Sam or the metal shop guys. I understood the janitor now. A smile was his way of saying, "Hey, I hope you're doing okay." And after the cigarette-match thing at the trashcan, something told me he wanted to know how I was doing.

Cathy pulled out a piece of paper. "Look, Dale, it's that prescription for Evan's inhaler that I thought I lost. I had it the whole time."

"Cathy, that's ridiculous. You should have tucked that into your wallet." He looked at her bulging wallet under her arm. "Well, maybe not. But Jesus, that's just absurd." Dale turned around, ran a hand through his short hair. There wasn't a hair out of place before or after. "I can't believe you had the prescription with you the whole time. Remember how I had to drive to get the new prescription form?"

"Well, I'm sorry, Dale, okay?"

He took a step her way. "Let me look inside." He reached for her purse.

"No, stop, Dale. Just call my cell phone. I'm sure it's in here." Dale flipped the flap on his leather phone holder that looped through his belt, started pulling out his cell. Instantly, though, Cathy stopped her search. "Oh dear, no. Never mind, Dale. I would have turned it off for the meeting. Did I turn it off? Or … Oh, that's it." She threw her head back and sighed, "You know what happened, Dale? I was talking to Becca by the window in the hotel where I plugged in my charger. Darn it! I remember setting it back down on the table." She reached for Dale's cell. "Give me yours to use. Remember Becca was going to call me right back about the Sunday barbecue, but then you rushed me out of the hotel room."

"Oh, so it's my fault. Good work, Cathy." He handed her his cell phone, shaking his head. "We'll meet you inside the cafeteria." He looked my way. "Tyler, come on. Let's go." I didn't have time to care about being called Tyler. I saw his eyes look down toward my knees. I had put the sole of my tennis shoe against the wall and was kicking back. "Don't put your foot up on the wall like that." He pointed to the wall. "Look." I leaned forward, off the wall, and twisted around to look. There was a dirt shoeprint on the white paint. "See, you left a mark. Let's go."

It was a weird feeling to have him correct me like that. He wasn't a backhand-across-the-face guy like Bob when he's sober, so I was questioning why I should take that kind of heat about a stupid smudge mark. I stopped myself and pulled back my irritation. I should try to be thankful because he was showing me what to do and not to do, normal "dad" stuff, I guess. And besides, thinking about the janitor having to wipe off the mark wasn't cool.

I could tell Dale didn't need me to show him where the cafeteria was. He walked through the doors like he owned the place and grabbed a tray for himself and one for me. Then he immediately headed over to the area where you picked out what foods you wanted. There was nothing hesitant about him. He grabbed two silverware packets turned to hand me one. "Here, *Tyler*." I got the message. I dealt with it by convincing myself I was an empty shell. I put my eyes to the ground, walked behind him, and nodded to his words. I wasn't going to be Landon in his eyes.

He had this kind of uptightness about him, too. Like if I responded to him with a mumble or stutter, he'd bark back, "Whaddya mean by that?" He would do it right at my face, too, whether it was just us two or in a room full of people. He didn't turn around when he spoke to me, either. He was happy knowing that I was following. Lucky for him, I thought;

Bob made me a master at hearing everything even though I stayed two steps behind.

"I don't know what they've told you in here, Tyler, but the attorney we've talked to agrees with us. If we have our way, you'll be out of here in a week. To think they can make you a ward of the court, take our rights away when we've done nothing wrong, is ludicrous. I have to agree with your mother on this: we're being victimized all over again."

"I guess they just want to make sure I'll do okay when I get back, you know ... I guess," I said quietly. That's when he turned around and looked at me. Either he was irritated that I had an opinion, or he knew what I meant but he didn't like how I strung the words together. "Well, that's all psychobabble. Don't listen to it. You need to be back with us, in our home, with our family. This Tracie Lodin lady just wants to make sure she gets her federal funding, that's all. When you get home, you'll put everything behind you. You can cooperate with Agent Drysdale's investigation from Colorado Springs. And whatever happened with that Robert guy, well, it's over; it's the past. Today is the day we move forward." He paused. I got the eye contact I was looking for in Tracie's office from him. "Am I right?"

"Well, yeah, I just ..." He was making sense, but I couldn't get over hearing him call Bob "Robert." The way he said it felt like the life I left behind in the trailer was in some distant country that Dale hadn't heard of, and because of that, it didn't deserve a spot on the world map. And also, at the same time, I knew he wasn't going to allow me to call him anything but "dad." I imagined accidentally mumbling a "Dale," and instead of getting a compassionate laugh about how we have to move on from that, he'd be the guy that would give a stern asshole-type correction: "I'm your father. That's what you'll call me."

Then this feeling came over me, yelling at me from my gut, saying, *Make sure you're really paying attention because something is about to go wrong.* In a weird way, even though Dale was taking me away from the trailer, the way I felt around him with his authoritative talk—it was like a part of me still felt like I was with Bob.

"Tyler, answer the guy. You want cheese on your hamburger?"

"Oh, sorry." I looked over the counter to the cook. "Yeah, please." The guy responded by turning back to the grill and slapping a slice of cheese on the patty. I started to drift back into my thoughts but was yanked into the present when Dale turned around to give me my first new-life instruction. "And I know about the school situation. You have to go back to school."

"Definitely. I have that worked out. Well, I mean I did before they took me out of there, you know, out of the trailer." It was the first full sentence I spouted out with no stuttering.

Dale kind of snorted. "Oh, you think you have that figured out? We'll talk about that later." He looked down at his watch. "Jesus, your mother is taking forever."

While I waited for my cheeseburger, Dale took a look at the desserts and said to the counter guy, "We'll take two of the peach cobblers." He walked back over to me, put one cobbler on my tray and the other on his. *What the hell? I'll never eat that crap*, I thought. I jerked my head a little, but he didn't notice because he turned to the cook and thanked him for me. Then he reached up and grabbed my cheeseburger, and put *that* on my tray. We walked toward the cashier, and I got the next direction: "Go find a seat while I pay for this."

"Should I, um …" I didn't want to say it. I wasn't sure the word would come out, or make sense. I knew I was betraying Bob, but I had to start somewhere. "Should I get, ah, you know, get *Mom* something?"

He didn't miss a beat. "No, just go find a seat. She'll get her own lunch." He pulled out his wallet, and I walked off to do as I was told. He would never know how difficult it was to say that sentence, that three-letter word.

I can't remember how I found a seat. I was kind of in a daze, frankly. I looked over at Dale, paying with exact change. His wallet fit perfectly in his back pocket. The ironed creases down his pants probably went right over the centers of his kneecaps. And the way his food was arranged on his tray: precise angles. I looked at the entrance door, hoping Cathy would come in before Dale took his seat. But he was heading my way, and there was no sign of her.

Deep breath.

I remembered being five years old. My mom was walking toward my dad. He was across the street, standing next to his car in a parking lot, yelling something to her. I ran up behind my mom, trying to hide from him. I was stumbling in her footsteps. I was wearing my Little League uniform. She reached behind her, grabbed my arm, jerked me forward, and forced me to walk at her side. I started to cry. I felt exposed. I needed her to stand between him and me.

I looked at the cafeteria door again. *No Mom.* She was our middle ground.

Dale took his seat next to me. And for the first time that afternoon, I had a good sense of what it was like to be home.

(17)

Cathy bolted through the cafeteria door and made a beeline straight for us. "Dale, did you tell him?"

"No, I wasn't going to say anything without you here."

Cathy was out of breath. She still clutched her wallet under her arm. She set that and Dale's cell down on the table. She plopped her huge purse on a nearby chair, took off her sweater and threw that on top of the purse, and then put the wallet on top of all that. She sank into the chair next to her stuff and leaned forward, smiling. I wanted to back away but I was sitting in a plastic booth and there was a wall behind that. "We have a surprise for you, honey," she said smiling. I didn't think it could be a gift, an actual gift in a box like the one they talked about from an Aunt Becca who I don't remember. I would have seen it when she emptied out all her crap from her purse in the hallway. "Are you ready, honey? Do you like surprises? You used to love surprises." She started to rock back and forth. I was getting motion sickness from it.

"Jesus, just tell him, Cathy." Dale sounded exasperated.

"All right, all right, all right." She sat still, paused, took a breath. Her smile got bigger, which I didn't think was possible. "You have a brother, a little brother, honey." I think she clapped her hands and squealed a little, even cried a tear of joy maybe, I didn't know. "Isn't that exciting, honey?"

The "honey" crap was gonna make me throw up.

"His name is Evan," she blurted out.

Now I knew who one of the people in the family circle was.

"So tell us, honey, what do you think?"

I wanted to say, "Stop the 'honey' bullshit," but that would get Dale pissed off and all up in my face. Honestly, I didn't have an answer for her.

"Tell me what you think, honey." Her lipstick was shiny, her voice squeaky. The mascara smudge was gone, but there was some kind of glitter crap mixed in with her eye shadow. I tightened my lips to make sure nothing came out. I just wanted to be left alone for thirty seconds to try to figure out how I was feeling.

She looked over at Dale and then back at me. "Well, when we told Ms. Lodin, she said you might find your relationship with Evan confusing. But once you and Evan get to visiting ... oh gosh, I can tell, you're really excited, aren't you?" Her eyes widened, and she was still grinning. She was waiting for an answer.

And ... she was gonna have to keep waiting.

She looked over at Dale, and her smile faded a tiny bit. He didn't say anything. She looked at me again.

Damn it. She still wanted an answer. I opened my mouth and forced out, "That's cool, I guess."

Her smile burst. "Oh, see, we knew you'd be excited. Didn't we, Dale?"

Dale was looking down at his peach cobbler. No reaction. Or maybe there was, but everything about me was shutting down. The voice in my mind was talking slower. Every movement I made was starting to take twice the energy. It's like I was riding on a teeter-totter by myself. I would jump up, get my end in the air, and that's when I would be happy, but because I didn't have a partner, I'd slam back to the ground. I was getting too tired to try to get myself back up in the air again. Nothing seemed worth the energy anymore.

"You are happy, aren't you, honey?" Her face felt like it was two inches away from me. "Evan can't wait to meet you. He's five years old and just started kindergarten."

"Cathy, give him some space. This is a lot for him to take in. Why don't you go get something to eat? Tyler and I didn't know what you wanted."

"Oh, okay. But before I go, I told Evan we'd call him in a little bit, okay, honey?" She patted the side of my arm with her hand. It was the same kind of hand-squeeze move that Dale gave her in Tracie's office. It wasn't helping me like it helped her. I just needed her to go get her food so I could sit in silence and try to bring my mind back to life. She wasn't leaving, though. She readjusted herself in the chair and put her sweater back on. "We left Evan with Ronnie. Do you remember Ronnie? Well, we all call her Ronnie, but Rhonda. Do you remember Rhonda, my best friend from college? She moved back to Colorado Springs about three years ago."

I tried to tune her out. I needed silence to process all the crap she was throwing in my ears. *A brother? How did I feel about a brother?* He couldn't replace K.C. It sounded better in my mind to say, *Cathy and Dale have a son, and I am linked to him by blood.* I couldn't get the silence I needed. She wouldn't stop talking. "We left Evan with Rhonda, and he sent this text message that—honey, are you with us?"

I murmured, "Yeah." I wasn't, though. And she didn't follow up with an, "Are you sure?" so I continued to drift away. But I was glad for it. The only way to survive the moment was to hope that emotional numbness would take over. I watched her lips move, but her voice was getting farther away as she prattled on. "Well, Evan wanted to come with us so bad." I tried to smile, and I think she thought I did. Some relief came when she turned to Dale. "I had five messages. Thank God I checked them." I tensed, again, though, when she turned back to face me. "Everyone can't wait to meet you. If we don't get you home in the next week, well, they'll all be here with us on the next visit." She turned back to Dale, but I wasn't sure if I should relax yet or not hearing her words. "The news has our story all over it, every channel. There's a nationwide search for ..." She looked at me out of the corner of her eye, lowered her voice. "... for Robert Starker. And Ronnie says there are reporters at our house, waiting outside the house. One of the messages was from—"

"Cathy, please. Go get your lunch," Dale interjected. "We'll talk about that later. Give him some time to absorb what's going on. We have other things to discuss, like how we're going to handle getting him out of here."

Cathy leaned in toward me. "I'm sorry, honey. My emotions are just all over the place. Your dad's right. I need to give you some space to take all this in." She looked over at Dale. He gave her a nod toward the cheeseburger station and ended the look with a wink. She finally left to plate up her lunch.

I put my head down, pretending I was picking at my food. I was sitting between Dale and a wall. The table was bolted to the floor. I wanted out. I wanted to leave. That's what I was going to do. I was going to slowly walk away. I knew I was too tired to run, because I felt this wave of exhaustion come over me every time I asked myself, *Where would you run to?*

"Tyler."

"Huh?" I looked up.

"You and your mom were really close when ..." Dale turned his head away. I could see his left hand reaching into his pocket for the handkerchief.

He lowered his voice. "Deciding to have Evan was something I really felt she needed." He ushered in some emotional control. The handkerchief stayed in his pocket. "You have to understand that these are things that parents go through, and, well, we just have to work at getting us all back on track." He took his fork and moved his salad around on the plate. He shook his head back and forth slowly. "That Robert Starker deserves to burn in hell. He'll be lucky if I don't find him first."

I don't know why I said it, but I did. "Bob tried to do the best he could with me, you know." I think it was a mixture of me trying to hold on to my trailer life as screwed up as it was and being fearful I couldn't fit into their family circle. But if I could have grabbed the words as they came out of my mouth, I would have taken them back …

My father has grayish-blue eyes. I saw them clearly when he turned to me and, in a voice that rattled my bones, said, "Don't you ever say anything like that again about that man. Do you understand me?"

I gave the table one quick shake just to make sure it was bolted to the ground; it was. I wasn't getting out. I was stuck. I stared down at my plate. "Yeah, you're right. I'm sorry. I'm stupid sometimes, you know."

He turned his head away, but I heard his words clearly. "I wish you would have thought about calling us, just once. Just to let us know you were alive." Every thought in my head mixed around and scrambled up. I was afraid to respond. Tracie's talk with me before meeting my parents flashed into my head. Another part of me thought, *How do you call someone when you know for sure they won't answer?* It was never a choice, as stupid as that sounds. I responded in the only way I knew how: "I'm sorry."

I guess it worked. He sat silently until Cathy made her way back to the table. She took note of Dale's mood. Her voice was calmer and slower as she said, "So, honey, I haven't had the heart to read what Agent Drysdale has given us. You know, the reports about what life was like with him."

The "him" was with a capital "H." "You mean Bob?" I asked.

Dale corrected me. "Robert Starker."

I could feel my anger bulging behind my ribcage, using up my last little bit of energy. *Why are you defining my world? You didn't live in it.* I wanted to yell out but the raging words stayed trapped in my mind.

She looked at me. "Yes, with Robert. What was it like, honey?"

"I don't know." I shrugged. "Not good, I guess." My lungs were freezing. I couldn't breathe. The word "it" really bugged me. *What was it like?* I asked myself. *My whole life … Why such a small word to ask about seven years?*

She looked to Dale, her forehead worry lines creasing. She looked back to me. "We've always kept the same phone number and, well, we just want you to know that you've never left our prayers. It's a mother's instinct, but I just knew that one day we would have you back."

There was silence, and I managed to loosen up my lungs enough to take in a deep breath, but she couldn't leave it alone. "Oh, but Agent Drysdale did tell us that there was another boy."

I didn't have to think to respond. "Yeah, K.C."

"Right," Cathy smiled, "that's the name. Was he nice to you?"

"He was like my brother." Dale coughed what I knew was a fake cough. I put my hands below the table and gripped them together so hard my knuckles turned white. My anger was going somewhere, and I was trying to keep it away from them.

She tilted her head to the side. "Oh, well, that's nice that the two of you got along."

Got along? What the hell does "got along" mean?

A memory popped into my mind of Bob beating K.C. There was something about K.C.'s mouth ... it wasn't clear in the memory. I remembered tears streaming down my face, begging Bob to blame me, direct his anger at me. It was at the bungalow, in the living room. I wanted to run to K.C., to shield him from Bob's rage, or at least be near to him, but something was stopping me. I couldn't help him. As the memory flooded my mind, the little voice in my head asked why I couldn't move toward K.C., what was stopping me. It's that voice that you don't listen to in the moment, but afterward you know it was talking to you, trying to get you to pay attention and figure things out.

I let the K.C. thought drift away because the intensity of the memory and hearing Cathy say we "got along" didn't match up. There wasn't enough room in my emotions to think of the two experiences at the same time, so I came back to the discussion at the table when Cathy asked how old "the boy" was.

Dale was eating, not looking at either of us.

I scanned the cafeteria. The external world was moving in slow motion, but inside, I was raging and ready to explode. I compared my memory of Bob beating K.C. to how Cathy and Dale were sitting there, nice clean people surrounded by the white walls of a cafeteria. Hearing her call K.C. "the boy" echoed in my brain. My lungs wouldn't expand. My ear muscles tightened. I bit my teeth together until my jaw was shaking.

How could they reduce my life to "it"?

How could they reduce my brother to "the boy"?

I snapped.

"Excuse me. I have to go to the bathroom."

Dale got up. Let me scoot out.

It was the only way I knew how to leave, and I was fine with not saying goodbye.

(18)

"Landon?" Tracie's voice echoed in the stairwell.

I didn't answer. The cold cement floor, brick walls and gray metal railings were the only company I wanted.

"Landon? Are you here?" Her heels were clanking on the metal stairs. She was alone. She wasn't rushing, but she was coming closer.

Finally she appeared. "There you are. Can I join you for a few minutes?"

I shrugged.

She sat down, cross-legged, with her back against the cement wall. It was like that first night when I sat in the chair and she was on the floor.

We sat there for like what seemed forever. She broke the silence. "I've always been curious, why the stairwell? I find more than half of the kids I see here in the unit in the stairwell at some point." At the end of every sentence she'd pause, I guess waiting to see what I was gonna say. I just sat there, staring straight ahead. I could feel her eyes tracing my profile. She continued on. "At first, I was so confused by this. Why not the atrium? Or the sundeck on the rooftop?" Her voice rose a little. "Oh, that's right, I wanted to make sure I asked you, did they show you the sundeck on the roof?"

They had, but I wasn't going to be tricked into talking.

"Well, if they haven't shown you yet, I'll make sure you know where it is."

Another pause.

"You know, I had one girl I was working with, her name was Ann, and I finally asked her, 'Why the stairwell? It's dark. Cold. Gray.' She looked at me, huge tears welling up in her eyes, and said, 'It's the only place where I feel comfortable.' I didn't get it. She had been with us for several weeks and was moving forward with the therapy, excited about her future. Then I saw a tear fall to the cement floor and puddle there. She took her fingertip and dipped it into the tear. It made me understand. She was still attached to the pain she lived with before she was brought to us. And so being surrounded by her tears would bring on a familiar feeling, and in here at the York center, we were always pushing her to step into the unknown."

Tracie stopped talking, and I guessed that was all she was gonna say about Ann. The silence was getting weird. I was worried that the next conversation would be about my parents, so I asked, "What happened to Ann? I mean, why was she here?"

"Ann was abducted by her mother, who had a drug problem and suffered from mental health issues. They were essentially homeless, living in and out of cars, public bathrooms. They would land in a homeless shelter here and there, but Ann's mom would be kicked out for drug use, or for leaving Ann unattended, and then they'd be back on the streets."

"Did her dad want her?"

"Oh yeah. But Ann's mom convinced her that he didn't, and that if he found them, he'd kill them both. That's how she explained to Ann why they had to live the way they did. But, yes, her father loved her very much and helped through the transition process as much as he could. I mean, he had his own baggage."

"What do you mean?"

"Well, while Ann was here at the unit her dad violated his parole and had to go back to prison."

The words "prison" and "dad" made me think of Sam.

"I'm glad Ann came to my mind, though. I need to check on her, see how she's doing. Her dad might be out of prison now."

I turned my head toward Tracie. I got this feeling that I hated. It was the feeling I get right before I decide to share something about myself, and that voice inside me would say, *You're stupid if you talk. No one wants to hear you.* But I kind of wanted to know if Tracie would have the same explanation as Bob as to why Sam's dad did what he did. "My friend's dad is in prison."

"Oh, really? What friend?"

"His name is Sam."

"Right, Drysdale mentioned a Sam the night you came in. Is that the same one?"

"Yeah."

"So Sam's dad is in prison. For how long?"

"He's doing life."

"That must be hard on Sam."

"Well, over the summer, this last summer, his dad wrote him a letter saying that he didn't want to hear from him again. Saying something like, you know, 'Yeah, I was your dad for a while, but now it's not working out, so goodbye.'"

"That's pretty rough, isn't it?"

"Yeah, that's what I thought. I was so mad at his dad, you know. Like, I didn't even know the guy, never even saw a picture of him. But I knew Sam, and he didn't deserve that."

"What do you mean 'he didn't deserve that'?"

"I dunno. I mean, it's like he was trying to throw Sam away, just erase him from his life. And, you know, Sam isn't a perfect kid but ... I dunno. It's stupid."

"What's stupid?"

"Like ... you know, it's not like Sam chose the life that he was born into, but everyone expects him to deal with it."

"I can hear in your voice that you're upset about it, aren't you?"

"I guess. It makes me sad to think about it. Like this one time, I got sick—throw-up sick—and Sam rode his bike over and did my chores so Bob wouldn't be a dick when he got home. I mean, I know Sam and I are screw-ups, you know, like getting busted with the weed and stuff, but deep down ... I dunno."

"Don't know what, deep down?"

"He knows how to care about people, Sam does."

"Like you? You know how to care about people, don't you?"

I looked at her, sort of annoyed. I was talking about Sam, not me. She met and held my stare, though, so I added, "When he was reading his dad's letter, I just couldn't stop thinking how he didn't deserve to be thrown away like that. I mean, doesn't his dad even want to know what kind of son he has? It pissed me off."

"Of course. That's really painful, for a son to feel like his parents don't want him. Did Sam feel the same way as you?"

"Well, he was just being Sam, you know, and telling me, 'It's cool, dude, whatever.' But I was mad. I hated his dad. I was even mad at his mom because she wasn't crying for Sam, you know, telling him that he didn't deserve that. Like, why wasn't someone showing him he didn't have to be treated that way?" I was getting worked up, so I tried the breathing that Tracie showed me earlier.

"What's your body feeling like right now, Landon?"

"I have this yelling feeling. Like you're on a cliff and you need to yell at someone far away but no matter how loud you yell, they're not going to hear you, so you're just frustrated because it's not even worth yelling, but you still want to."

"Do you remember feeling that way when you were talking to Sam?"

"I don't know. I mean, when Sam was reading the letter, all this anger came out of me, and I turned and hit the side of the trailer with my fist. Sam was like, 'Dude, it's no big deal,' but I couldn't stop yelling that his dad was an asshole. I mean, how can you do that to your kid?" My chest started tightening. "Whatever, though." A sliver of calmness crept in. "I don't know why I get so upset over the Sam's dad thing anyway."

"Maybe you do have a good reason. Can I ask you a question?"

I nodded.

"Can you see any similarities between what happened to Sam and what happened to you?"

"What do you mean?"

"Well, when we first met, you told me that your parents didn't want you, and that's how you ended up with Bob. Is there any similarity in that reality compared to what Sam's dad did to him?"

I resisted the urge to roll my eyes. "I dunno, maybe. But that doesn't matter anyway, because, like you said, I was taken."

"Kidnapped, yes. But whatever your feelings were when you believed that your parents didn't want you, they're not going to just go away or disappear. They're real. They want to be heard. Does that make sense?"

"No. Well, yeah, I guess."

"You lived for seven years believing that you weren't wanted, didn't you?"

The memory of me sitting under the dining room table staring at the front door popped into my head again. When Tracie asked me that question, it was weird how all of sudden I knew what I was waiting for as I was staring at the front door.

"Landon, what are you thinking about?"

"The first time Bob told me that my parents didn't want me."

"Where were you?"

"In some apartment ... I don't really know where. It's dark inside but daylight outside. I was sitting on my knees, waiting for Bob to come back, because he said he was going to go talk to my mom and dad. I can see the front door opening and ... and I really think that my mom is going to walk in behind Bob. I just really figured that Bob would ask her, 'Are you sure you guys don't want him?' and she'd say, 'Yeah, we'll take him back.' But … but … eh, it's stupid." I wanted to stop talking in order to stop my pain.

"Maybe it's not stupid. Can we just go with it?"

I shrugged.

"So the door opens, and who walks in?"

"It's Bob. First I saw the light from outside come through the open door, and then his boots, and then the door shut. My mom wasn't there." I felt a stream of tears trying to leak out the corners of my eyes. I felt embarrassed that I couldn't squeeze them back, but I stayed with the memory. "I wanted to yell so loud to my parents, you know, like, 'I'm sorry, please take me back. I didn't mean to make you guys hate me.' But I couldn't scream."

"Is that the same feeling you were describing about standing on a cliff and wanting to yell?"

"Yeah, like I wanted to yell loud enough for my voice to reach my mom and dad at our house."

"Did you try yelling when you were in the apartment?"

"No, because I had to keep the mouth cover on."

"What do you mean? What's the mouth cover?"

"Bob wanted to make sure I didn't yell, you know, and get the police involved, because that would ruin any chances for my parents to ever want me. The police would separate us all and get my parents into trouble. And, you know, Bob would come back and make sure the knot on the mouth cover wasn't messed up. He'd know if you took it off or something while he was gone."

"Of course."

"And my parents weren't going to hear me anyway."

"How do you know that?"

"Bob told me they were never going to hear me. It hurt Bob to tell me that, too. I remember he sat down in the living room, and I was still under the table. He turned on a light and told me to come over and sit by him. When I got close to Bob, I could tell he was sad."

"Bob was sad?"

"Yeah. I sat on the coffee table in front of him. My feet were barely touching the ground. He took the mouth cover off, and I looked at Bob's face. I knew right away he was sad because my parents told him they didn't want me, and he didn't know how to tell me. I reached out to his hand, and I told him, 'It's okay. Maybe they'll want to come get me later.' But he just shook his head at me and said, 'No, kid. I tried to get them to take you back, but they're done with you. They hate you.' I remember there was this chip in the wood on the coffee table, and I just tried to stare at it and not cry, you know. I was worried I'd make things worse for Bob if I cried like a baby. I didn't want to hurt his feelings and make him feel like I didn't want to be with him because he was trying to help."

My nose was running. Tears streamed down my cheeks.

"You worried a lot about how Bob felt, didn't you?"

"Yeah, Bob really had a rough life, you know. He wanted to help K.C. and me both. It was weird how he did it, but where else were we going to go? I think a lot of his beatings were just from the stress of raising us. I always knew he was trying to do the right stuff because he felt bad after he'd lose control."

There was silence in the stairwell, and the whirring in my mind started to slow down.

Tracie's voice was soft and didn't echo. "You know that feeling you have of wanting to yell, Landon?" I nodded. "It might help, if you felt comfortable enough with me, to try to yell for your mom and dad now."

"I don't know. That's weird."

"It's just us here. I've seen it help others before. Would you maybe want to try?"

"I don't know."

"Picture in your mind being under that dining room table, okay? Now, I'll assure you that the police are not around, they're not going to hear you, so if you yell, no one will get in trouble. If that were the case, what would you yell?"

"Come get me. Take me back. I'm sorry."

"Of course you would. How loud would you yell it?"

"Come get me." I raised my voice a little. "Take me back."

"Louder."

"Come get me! Take me back."

"Louder."

"Come get me! Take me back! You can't throw me away! I'm your son! I'm sorry! Please ... *just come get me!*" My voice turned hoarse. My fists clenched so hard my fingernails bent backward. My stomach muscles tightened.

"And if you brought back into your mind the moment when Bob entered the door, and imagined that your mom walked in behind him, that same woman that was in my office earlier calling you 'honey' with all of her bracelets jingling around, what do you think she would do if she saw you under that dining room table, Landon?"

"She would have taken me home."

"I think you're absolutely right."

I didn't have any more words. Tracie didn't either. I sat there with the feeling of seeing my mom walk through the door, running over to me, hugging me. And even though it was fiction in my mind, I relished the thought, bringing it as close to my reality as I could.

"Landon."

"Huh?"

"It's amazing to me that through everything you retained a sense of self-worth."

"What do you mean?"

"I work with kids who truly believe that they are worth throwing away. Their reaction to Sam would have been, 'Just deal with it.' But somewhere inside you, you knew that you didn't deserve to be left behind."

Tracie's footsteps were softer on the way up the stairs.

I didn't understand why the yelling thing helped, but I could tell I wasn't as angry at Sam's dad. And, I think, I started to miss my mom a little. It was a new feeling. I wasn't sure if I wanted it, though.

(19)

"So the meeting with the parents the other day didn't go too well, did it?" Drysdale cocked his head a little, and the side of his mouth rose. I couldn't gather if the look was saying it's no big deal, or it went how he expected it would.

"I don't know. I guess not."

He didn't just have a folder this time. It was a box, one of those ones that you assemble yourself. He flipped the top off and started unpacking. The folder that he had from the first night was thicker now. He pulled out four thick three-ring binders, a laptop, his normal yellow pad of paper and three pens. He organized it all on the table. All of a sudden the place felt like he owned it. It wasn't just the room down the hall from Tracie's office. His jacket came off as usual. He swung it around the back of the chair, loosened up his tie, looked over at me, and asked "Are you comfortable?"

"Sure."

"Looks like they got you some new clothes. Do you like them?" He was referring to my new hoodie and baggy jeans. I didn't know who at Tracie's place got them for me, but the cool thing was that the hoodie had the same green John Deere logo as the one I wore at the trailer.

Drysdale's comment reminded me of how Dale thought that he and I dressed alike. It was the first sign from Dale that it was going to be his way or no way; the world through his eyes was the only right world. And yeah, it's true that I lived Bob's way and didn't get pissed off at him all the time, but that's probably because Bob had guns that he used. I couldn't imagine that that would be Dale's style.

"We gave Tracie's assistant a list of some of your clothing articles that we took into possession from the trailer." *That solved the hoodie mystery*, I realized. I thought it was a weird coincidence when I saw the hoodie in my room that morning, and it was the same as my old one I left at the trailer. Thinking about the trailer reminded me of all my other crap. Not like the stuff was priceless or anything—I mean, honestly, I felt like a bum who cares about his shopping cart full of trash pickings—but it was my stuff and I missed it all. "Will I get any of my things back?"

"I doubt it, but you never know." There was a pause, like Drysdale was checking me out to see how I took the statement. "I'm sorry, Landon." I shrugged. His eyes were still on me. "I don't know if Tracie shared this with you, but most of the kids we come in contact with are parent abductions."

"Yeah."

"Well, when they do the trauma research for these individuals, usually as follow-up years later, they find that although the children were reunited with their loved ones, they more often than not were traumatized during the abduction recovery by being ripped away from their belongings, school, friends … the life they had adjusted to, the identity they formed to survive. Hopefully we've learned a little from their experiences and are helping to make the transition smoother, even if it's a small thing like a sweatshirt."

I looked down at the green logo on the sweatshirt. It was the first time since all the crap started that I recognized something about myself from the outside looking in. I was kind of cool with not seeing Sam, like I'd learn to deal with it, but to have all my stuff taken away from me made me feel like the world would have no idea who I was when it looked at me. It was a weird feeling, but the sweatshirt helped make it go away a little. I don't think Drysdale got that I was feeling okay about it, though, because he asked, "Has Tracie been helpful?"

"Yeah, I think so."

"Good. I've seen them do some amazing work here with children and teenagers."

"She's told me about some of them."

"Tragedies, aren't they?"

"I guess." I really wasn't sure, even about that word, so I quickly asked, "What do you mean by a tragedy, though?"

"What I mean by that is an event took place in a person's life that shouldn't have, and because of that event, the person has suffered a great deal."

"Oh."

"If you think about life as a straight line," he went on, using his hand to indicate what he was saying, "you can kind of sense what the future is. I think this is true for any age, young or old. An infant can't comprehend what the path looks like, but he knows his mom is on it, right?"

I shrugged.

"But when a tragedy happens, your life takes a drastic turn." He used his hand again to make a sharp L-shape. "It can be devastating when a person must involuntarily turn away from or detach from that original straight line. That's how I think of an event being tragic, especially for children who have so little control over their life. Does that make sense?"

I nodded my head. I was thinking of the way he described it all. I didn't see how it applied to me, though.

Drysdale grabbed his writing pad, crossed his legs, and leaned back in his chair, looking my way. "What are you thinking about, Landon?"

"Nothing."

"Nothing?"

"Well, not nothing, but I dunno, like, how do you know if you're off that path, that straight line that you're talking about? I don't feel like I am."

"I suspect that's because you don't remember enough about your original path in life. It's not alive in your mind. You don't quite know what you missed out on yet. In other words, you may not recognize or feel the loss that you've experienced from being removed from that path."

"Oh." The memory of scratching my cheek on my mom's belt as a little kid popped into my head and then faded right away. I nodded at Drysdale. "Maybe, huh?"

He had this look about him sometimes, like he was happy with your thoughts even though he didn't know what exactly you were thinking. He kind of nodded back at me and said, "I'm glad you stood up for yourself."

"What do you mean?"

"With your parents, in the cafeteria. I interpreted your actions as taking care of yourself emotionally."

"Really?"

"Of course. You need to let people know what you want from them. We all do. And if I understand what happened correctly, you didn't exactly communicate it the best way, but I think your actions indicated that you weren't getting what you needed from them. Maybe they need to understand you better."

"Do you know if they're mad at me?"

"I don't detect any anger from them. Tracie talks more to your mother than I do, but I've talked to your dad several times. My sense is that they love and care about you, and they're starting to realize that they were not grasping the gravity of your situation. Maybe they were more focused on the celebration and not the reparation."

I shrugged. I didn't understand the last word, but I pretty much knew what he was saying. It felt weird to say it out loud, but I knew the part that really bothered me about the cafeteria thing with my parents. I wanted to share it with Drysdale, but not for Drysdale, you know. I think I wanted to tell him because he said he talked to my dad, and deep down I was hoping maybe Drysdale would tell my dad what I couldn't say to his face. I was still thinking whether I wanted to say it or not when the words just came out, all by themselves. "They called K.C. 'the boy.' And then I said his name and my mom was like, 'I'm glad you guys got along,' like we were school friends or something. And when she said it like that, I started thinking about K.C. and how we always tried to be there for each other, you know, when Bob was—you know, like when Bob was being Bob. I mean, K.C. and I helped each other. That's all I ever wanted to do, was help K.C. And he helped me. That's not just getting along."

I wanted to say more. I was trying to say more but just like they started, the words just stopped, and I was worried Drysdale would start talking before I got the courage to say more.

Deep breath.

There was a wall clock ticking.

Another deep breath.

Drysdale was waiting for me to continue. The words started again. "How can they say 'get along' and that's all? K.C. and I were there for each other. It's stupid, I know. But like when Bob would do his stuff, it's like you gotta leave your heart somewhere, you gotta leave it with someone who takes care of it. You can't keep it with you, or it fills up with anger and hatred because everything around you is too ugly. Bob can be ugly inside. You don't want to end up that way too, you know. And that's how it worked with K.C. and me. I'd keep that part of him safe, and he did the same for me. It didn't matter what happened to us, because we knew that between the two of us we could make things okay for one another. That's why there's a part of me that's still okay inside."

The wall clock was still ticking.

This time Drysdale took a deep breath.

I looked up at him … looked into his eyes. Finally he said, "I heard everything you said, Landon. Thank you for sharing that with me."

He gave me a couple seconds of silence so I could figure out how to give more. "K.C. wasn't just like my brother—he *was* my brother. And I think when I was talking to my parents I wanted them to be happy that K.C. was there for me. I know they never met him, but I wanted them to be proud of K.C. But it's like they only cared about how their new son was going to be there for me."

Drysdale nodded. "Right. I understand. All I can say is that some people have to be taught to listen, not just hear. And I think that your parents are not an exception to that rule. I know they want to help. But I'll be honest with you, I don't know what they're capable of emotionally. Everyone loves in their own way. And in my opinion, I think that the parent-child bond is so strong, quite often it's the parents who have a harder time dealing with the child's pain than the child does. It's like the parents can't detach themselves so that they can recognize what exactly the child went through. Does that make sense at all?"

"I guess."

"Would you mind if I shared with your mom and dad what you just told me?"

"No, it's fine. Sure." I looked down, saw that my shoe was untied. As I bent down and tied it, I couldn't help but to bring on a small smile. I wiped it away before I sat up.

I liked Drysdale.

"So, are you ready to get to work here?" Drysdale asked.

I nodded.

"Our focus today is going to be on K.C. No surprise, right?"

"Yeah. I mean, right, no surprise."

"These binders here are full of missing children pictures. We haven't been able to identify K.C.'s physical description. There were no pictures of him in the trailer."

"What do you mean?" I looked over at the binders. There were four of them, filled with pages.

"We're doing things a little backward. We have what we believe to be K.C.'s DNA. You know what DNA is, right?"

"The science information about a person?"

"Yes, exactly, in simple terms. But we don't have a picture of K.C. or know anything substantive about him. For instance, where his family is from, if he was abducted, if he was abandoned by his mother like he and Bob told you. I know what you've told us, but we need to confirm that. And sadly, as you see from these binders, there are thousands of missing children out there. So what I'd like for us to do today is ... well, what I'd like for *you* to do is to go through these pictures and see if any stand out to you as being K.C."

I had that feeling like when my parents first came into Tracie's office. I was afraid that maybe I wouldn't remember what K.C. looked like.

"You look a little nervous, Landon."

"It's just, um, what if I just pass him up, you know, or pick the wrong person?"

"Picking the wrong person isn't a concern. You can pick twenty people that you think may be K.C. We'll be verifying the identification with a DNA match, hopefully. And as far as passing him up, why don't you wonder about that after you finish going through all the books. Sound fair?"

"Okay."

He reached for a binder, opened the flap, and turned it around to face me. "Just take your time. We're in no hurry."

"Was I in here?"

"Of course." No hesitation in his answer.

I nodded … and turned the first page.

(20)

I was almost done with the second binder and had been turning pages for what seemed forever. Drysdale was typing on his laptop computer. Reading stuff. Typing. Writing. Typing. I was focusing so hard on all the pictures, at times it felt like it was just me in the room. I looked at so many that they weren't people any more. They were just eye and hair color, last seen date, age. City. State. The first sign was a tingling feeling that rushed through my body. My eyes were staring but my brain wasn't registering.

That's K.C.! I gasped for air. Then everything about me popped back into place. I asked myself if I was really sure.

I'm sure. It was really him. It was K.C.

Drysdale looked up at me, "You recognize one of the identifications?"

"Yeah, that's him. That's K.C."

There were two pictures of him side by side. One looked like a school picture when he was really young, maybe around six. The other one next to it was more like a drawing. The drawing one didn't look exactly like K.C., but I knew it was K.C., especially with the school one right next to it. K.C. had this weird flip to his hair where the bangs were. Bob called it a cowlick, but K.C. and I never knew if we should believe him because that was such a strange word.

Drysdale pulled the binder his way, flipped it around, and pulled out the paper with K.C.'s picture on it. I saw on the back there was some typed information. Drysdale turned it over and read what it said to himself. He put the paper down, picture side up, and leaned into his computer.

My heart revved from zero to sixty. I was leaning over so far toward Drysdale that the skin below my elbows dug into the corners of the table. Drysdale stopped typing. I could see in the reflection of his glasses there was a lot of stuff written on the computer page that he pulled up on his screen. His eyes were moving side to side slowly, as if reading every word twice. I held my breath trying to hear what he was silently reading. He nodded. "Yes, this makes sense. This makes a lot of sense."

I couldn't take it anymore and blurted, "What? What do you mean?"

"There's no doubt that you're right. His birth name was Kennedy Charles Nelson." It was strange to hear him not called "K.C." I thought I knew everything about K.C., or maybe it was that he knew everything about me and because of that I assumed that I knew so much about him.

Another memory flashed into my mind. We were in a tent made of sheets. We used to take the lamp shade off the coffee table light so it was just the light bulb, and then we'd put it next to our sheet tent. When Bob was happy with us and let us build our tent, K.C. would give him the end of the cord to the lamp and tell him to plug it in when he thought we should wake up. We wouldn't be really, really asleep, but we'd get into our tent area and yell out, "We're going to bed." Then Bob would plug in the lamp after a couple of minutes went by, and we'd act like the bright light bulb was our rising sun of a new day. We'd slowly open our eyes, stretch, let out fake yawns, and pretend we were soldiers waking up for battle. It seemed kind of dumb to think about it, but it was our fun. On a good day, Bob would join in, yelling out to us, "Come on, brave soldiers, time for battle. Captain K.C., Captain Landon, report for duty." We'd laugh. We'd *all* laugh.

My curiosity brought me back to the room. I couldn't wait for Drysdale to finish what he was reading. I had so many questions. "Why is there the drawing?"

"It's a sketch of what K.C. would look like at approximately twelve. The file says that his grandmother, Ruth Nelson, reported him missing, so the younger picture probably came from her. It looks like he may have been with his mother when he went missing. His mother was picked up for drugs and prostitution, and K.C. was last seen with her ex-boyfriend."

"Does it say her boyfriend's name? Does it say Bob's name?"

Drysdale leaned past the side of the computer screen and looked at me over the rim of his glasses. "I'm sharing with you what I can, Landon."

"Okay. Okay." I backed off a little bit. "Well, what else does it say?"

"It says that Deborah, K.C.'s mother assumed that the boyfriend would eventually take K.C. back to her mother, K.C.'s grandmother, whom he lived with at one time. After being incarcerated for several months, Deborah called her mother and learned at that time that K.C. was never returned. The boyfriend never contacted the grandmother. That's when K.C. was reported missing." Drysdale inhaled slowly. Let out a sigh on the exhale. I knew of K.C.'s grandma. She taught K.C. how to make French toast and tuna-fish sandwiches. Drysdale's voice trailed off, but I knew he was reading to himself. He had a dazed look on his face. "This tells us a lot, Landon. I need to get back to the office, get some agents on this, and I'll see what I can let you know, okay?"

"All right."

There was a pause. He started to read again to himself.

"Agent Drysdale, can I ask you something?"

He looked up. "Sure."

"If it says she left him with her boyfriend, doesn't that mean that Bob was right, that K.C.'s mom just left in the middle of the night?"

"I don't know what it means." He nodded lightly, stared at his computer screen. "But this is very helpful information."

I looked over at K.C.'s picture, lying next to Drysdale's computer. For a second, I was kind of excited, because it was like a missing piece of the puzzle had been found and it fit into place exactly how K.C. and Bob said it did. Something about that felt good. It's like I needed everything I knew about K.C. to be real, because that was the reality that meant the most to me. I didn't want to lose it.

I looked again at the picture. It ushered in the thoughts about how K.C. and I used to play. The way our laughter melded together echoed in my mind. A twisting feeling started in my gut. I missed K.C. Deep down, even though he hadn't been a part of my thoughts for so long, I knew I had been missing K.C. for years. I cared about him so much that I was mad at myself for not thinking about him every single day since he left. I felt guilty for trying to forget about him. I wanted to keep that picture of K.C. with me so I would never force him out of my mind again. "Can I have that paper with the pictures on it?"

Drysdale smiled at me. "Let me work on getting you a better picture. Maybe it'll be a copy. We'll see. I have to keep this one because of the information on the backside. Okay?"

"Yeah, okay." I was a little bummed out, but I knew that Drysdale would try to come through for me. As Drysdale started packing his stuff up, I could tell he was deep in thought. I could see his mind spinning with information. He put everything back in the box and then put the lid on and let out a big breath. "I've got to get back to the office. I won't see you for a couple of days, but I'll be talking daily with Tracie and of course continuing to speak with your parents as I'm sure Tracie will, too. You do know that your parents want to talk with you, right?"

I shrugged.

"Don't shrug, Landon. Do you know it?"

"I think so." The whole cafeteria scene ran through my head, but then I focused on the feeling I had after my talk with Tracie in the stairwell, how I missed my mom for the first time in years. And for a second, I relived the flash of emotion I had seeing my mom's mascara smudges and Dale's swelling tears after our first handshake.

Drysdale's voice swept the recollections away. "I know that K.C. was your family then. He will always be part of your family. But I don't want you to give up on the family that's waiting for you. No family is perfect. You've got to have an open mind as to how it gets patched back together."

I didn't really know how to respond, but I knew he was right. I had to patch stuff together, like a collage project in school. I had to bring all my random experiences together to create one big, unified self that hopefully wasn't too screwed up and could one day survive in the world.

(21)

I talked to my parents every day for the next several days. Actually, it's more like they talked to me, but I was the one who made the call. It was an okay compromise. When I thought about Bob, I tried not to get too worked up about how upset he must have been with me. I didn't tell Tracie this, but my biggest fear was what would happen when Drysdale's people found Bob. I mean, I wasn't in reality worried about what would happen to me, physically, but when I thought about Bob being mad, I got worked up, almost scared, like it was hard to think straight. I just wanted everyone to be happy, you know, as best they could: *me in here, Bob out there, and my parents on the phone.*

Drysdale hadn't been by in awhile.

The smiling janitor, it turned out, was named Palmer. He had two great-grandchildren in college, he loved Wikipedia, his bowed legs didn't hurt when he walked, and he listened to jazz on his iPod. He'd had the same wife for fifty-one years. I didn't know her real name. He just called her "the wife." And the way he said it, I bet her kids called her "the mom." Palmer's janitor room was on my floor, right by the stairwell door. If he was there, the door would always be open. If he wasn't there, well, he was the kind of guy you could go find and he'd open it for you.

Joseph, the kid next door to me, went home to his grandmother's. He wasn't really a talker, but he was a good basketball player. He and I were hanging out the morning before he left, and in a split-second, I understood what he was about … or what his tragedy was, as Drysdale would say. Joseph said he used to be a talker and sucked at basketball, until his father came home one day and checked out—as in suicide—and took his mom with him. After that he talked less, understood himself more, and developed his love for playing basketball. He was a cool guy. I hope he would say the same about me.

We would both say the same about Tracie. I liked my talks with her, except when she rambled on forever. I really liked my talks with Palmer, though. We would just talk about regular stuff, just stupid stuff: Arnold Palmer was a famous golfer, Michael Landon was a famous actor, you can't mix ammonia and bleach, there are seven continents and in each continent there are countries, and then the countries have states, like Nebraska, and the states have towns or villages like where we were in Omaha. But we'd talk, and I'd find my mind traveling away from all the crap I had been through.

The other day he said the wife wasn't gonna believe it when he told her I was fifteen and didn't know about all the countries and stuff. But the way he said it never made me feel stupid. Instead, I started getting worried that I was missing out on information, and that I was smart enough to learn about things.

Palmer was mad at the schools because I didn't know that Lincoln was the capital of Nebraska and Washington DC was the capital city of the United States. I told him how I always had an attitude and maybe it wasn't the school's fault. I mean, like the nerds in school, I'm sure, knew all that stuff. But his raspy voice only responded, "Nope, I'm not gonna hear that excuse from ya, little man. You're a bright kid. You learned how to walk, didn't ya? Your only problem is no one showed you how to use your brain." He went on about how he pays his tax dollars for kids like me to learn, and he gets mad when he sees one slipping through the cracks.

I wasn't sure what he was saying, but I did start wondering if maybe I was smart enough to know what the nerds in class knew. I mean, like, not the hard math stuff, but maybe I was smart enough to read a book and get it.

The York center had some weird rules, but they weren't really that big a deal. On the third day, I had to write up a schedule for myself. Like, what time do I wake up, eat lunch, and use the PlayStation—stuff like that. The schedule paper thing that I filled out was broken down into thirty-minute slots, and they didn't care what I did except for keeping my appointments with Tracie and Dr. Williams. The only thing was that I had to stick to my schedule. If I couldn't manage the schedule I made up, the lady at the counter downstairs said that wasn't a big deal either, I just had to make sure I revised it. I don't remember her name, but she's a blonde lady. And it's not like I was talking to her for fun, either. Part of the scheduling thing was that I had to put in a meeting with her every day to go over the schedule and whether or not I was sticking to the schedule. I couldn't decide at first if it was stupid or not, but I did it regardless.

Tracie said the whole schedule thing was an exercise in being aware of the here and now. If that means always knowing what time it is, she was right. I kept the schedule folded up in my pocket, and I folded it and unfolded it so much that by the end of the day you could almost see through where the creases were.

I didn't know this about myself, but I hate being late. Like for instance, if I was due to meet with Tracie in eight minutes, then even though I could make it down the stairs and to her office in sixty seconds, I liked to head out five minutes before just in case I saw Palmer.

"Hey there, little man. I got somethin' for ya." I stopped at Palmer's door, hearing his voice. "Whoa, am I that ugly to look at?" He was referring to my hoodie. I still liked to pull it down over my face. I usually pulled it away when I saw him walking down the hallway. I was thinking about my visit with Tracie too much, and Palmer caught me off guard, I guess. I pulled away my hoodie. Palmer smiled. "That's better now." He waddled over to his desk.

Palmer had the bowed legs since he was a kid. I asked how he got them and all he said was, "Thankfully, it's the only scar from a rough childhood." His room was cluttered with cleaning supplies, baseball memorabilia, and a corkboard that was basically completely covered with holiday cards. I wanted to know more about all the cards, like what the people wrote inside. Some of the cards toward the middle of the corkboard were yellowed around the edges, like they'd been tacked up there forever.

He opened a bottom drawer to his desk and pulled out a piece of paper and a brown bag. "I had the wife pick this up at the store for ya." He handed over the piece of paper. It was a world map. "I'm not gonna quiz you on this, but I thought that if you're curious what the big picture is, well, I wanna make sure you can figure it out. And here, this is for you, too."

In the brown paper sack were three cookies covered in plastic wrap, with a bow tied around the top where the plastic wrap bunched together. It made the cookies look like a gift. I wanted my hoodie back on because I felt weird accepting it, but his raspy voice took my eyes off the gift. "Don't feel too special now. She makes them for everyone."

It was kinda like he could read my mind. It was weird, but I calmed down. "Will you tell her she didn't have to do that?"

"Nope, I can't do that, can't tell her that." He had this belly laugh that made you wonder what his voice would sound like if it wasn't so raspy. "I'll have to tell her that you liked them so much you're hoping for more."

"Why?"

"How do you think I get a belly this big when she packs my lunch every day? It's hard work." He arched his back and rubbed his tummy. "She isn't gonna sit around and bake cookies just for me after fifty-one years of marriage. And if she did, I'd have to do all kinds of stuff around the house. So you want more cookies, don't you?" He winked and yanked at his pants. He always pulled up his pants when he was making a joke. I really liked him. "Yeah, I guess I do." I smiled back.

"That's right. See, you're a smart kid. Where ya headed?"

"I have a session with Tracie."

"Tell her to stop throwing her coffee cups in the trashcan when they still have coffee in 'em. Will you do that?" I shrugged. He laughed. "Anyway, you know why I got that map for ya? Smart people are self-taught."

I looked up at the baseballs lining the shelf above his desk. "Hey, are those famous people who signed all those baseballs?"

He followed my gaze. "It depends, I guess. When my girls were younger, I coached their softball teams. And at the end of our season, I'd have the players sign a ball for me."

"That's cool." There were like thirty of them, each in its own little glass case. "Well, I gotta get to Tracie's."

"Yup, I'll see ya tomorrow."

I went to turn toward the stairwell but looked down at the world map. I knew myself and how bad I kept track of my stuff. Plus, after losing all my crap from the trailer, everything I owned was twice as important to me. I didn't want to lose it … but in a weird way, I didn't want Palmer to know that I cared that much about it. "I forgot something in my room," I called out as I turned around. I didn't know if Palmer heard me, but I jogged back to my room and placed the world map he gave me next to the Ameritek ID card that's in the top drawer next to my bed.

When I was heading to the stairwell again, Palmer was locking up his office, his iPod earplugs in, and he gave me his signature smile. I felt like saying, "Yeah, I'm doing okay. Thanks for caring," but it felt safer just to say, "I'll see you tomorrow."

(22)

I took a seat in Tracie's waiting room and picked up a magazine. *National Geographic.* I flipped the pages, and there was a section on panda bears with all these pictures of the baby pandas hanging out in trees. I looked where they lived: some place called Chengdu, China. I didn't know how to pronounce the town but I wondered where it was.

I thought about the map that Palmer gave me. If I had brought it with me, it would have been cool to look and see where the pandas were. I mean, like, I knew China was far away, but it would have been cool to look at the pictures and know that the pandas were alive and then see on the map where they were in relation to me. It's hard to put it into words, and, I don't know, maybe I was being stupid.

The door from the hallway into Tracie's waiting room opened and Tracie bustled in, with files in one hand and her paper coffee cup in the other. After what Palmer said, her coffee cup had meaning to me. I smiled to myself. She almost sounded out of breath. "Am I late? I'm so sorry. I just came from an administration meeting. Come on in." I tossed the magazine down and followed her. "Your name came up in the meeting. Everyone is so impressed with your time management skills." She was at her filing cabinet with her back to me, putting some files away.

"My what?"

"How you stick to your daily schedule."

"It keeps me busy, you know."

"It's a strong sign of responsibility. Carrie, the lady you see to revise the schedule, mentioned you've been making use of the basketball court."

"Yeah, I was hanging out there with Joseph yesterday."

"Oh, that's good. I'm going to miss Joseph. Anyway, in the meeting, we were discussing that maybe toward the end of next week you'd be ready for a community service assignment, outside of the center here. The community assignments are designed to promote positive experiences for you. They're meant to be rewarding." She slammed the filing cabinet door, locked it up, and tossed her coffee cup into the trashcan. I got a mental picture of Palmer picking it out, shaking his head. I didn't know why, but it put me in a good mood. I could tell by then that when I was happy, there's this kind of bigger feeling in my ribcage, like its inflated, that makes me feel like I'm floating away. My spine even gets straight and my chin lifts. That's what Tracie and I worked on the other day; paying attention to how my body feels when I have emotions.

I took a seat on the couch that time. Something new, you know, instead of the chairs. The office looked different from a new perspective. She had about five or six shelves on the back wall lined with books. "Do you read all those books?"

"Oh gosh, no. Most of those are reference books."

"What do you mean?"

"If I have a certain topic I want to read about, I just pull the book that I think will have the information I need, or which one will help refresh my recollection on a subject that I need to brush up on."

"Oh … right." I paused before adding, "Was that a stupid question?"

"No, not at all. How would you know otherwise? I'm glad you asked. If you made the assumption that I had read all those books, you'd have the wrong idea about me. I mean, I like to read in my spare time, but not psychology books. I'm not that boring." She smiled. "Do I look that boring?"

I sort of smiled back. "No. That makes sense, I guess. It makes sense about the reference books, I mean." There was a little pause. She was smiling at me. I knew what the smile meant. She was wondering what was on my mind. I went ahead and offered my thoughts. "I've never read a book before."

"How many children do you think have read books for pleasure?"

"I don't know."

"Give it a guess for me."

"Most of them, probably."

"Would you be surprised if I told you that illiteracy is a crisis in our nation? Or worse, that some high school districts report a 30 percent dropout rate?"

"Is that a lot?"

"Out of every hundred students, a little more than thirty are not graduating. It's estimated that nearly one out of every five teenagers can't comprehend the meaning behind a written paragraph. Their local newspaper articles are too difficult to comprehend."

"Do you think I could?"

"Could what?"

"Understand a book, like, care about reading it?"

She laughed. "Of course I do, Landon. The brain is like a muscle, so you may have to work on strengthening your comprehension skills to get it into shape, but absolutely."

Her phone rang. I thought about what she had said. I didn't know whether to believe her or not. I mean, I wanted to, but the kids I knew in school seemed like they had something that I didn't. And thinking about me reading a book and really liking it was about as clear a vision as seeing my hands in front of myself in a black hole.

The phone was still ringing.

"I'm sorry about that." She looked toward the phone on her desk. "I didn't silence it. I guess I was in a rush wanting to make sure we started on time." It kept ringing, and she made a face. "It'll go to voicemail in a sec." She picked up her pad of paper and a pen, which was the sign that we were going to go ahead and get started. "You bring up a good point, though, Landon. If you're willing, I'd like to do a little exercise with you so you can work on learning to question how you arrive at what you believe. But first …" She lifted her index finger. She was funny like that. She used her hands to talk a lot, which made you keep your eyes on her when she was saying stuff. "Let me silence my phone." She got up and walked over to her desk. "And while I'm doing a little housecleaning here and before we start, did you have anything to add about the conversation you had with your parents earlier today?"

"What do you mean by housecleaning?" I asked.

Her phone started to ring again. She ignored it and put it on silence halfway through a ring; that made me feel good that she didn't interrupt our time by answering it. She took her seat and looked at me. "Does that mean you don't have anything to add?"

"I don't know. I just, well …" I didn't mind talking to them, honestly. I just didn't want to talk about how it *felt* to talk to them. I was doing okay with it all.

Tracie put up a hand, like to stop me from moving. She could tell, I guess, that I was trying to figure out what to say. "Landon, you don't have to explain. I'm here to talk about it only if you want to, okay?" She gave a friendly smile and waited to see if I had a response. I didn't. She sat back down. "Okay. So can we try this exercise?"

"Sure." And I was fine with it. The exercises were kind of fun. At first, I always wondered why she asked what she asked, and then when she was done, it gave me something to think about, or something to pay attention to.

"Consider this. If we worked on a model of one hundred kids, how many of those kids would you think that their parents just left them, got rid of them as you say?" It was a weird question. The last exercise was learning about how different parts of my body felt. Or closing my eyes and learning to lower my heart rate.

"Um, I dunno really." Deep down I kind of always thought that that's what a lot of parents have to do, you know, like maybe it was natural, or something. And all those pages in Drysdale's book popped into my mind, the book with K.C.'s picture in it—like, *How did all those kids end up in the book if their parents didn't get rid of them?* I asked myself.

"Well, how about if I phrase the question this way: do you think it's a common thing that happens in families?"

"I told you about Sam, but his mom was still there. Does that count?"

"Sure. How many children would you say have a father *or* a mother who just walks away from them?"

"It's hard … I mean, you talk about the kids you see in here. I never thought about how many."

"You say you never thought about how many. Okay. Is that because you already have an idea how many parents do that to their children?"

"Maybe. I never really thought about it, like, directly."

"Well, would you say that it's common or uncommon for a parent or both parents to give up or give away their child?"

She let me think about it. It took like a minute for it to really go through my mind. It's weird to question something that silently sits in your mind as a fact, you know. "It's—I mean, well, isn't it pretty common? Right?"

"Is that what you think?"

"Kind of. Yeah."

"And so when you told me about your anger toward Sam's dad, you were yelling out at a lot of parents, weren't you?"

"What do you mean?"

"If I understand your thinking correctly, when you shared with me about how Sam's dad just can't throw his child away, you weren't referring to just Sam's situation, or your own feelings like we explored in the stairwell. Instead, you were referring to a lot of parents. You were angry at a lot of parents, maybe even most if I hear you correctly, with regard to how they treat their children."

"Yeah, I think so. You can't do that to your child, that's what I think."

"And Landon, most parents don't. Most parents take care of their children and make tremendous sacrifices for their children, even in divorced situations. Millions of mothers and fathers fight in court to be a part of their child's life. Parents are not perfect, and a lot of them do build resentment toward their children because they sacrifice what they believe is too much, but only very, very few go to the extreme of abandoning their children."

That eighth grade Back to School Night with Bob popped into my head. Those parents weren't like Bob, or like Sam's mom. I remember being pissed off at them that night because they were acting like they cared about their kids and were asking stupid questions about homework and if the books that were assigned were age-appropriate. I told myself then that they were all lying about caring for their kids.

"What are you thinking about, Landon?"

"Nothing really."

She didn't say anything.

I shrugged. "All right, well, Bob and I went to this school thing where the other parents went also, you know, a Back to School Night. The classroom was full of kids and their parents, and then you could go to the cafeteria afterward. Bob and I left early, but I saw all the parents in the cafeteria, and I remember being confused about seeing so many parents in one room. I was thinking, basically, how could so many parents show up when parents don't care about their kids, you know? And now what you just said … I'm thinking, maybe what I was thinking then was wrong. It's strange."

"So you're questioning why you think the way you think about some things?"

"Yeah, I guess."

"That's wonderful. And in that instance, I think in time you'll follow through on learning why you developed that thought pattern about parents not caring and why it probably lessened your own emotional pain to convince yourself of that. But that's the exercise. I can't stress enough how helpful in life it can be to learn to question your thinking patterns and how you arrived at conclusions. In other words, learn to question *why* you believe what you believe. Get rid of beliefs that are wrong. A lot of us walk around every day with wrong assumptions that cause unnecessary emotional pain, anger, sadness—a great number of burdening emotions. And if beliefs are true, then there's no harm in exploring them, right?"

There was a knock at Tracie's door. It caught her off guard. "That's odd. I don't have another appointment. I'm heading out after our session." She walked over and opened it.

It was Dr. Williams.

"Oh, wow. Hi, Steve. What's going on? Come in."

"Sorry, Tracie. I called over but I must have missed you before you started with Landon. Can I speak to you real quick, outside?"

"Sure." She turned to me, shrugged her shoulders, lifted her eyebrows. "I'll be right back, okay?"

"Yeah, okay." I put my hoodie over my face, leaned my head against the back of the couch, and closed my eyes. I still hated the parents I saw at the Back to School Night who made Bob and me feel like lowlifes, but what Tracie said kind of erased in my mind all those faceless parents who I wanted to yell at so bad. For a second, I thought about what it would have been like had I lived with one of those parents, the ones who seemed to care about homework and age-appropriate books. But I dismissed it because I knew, just by looking at them, that my hoodie and I wouldn't have ever fit into their families, the same way, at the core of me, I worried that I wouldn't fit in with Dale and Cathy.

They were gone for maybe a minute. Then Tracie and Dr. Williams came back into the room together. They both took a seat. Looked at me.

Weird.

I slid my hoodie back, off my face. The vibe in the room was serious. Somehow, I knew I needed to sit up straight and look at them. Dr. Williams spoke first. "Landon, I received a call from Agent Drysdale a short while ago. He informed us that Bob Starker was taken into custody earlier today."

(23)

I'm sitting cross-legged under the dining room table. *Am I back in that apartment?* I'm too tall to sit on my ankles. My back hunches over. I feel my curls rubbing against the underneath of the table. The vertical blinds shift back and forth, hypnotically. Calmly. I can see through the slits to the outside world.

It's daylight. Sunny.

I hear Bob's work boots. I look through the blinds. I don't see the boots. I see high heels. She's walking up to the apartment front door! She came by herself! A sense of joy washes over me.

The door opens. Light floods the whole apartment. I turn my head, but it won't turn. There's an invisible force holding my cheek from turning. I want to look everywhere. I'm curious. I want to see the furniture in the apartment … what kind … how it's situated. And my mom … I want to see if she's standing there with open arms.

When I do get my head turned, I'm blinded by the light from the opening door. I only get a quick glimpse of the shelves across the room. *What's on the shelves?* I never knew they were there. I like seeing new things around me.

The door slams shut stealing away the light. It's dark. The air is heavy. This lost feeling starts to creep up from the floor like a fog rolling along the ground, surrounding me.

Where is she? I want to call out but the words are stuck in my chest.

A sweet smell swirls around the room. Someone is cooking, and the aroma tells me I am safe. I look to where I think the kitchen is. I squint. I try to inhale the sweet smell. It's getting less and less … and then it's gone.

The lamp across the room goes on. I turn my head that way. It's Bob. Not her—*not Mom.* He sits on the couch and pats the cushion with his open palm. "Come here, kid." He's not sad. I am so relieved.

I sit on the coffee table. I'm trying to look around. *Where is she? Maybe in one of the dark corners? Maybe in the kitchen?* I look into the darkness at my right. Bookshelves. She's not there. *I saw her walking up, right? Maybe she forgot something, but will be right back?*

I feel the carpet between my toes. I'm so much taller now. *Why did I have to come back here now that I've grown?* I look down. It's the dirty carpet from the trailer. I feel a thick, creamy liquid between my toes, but the carpet looks dry.

I look at Bob's kneecaps. My eyes drop to the ground again. *Bob's wearing her shoes? That wasn't her outside the window?* Panic surges up my spine. I need to run away

No! Stay! My neck freezes in the down position. I can't swallow my saliva.

"Look up, kid." Bob's voice.

My ribcage contracts. My chest starts to cave in. I can't move my head.

"Landon, look at me." His voice grows stern.

I look for the missing wood chip in the coffee table. I just need to focus. It's not there. It's a different coffee table, made of white marble. *I've seen this table before, haven't I?* The palms of my hands rest on the white surface. It's cold. There are gray veins streaming through the marble.

My eyes wander around with my neck still frozen. I can see the side of my nose. The brow bone of my eye socket. One of my curls resting at my temple. The muscles that hold my eyeballs start to tire. I look to the right. My eyes want to relax, but I am telling them to look, to see what's over there. *I'm not in the apartment; where am I?* I keep straining my eyes. I want to figure it out.

I try to bring the shelves into focus. *What's on the shelves?*

"Landon, look over at me." My body tries to turn toward Bob's voice before he gets mad, but I want to know about the shelves.

Suddenly ... I see them. Reference books!

I gasp, slam my eyelids shut as hard as I can. We're in Tracie's office. It's Tracie's white marble table.

"Landon, look here. I have something to show you." My neck tenses even more, and I feel it trying to jerk to the left. "I'm not going to hurt you, brave soldier. You know I never meant to hurt you." I nod like I'm supposed to when he says that. "But look, kid, they sent you evidence." My neck starts to loosen a little. I lift my head slightly. I see the couch better—Tracie's couch.

Why did Tracie do this to me?

Why would she let Bob in her office?

"That's it, brave soldier. Look at everything in the room. Yeah, look up. You need to know the truth. No one is here for you except me. I've always been there for you."

I see the wrist of his right hand. There are indentations where his handcuffs bound him. *Drysdale let him go?*

"Look, kid. Look what your mom gave me."

"How did you find me here?" It's weird to hear my voice.

"I always know where you are. I'm helping you. You need to see what I brought you."

I'm overwhelmed with sadness, fatigue. My chest heaves, but no tears come. I look at what he holds in his hand. It's my mom's calendar, from her purse. "How did you get that?" I ask him.

"She gave this to me to show that you need to trust me. They don't know how to tell you the truth."

"What's the truth?" I hate it that he is the only one I can ask.

Bob tilts his head to the side. His worry lines crease. "Landon, I could have treated you better. I'm sorry. You have to forgive me. I was trying to do the right thing for you and K.C. You know that, don't you?"

I nod because that's what he wants me to do.

"Look what else I have, kid."

My eyes look away nervously.

His words command me. "No. Look at me. Show me your courage, brave soldier." Then I see it. Next to his thigh, on the couch, my mom's wallet. Bob's hand caresses it. He takes between his thumb and finger a stray paper sticking out of it. I hear the sound of the paper being rubbed; it's loud. His voice has laughter in the background. "Yeah, go ahead, feel it for yourself. It's Evan's prescription she thought she lost." Bob's hand reaches up to my chin. I freeze again. I know better than to flinch. He takes my chin between his fingers. "I'm so sad for you, kid. No one tells you the truth."

I look away. I don't want to see his tears. *They hurt me more than my own.*

By my side, I see my mom's key ring with all those weird decorations. I didn't see it before, but there it is. Bob leans into my ear and gently pushes a curl to the side. "Pick it up, Landon."

I look at it closer. It's hers. I recognize the decorations. *I love her.*

"I see you staring at it, kid. Pick it up." I start to reach for it. "That's right. Take it in your hand, Landon." My reach is moving slow. I'm getting closer to touching it. Bob laughs softly, "Yeah, that's it." I reach it and hold it in my hand. I think about smiling. It's hers. It's my mom's. I love her. *I know I love her.*

I hear Bob's breath at my ear. "Now look closely, Landon. Look at how she took off all the keys to their house. There's no keys on it, only decorations. You know why?"

I shake my head in confusion.

Bob's voice intones, "Because they don't want you in their home."

My eyes popped open. The dream felt real.

My neck hurt.

I was awake, but I felt dead.

(24)

I knew that I was resting on my side. My eyes weren't blinking. I just stared at the wall, at a random picture of some old farmhouse with a broken, sinking roof. Horses were grazing. Chickens were pecking at their food. The grass was green and tall. A field of sunflowers waved off in the distance. It was all fiction. Ugly, unbelievable fiction. My focus would go in and out. Blurry. Double vision. Clarity. Then I'd release my vision and lie there with my eyes open but blind.

At one point the phone next to the bed rang. My body didn't react. My ears heard it, but my brain was closed off. I thought I was numb when I went to the stairwell after the visit with my parents in the cafeteria, but in that room, at that moment, I didn't know if I'd ever physically react to my senses again.

The door to my room opened. Whoever it was, she pulled the curtains back and let the daylight in. I had no curiosity. I couldn't give a damn who came and went. I had no use for my peripheral vision. My eyes remained open, even though the rays of sunlight dried away the moisture. The person in the room walked in front of my bed. At first, I only saw her at waist level. I knew it was a woman by the pink shirt and flower-like belt buckle. "Landon, are you cold?"

I heard my name, but there was nothing inside me that told me how to respond. I was a million miles away. A thin thread kept me attached to the Earth, but it was pulling tighter and tighter, ready to break at any moment. I didn't care if I ended up in space, floating around, unable to come back to the world I was once a part of. In fact, the only happiness about my future was the thought of looking at the world from a distance, far enough away to only recognize people's happiness or sadness, but not be a part of it.

The lady walked over to the wall where the thermostat was. Dry heat started flowing through the wall vents. The first night I was in the room, the wall vents reminded me of the trailer. But the mind I woke up with then, thankfully, refused to go anywhere in the past or future.

She walked around the room and passed in front of my eyes again. I didn't know her voice. I felt her hands straightening the sheets, pulling the blanket up around my chin. She turned the television on, lowered the volume and put the remote next to my arm. Her hand ran over the blankets, along the side of my body. I didn't flinch. My nerve endings were dead. I wanted to be dead. I hated my body, my heart, for continuing to live.

She bent over in front of my face. I saw then that it was the blonde lady who did my scheduling. She tucked one of the lonely curls that fell in front of my eyes behind my ear. "Sweetie, everything will be okay. Tracie's on her way right now. Just hang tight. Okay?" She covered her index finger with a part of the sheet and soaked up a tear that nestled its way in the corner of my eye. I didn't remember shedding it.

She walked away and returned with a can of soda that she placed next to my bed. "I'll be back shortly. But like I said, Tracie is on her way." I heard the door shut. Knowing that I was alone in the room gave me hope. I tried to promise myself that if I pulled out of the numb feeling, I would learn my lesson. I promised myself not to trust anyone. Ever. I said it out loud. "I promise." I made myself repeat it. "I promise."

The door opened again. It was Tracie. She pulled a chair over to my bed. "Landon, did you have a memory or dream that disturbed you?" I took a breath to show her I was alive. "Whatever happened last night, we can deal with it. Remember where you are, Landon. Yesterday we were talking about the books. You told me about playing basketball on the sundeck with Joseph before he left. We were talking about community service programs. It's imperative that you bring your thoughts to the present, to your reality here at the center."

I felt her eyes on me. I saw that she was wearing jeans and a flannel shirt, with the sleeves rolled up. I started to wonder where she was when they called for her to come over, but I stopped myself. I didn't want to care, and I didn't want people caring about me.

"Whatever thoughts came to your mind, Landon, they are not here. They are not part of today." *That's not true.* The white marble table in her office flashed into my mind. I never looked at the table that close during my sessions, but in my mind's eye, I could see it clearly. I could have traced it in the air with my finger, right then, in front of Tracie, the gray marbling veins to prove I knew exactly what it looked like.

Bob's words from my dream boomed in my ears. His voice was real. The sound of him was in the room without his body. For the first time that morning my eyes looked side to side, around the room, looking for him in the flesh.

Tracie's face came into my view. She was leaning forward in her chair. "Landon, it's clear that you're shaken up over whatever happened during the night. It can be helpful if you bring your thoughts to what's happening around you today, yesterday. Run through your mind all the things you did yesterday." I couldn't do that. I wanted to stay with the dream, understand why I had it. Understand in that moment how Bob's voice could hover in the air, separated from his body. "If it was a memory that flashed in your mind, I can help you work through it. Do you remember when we talked about reliving trauma? I'm here to work on these things with you. Or if you had a nightmare, you have to understand that the mind can do strange things."

I wasn't listening to Tracie. I had my own thoughts. Like how my dream was smarter than me, stronger than me. It came from somewhere inside me that I had no control over. I stared at the farmhouse roof in the picture. I tried to freeze my mind, stop any new thoughts, send the old ones away.

"Landon, I can't tell you how important it is that you bring your thoughts to the present. For instance, you've shared with me that you enjoy talking to Palmer. Think about the last time you saw him. The mind is like an engine; you have to restart it, fuel your thoughts. Think about the here and now, the positive things around you."

I just lay there, staring at the picture, not consciously thinking of anything, but then my mind would flip over, and I'd be back in the dream. I couldn't stop going over in my mind the fabric of her couch, how it felt in the dream. How Bob was sitting on it. How my mom's wallet was next to him.

My thoughts and Tracie's words weren't mixing right. It made me feel queasy, weird, heavy. I needed her to stop talking. I needed time to understand why my mind did what it did. Why it was doing what it was doing. Why Bob felt so close to me. My first words to her were a mumble. "Can you just let me be, leave me alone?"

She sat there staring at me. "Okay, that's fine. But let some new thoughts come into your mind. Can you do that? It's important that you don't keep your mind on whatever invaded your thoughts last night." She looked at my face for an expression.

I didn't have one.

"I'm not saying forget what you saw last night, whatever that was, but try to detach yourself from what went through your mind so you can stand back and take a clear look."

I wanted her to hear me, to listen to me. "Please. Leave. Me. Alone." When my voice loosened up, my tears unfroze too, but I kept them silent. I didn't want them to be a sign that betrayed my words. I wanted to be left alone, like in those minutes before Bob would come home from work, and I would prepare myself for whatever the evening had in store for me.

"What happened last night, Landon?" I shook my head. I didn't want to share. I wanted my own space. "Was it a dream? Can you tell me what the dream was about?"

"No. Just stop. Please. I can't share anymore."

She sat up straight. Paused her breathing. I couldn't raise my voice, but I tried to send the message with force behind my words. "All you guys do is cloud the truth for me. I want to be by myself."

"I don't mean to trespass on your privacy. I'm sorry." She put a gentle hand on my knee and stood up. "I'll check back later. I'm here if you need me." She held her gaze on me for a second and then walked away.

I felt relief. My tears were no longer droplets falling from the inner corner of my eyes. They melded together to create a blanket of water that coated my cheeks. I knew one truth that came from the dream: Bob was never leaving me. His spirit lived inside me, and it was time for me to accept that.

(25)

At one point while I was lying there, I imagined that if I told my parents about the dream and asked them, "Why did Bob have your things?" they would answer, "It's just a dream. Forget about it." I argued with them in my mind: "But why did those thoughts exist in my head to begin with? What is it about my reality that would make those thoughts come to me?" I could hear my dad's response, too: "You're reading too much into it all. Just put it out of your mind."

But it wasn't a dream like those balloons they draw in comic strips above the cartoon person's head. The dream wasn't fiction; I *lived* it. I kept thinking over and over in my head how I felt that rush of excitement when the dream started, and I saw my mom's shoes. How I felt the warmth from the sunshine outside. How I heard Bob's voice, his real voice. I couldn't see the kitchen but I sensed it, smelled it. I saw the shelves like they were right in front of me. I remember the coldness of the marble against my open palm.

I felt sadness.

I could still feel the sadness.

I could still feel Bob's presence.

And I could still feel the fear of Bob being mad.

I laid in my bed for probably close to three hours after Tracie left. I finally got up, started moving around, but for no good reason. Tracie left my door open, not all the way, but cracked open. When someone was walking by in the hallway, I could hear their footsteps. I heard Palmer's mop bucket wheeling by my room.

I started focusing more on the details of the random picture on the wall. I looked closer where the two corners came together to make the frame angle. There was some chipped paint, and I could see where someone tried to paint over it. I don't remember doing it, but at one point I pulled off my covers and sat up. The only way I can explain it is like how when you take a long, hot shower and you're in there thinking about stuff, and while you're still thinking about everything, you reach over and turn the water off without thinking about it. It was like that. I didn't just snap out of lying there, staring at the wall. It's like there was this ghost part of me that started to get up and move around, and then my body followed. After an hour or so, my brain was back in place and I started feeling like myself. It sounds like I'm a freak, but whatever. It was strange. I just didn't want another dream.

For a minute, I thought about talking to Palmer about the dream, but I didn't know if I should trust him with that kind of stuff. If he talked to me, maybe he talked to everyone. And like, if he said to me I should share that with Tracie, I don't know what my attitude would say back. I didn't want to be a smart-ass and ruin my talks with him … I just didn't know what to do, but it seemed, well, safer just not to talk to him about it.

In the end it didn't matter, because I did finally tell Tracie it was a dream, but I didn't tell her that she was a part of it. I know it sounds stupid, but I was afraid if I told her about being in her office in the dream, she would blame it all on Bob, and I couldn't handle that. I didn't want Bob to be upset no matter where he was. So Tracie and I just sat there in her office not saying much at all.

She had promised if I came down to see her she wouldn't ramble on about helping me with the dream. It was weird, though, to be in her office. I was nervous. I didn't want to look around the room. I was worried, like, if I looked at the books on the shelves, it would put me back into my dream. I knew I wasn't going to forget about the dream, but I wanted it to die down in my head, become flat like my memories.

"Landon, are you with me here?"

I looked her way. I had my hoodie pulled down below my eyes. I was sitting in my loner chair, the place where I started out in the first sessions with her. Tracie didn't ask any questions about where I sat. She simply sat across from me, calm, like we had all the time in the world. She broke the silence asking, "Do you still feel up for your meeting with Drysdale?"

"Yeah, it's cool." I wanted to hear about Bob. I didn't want to say this to Tracie—and I knew I wouldn't say it to Drysdale—but I wanted to talk to Bob myself. I felt so confused about what the truth was, since everyone had a totally different version, it seemed. In a way, I kind of wanted Bob to repeat in one single paragraph all the things he had been telling me the last seven years. Just go through it all and slowly explain how everything happened. I wanted to listen to his every word and link it up with a memory so everything would fall into place and start to make sense.

Tracie looked up at the clock. "I think he'll be here shortly. I'm not going to talk about the dream—" *That's a lie*, I thought. *You did it right there*. But whatever, I just stared at her. I knew she was just trying to do her job and so I sat there numb and just listened. "—but it obviously really impacted you. Do you think what we've been working on together so far has been useful to you?"

"I guess." It had, but also, it hadn't. It had, because I was able to live in a bubble, you know, just thinking about my next thing to do. But it hadn't helped because Bob was going to forever be a part of me, and there was nothing the York center or Tracie could do to help that. I just had to live with it.

She leaned forward and inched her body to the front of her chair. "Are you sure you don't want to share with me what you went through last night?"

I shook my head, sighed, and replied, "You won't understand. I'm trying to get over it, you know, if you guys let me."

She stood up from her chair, took a couple of steps, and sat on her white marble coffee table right in front of me. I looked down at her open palm against the surface. One of the gray marble veins flared out under her ring finger. The same vein that I saw in my dream. My body flinched.

Why would she sit there?

The world started closing in on me. My chest started sweating. My undershirt stuck to my body. I couldn't take my eyes off the gray veins running through the marble surface.

Why would she sit there?

"What's going on, Landon? Let's see if I can help." She reached up and inched my hoodie back off my face.

Mistake.

I jumped out of my seat. I don't know why I didn't just bolt out of her office, but I stayed and started pacing. "No! I'm not sharing anymore. What the hell? Can't you let it go? Let me try to deal with it. I need to get out of here." I wanted to leave but I didn't have anywhere to go. My pacing got quicker. I ran my hands through my hair. I wanted to hit something, to explode. I started turning around and around, spinning.

"Landon, I'm here for you."

"No, you don't understand. I can deal with my own stuff. I don't need you guys." I started pacing again. Every time she asked if she could help, the dream flooded back into my mind, like in a way Bob was fighting her.

I wanted—no, I *needed* to hit something.

I sat down and then stood up again, started turning in a circle. I wound my fists in my hair. All these random memories started flooding in, crowding and overlapping in my mind:

I saw K.C. being beaten, and I couldn't help.

I saw Bob asleep with his gun on his lap.

I saw myself playing Little League baseball.

I saw the bathroom in my room upstairs; I felt that pressure, like a vice grip on my throat, that freaked me out.

My skull felt like it was pounding, my brain tissue swelling and pushing against it. I wanted the world to stop spinning, but the memories just played over and over, intensifying:

I was sitting under the dining room table waiting and waiting.

I heard Bob's gun firing over and over.

I knew I took a deep breath, trying to slow everything down, but the thoughts wouldn't go away.

I was meeting my parents and then leaving them in the cafeteria.

I heard the clicking sound of Bob's gun.

My parents.

The cold metal of a gun pressed against my temple.

My mom.

Trying not to flinch when the gun pressed against my temple.

Red police lights flashing.

Sam.

The letter from Sam's dad.

My mom.

My mom's key ring.

No keys—

Tracie's voice was raised. "Landon! Please! You're in pain. I want to help. *Let me in.*"

I opened my eyes. I wasn't standing anymore. I was huddled in the corner of her office, behind her desk area. When I looked around her office, in silence, my first thought was that I had no idea if the memories racing through my mind would ever stop.

"What you were just going through? Were they flashbacks? Painful memories?"

"I don't know. I just want out of here. I want everything to go away."

She was kneeling, leaning over me with her hand on my back. "There are ways to confront the memories and deal with the dreams. You don't have to go through this alone, Landon."

"Please, I just want to go. Can't you guys just let me leave? I want to be alone."

A tear streamed out the corner of Tracie's eye. "When the time is right, maybe that's what you will do, end up on your own. I know that you're the only one you can trust, but right now, while you go through this, I'm here to help."

I shook my head. "I don't want help."

"What does getting help mean to you?"

"I don't know. I just don't want it. Can't you guys understand that? My life was okay before all this, you know. It was screwed up but in an okay way. I dealt with it."

"Was it? Are you sure? Don't you see what Bob did to you?"

"No! Don't say that." I tried to get up.

"Wait, wait, wait. Why can't I say that?"

I didn't want to hear comments like that. I didn't want Bob upset. "I don't know. Just stop. You don't understand."

"Bob is not here, Landon. What's wrong with exploring whether Bob hurt you or not?"

There was a knock at her door. Someone was on the other end, blocking my escape. I couldn't get out. Panic rose in my throat. "I don't know. Just stop, all right? I have to learn to deal with stuff my way."

"But last night, and what you went through right now, I don't take these as good signs. You're going through trauma. I can see it on your face. Bob is *not here*; you know that, right?"

I shrugged. *She's wrong*, I argued back in my mind. There was another knock, and the door opened. It was Drysdale. He looked our way. "Oh, excuse me. Do you guys need a few more minutes?"

Tracie looked to him, standing halfway in the doorway. "Yeah, please." Drysdale shut the door. Tracie looked back to me, going for another round of "Can I help?" No dice, though. I was done talking. I wasn't going to do anything that would anger the part of Bob that lived in me.

(26)

Drysdale was sitting in the conference room with a woman I had never met before. Both the new lady and Drysdale stood up when Tracie and I entered. The lady wasn't as tall as Tracie, or as thin. I mean, she wasn't big, either, but her lower body looked like she sat a lot. Maybe she worked long hours and always ate at her desk, I don't know. She had black-rimmed glasses, a nerdy suit, and wore her hair in a messy ponytail. Tracie was surprised to see her. "Lindsay, why did you come over?"

So her name was Lindsay; not what I would have guessed. She seemed weirded out by Tracie's question, kind of half mumbling and looking my way while she answered, "Yeah, sorry, but there was—well, the motion, the custodial motion got moved up because of yesterday's—the events that took place yesterday."

Tracie walked over to Drysdale. "Leon, can I talk to you outside for a minute about this?"

"Yes, of course." I had forgotten that Drysdale's first name was Leon. Hearing Tracie call him that, it almost sounded like she was talking to a different person. As Tracie and Drysdale were heading out the conference room, the Lindsay lady looked over at me and introduced herself. "Hi, Landon. My name is Lindsay Crandall. It's nice, I mean really nice to finally meet you face to face. I don't want to scare you, but I'm here as—well, the court has appointed you an attorney, and that's ..."

I just wanted her to spit out what she had to say. When she said the word "attorney," the door to the conference room shut, and I could see through the window into the hallway where Tracie and Drysdale were talking. Actually, it was Drysdale doing the talking. He was his usual calm self, with one hand in his pocket and the other one moving around like it does when he talks. I looked back at the Crandall lady. "My attorney? I don't get it. For the stuff that happened with Sam?"

"Who?"

That answered my question. "Why do I have an attorney?"

My eyes left her and looked back toward Tracie and Drysdale. Tracie was standing with her arms crossed, shaking her head. Ms. Crandall saw I was looking out there. "Well, actually, it's a procedural appointment, really. The court, that is, the judge handling the case, he ruled under what they call the Uniform Child Custody Act and by appointing me—well, by appointing you an attorney, it's to make sure that your best interests are represented." The way she spoke made it hard to focus on what she was saying. You could hear the words but you couldn't get the meaning out of them. It was sorta like if the words were beads on a string and they were strung together side-by-side to give them meaning, her string was crooked and tangled up. Whatever though, the word "custody" made sense. My dad had said it in the cafeteria that day and also on the phone that he was going to get an attorney. I remembered Tracie telling him something about petitioning the court for custody. I couldn't think about all that, anyway. What was really getting my attention was watching Tracie and Drysdale through the window. Tracie looked upset, leaning into Drysdale, her mouth moving fast and pointing her finger toward the room where I was.

"Landon?" I was so focused on Tracie and Drysdale that when the Crandall lady said my name, I jumped.

"Yeah?"

"I need—while Agent Drysdale and Ms. Lodin are out of the room, well, I'd like to explain to you how—" She took a breath, and then finally a whole sentence came out in one piece. "It's important that you understand what an attorney-client privilege is."

"Okay."

"Well, you should know that whatever you say to me will remain—it has to stay between us. That's for your protection."

"What do you mean?"

"Well, I know that Ms. Lodin and you talk about things, you know, that you share your feelings with her, but—well, there might be things that are better, or not better, but that should only be shared with me. Things that you think, maybe, the law would be upset about."

"Like what?" I asked, but my eyes weren't leaving Drysdale and Tracie. Having them in the hall talking like that and trying to understand this lady's way of talking made it hard to focus.

"Oh, just—well, you and I will learn how this works as we go along. I've spoken with Leon, that is, Agent Drysdale, before you joined us, and what I'm explaining is—well, I don't think there's going to be a problem, but if you start to say—I'm going to keep my hand right next to yours, and if you feel a little tap from me, I want you look to me before you go ahead and answer, okay?"

The door to the room opened. Drysdale and Tracie came back in. They took their seats: Drysdale across from me and Tracie on the side of me. Ms. Crandall rolled her chair closer to me, sitting on the other side, with her arm where she said it would be. I had only known Lindsay Crandall for maybe five minutes, so I couldn't read her mood. But for Tracie and Drysdale, things were different. Tracie sat there with her legs crossed, her back straight and tall. She kept her eyes on Drysdale and her mouth tightly closed.

"So, Landon, I assume you've met Lindsay, Ms. Crandall?" Drysdale still had his jacket on and his tie tightened. He had an intense look on his face, which made me doubt that the suit and tie was coming off at all.

I responded, "Yeah."

When Drysdale made the reference to the attorney, she patted my arm, smiled at me, and then piped up, "Yes, Leon. I explained … well, in the short time when you were in the hall there, I told Landon about the court appointment and explained, or, I briefly talked about the attorney-client privilege. I told him that we'd become more familiar with the process as we proceed."

"Very good." Drysdale leaned to the side, over the chair arm. I heard his briefcase locks unlock and the leather flaps flip open, hitting the side of the briefcase. He pulled out his normal writing pad, the file that kept getting thicker and thicker, and a tape recorder. He organized all the stuff and put the tape recorder in the middle of the table, facing him.

Why the tape recorder? The mood in the room was too serious to ask, though.

His hand rested on the play button but he didn't press it. "Landon, Tracie was speaking to me in the hall about what you've been going through the last twenty-four hours. I know that it's Tracie's wish that we hold off on this interview—" *Wait, this is an interview? I thought you were gonna tell me about Bob.* "—until things settle down for you."

I was listening to Drysdale so intently that when Tracie spoke up, the tone of her voice caught me off guard. "Or at least wait until tomorrow, Leon."

Drysdale looked her way. He gave her a polite smile and nod, and I knew it meant he wasn't taking her advice. It was obvious that he had come out to the York center to talk to me, and he wasn't leaving until he got his way. "I'm sorry, Landon. As you know, we have Bob in custody, and I need some answers."

When he said Bob's name, there was a small pang in my chest, and I tensed up. Drysdale didn't notice. He just continued on with what he was saying. "I'd like to wait until tomorrow as Tracie is trying to suggest, or the next day even, but that's not an option when we have an active investigation and the answers we need right now are out there. Okay?"

I shrugged.

"Okay?"

I forgot I was talking to Drysdale. "Yeah, that's cool."

"Good."

The way that Tracie looked, the feeling of the new attorney lady at my side, and the sight of Drysdale sitting across from me with his give-me-the-truth brown eyes made me nervous. I felt small. I felt … well, I felt fifteen years old.

Drysdale's finger was about to press down on the play button. He looked at me and said, "I'm here because I need to know more about K.C." I felt my intestines spasm. I felt Bob standing behind me, with more control over me than the two women at my sides. I took a deep breath and tried not to show any emotions. Drysdale nodded and pressed play.

(27)

"First of all, Landon, the information you gave me the other day was very helpful in understanding how K.C. ended up with Bob. We've been in contact with both K.C.'s mother and grandmother, and it appears that what K.C. told you is more or less true—that his mother left him with Bob."

"That's good, right? I mean, that K.C. and Bob were telling the truth?"

No one responded to my question, except my attorney patted my arm. I guess that was to shut me up, but I couldn't. I wanted to know more. I was thirsty for details. "How did you find K.C.'s mom? Bob said she just took off."

"We actually found his grandmother," Drysdale responded.

A memory of K.C. and me making sandwiches in an apartment kitchen popped into my head. Well, I wasn't making the sandwiches, but K.C. was teaching me. Like how you have to drain the water in the tuna can so you use the lid to push the juices out. We were happy, and the memory made me happy, but I didn't dwell on the thought. I wanted to be in the moment, listening to everything Drysdale had to say.

"K.C.'s grandmother has been active in the search for K.C., and she is the one who put us in touch with her daughter, K.C.'s mom, Deborah, who is currently at a drug rehabilitation facility in Lexington, Nebraska. But before I go any further, Landon, do you remember K.C. talking about his grandmother?"

"I don't remember her name, but yeah, that's how I learned to make tuna-fish sandwiches."

"What do you mean?" It was the first time that Drysdale smiled since I saw him. It helped relieve the tension that I sensed between him and Tracie.

"K.C. said he learned how to make tuna sandwiches from his grandma."

Drysdale chuckled. Tracie smiled, but not at Drysdale.

I quickly thought about how I hadn't made the canned tuna stuff since K.C. left. It's weird how when it's too painful to remember someone, you stop doing all the things that remind you of them. But again, I was too anxious that Drysdale wouldn't remember what he was about to say, so I asked a question to try to keep him on track. "Why did his mom leave him with Bob?"

I got another pat from the attorney, but whatever. It was important for me to know everything about K.C., whether it was when we were brothers or before we became brothers. Drysdale nodded to Ms. Crandall, like he was saying she didn't have to do her job quite that well, and then gave me my answer. "Deborah had a drug problem at the time, a methamphetamine addiction, and when she met up with Bob, they entered into an arrangement wherein Deborah and K.C. could live with Bob, and Bob would provide financial support, which Deborah used to satisfy her drug addiction. Deborah has told us that she and K.C. stayed with Bob for about six months. During that time, Deborah started prostituting again, leaving K.C. alone with Bob at night. She noticed that Bob was taking a liking to K.C., and although she knew what Bob was doing to K.C. was wrong, she was trying to survive and didn't know how to deal with her drug addiction."

Drysdale looked at my attorney and then at Tracie. I heard mumbles of sadness under Tracie's breath. I couldn't feel the same sadness, though. I already knew everything Drysdale was saying. I chimed in with, "Yeah, I remember when K.C. told me all this stuff. He said his mom used to tell him that they were lucky to have Bob, and that whatever K.C. had to do, it was better than being on the streets. And also after his mom left, he didn't want her to get in trouble, you know, like get arrested for leaving him."

Everyone in the room was looking at something different. No one made eye contact with anyone else. I was looking at Drysdale, though, hoping he had more information. It seemed like forever before he said, "With everything that he encountered at such a young age, I guess it's understandable that K.C. would have reasoned out the situation that way, trying to protect his mom or the adults around him." He gave me one of those weird, quiet stares, like he wanted to see my reaction to his words. I didn't have one.

His pause seemed to last forever. Finally, he went on. "So what we've learned is that K.C. lived with his grandmother while Deborah was in jail, before they ever met Bob. That's probably when he learned to make the tuna sandwiches." His comment didn't get the smile I think he was looking for from Tracie. She just sat there, stunned or something. I wanted to check in with her like she had with me so often, but I couldn't take my attention from Drysdale as his words flowed out. "And his grandmother actually wanted to raise K.C. She became attached to him when he was living with her. She's been helping us with the identification process. It seems, in fact, that K.C. lived with his grandmother from the time he was about three years old until he was six, the end of his first year in kindergarten. That's when Deborah was released from jail, and because K.C.'s custody issues didn't go through foster care or a social worker, Deborah had the legal right as a parent to come and take K.C. from his grandmother.

"That was the last time that K.C.'s grandmother—Ruth—that was the last time that Ruth saw K.C., when Deborah was released from jail and said she needed to take K.C. with her so she could get her welfare check from the state. After Deborah took K.C. from his grandmother's, they bounced around between shelters, the streets, and friends' houses, and eventually ended up with Bob. Deborah has told us that at the time of her arrest, she thought Bob would take K.C. back to his grandmother's because he would not want to take care of K.C. She said she didn't tell the police right away about K.C.'s whereabouts for fear she'd be booked with a child endangerment charge as well. Bob, of course, didn't take K.C. to his grandmother's.

"At the time Deborah was picked up for prostitution, her welfare check was sent to an apartment. The lease for the apartment where that check was sent to was under Robert Starker's name. The records for the apartment, which we've been able to obtain, indicate that the property was abandoned by the tenants—Bob and K.C. we believe—a week after Deborah was arrested. That was close to ten years ago, and about three years or so before you ended up with them."

There was this heavy silence in the room. Maybe for everyone else there was confusion why things like this happen in the world. I mean, if that's how they felt, it was because they never lived in my world, or K.C.'s world. For me, though, everything Drysdale said made sense. It clicked with all my memories, and this feeling of relief came over me because I knew, for once, that what I thought was the truth, really was.

(28)

I waited as long as I could for everyone's face to lighten up—for their worry lines to fade. After hearing Drysdale confirm the truth about K.C., I felt a boost of confidence that maybe I would eventually get enough information to bridge the gaps in my mind about what happened to me. There were missing pieces, blank pockets of space in my memory when I thought about my life in a linear way. K.C. told me about his life, but it wasn't the same for me. I always had to ask people what happened to me instead of knowing the details through a memory.

The feeling is kind of like what you get when you lose something and you can't find it, but when you do find it, it blows your mind how it got to where you found it. Like you know you put what you lost somewhere, but you can't remember how it happened or when you put it there. You would never know the whole story unless you asked someone who saw you do it and had them explain it all to you. That was me. And the interesting thing is that when they do tell you what happened to you and it's the truth, it fits that blank space in your mind just right, and the missing puzzle piece clicks in right away.

I started the questioning back up. "And did you ask Bob about me, how he found me?"

I didn't like the look that Drysdale gave me when I asked the question. "We did ask, Landon. We've spent a lot of time questioning Bob on your kidnapping, and we believe at this point he's being fairly forthright with the details. I'm hoping that out of our meeting here, you can confirm some of the information he's given us. I know that Tracie doesn't feel comfortable prodding you for memories, and if at any point you feel uncomfortable, we'll stop and take a break. Okay?"

I nodded. "Okay."

Drysdale looked over to Tracie and gave her a nod. It reminded me of the nod that I saw between them the first night in the FBI room, except this time Tracie didn't nod back or flash a polite smile to indicate they were on the same page with what was going on.

The lawyer leaned in closer to me. She was almost sitting on my lap. "And if you, well, if you have any questions that come up, just remember to ask me first. We can step outside, okay? And if Agent Drysdale asks a question, and I don't think that the—if I don't think you should answer it, I'll tap you on the arm like I've been doing. Okay?"

"Yeah, okay." *What else could I say?* I mean, I wanted to ask why the interview was different this time and why this attorney lady had to be breathing down my throat, but before I could say anything, Drysdale started in with what he had to say. "Landon, Bob has given us a full confession with regard to your disappearance."

"What? What do you mean?" I ignored Ms. Crandall's tap on my arm. "I don't get it. You mean he knows how everything happened?" Time started to speed up.

"No, Landon. I mean that he's given us the details about how he kidnapped you."

"No, I don't understand. Bob said he found me." I looked to Tracie. She sat there just listening to me. "I know what you said about the kidnapping, you know, but that's—that wasn't Bob, right? I mean, I know you don't know, but ... well, I just ... wait."

Tracie finally offered her advice. "If this feels too strange to think about, Landon, like Agent Drysdale said, we can stop and take a break."

"No, no, I don't want to stop. I don't get it, though." I looked back to Drysdale, who in his normal calm way of talking asked, "Well, what do you think happened? Based on what you just said to Tracie, what do you think happened to you?"

"I kind of didn't think about all of it, I guess." It's like this heavy fog that lived in my mind started to thin out. The coffee table memory of how Bob said he talked to my parents and they told him they didn't want me flashed into my mind, and it stayed there while I compared it to what Drysdale was saying that Bob confessed to. Like, in a weird way, I knew I was trying to accept the two facts as truths even though I saw they canceled each other out. Bob couldn't have ever talked to my parents if I was kidnapped, no matter who kidnapped me. It's like a curtain on a stage opened in front of me. Before it opened, I knew what was backstage and I knew what was front stage, and I just accepted both realities until I saw both stages simultaneously, and right then it dawned on me that both of those truths can't exist at the same time.

"Landon? Are you okay?" It was Tracie.

Drysdale's face came back into my view. He sat there, staring at me, waiting for what he said to sink in. When my eyes settled back on him, he continued, "Do you really not want to believe that Bob was the one who kidnapped you, Landon? Is the denial that strong?"

"Leon, give him time to process it, please."

I responded right after Tracie's comment. "I don't know. I mean, didn't he tell you about the shelter? I know everyone says I was kidnapped, but maybe whoever did it, you know, they are the ones that gave me to Bob."

The second I heard the question that I asked Drysdale, I wondered why I asked it. I didn't need anyone to point it out for me. I saw what I was doing—I was still fighting to keep both truths alive, but Drysdale's words carried with them that there's-only-one-truth tone when he said, "Landon, what you just said doesn't make sense. And you heard what I told you about K.C., you know what kind of person Bob is. I don't mean to jolt the foundation or reality that you've created to define your past experiences but ... Landon?"

I was shaking my head, not at what Drysdale was saying but at myself. At how stupid my mind worked. *Why didn't I see this before?* I kept thinking back to Tracie's office the first day at the center, to her telling me I had to accept that I was abducted.

"Should we take a break?" It was Tracie again.

"No," I said as I shook my head more, "No, I'm okay. I mean, I just don't understand this." I looked up at Drysdale. "Are you totally sure? Could it be that Bob is just telling you this because it's what you wanted to hear? Never mind. It's like, even when I say it, I know that's not true. It's just that, I don't know, I'm just stunned and don't understand why I didn't question it myself, in my own mind, like when I was in Tracie's office last week. I don't get why I never questioned if it might have been Bob who kidnapped me, unless maybe there's something missing, you know, something that hasn't been solved yet."

Drysdale responded, "It's true, Landon. Bob confessed that he was the one responsible for your abduction. He's told us how he did it, and where you were when you were abducted. He knows details that only the perpetrator and the police could be aware of. He's volunteered his DNA so it can be tested against the physical evidence taken from the recreation center where you disappeared."

I couldn't stop the words from pouring out. "But why didn't I leave then? Why would I call him my dad?"

I heard Tracie's voice. "But Landon, in fairness to you, you don't remember the day you were abducted. It's been blocked from your mind. So it's reasonable that you've been patching together made-up beliefs to make sense of how it all happened." I couldn't absorb Tracie's advice. The thought that I had been living with so much fiction was too weird to keep in my mind. My words started streaming out. "I thought he found me. I mean, I remember him finding me. I just—like, I remember the shelter. Wait. Yeah, that's right. Didn't Bob talk about the shelter?"

My attorney's hand patted me again. I jerked away but not in a rude way. I just wanted to feel like I had my own space to think. All she said in response was, "Again, let's—well, I want you to just listen, okay?"

Drysdale's voice was solid. "I'm sure there was no shelter involved, although I may know what you're referring to. And we believe strongly that there was no one else involved in your disappearance."

"Yeah, but I remember the shelter. I told you guys about the shelter, remember? I remember the closets there. Like, I don't remember the people, but I was there. I remember being there. Maybe you guys scared Bob, and he's just saying stuff to you."

"No, Landon. The agency is confirming the facts of his confession as we speak. You are the only one denying it. Keep trying to come out of the denial like you're doing right now." It was weird to hear Drysdale's words. I sat there, stunned. My shoulders slumped, my spine curved forward. I was more freaked out with how my brain accepted things than I was with the information I was hearing.

Drysdale remained calm. "If you feel comfortable, I can show you some pictures that may help your recollection. Are you okay for this?"

I felt Tracie's hand on my back, like the night when I threw up in Drysdale's interview room. I stared forward, across the table at Drysdale. Tracie murmured, "I really don't like this approach, Leon."

Drysdale didn't waver in his actions. He flipped open the file, pulled out some computer-printed pictures, and pushed them in front me. "Do you recognize this place, where these pictures were taken from?"

I knew immediately. "Yeah, that's the shelter." It looked a little different, like all the cluttered stuff in the photo wasn't the same in my memory, but I saw the cots, or what I was calling beds, and then the wooden closets behind the cots. And on the opposite wall, this other wooden panel stuff, I remembered that. I didn't recognize the pictures on the wall, but I knew the room. "Yeah, that's the place, that's the shelter. See. Didn't Bob tell you about this place?"

"Yes, we found this location because of Bob. He told us that after the abduction, he took you to his sister's ranch in Scottsbluff, Nebraska, up near Wyoming. It's about a five-hour drive from Colorado Springs. The ranch was vacant at the time of your abduction. We've confirmed that through his sister. And these pictures are from the tack room located on that ranch. Apparently the cots and closets are there for the ranch hands who stay onsite for more than a day. It's something like a lodging area for the hired help. But, Landon, to make sure we understand each other, what you're telling me is that you recognize this room. This is the room you have been calling a shelter?"

I looked at the tape recorder, slowly spinning.

I looked again at the pictures.

"Is that what you're telling me, Landon? You've been in this tack room before and when you refer to Bob finding you in a shelter, this is the place you are talking about?"

I nodded.

"Is that a yes?"

The closets in the pictures looked so small, but in my memory they were huge. Then it dawned on me that that's because I was so small when I was put in the closets. I moved the pictures out of my sight. I didn't need them anymore. The memory was flooding in. "Yeah, that's the shelter. Or what I thought was the shelter." The memories were back in vivid detail. The closets were made out of plywood, and the doors didn't close flush, like a regular door. The wood was warped at the bottom, and you could see out into the room during daylight. I remember staring for hours at the knots in the plywood. I remember the flooring stained with dirt, and the smell of fertilizer and hay mixed together.

Drysdale took the pictures away. "What's going through your mind?"

"The closets."

"What about the closets, Landon?"

"I was in them. They put me in them."

"They?"

"I didn't see them, but, I mean, when I was in one of the closets and I looked through the crack, you know, at the bottom of the door, I could see people walking back and forth. Like I never knew who they were, but I knew people were there."

"And did you see Bob?"

"Leon, don't take him there. You got the identification of the location. Isn't that enough?"

"No, Tracie. This is too important." Drysdale directed his attention back to me. "Landon, think about seeing Bob there. Can you?"

A quick, choppy picture flashed in my mind. It was a boot kicking me. I kept yelling out, "I'm sorry. I'm sorry." The boot kicked me into the corner. My hands were bloodied from being kicked and from feeling around my body trying to soothe the open sores. I could feel the rough wood of the closet walls rubbing against my arms, how the splinters pricked at me. The swollen bruises that hurt to lean against were pressing on the warped wood surface of the closet walls. I wanted the boot to stop. I yelled louder, "Please. I'm sorry. I'm sorry."

"Are you okay? Landon?" It was Tracie's voice. I nodded. She looked to Drysdale and said, "I think we should take a break, Leon."

The memory wouldn't cease. I heard the boots walking my way. When they stopped, the latch on the closet door clicked. The plywood door flew open. As fast as I could, I ducked my head under my stomach and brought my knees under my body. It was my only way to fight and defend. My hands clasped behind my neck. The hard heel of the boot kicked against my spine nubs.

"Landon, do you see Bob there?" Drysdale wasn't giving up.

Something about the memory didn't make sense. "I don't understand."

"What's that?" It was Tracie responding to me.

"I remember the closet, you know, being in there. Even though it was latched shut, the door wouldn't close all the way at the bottom and there was a crack I could see out of. And when I'd look out and it was daylight, I could see people walking by. There were people there."

"But you said you never saw what they looked like." It was Drysdale.

"No, I could only see through the crack at the bottom. I could only see their—" I stopped midsentence. When I had the memory clear in my mind, I questioned what I saw. "*Oh* ... I get it."

Tracie leaned toward me. "What? What is it, Landon?

"The person walking by, he did it a lot during the day. That's why I thought people were there. But it was just him. It's the same boots walking by throughout the day."

"Who is it?" Drysdale asked. "Is it Bob?"

The epiphany shattered the foundation of truth I had been trying to live on. I closed my eyes. My body rocked back and forth. "All he did was kick me. I kept trying to say the right thing, you know, so he'd stop."

Tracie made a circular motion on my back with her hand. It didn't comfort me. Instead, it replicated what was happening in the memory. More details flooded in. "The cots, I remember waking up on the cot."

"And do you see Bob?" Drysdale pressed.

"Yeah … he's there." The memory entered my mind so clearly that I could see the air particles floating in front of my eyes. I would lie on the cot, trying to be still, trying not to press against any of my bruises and open sores.

"Where is he, Landon?" Drysdale put the question to me again.

"He's rubbing my back. Like, I don't know when I left the closet, but I woke up on the cot. And Bob was there. I remember looking at the pillow under my head, and my blood was smeared all over the pillowcase. The closets were there, just like you see them in that picture. And I could see them out of the corner of my eye, right next to the cot, at the head of the cot. I kept trying not to look that way toward the closets because I didn't want to go back in. I was afraid that if someone saw me looking at the closets, they would have an excuse to put me back in. I just didn't want to go back in."

"And you said it was Bob rubbing your back?" Drysdale asked.

"That's when he said he found me. He felt bad for me, and kept asking who would do this to me. He wanted to know. He was sad for me. And I couldn't—well, my voice was frozen, and I couldn't say anything because I didn't want to go back into the closet. I didn't want to say the wrong thing. But he kept asking me who did this to me, like he was mad at them, and he said he would save me. That no one wanted me. He kept saying he was going to take me away to be with him and his son. He was sitting there on the side of the cot, telling me he was going to save me and not to worry."

Everyone took in a deep breath.

Everyone exhaled.

There was this silence that allowed us all to ponder the vision that my words created.

"Leon, I think we should take a break," Tracie murmured, taking her hand off my back.

"Yeah, that's a good idea." Drysdale pressed the pause button on the tape recorder. Tracie and Ms. Crandall started to move around. I sat there, holding my chest, slowly nodding. I had more to realize from the memory. "You know what's really strange?"

"What's that, Landon?" asked Tracie. Everyone stopped their movement to hear my words.

"I remember looking down to the ground when I was on the cot while Bob was rubbing my back. I saw Bob's boots. They were covered with dried blood. And when I saw the blood on them, I knew it was my blood, and that those were the boots that ripped my skin open and bruised my spine. But at the same time, I ignored what I saw and didn't question it because I just wanted him to save me and not let me go back in the closet."

I looked over at Drysdale. Silence.

I turned to Tracie. Silence.

My attorney sat there, frozen, with her hand no longer on the table next to my arm but instead resting limply in her lap.

(29)

We took the break Tracie recommended. I could feel Drysdale, Tracie, and Ms. Crandall's eyes all watching me walk out of the interview room. No one said a word. The silence actually helped. I wasn't sure where I was going: the stairwell, my room, the atrium. I ended up on the rooftop where the basketball court was. I lay down on a bench, and looked up at the stars, letting my thoughts drift.

Why did I call Bob "dad"? Maybe it was some kind of made-up belief that I created to help cope with my reality. I thought about that twelve-hour road trip Bob and I took to hand-deliver the Burnside Breech-Loading rifle that he restored. Bob was happy. I was happy. For the two days of the trip, I had a sense that we were father and son. *I hate myself for allowing it to happen*. This feeling of embarrassment came over me. I wanted to roll off the bench, crawl over to the corner, and chant, "Why did I let that happen? Why?" *I'm so disgusting*, I yelled in my mind.

I tried to brush the emotions off to the side and stay with the question: why did I enjoy moments like that when something at my core should have been prodding me that he was never my father but always my abductor? The only way I knew to help myself out was to tell me that maybe it wasn't about Bob as much as it was about me wanting a father, wanting a parent, wanting a family, wanting closeness, wanting to know I could still connect with another human. Maybe deep down, in that part of my mind that blocked out the pain, I wanted to somehow make sure I stayed able to love. The thoughts did make sense to me, but I still hated myself that I ever cared about Bob at all, and I feared how I still might care about him.

"Hi." I didn't hear the footsteps or the stairwell door shut behind Tracie. I didn't register her presence until she spoke. I sat up, turned around, and gave her a nod. When I saw her eyes under the rooftop lights, the worried look on her face came into view.

I didn't feel like explaining it to her, but the weird thing is that when the memories flooded into my mind it was like I already knew them, in a hazy way. They weren't totally new to me. It's more like they had always been in my mind, but off to the side where I refused to think about them. And when the new memories of old stuff came back in, there wasn't this worry, like, "Am I sure this memory really happened?" I knew it did. I remembered living it. The screwy part was that when I examined the new memory there was no label attached to it that gave a description of the time, place or reason it happened. And not knowing the reason behind it made me feel dumb. Like when I thought about those closets all that time, why in the hell did I call that a shelter? How many other times had my opinions been so positive that I knew the "why" part of a memory and because of it, I ended up defending the lies and deceptions of other people? *Why am I such a stupid-ass fool?*

I almost forgot Tracie was there until she said, "You look like you're in deep thought. Are you handling everything okay?"

I shrugged. I wished that she'd stop asking that question.

"Can I have a seat?"

I moved over.

"Agent Drysdale would like to continue with the questioning. It's getting late, but it's up to you. He's pushing to finish tonight because Lindsay, your attorney, can't come back out tomorrow."

"Why is she here?"

"Just a precaution to ensure that if you were a witness to any of Bob's criminal activity, you don't by accident say the wrong thing that might appear to make you involved. Does that make sense?"

"I guess."

"It's been a long day, hasn't it?"

"Yeah." I looked over at her clothes. She was in the same flannel shirt and jeans that she showed up in at my room that morning. Her makeup was gone and her hair wasn't as fluffy as it usually is. She still looked okay, though, for her age and all.

"Do you want to talk about anything?"

"What? Like how stupid I am?"

"Stupid? Really? What do you mean?"

"Like calling that ranch place a shelter."

"You were seven years old when that happened. When you think about what you went through, try to remember what your mindset was at the time, not what it is today. Or consider what we talked about the other day.

It's more helpful to just ask yourself why you remember it that way. Don't be so hard on yourself."

"Yeah, I guess. I don't know." I looked behind us and all around the rooftop to make sure no one else was there. "But that's not just it, you know."

"What do you mean?"

"Like when I hear stuff about Bob, my mind will think about how bad he is, and if someone else went through all that stuff, I would hate Bob for it if I didn't know him. But then there's this other part of me, you know, that's like … just really stupid."

"Stupid how?"

"I still don't want him to be too mad at me. Or like, I think that maybe people just don't understand him, and I feel like defending him. I mean, this is stupid, but it's like a part of him is in me and even after all that stuff with Drysdale, even though I hate Bob, like Bob in the flesh, there's a part of me that still feels attached to him. I don't know why I'm even saying this. It's stupid."

"It makes sense."

I stared at Tracie. I wanted her to be right. "It does?"

"Sure, it does. It's the territory of abuse. But it's not that Bob is a part of you, Landon. That's important for you to understand. It's more like there's a part of you that has programmed yourself to look for or to try to detect situations that might bring on the abuse. This doesn't happen in a thinking way, wherein you recognize that that's what you're doing. Those reactions of wanting to defend Bob or not make him mad are your way of trying to prevent the abuse."

"I don't understand."

"Let me try this with you. If I asked you to think about Bob being mad, tell me what you feel like, what your body feels like." I pictured standing inside the trailer by the front door, knowing that Bob just got home, and hearing his van door slamming shut like it does when the world pissed him off. "Are you thinking about Bob being mad?"

"Yeah."

"What is your body doing?"

"My chest is tense, actually my whole body is, and then I get this feeling like I can't swallow."

"Anything else?"

"I don't know."

"Do you see that you've made your hands into a fist?"

I looked down. "Oh."

"Bob isn't anywhere near us, but if you just think about the possibility of Bob's rage, you see that you start to defend against the abuse. You prepare for it in a way."

"But you asked me to think about it."

"Right, as a way to show you. But let's now come back to what you were saying before, about wanting to defend Bob when people say bad things about him. What happens is that when you hear something you know would make Bob angry, that programmed part of you sends the message to your thinking mind to defend Bob. It knows that if Bob isn't angry, it's less likely that you will be abused by him. Is that helping to explain it?"

"But Bob isn't around. I mean, I can see that Bob isn't anywhere."

"That's a big issue for traumatized people. It's hard to convince that part of the mind that the trauma is not around. In a funny way, it's as if that part of you, the part that wants to protect you from the abuse, doesn't trust your thinking mind to recognize that the abuse is actually over."

"That sounds weird."

"People can experience the panic or attachment like what you're describing for years after being removed from the trauma." *That's not what I wanted to hear.* "Landon, think of it this way. You were sharing with me the other day about the sound of crunching leaves and what that represents. To you, it means that Bob is coming, right? And any time Bob is coming, abuse may be coming as well, right?"

I shrugged.

"Now fast forward in life, let's say five years from now. You're a busy guy, I don't know … let's say you're on a college campus, talking with a group of people, and you're focused on listening to what everyone is saying. You also see in the distance another friend you need to talk to. In other words, your thinking mind is occupied with the things going on around you. Yet there's still that other part of you that always wants to keep you safe, and to do this, that part of you continually monitors, through your senses, signs of danger. Are you with me so far?"

"I guess."

"So go back to the campus thought where you're focusing on everything around you. While that's going on, a random person walks behind you. You don't turn around to see the person. Your thinking mind doesn't even sense that the person is there, okay? But at the same time, this fear comes over you. It's an intense panic like something bad is going to happen. The feeling is so intense that it interrupts your focus. You can't see the danger. You just *know* it's there."

"Okay. I don't get it, though."

"Well, hold on. I'm not finished. Now imagine that you could freeze-frame that exact moment when the fear came over you, okay? You go back in time and take a look at everything that was going on around you when the panic feeling came over you. What you find is that the person who walked behind you—that you didn't pay any attention to—was walking over dried leaves that made a crunching noise. To that part of you that protects you, the crunching sound of leaves means Bob is coming. Immediately, the message is sent to your thinking mind that danger is nearby. No explanation. Just the warning that *danger* is in the air."

"Yeah, I don't know. Maybe I get it. But it's too much to think about. I just want everything to be over." I leaned forward like I was looking at the stars, but I was really trying to go over in my mind what Tracie said. I felt her stare at my profile. She didn't say anything, probably because she knew nothing was ever going to be over for me. Because even if she was right and Bob wasn't a part of me, his voice spoke louder than my own, which meant that a part of my destiny would always belong to him somehow.

(30)

Before I went back to the interview room, I stopped on my floor. I just wanted to double-check that Palmer's door was closed. I knew before I got there that for sure he was gone; it was almost nine o'clock. But this little part of me thought maybe something strange might have happened and maybe there was a small, slight chance he was there. Other than hearing his mop bucket go by my room earlier in the morning, I hadn't seen him. It's not that I missed him, like I was totally sad he wasn't around. It's that I missed how I felt talking to him. When we talked, he never made me think about all the crap that I was going through. I called it Palmer talk.

His door was closed. The hallway was quiet.

Drysdale and the rest were waiting downstairs.

I sighed a tiny sigh and headed toward the stairwell.

Drysdale was on his cell, standing in the corner of the room talking. Tracie and Lindsay Crandall were whispering gossip about an office person I didn't know but slowly stopped when I came in. The two of them pushed their seats apart, indicating for me to have a seat in the middle chair.

Drysdale was off the phone and sat down almost at the same time as me. "Okay, Landon. I hope to have you out of here in just a few minutes. You've been a real trooper tonight. Thanks."

I felt Ms. Crandall's wiggling fingers on my forearm. "And remember, I know you probably didn't forget, but if I think you should, maybe should not answer a question, I'm going to—well, you'll feel me tap you, okay?"

I nodded.

Drysdale turned on the tape recorder. He lowered his head to it and stated what time it was and who was in the room. He grabbed his yellow writing pad and flipped back to the front pages of his notes. He looked up after reading for a couple of seconds. "Landon, I just want to go over a few statements you made in one of our first meetings. It's about K.C. This was something you said on our first meeting. Do you remember I asked you who moved into the trailer with you?"

"Yeah."

"And do you remember what your answer was?"

"Yeah, Bob and me."

"But that's not true, is it?"

"What do you—" Before I got the whole sentence out, there was a tap on my arm. "Mr. Drysdale, you'll need to rephrase that without the suggestion of dishonesty." There was no stuttering. Lindsay Crandall's voice was strong and direct. For the first time, I felt like I had an actual lawyer next to me.

Drysdale didn't hesitate. He looked at me and said, "That's not what I intended. Ms. Crandall is right. I'll rephrase. Do you think you remembered that incorrectly, Landon? Could it be the case that K.C. did move into the trailer with you and Bob?"

Again, there was the tap on the forearm. I couldn't focus on the attorney's words because the packing boxes from the spare room of the trailer popped into my head. Then blotchy thoughts pulsed in my mind, thoughts about Bob asking what happened to K.C., and I was in the trailer living room, confused, afraid, not knowing what happened to K.C. I looked at Drysdale, stared at his moving mouth. I wanted to leave the memory. My heart was free-falling to the bottom of my chest.

"Landon, are you with us?" It was Tracie.

My mouth was hanging open. I blinked rapidly to clear my vision. "Yeah. Yeah, I'm good."

Drysdale looked me in the eyes and started up his questions. "Let me explain where my confusion lies with your previous statement about who moved into the trailer with you. During our first interview at my office, you told me that K.C. lived at the Cordia Bungalows in Coleridge with you and Bob, did you not?"

"Yeah."

"And you said that it was only you and Bob who moved into the trailer, right?"

"Right. I mean, I think that's right."

"Good. And then when I asked you what happened to K.C., you said you didn't know and you remembered that K.C. wasn't at the trailer when you came home on the first day." What Drysdale was saying matched my memory. I opened the front door to the trailer and Bob was in the living room, pacing back and forth in a rage, waiting for me. I was confused by

Bob's anger, not knowing what happened to K.C., but the more I pleaded with Bob that I didn't know what happened to K.C., the angrier Bob got. "Yeah, that's right. I was confused about where K.C. was." The memory of that day expanded. I was leaning with my back against the refrigerator, running my hands through my hair, telling Bob I didn't know where K.C. was. But Bob continued his pacing, letting his rage build while my confusion grew.

"Well, hold on, Landon. Do you see the inconsistency there?"

"What do you mean?"

The Crandall lady gripped my forearm. "No, Agent Drysdale. You will need to point out the inconsistency. It's not Landon's job to clear that point up or support it. Ask your next question." She was a different woman. I felt like telling her to go easy on Drysdale. He wasn't trying to hurt me. But more of the memory flooded my mind.

I was eleven, maybe twelve. I was walking up to the trailer. It was daylight. Through the window I saw Bob pacing in the living room. I was scared. I went to grab the doorknob but the door flew open. Bob grabbed my arm and yanked me inside the trailer. I fell to the ground and crawled behind an open kitchen cabinet. I looked up. Bob was pacing. Yelling. He started asking what happened to K.C. He was yelling … pacing … his spit was spewing and veins bulging. I crept away from the open cabinet. Stood and backed up against the refrigerator, fearing his rage.

"Landon, we have a witness—" I knew Drysdale was talking, but nothing was registering. His voice couldn't overpower the memories.

"I'm sorry, what did you say?" I asked.

Tracie asked if I wanted a break. I shook my head.

Drysdale repeated his question. "Landon, we have a witness who has told us that she saw K.C. when you moved into the trailer with Bob."

"I don't remember that, really. I mean, maybe it happened? I don't think so. I'm confused. I don't remember K.C. ever living in the trailer."

"I think we're just going too fast here. Let's slow down." Drysdale dropped his pen, clasped his hands, and looked at me. "We'll take it one step at a time. Okay?" I nodded. He continued on. "Do you remember the day that you moved out of the bungalow in Coleridge?"

"Not really."

"What does 'not really' mean, Landon?"

"I don't remember in detail, but I know we did. So, like, I can remember memories of the bungalow in Coleridge, like the sidewalk outside the door.

Then I know when the first day at the trailer was, but I don't remember in between moving out of the bungalow."

"Do you remember driving with your belongings to the trailer, knowing that you had moved out of the bungalow in Coleridge?"

I shook my head and closed my eyes. I was able to bring a picture into my mind of driving in the van at night with moving boxes in the back.

"Is that a 'no'?" Drysdale's voice rose slightly.

"I don't know."

"What do you mean you don't know?" I could tell Drysdale was getting irritated. I had never seen him like that. It made me nervous. I wanted to have more answers. I had wanted those answers since I walked into the trailer that day, confused about what happened to K.C. But as the years went by and the memories of K.C. faded, the questions of what happened to him faded as well. "Explain yourself to me, Landon." Drysdale's command made my heart race.

"Well, when you say that, you know, do I remember driving after the move from Coleridge, it's like I can picture boxes being in the van, the moving boxes that I saw in the trailer when I came home that day looking for K.C. They're the same boxes that were in the spare room for all those years, right? But like when you ask me what I remember about moving, it's not really a memory like you'd expect. It's more like I can *imagine* those boxes in the van, and I'm *thinking* about us driving, but I don't know for sure if that's the memory, the real memory, or if I'm like patching it together like—"

"Don't say anymore, Landon." It was Ms. Crandall. "It's clear, Agent Drysdale, that he's trying to construct an answer to help you out. I'm not going to let him do that. Maybe you need to explain to us why this is so important."

Drysdale took in a deep breath. He leaned back in his chair, crossed his legs and arms, and looked at me.

Stared at me.

Then he leaned forward and pressed the stop button on the tape recorder. "Here's the deal, guys. Bob surrendered with an attorney present. He's asking that if he confesses to the kidnapping charge and fully cooperates with the murder investigation of K.C., in turn, he wants us to recommend a plea deal of twenty-five years."

Tracie's upper body moved forward, over the table. Her voice was raised. "I don't get it, Leon. Why are you sharing this with Landon? Why would you bring up what Bob is facing with regard to prison? You saw

Landon's state of mind earlier tonight when we spoke about Bob. I'm sure your office is qualified to make those decisions on its own. Why are you involving—"

"Tracie, hear me out."

She relaxed in her chair a little and threw her hands in the air. "Go ahead. Let's hear it."

"We have a confession for the kidnapping."

"Yes, I've listened to everything you've said." Tracie's voice was still raised. "What does that mean, though, with regard to—"

"That means he confessed to the *kidnapping.*"

"Right, Leon, you told us that."

"*But* we have a murder investigation that is still open."

Tracie gasped. The Crandall lady's hand slipped off my forearm. Everything they were saying was over my head. I was straining to try to understand Drysdale's words. "Bob has told us—"

Tracie jumped up. Her chair flew back toward the wall. "Don't say it, Leon!"

He did anyway. I heard every word loud and clear. "Landon, Bob has told us that you are the one who killed K.C."

Before the Crandall lady's hand could grip my arm, the words slipped out of my mouth. "Did I?"

"Don't say another word." It was my attorney gripping at my forearm. She spun my seat around to face her. "I'm instructing you not to say another word."

Tracie swung the door to the interview room open. "Let's go, Landon. We're done here. This line of questioning was inappropriate, Leon. I can't believe I witnessed this without his parents involved. This wasn't right."

"He has a court-appointed attorney, Tracie. She is here to protect him legally."

While Drysdale was talking, I felt Lindsay Crandall's hand pulling at me to stand up. I was in a daze. She guided me out of the interview room. I looked back at Drysdale through the window once I was in the hallway. He didn't look my way. He had his head down, shaking it back and forth slowly.

Tracie was clearly upset, her voice agitated. She looked at me, looked at Ms. Crandall. "Landon, don't say a word. Don't say anything. Do you hear me?" I think I nodded. I was trying to rethink everything that happened in the last thirty seconds.

The attorney barked back to Tracie, "No, Ms. Lodin. I'm his attorney. I will advise him on what to say and not to say."

Tracie's voice rang out, even stronger. "I want his parents here. I want his parents advised first. This isn't happening in this way in front of me."

We were at the exit doors to the center. I couldn't focus enough to hear the details of Tracie and Lindsay Crandall's conversation, but I remember hearing, "See you in a few days," in the attorney's voice. Tracie buzzed Ms. Crandall out the exit doors and then indicated for me to walk toward the elevator.

Tracie and I were in the elevator heading up to my room. To go three floors up seemed to take forever. I kept replaying Drysdale's last words in my mind. I looked over at Tracie, who stood perfectly still, staring at the elevator buttons. She didn't blink.

"Tracie?"

She sucked in a huge breath. Held it. Finally exhaled and, in a voice that was almost a whisper, asked, "What, Landon?" She wouldn't look at me. The elevator chime went off. The doors opened. I couldn't hide the sadness in my voice. "I don't remember saying goodbye to K.C."

(31)

I learned later that night what the word "incriminate" means. When Tracie and I got back to my room, we made the call to my parents. As soon as Tracie explained to my dad the conversation with Drysdale, she gave the phone to me, reminded me that I could reach her through the operator, and then left the room. Still dazed, I held the phone to my ear, ready to sit silently and listen. I had learned that that's the best conversation to have with my dad. This time I was wrong.

"Tyler." The way he said it didn't challenge my identity. He put me in my place. I was his son. He was my father. His voice—so many miles away—was giving me guidance, and I wanted it. "Yeah."

"I need to make sure you understand what's happening. This is a very serious situation, and I don't want you talking to anybody. Are you listening to me?"

"Yeah."

"Whatever you say, even to your attorney, can be misunderstood. It's important that I make sure you understand this, Tyler." His voice paused. "Is Tracie gone?" I knew she was but I looked around the room anyway. "Yeah, she said she'd see me tomorrow."

"Good." There was another pause, like maybe the phone call woke him up and his thoughts were coming slow. "Yeah, yeah, that's good that you're alone." The silence was strange, unlike his way of talking. But when he broke the silence, his voice was stern and resolved. "Tyler, I'm going to ask you something, and I just want a yes or no answer, okay?"

"Okay."

"Did you see Robert Starker kill K.C.?"

"I don't know."

"What do you mean you don't know? This isn't the time to feel like you have to protect Robert. I understand those feelings, but that can't happen now. This is the rest of your life that we're dealing with here." My dad didn't know that I never protected Bob when it came to the things he did to K.C. I answered honestly. "No, I know, but what I'm saying is that I don't remember anything about when K.C. left."

"What do you mean, 'left'?"

"Well, I mean like what you're saying."

"Killed?"

"Yeah, I guess."

"But listen, you know that whatever happened to K.C., Robert Starker is responsible for it, right?"

"I don't know. I don't remember what happened to K.C."

Instead of raising his voice, he lowered it and moved the phone closer to his mouth. "If you don't remember, then you didn't have anything to do with it. Do you understand? That's what we're going to tell everyone: your attorney, Drysdale, Tracie, Dr. Williams—everyone. You had nothing to do with it. Okay?"

"But I'm worried that what Drysdale said is right, you know. That what Bob is saying is true. Maybe I did do it."

"No. Stop. That's what I mean by saying things that can be misunderstood."

"But I remember Bob yelling at me when I came home that day to the trailer."

"That doesn't mean you did anything wrong, Tyler."

"But I don't understand why, when I came home to the trailer, I was so confused about where K.C. was. And Bob just kept asking me where K.C. was and what happened to K.C., like maybe I was trying to lie to Bob about something, about what happened to K.C., you know. I don't know."

"You're making it all too confusing, Tyler. All that means is that the last time you saw K.C. he was alive. It means that you didn't see what Robert Starker did to K.C. That's what I hear you saying. And that's what you have to understand. The last time you saw K.C., he was alive, and you don't understand why you didn't find him when you came home to the trailer. Don't let what Robert said to you at the time twist your thoughts now."

I paused. What my dad was saying made sense, but confusion clouded my mind. What I remember Bob saying on that day in the trailer didn't feel like the same type of lies that Bob was using at the shelter. I remember how I felt looking at Bob when he was yelling at me the day K.C. left.

"Tyler, do you understand the significance of all this? We've got to be very careful how we talk about this. People can misunderstand what you mean."

"Maybe. I guess."

"No, I'm telling you." He paused again. "The truth is that Robert Starker killed K.C."

I couldn't absorb what my dad was saying. Instead, I was trying to rewind that memory, starting from the moment when I walked up to the trailer that day. But the more I tried to think of what happened, the louder Bob's voice got, yelling at me, wanting to know what happened to K.C. "But I don't remember—"

My dad cut me off. "No, Tyler. There's no explanation here. Listen to me. Robert Starker killed K.C. The real truth is that it doesn't matter what really happened, and who did what."

"What do you mean? K.C. was like my brother."

"I know that. We've talked about this with Tracie. Your mother and I accept how much you cared for K.C. But, Tyler, you were our child, our son, and you were never supposed to be in that trailer. You were never supposed to be with Robert Starker. And whatever happened to K.C., it is *Robert Starker's doing.* He is the one to blame, regardless of what happened in the trailer."

I heard my dad's words but they didn't stop my desire for the truth. "I just want to know what really happened."

"This is not the time for trying to bring up recollections, like what Tracie works with you to do. That's how things get misunderstood."

I couldn't stop the memory, though. How Bob yanked me through the front door and my shin got cut open on the corner of the door's threshold. How I ignored the pain and crawled away into the kitchen as quickly as I could, trying to hide behind an open cabinet door. The fear for my own life swelled inside me, seeing Bob's neck veins bulging and the blood beneath his skin gushing into his face like fuel, feeding the rage coming from his mouth. His words rattled the trailer windows as he yelled, screamed, "What happened? *What happened to K.C.?*"

"Tyler, are you hearing me?" I heard my dad's words but I couldn't respond. My senses were frozen like they were that day in the trailer. How I stood dazed against the refrigerator, watching Bob turn to the gun rack above the television and pull down his rifle. I knew that I didn't have anywhere to run. I just stood there, pushing my back against the refrigerator, hoping somehow that I'd meld into the metal. All the while, my eyes didn't leave the butt of the rifle as Bob jammed it into my ribcage.

I remember that I fell to the ground. My ribs ached with a sharp, stabbing pain. My vision blurred, faded, returned. My cheek pressed against the cold kitchen linoleum. My mouth hung open, saliva dripping out. The filthy carpet served as my only horizon. Bob's stomping feet pounded the flooring beneath my ears. My fear started to gurgle up even as the darkness of unconsciousness crept over me. I looked for something to focus on, to keep my mind alive. My eyes landed on the moving boxes in the living room. The bottom one in a stack of three had K.C.'s name written on it. Tears escaped the corners of my eyes at the sight of the letters that symbolized him. Only then did I let the blackness overcome me. It was the only way to leave reality and avoid my own sadness, my own despair that somehow K.C. got to leave, but I was still there. Still alive.

"Tyler, talk to me. Are you still there?" I heard my father's concern.

"Yeah, yeah, I'm here." And I was. I didn't want to go back to my memories, ever.

"Do you understand what I'm saying, Tyler?"

"Yeah ... but ... I don't know how to stop remembering."

"The first step is to stop talking."

(32)

I took my dad's advice. Tracie knew it, too. I stopped volunteering details. When a memory would flood in, I'd just go and do something. Shoot hoops, fire up the PlayStation, talk to Palmer. Pretty soon, K.C.'s name stopped coming up. I told Tracie that my dad's advice was, "Don't talk about what you don't remember." She just smiled, didn't say that was good or bad thinking, and then changed the subject. That's how I figured out that the Drysdale issue was serious, like jail-time serious. No one knew if my memories would hurt or help.

I had a new attorney, also. He worked for my parents, not the court. He didn't stutter, but he yelled and pounded his fist on the table, saying that I'm not guilty. The stupid part of my mind liked it when he said that. But my brighter side wondered how he knew what he was talking about when he never asked any questions. My dad said, "Don't worry. We're proving Bob's guilt, not your innocence. The evidence is there."

I still caught myself wanting to know what really did happen to K.C., but I stopped the thought. It wasn't the right time, and maybe it wouldn't ever be. I kept having this thought about my life. When I first got to the York center, I looked at my mind like a house. I wanted to visit all the rooms and see how I once lived in them. When I explained it to Palmer, he said, "Move out and look for a new place. Just like an old house, drive by when you need to, but don't go in." When he first said it, I thought it was funny, like in a goofy way. But he was right: I can't go back and revisit every minute I lived. I had to move forward.

I knew I was going to miss the Palmer talks.

And also knew I was going to miss Tracie. Not her talks, although I knew they helped me, but her as a person. I didn't say this to anyone, not even Palmer, but she's the first person I met that I think would make a good mom. I didn't mean to put down my own mom, but it's true. After my first home visit, I learned a lot about my mom. She's good with kids who are tall enough to scratch their cheek on her belt buckle, but it's a different story with kids taller than her, like me. I learned that she's the kind of parent that you should only tell stuff to after it happens, because she gets too worked up about the what-ifs. Like she jumps ahead when you talk to her and she gets weirded out when she hears about things that already happened, whether yesterday or seven years ago.

Tracie just had a whole different way of listening. It was always about what I was going through and where I thought I was headed. She heard what I was saying and didn't spit it right back in my face with stupid, wacked-out emotions. The strange thing was that, in the whole time I was at the York center, I never had the courage to ask Tracie if she had kids. I think because deep down even though I would have been happy that she's a mom, I would have also been kind of jealous that I didn't have a mom like that.

Saying goodbye started to be harder than I thought.

It only took me like ten minutes to pack up my stuff. I had two hoodies, shirts and jeans, the Ameritek ID picture, Palmer's world map, two old *National Geographic* magazines from Tracie's office, and a bottle of antidepressants. I laid everything out on my bed before I packed it up. Looking at all the stuff together, to a stranger, it probably looked like random belongings, but to me it symbolized where I had been, and I kinda hoped it was showing me signs of where I was going.

Before I shut the door to my room, I took one last look at everything. The stupid farm picture hanging across from my bed, the fluffy chair that looked out over the river, the bathroom door that I always kept closed, and the PlayStation with only one controller.

I met other kids at the center, but it's like we were always in our own little worlds, you know, trying to fix our own crap. At least that's how I looked at my stay. I was there to work on changing myself. And I think I did. The guy I was in English class way back when … well, he looked the same, with a John Deere hoodie, dark curls and unlaced shoes, but my attitude was different. When Tracie and I talked about the jerk I was then, I felt embarrassed, like how I treated the overweight kid behind me. But I can't change the past, only learn from it so I can change the future.

Palmer's door was open. It didn't matter. I was going to find him wherever he was to say goodbye. "Hey, what's up?" I asked as I pulled my hoodie off my face.

He was his usual calm self. "So today's the day, huh?" No matter what he was doing in his office when I showed up, it always seemed like he was expecting me.

"Yeah, I think my parents and little brother are here already, you know, downstairs."

He was leaning over his sink in the corner washing something out. I stepped into his office to look at the corkboard with all the cards tacked to it. It looked the same. And the signed baseballs in their cases above his desk, looked the same. He finished what he was doing in the sink and waddled over near his desk. I remembered how I wanted to hate him the first time I saw him in the hallway by my room, because I didn't believe strangers could care. *Another thing I was wrong about.*

"I have somethin' for ya, little man."

"For me?"

He reached down and opened the bottom drawer. I knew right away what he had for me. He was saying goodbye with more of the wife's cookies.

But it wasn't a brown bag that he pulled out. *I was wrong again.*

"Here," he said. It was a gift, a wrapped gift. It was pretty. That was a strange word my mind was using lately, but true. It was wrapped in pretty paper with a tied ribbon. It was clean. Perfect. "Here." He wiggled it in front of me. "It's for you." I slowly reached out and took it in my hands. I turned it upside down. Looked at how the corners were nicely folded. Only a couple pieces of tape. The little bow on top was centered. And the ribbon strands were cut evenly. "The wife wrapped it."

That explained it, but I was confused about why she would do that for me. I pulled out Palmer's desk chair, took a seat. I couldn't think of any words to say. "Thank you."

"You haven't opened it yet."

"Oh."

"Go ahead. Rip it open."

I gently pulled away the ribbon and lifted up the tape in the back. As the wrapping paper unfolded, I recognized the box, the logo. I didn't get too excited, you know, like maybe the box wasn't what the gift was. But then I saw the plastic wrapping around the box. "You bought this for me? This is for me?"

He flashed me a Palmer smile.

I hadn't felt the joy that comes with a surprise in a long time. It was an iPod. My own iPod. I looked down again at the packaging, the box. It was new. It had never belonged to anyone. I looked back up to Palmer. "Are you sure?" I don't know why I asked that. I was scared of the wrong answer. I was worried I didn't deserve it. "I'm going to really take care of this."

"I know you will. Pick the music that feels right to ya, that's all."

I nodded.

He gave me a pat on the back. I was stunned. I never saw that coming, would have never asked for it. I thought he was so weird to have an iPod when he was so old, but I never thought I deserved to have an iPod instead of him. But here it was. I felt happy, really happy.

Right then, I missed Palmer. I mean, I knew he was in front of me, but I knew that when I left the York center that day, I was gonna miss him. Tracie, my room, Dr. Williams, the rooftop, the schedule lady—everyone, I was going to miss everyone.

I looked again at Palmer's corkboard. "I'm going to write you."

We both stood there looking at his corkboard. Then he waddled behind me and pushed his cleaning cart into the hallway. He threw me a wink and his last words, "Close the door behind you. Remember, don't sell yourself short." And he was gone.

I stood there in his office for a minute, not wanting to see him again and have to say goodbye another time. When I'd waited long enough, I made my way to the stairwell like I had every day that I was at the York center. But this time I knew I wouldn't be coming back up. I was leaving.

In a funny way, I was happy that I was sad.

When I exited from the stairs, I saw my parents and my little brother at the end of the hallway by the security doors. My little brother doesn't look like me. When I first met him, I thought that it was probably a blessing for my parents that they had two boys who didn't look alike. Plus, I think it helped me see that Evan wasn't my replacement. He was an addition.

The way they stood there in the hallway, I knew it wasn't going to be the perfect match, but I think that's what made them my family. It's like, because we were kind of mismatched, it took away this fear that life with them had to be perfect, you know. I'm not perfect, and I can't be around perfect people if I want to keep my attitude under control. I took a deep breath and let the stairwell door close behind me.

My mom let out her normal gasp of joy and a couple of hand claps. She had her jewelry jingles back on. I could smell her perfume like she was standing right next to me. Evan ran up to me to hold the duffel bag that had all my stuff. He talked a lot. I mean, like, a *lot*. I tried to listen as long as there was nothing else going on. I felt kinda bad for him, you know, because I saw at the family barbecue that the adults didn't really listen to him. They just responded with "I don't know" and "Maybe" to any question he asked.

I met Evan halfway down the hall and his questions started coming at me, but I told him I couldn't talk yet, so he should wait until we got in the car. I think he liked the truth. He said, "Okay," and shut up. I gave him my bag and then wiped my sweaty palms on my pants, getting ready to deal with the hello handshake from my dad.

When I was close enough for a handshake, I looked him in the eyes. He had his normal stiff look, with his hairy arms, creased pants, and leather loafers. He lost my eye contact for a second when he barked at Evan to hold my duffel bag with both hands.

That was the thing about him that I still had to deal with. He was always going to be an asshole in a father way. But like Tracie and I talked about, I was only fifteen, and if I didn't have an attitude about everything that pissed me off, I'd do better in the world and be okay with my dad. He was forty-seven and wasn't changing his ways. In a couple of years, if I got my act together, I could be on my own. Anyway, the good thing about my dad always being a jerk was the "always" part. He was stable that way. I could tell already he would always be there for me. It's just that the help he would give would always have to be on his terms.

He turned to my mom while he was still shaking my hand. "Cathy, take Evan, and we'll meet you in the lobby." Evan didn't want to leave. He started whining, but my dad took care of it right away, saying sternly, "Evan. Now. Go with your mother." And the way he said it, I would have done what Evan did. Actually, I probably did what Evan did when I was his age, and that's why I remember my mom's belt buckles so much. As soon as my mom released her bear hug around me and said, "See you in a minute, honey," with all her bracelets jingling, the two of them exited the security doors.

My dad gave me a pat on the back. The kind that turns your body a little, like it tells you where to go. "Tyler, we have some paperwork to finish up." I turned into the blonde lady's office, Carrie, who did my scheduling and helped me figure out my community service work, which was kind of a joke but I liked it. As she finished all the paperwork for me to leave, Dr. Williams, the cafeteria people, and everyone else I saw all the time came in to say goodbye ... except for Tracie. We said goodbye the day before so it wouldn't be a sad thing. And anyway, with Tracie, it was more like, "See you later," and not a goodbye. I believed her when she said she'd always be there for me.

When we finished the paperwork and they buzzed us out the security doors, my mom and Evan stood up from the lobby couch. The moment felt surreal. Time seemed to slow. Everything in my peripheral vision started to blur. I walked straight for the exit and sensed my parents walking behind me, holding hands. Evan ran up next to me, struggling to walk at my speed while still carrying my duffel bag. I reached over and took it from him. The sliding doors to the outside opened. I went to turn my head to see where my parents were but instead my eyes landed on Evan, my little brother. He smiled at me and grabbed my hand. I was glad I didn't jerk away like I would have months ago. I smiled and gave him the big brother he was looking for.

(33)

The first few weeks of being back with my parents weren't easy. When I was at the York center and would have family visits in Colorado Springs, that's just what they were: visits. Living together was a different story. And it wasn't anyone's attitude that made things hard. It was more like this feeling that I was a guest in their home.

Like on Sunday nights, it was a ritual that my dad would rent a DVD for everyone to watch; family night at the Roberts house. On the first Sunday when I lived with them, my dad asked what movie I'd like to see. I shrugged. Evan chimed in that he wanted to pick out the new release. My dad said, "Fine, go get in the car," and the two of them drove off. I wandered around the house thinking to myself how I would have gone with them but I wasn't invited. Maybe they didn't ask on purpose.

When they got back, I recognized the movie title because the metal shop guys talked about seeing it in the theaters. Bob and movie theaters never happened in my lifetime. Our luxury was basic cable, and that was only because the main house had it. Even then, it was hard to get Bob to watch anything other than war movies.

As everyone started settling in to watch the movie, Evan grabbed a pillow from his bed and plopped down on the carpet. My first thought was how lucky Evan was to have clean carpets in his home. Then I caught myself: *his* home. I couldn't correct my thought, though, by saying *my* home, too. The best I could do was to keep my emotions flat and accept that that's how I saw my surroundings: *their* home.

As soon as the DVD was in, my dad yelled that the movie was starting and my mom was already holding it up. She rushed out of the kitchen with a bowl of popcorn and sat on the couch. My dad was on the other one. There might have been room for me, but when I went to ask, the question wouldn't come out. My mom looked over at me standing nearby and asked me to go get the salt for the popcorn.

On my way back, with the salt in hand, I brought a chair from the kitchen table and placed it behind the couches. When my mom grabbed the salt from me, she asked if I was comfortable. The chair wasn't, but the feeling felt right, felt safe. I was sitting on the outskirt. I shrugged and gave her a nod. I guess she accepted it, because she didn't move to the side and tell me to sit next to her. And all my dad did was bark a complaint that he couldn't hear the movie over everyone's whining. Halfway through the movie, I went to the room where I slept. I wondered if anyone noticed.

The room I slept in was once my room. But at some point, it had turned into more of a guest room and storage place for my mom's crafts. When I unpacked my stuff from the York center, I asked my mom what I should do with the woman's clothes in my dresser. They were Ronnie's clothes, my mom's best friend, who used to stay at the house a lot during visits before she moved back to the area for good. I thought my mom would take the clothes from me and put them in the garage. Instead, she said to place them on the shelf in my closet. And I didn't know why that bothered me, because it's not like I had my own space back at the trailer.

The first day that I was at their house by myself was the hardest. My mom volunteered in Evan's kindergarten class, so she left when he went to school. And my dad, he hadn't missed a day of work since I was home, not because he didn't want to help with my transition, but because when my trial started, he needed his engineering projects to be on track. That's the only way he could be out the office for so long. At least that's how he explained it. Maybe it was an excuse, who knows. At times I still saw him and Bob as similar. They both showed that they cared about you by reminding you of the burdens and sacrifices you caused them.

My mom left out the cereal box with a note that she'd be home around one o'clock. I turned around to get the milk from the fridge, but it didn't feel natural to just open the door like it was my house and my food. I hesitated.

The front of the refrigerator was a collage of pictures. I stared at them. In the top left there were a couple of pictures of me as a baby and then a young child, like the school picture that was on the Ameritek ID card, and then it was like I dropped away from the earth. When the pictures started up again, it was a couple of years later. There was one of my mom pregnant with Evan during the holidays, another couple of Evan as a newborn, a preschool photo, and then tons of pictures of random family members and friends.

I felt left out.

I moved away from the fridge until my back hit the kitchen counter. My eyes stayed on the photos. *Why can't I fit in? I want to belong.* I quieted my mind and ushered in Tracie's voice, "Learn to question why you feel the way you do." My eyes didn't leave the refrigerator, though. I focused on the empty space after the Ameritek ID photo but before the first photo of my mom pregnant with Evan. It was that blank space that was making me feel left out. I needed to understand that blank space so I could stop reacting to it. My heart started racing, but for the first time that I could remember, in a good way. I pulled out the phone book and looked up the number for a taxicab company.

As I waited on the porch for the guy to arrive, I felt adrenaline rushing through my body. I saw the yellow cab turn the corner and head toward the house. I met him at the curb as he pulled up.

"You called for a taxi?"

"Yeah, can you take me to the Arthur Black Recreation Center?"

"Huh? Are you sure?" His question caught me off guard, like he was worried for me. I didn't recognize the guy, but on my second family visit to Colorado Springs, my parents and the search and rescue organization that was involved in trying to solve my abduction threw a big barbecue at the Chamber of Commerce place. I met so many people that day. I guessed by the concern in the taxi driver's voice that I had met him there, too.

Maybe he was right to question whether going back to the location of where I was kidnapped was a good idea. But what he thought didn't matter; it was something I needed to do, something that just felt right. "Yeah, I'm sure I want to go. Will you take me?"

"All right. If that's what you really want, hop in."

(34)

The taxi driver didn't know who I was. We had never met. The concern I heard in his voice wasn't concern, it was confusion—because the Arthur Black Recreation Center was only four blocks away from our house. He just thought it was weird that I didn't walk over.

But when I pulled up, I learned something about my parents. My dad's advice from the first day in the cafeteria played over in my mind: "We have to move forward and put everything behind us." At the time, I was angered by his words, like how can you leave behind an entire existence and write it off as if it never happened. But now I understood what he was saying, even if his advice didn't work for me. I looked around at the front of the park, the trees, the playground, the picnic tables. This place no longer existed in my parents' mind. They moved on from it, even though it was pretty much in their backyard. I knew that for sure because I went to Evan's Little League game the day after I got to town. And the recreation center where he played baseball was like ten miles away. *It wasn't this place.*

When I stepped out of the cab, the driver took off. I looked around. Nothing about the place felt familiar. I walked toward the gym building.

I walked away from the gym building.

I did a full turn, saw the office door. It was open, but I decided to walk around a little.

There weren't a lot of kids, probably because it was during school hours. There were just moms and daycare people helping on the slides and pushing the swings. My eyes scanned out to the baseball field. A quick memory revisited me: I was in the dugout and looked over to the bleachers. There was my mom sitting with a group of women. She looked my way when she saw I was picking up the bat. Her hands went into the air and her cheers drowned out the advice of my coach.

The recollection came to a screeching halt at the sound of a metal trashcan scraping against cement. I looked around, startled. My heart banged against my ribcage. A small kid on a scooter was trying to get out of my way, and he used the metal trashcan for brakes. I went to help him get back on his scooter, but he didn't need a helping hand.

I finally made my way over to the open door of the gym. It's what I came there to do, I told myself. The rec center guy at the counter spoke up before I stepped over the threshold, "Can I help you?"

"Oh, yeah, I—is there—" I gulped down my nerves and threw my hands into my pockets. "Yeah, can I use, um, is the bathroom in here?"

"Yeah. On the right side, halfway down the gymnasium." He pointed toward the bathroom door and then took a seat at his desk. He didn't hesitate, didn't hold me back, just sent me on my way and went about doing his business.

The walk across the gymnasium took forever. The closer I got to the bathroom door, the more that's all I could see. It was painted a glossy dark blue color, and it didn't have a doorknob. It was a metal pull handle where you gripped it and pulled it toward you to open it. I stood in front of the door. I was about to turn to look at the gym guy, but I stopped myself. I didn't need his reassurance. I didn't need the taxi driver's concern. I just needed myself. I needed to be there for myself.

I grabbed the handle. Pulled. Stepped in.

Green tile.

A hanging light.

A metal framed mirror.

The door shut behind me. The sound seemed like a shotgun. My eyes closed. My neck tensed. My nerve endings fired off, tingling, crying out for me to save myself. A black force wrapped around me, pulled at me, wanting to suck the life from me.

I had to get out.

I pushed with all my weight against the door. It flew open. I jumped out, gasping for air. Leaning against the gymnasium wall, I bent over and grabbed my knees, slowed down my breath.

When I stood up, still leaning against the wall, I looked over at the rec center guy. He was at his desk. Calm, totally oblivious to my panic. I gently rested the back of my head against the wall. I wanted to confront this. I wanted to know the pain I felt when I was severed from the world. This was the blank space on the fridge door. I looked again at the rec center guy. He didn't look my way. He had no reason to. He didn't sense anything was wrong. I was the only one around. I opened the door again …

… stepped in.

I ignored my pounding heart. I let it throb while my mind tried to discredit my worries. I took my open palm and touched the green tile on the wall. I felt its coldness and smoothness. I traced the grout lines. I took another step forward and reached out to the bathroom stall door. The stalls were empty.

I kept repeating in my mind, *It's just a bathroom … just a bathroom. No one is here. And if the memories come, I'll be ready.*

On the other side of the bathroom, opposite the door I came in, was another exit door. Drysdale's words from the interview room played in my mind: "You entered the bathroom from inside the gym. We believe your abductor took you through the outside door." I traced the metal bars that permanently locked the door shut. *They were there because of me.*

I stepped in front of the mirror. My neck started to tense. It was the same reaction I had from the bathroom in my room at the York center. I promised myself I wouldn't run away. I stayed in the moment. I exhaled and let the panic run through my bones. It had to leave at some point. I reached my hand down to the sink. I touched it. Moved my hands all over its surface. *See? It's just a bathroom.*

I forced my eyes to look up at my reflection in the mirror. At first I saw my face, but I stared for so long that eventually all I saw were my eyes, and it was at that point that I looked beyond, into the person I was on the inside. *I want to win the battle. I want to give myself happiness. I want to see the world as a place I belong.*

Not one memory inched into my mind of the day I was abducted. But that didn't invalidate anything about me or my experiences. Instead, it proved that the tragedy was too extreme.

I walked back home. I was there when my mom came back from Evan's school. I didn't share with her that I went to the rec center. Instead, I packed up all the woman's clothes and craft crap in my closet and showed my mom where I put the stuff in the garage. I made it my room, my space. And then that night, I asked my mom to move over because I was gonna sit on the couch next to her.

On Sunday night, I told my dad I wanted to go to the DVD store with him. When he, Evan, and I got back, I asked Evan to go get the pillow from my room. And when my dad pressed play and he barked his complaint that we all needed to stop whining so he could hear, I smiled and replied, "I'm not whining." He acted like he didn't hear me, but my mom gave me a wink.

(35)

It took close to a year for my trial to start. The courtroom didn't look like the ones I had seen on TV. Like for instance, there were no chairs for a jury to sit in. I learned juveniles don't get juries. I also thought I'd see Drysdale, but when I asked if he'd be showing up, my attorney answered by saying my case was moved from federal to state. *Whatever that meant.* I felt the smart-ass side of me knocking at my lips. I wanted to say in a really dumb voice, "Excuse me, I guess I don't understand, does that mean he's not showing up?" The new attorney guy, Randall Braide, irritates the hell out of me, but no surprise—my dad loves him.

I looked over at my dad. He looked exactly the same as that first visit in Tracie's office. His voice was as solid as the night on the phone after the Drysdale interview. He stood on the other side of Mr. Braide, hunched over the table reading some court document. He read everything, even when Braide said, "It doesn't really say anything."

I was bored out of my mind, which was stupid, and I knew it. I mean, there I was, starting down a dark tunnel, and as confident as my dad was, something about the future didn't feel stable. And yet, I was yawning, almost unable to stay awake.

The funny thing was that for the first time I was glad to be wearing nerdy clothes: a tie, creased pants, leather loafers, the whole shebang. I knew that looking like the hoodie loner from Clarkson High would have only hurt me. I almost laughed to myself about how, in all those years with Bob, I hated the world for judging me on the outside, and now with my nerdy clothes on, I was praying for it.

I knew what Braide and my dad were talking about, though. The district attorney, the guy who's trying to prove that I hurt K.C., offered me a plea deal saying that the trial wouldn't go forward. Instead, I'd serve time in a juvenile detention center as a delinquent, not a prisoner, if I told them I was guilty. I wasn't really sure what the difference was between a

171

detention center and prison, but I knew Braide was telling my dad that if I took the plea deal and my psychological evaluations at the detention center went well, which they should because of Tracie's recommendations, I could possibly be out in less than six months, maybe a year. Worst case, definitely by the time I turned twenty-one.

Twenty-one, more than four years away—a long time. But my first thought was that I could probably make it work out. It couldn't be worse than living in the trailer, dealing with Bob's stuff. I went to start to shrug, you know, to let Braide know I was thinking about it, but I froze before my shoulders lifted. It was the tone of my father's words: "No. Absolutely not. Tyler's not going anywhere, not for one single day. Our family already served a seven-year sentence. Where's the compassion for that? I can't believe they're putting us through this. The only sanity in all this is knowing that Robert Starker will be found responsible for the crime one way or the other." My dad looked over at me. "Tyler, two weeks from now, we'll be walking out of those doors, and this will all be behind us. You're not taking the plea deal."

I couldn't hold his stare. My dad's confidence made me nervous. He didn't know the truth. I mean, jeez, *I* didn't know the truth. He didn't know how a memory can just flood in, like when Drysdale showed me that Ameritek ID photo, or how the shelter place came to life in my mind when I heard the truth.

"Tyler," said Mr. Braide, turning his chair around and leaning toward me, "I hear what your father has been saying." Over his shoulder, I saw my dad stand up straight, cross his arms, and start his normal slow pace. I brought myself back to Braide's moving mouth. "But one other thing I want you to consider is how you'll feel seeing Robert Starker testify, if you can handle going through that. It's important that you weigh all your options, for your own well-being. Part of the decision-making process needs to involve thinking you can get through this the best you can. All right?"

I nodded. When he mentioned Bob's name, my heart jumped forward and crashed into my chest bones. I didn't want to see Bob. I didn't want to think about Bob. I was scared of Bob. I looked over at the bailiff; it was a woman, way shorter and smaller than Bob. "Maybe, you know, the plea deal is the right thing to do. I don't know." I heard my dad clear his throat from across the courtroom. I dropped my hands to my lap, wiped my palms dry. "But, you know, my dad's right, I just want to get going with my life and stop dealing with all this."

Braide put his hand on the back of my chair. He reminded me of Drysdale, kind of. "I really believe you're not guilty of the crime as charged, Tyler. I don't believe sending you to a juvenile delinquent detention center for any amount of time can help in any way. And as much as a pest your father is—" He smiled at me and rolled his eyes toward my dad. I gave him a nervous smile back. "—I think he's right, we'll be able to prove that Robert Starker was responsible for K.C.'s death. But I need to know you're strong enough to get through this."

I nodded.

"So are you saying you want to move forward with the trial?"

"Yeah." I saw my dad's hands fall to his side. He let out a huge sigh. It was a glimpse that under his skin he wasn't as tough as his voice sounded. I took my own deep breath. "Yeah, I do want to go forward."

(36)

Everyone sat in silence waiting for the judge to come out, except for Braide. Any spare moment he had, he would write stuff down on his yellow pad. While the district attorney, Mr. Hagger, gave his opening statement to the judge, I think Braide wrote a whole book and went through the ink in three pens.

The judge was pretty. I mean, I didn't know what she looked like up close, but from my chair, she was pretty. She had brown eyes and fair skin. It made it hard to focus on her words. Her makeup wasn't too heavy, like my mom's, and her brown hair fell to her shoulders, except when she looked down to read something—then she would tuck it behind her ears out of the way. I also liked how, when she talked, she knew what she wanted to say. And all the men in the room listened, but they probably couldn't focus on her words either. Except for my dad, of course. He'd take *Reader's Digest* over *Playboy* any day of the week.

I realized not that long before my trial started that I was noticing a lot of stuff about women, older women, like twenty-five, twenty-eight. I mean, I was gonna be seventeen in a couple of months, so it made some sense. It started when I got my job at the grocery store by our house. Kirsten was twenty-six. She was the lead cashier. She'd just finished grad school and moved back with her mom and dad to pay off student loans while she wrote her federal research grant. I didn't know what any of that meant, until I learned about it all when someone from her high school came in and asked her what she had been doing. Lucky for me, the high school friend bought like three hundred dollars in groceries so I was standing there bagging for the whole conversation. But anyway, ladies like Kirsten didn't spend all day talking about empty, meaningless crap or complain about stupid stuff like nail polish colors. I also liked it how when Kirsten needed a price check, she would just call out my name, lift up the item, and that was it. She knew I knew how to do my job.

The door to the judge's chamber opened. The bailiff stood. "All rise."
We did.
The judge sat.
We sat.

She asked for both attorneys, Braide and Mr. Hagger, to come up to the bench where she sat. It's hard not to yawn when your only view is two guys standing with their backs to you, but I tried to yawn through my nose so my dad wouldn't see. He was sitting to my left at the attorney's table, and I could sense his jaw clenching because he didn't get to hear what the judge was saying.

Sometimes he did the weirdest crap. Like when we would stand for the judge, he would always reach over and smooth out my pants, where the creases were. When I would turn to him say, "What the hell's going on?" it was like Tracie was on my shoulder, telling me to only blow off steam when I really needed to.

About a month after I got home to Colorado Springs from the York center, my dad sat me down to talk about my schooling issue. I slumped my shoulders and dropped my eyelids, trying to give him the "I don't give a shit" attitude. But he surprised me. He said he looked over my school transcripts and because of the trial, the best thing to do was for me to study for my GED, get the trial over with, and when it was done, he'd have me enroll at the community college and work on transferring to the university. Meanwhile, though, I had to have a job and stay in counseling.

That's where Henry Schlick, my new counselor, came into the picture. He's not like Tracie. He's a jokester. He liked twenty-five-year-olds when he was my age, too. Now he's fifty-five and says he still likes twenty-five-year-olds. He gets the guy thing. He also gets my parents, and doesn't talk behind my back when I spend my sessions complaining about them.

Lately, because the trial was getting ready to start, I'd been talking about K.C. to Henry, and how my relationship with Evan sometimes made me think of how close K.C. and I were when I first ended up with Bob. I think that's why I'm such a good brother to Evan. I want to be the big brother that K.C. was to me. Otherwise, Evan would drive me crazy, because he talked about everything, and talked too much. He was a lot like our mom.

The powwow at the judge's bench broke up and the attorneys came back to their seats.

"Mr. Hagger," said the judge, "would you please call your first witness?"

"Yes, Your Honor, thank you. The State of Nebraska calls Deborah Nelson to the stand."

The bailiff stood, walked to the door, and called out the witness's name. Everything was moving quickly; I couldn't quite place the name with the person, like who exactly she was. I just knew I had heard the name before. The bailiff held the door open as this thin, mousy-brown-haired woman walked into the courtroom. I'd never seen her before, I knew that for sure ... or maybe I had and didn't remember. She walked down the middle aisle where the courtroom audience sat, and when she passed our table, the judge indicated where she was to go. "Ms. Nelson, please step forward to the witness stand and raise your right hand to be sworn in."

When the woman passed by our table, my nerves spiked like a seismograph registering an earthquake. It dawned on me that for the next two weeks every person who walked through the courtroom doors would add to the picture of my past. Each witness would add a detail that, collectively, would tell the story of my life over the last seven or eight years. My fear was that it would be a clearer picture than any recollection I'd had so far.

(37)

"Ms. Nelson, my name is Keith Hagger. I'm a deputy district attorney for Colfax County here in Nebraska. Thanks for coming down today. I know you drove quite a way from Lexington. Now, we've met before today, haven't we?"

She leaned into the microphone. "Yeah."

I had been watching everything about her, but none of her actions jogged my memory. She was really thin. She was wearing a short-sleeve blouse and her elbow joints looked huge because the arm part below and above the elbow was smaller than my wrist. Her hair was kind of long, with gray strands, but it wasn't styled like she had had a haircut. It was more like she just grew it. She might have been pretty once, but it was hard to ignore the brown scars on her face that you get from picking at your skin too much.

"Ms. Nelson, I'd like to show you what we've numbered Exhibit One in this case." The district attorney walked up closer to the witness and handed her a piece of paper. Her arms were so thin that when she reached for the paper, the sleeve part of her shirt just hung on her, like how a scarecrow's clothes hang from broomstick handles. "Take a look at the exhibit and tell us if you see your name anywhere on it."

She stared at the piece of paper and nodded her head. I saw her grab for the tissue box that was right in front of her. She dabbed at each of her eyes.

"Do you recognize this document?"

She nodded. She was starting to get worked up.

"What is this document, Ms. Nelson?"

"It's his birth certificate."

"And do you see your name on it, Ms. Nelson?"

"Yes, in the mother's name box."

"And you said 'his birth certificate.' To whom are you referring?"

"My son."

"And what was his name?"

"Kennedy Charles Nelson. I named him after my dad. My dad passed away when I was young and …" Her tears started streaming down her face. She grabbed for more Kleenex. "And then my mom started calling him K.C., instead of saying my dad's name, and it just stuck with him, the nickname K.C." I realized then that I never thought about being face to face with K.C.'s mom. K.C. never hated her, and it's weird how I never thought to hate her either, like the same way I hated Sam's dad.

"Ms. Nelson, I'd like to show you another exhibit. It's a picture, and I'd like to know if you can identify the man in the picture."

Her frail arms reached out to the 8x10 photo. I recognized the photo. It was the jail photo of Bob that Drysdale showed me. When she looked at the photo, her tears dried up and she sat straight up in her chair. "Yes, this is a picture of Bob Starker."

She called him "Bob," and the way she said it was how I said it. She knew Bob. She and I were linked in a weird way. We both had at one time been a part of Bob's world. I leaned forward in my chair, feeling a connection with her.

"Ms. Nelson, when was the last time you saw K.C., your son?"

"I wasn't really with it then, you know."

"Can you explain to the court what you mean by that?"

She looked at the judge. I compared the two women's profiles. They were probably close in age, but because of their different paths, K.C.'s mother lost all her softness. The creases at the corners of her eyes were hard, her cheekbones sunken, and the area below her eyes darkened. *K.C. would be sad to see her now*, I thought.

"After my son was born, I got mixed up with the wrong crowd, but my mom was helping me out by taking care of K.C. here and there. I was trying to get my act together, so I went through a court-ordered rehab center for meth, and when I came out I wanted to be on my own with my son, you know, to prove I could do everything myself. So I took K.C. from my mom's house, and I tried to live on my own, but I couldn't get a good job. Then I met this guy through some friends, Bob, and he started letting K.C. and me stay with him." Her eyes drifted away, to a random corner in the courtroom, and her voice trailed off. I assumed that she was thinking of that final goodbye with K.C.

"Ms. Nelson, again, when was the last time you saw your son, K.C.?"

"I was always trying to get things right, you know, and Bob at first seemed like he was helping and then he gave me the meth, like he wanted to party with me, and then I lost control of stuff again. I didn't want to show back up at my mom's with K.C., because it's like my family only saw me as a failure, and Bob was giving me money when I needed it to buy more drugs, but I was trying to fix things, you know, and be on my own with my son, so I went to the streets and I was picked up again, and I wasn't released."

"You were picked up for …?"

"Yeah, prostitution. And when I was picked up, K.C. was six at the time, and I thought Bob would drop him off at my mom's, you know, give him back to my mom, but that didn't happen."

Mr. Hagger, the district attorney, took a paper from a box on his desk. It was some document that had K.C.'s mom's arrest date on it. He was asking the court to look at the date of her prostitution charge so they would have the exact date when she saw K.C. last.

I couldn't stop staring at K.C.'s mom. She looked my way, but the look we shared wasn't about two people caring for K.C. Her eyes said something else. I looked away, afraid I might guess what she was thinking. After all, it wasn't Bob on trial for her son's death.

My attorney didn't have any questions for her. As she stepped down, the judge called a recess. The courtroom started to stir. The judge disappeared behind her door. As I saw the exit door to the courtroom close behind K.C.'s mom, I almost wanted to yell out to her how sorry I was that she lost her son, you know, that she lost K.C., but my attention came back to the table when I heard my dad whisper, "Some people don't deserve to be parents."

My thoughts came back around to Sam's dad, and I wondered again why I wasn't angry at K.C.'s mom like I had been at Sam's dad. I connected those thoughts with how my dad and mom proved to me that they were the kind of parents like I'd seen at that Back to School Night in eighth grade, the kind that Tracie told me about who make sacrifices for their kids and don't just abandon them. At that point, it didn't matter what that sadness in K.C.'s mom's eyes was about. She didn't deserve to be K.C.'s mom just like Sam's dad didn't deserve to be his father.

I felt my dad's hand on my back. "Tyler, let's go get some lunch."

"When's Mom supposed to be here?"

"She's flying in tonight," my dad responded, not missing a beat.

She had all these weird quirks about her, you know, the makeup, the bangles, drowning herself in perfume, always losing her stuff, but that seemed trivial all of a sudden. She worked hard on being a good mom in her own way. I looked up at my dad. "Can we pick her up at the airport?" My dad smiled. I tried to keep my face blank, but I knew that he saw through me. I was missing my own mom.

(38)

"Mrs. Katoundsky—I hope I'm pronouncing that right. I'm Keith Hagger. We've met before, haven't we?"

"Yes, you came up to Coleridge to interview me."

She was an older woman. Nice, like you see volunteering at libraries, you know. I'd never seen her before; at least, I didn't think so. The way her eyes shifted my way when she talked, it seemed like she was confused about me, too.

"Mrs. Katood—Katoundsky, right?"

"You can call me Kat." She had this smile that I'd seen on old people before at the grocery store. Like you can tell with some people, the old ones especially, that they've seen too much in the world to ever have their smiles taken away. She had lots of wrinkles that probably told about a lot of heartaches, but they cleared away when she smiled. By the third or fourth time she looked my way, I was smiling back.

Hagger's questioning continued on. "Thank you for driving down today. I know it was a long trip from Coleridge down to Omaha."

"My daughter drove me. I'm glad to help." She looked my way again. I did know her from somewhere, but I couldn't place where.

"Mrs. Katood—I'm sorry, Kat, I'd like to call your attention back to approximately five years ago. Where were you living at the time?"

"Yes, of course. I was living by myself. My late husband, George, passed away about eight years ago, and a couple of years after that, I moved into the Cordia Bungalows on Bloom Street in Coleridge. I've always lived in Coleridge."

When she said "Cordia," a wooden sign popped into my head. The word "Cordia" was carved in it and the "C" had this long tail that stretched under the "ordia" part of the word. And there were lots of trees.

"And Kat, did you have a job at the time?"

"Oh, yes, it was at the Cordia Bungalows. I was the manager there. I live with my daughter and her husband now, though." The separation of time changed what she looked like in my mind. When she said "manager," the truancy officer that came to talk to Bob popped into my head. She was the manager that Bob was mad at because she called the truancy officer about my not being in school. It's not that she looked different sitting on the witness stand. It's that my memory didn't hold onto the details about her. Like I remembered there was a manager at Cordia Bungalows, and I knew that was her on the witness stand, but if I had walked past her on the street before that moment, I would have never thought to think about whether I knew her or not.

"Kat, I'd like to show you a picture and have you tell me whether you recognize the person in it." Mr. Hagger took Bob's jail picture from the stack of exhibits. The manager lady reached out, and as she was bringing it closer, her smile fell away. "Yes, that's him."

When Hagger saw the reaction on her face, he took the picture back. "Do you remember his name?"

"No. But he lived in the back bungalow that had the alley access. He had been living there before I started managing the place. I never liked him. There was something about him that I knew just wasn't right. He'd never look me in the eyes, and I remember once we wanted to paint the interior of the bungalow that he rented, but he threw a fit and refused. I didn't—" Her voice dropped off. It's weird to see an old person sad; I didn't like it. I leaned forward to hear her words as she added, "I regret I didn't do anything about him. If my husband had been alive, we would have done something."

Hagger didn't ask his next question right away. There was silence like he was letting her thoughts play out in her mind. Her smile came back, but only halfway. Hagger nodded at her. She nodded back indicating it was okay to move on. "Kat, do you recognize the young man sitting at the defendant's table, Tyler Roberts?"

The question caught me off guard. I looked up without thinking. The old lady and I locked eyes. She nodded quickly. "Yes, that's him. That's the little boy that lived in the bungalow with him."

"And by 'him,' you're referring to Robert Starker, the man in the photo?"

She nodded at Hagger and followed up with a quiet, "Yes." Then her face turned my way. "But his curls ..." She titled her head to the side. Her smile expanded. I had to look away. I could tell I was a clear part of her memory. She had details about me that I didn't have about her. "He didn't have the curls. They used to shave his head. They didn't let his curls grow. They're so precious. They remind me of my grandson's."

There was a light laughter from the audience in the courtroom, and Hagger's next question took her eyes off me. "And Kat, do you remember a specific evening where you had an opportunity to talk to Tyler without Robert Starker around?"

"Yes." She reached for a Kleenex.

"Could you please describe that evening for us."

"Yes. I was sound asleep and I heard a knock on my door. I grabbed my robe and went to see who it was. It was the boy, Tyler. I mean, I didn't know his name, but I knew it was the boy who lived in the back bungalow. I had seen him several times and called the truancy agency to have it checked out as to why he was out of school." Her voice came to a halt.

"Go on." Hagger was trying to keep her testimony on track. "This was the middle of the night and Tyler was at your door?"

"Oh, yes, I'm sorry. I didn't have my porch light on, so before I let him in, I turned the light on because I didn't want his dad—I assumed that the man he lived with was his dad. But anyway, I turned on the porch light, and when I saw he was alone … he was in an oversized man's T-shirt, like what the kids wear for their sleepwear. And so when I saw he was alone, I had him come inside. His eyes were red and puffy, like he had been crying, but he was very calm."

"And again, this is Tyler?" Hagger pointed at me. "The young man seated at the table there?"

"Yes. Yes, that's him."

"Do you remember what he said?"

"Of course. Like it was yesterday. He was worried about his brother, he said."

I didn't remember a single thing she was referring to. All I could bring up in my memory was the "Cordia" sign, and how that fancy C was carved into the wood. Hagger's words brought my attention back to the courtroom. "Please, go on, Kat. Tell us what Tyler said to you."

"He was very worried about his brother. When he first said his brother, I thought maybe he had a bad dream or heard some news about his brother, because I had never seen another boy living in the bungalow. But I reached out and hugged him, and I'll never forget how he pulled away, like my arms were some kind of enemy." She wiped at her nose and then held the

Kleenex up to her mouth, above her lips. I still had no recollection to link up with her words.

"Can you go on, Kat?"

She nodded. "I kept my space from him because I saw he was very worried, and I wanted to help him. I asked him what happened to his brother and he said his head was hurting and that his dad can't help, that his dad was sleeping and can't help him. He wanted me to come over to the bungalow and help his brother. I was confused at first and tried to ask him when his brother moved in, but then he started to get worked up. I could tell he was getting worried that I wouldn't help him. And I could tell he had been crying."

"And what did you do next?"

"I followed him to his bungalow in the back there. I didn't want to go inside at first, because that Robert character, the man, always made me feel so uncomfortable. But my heart was aching, seeing the pain in the little boy's eyes, Tyler's. He was whispering that his brother was on the couch. I followed him into the bungalow there and left the front door open, just in case. That's how nervous I was. The place smelled horrid, and at first I put my bathrobe over my mouth to guard against the smell, a rotten food smell. There was trash on the floor everywhere and boxes stacked in random places like they had never fully moved in. But Tyler took my hand and walked me over to the couch. They had a flashlight there." She wiped at her nose again, clenched the Kleenex, her hand shook as she held it against her mouth.

"And can you tell us what happened next?"

She inhaled. Her fallen tears landed on her shirt, leaving wet blotch marks. She looked at me and said, "You were so worried about your brother." I looked to my lap. Her words weren't sparking any memories, but I knew my emotions were nearing a collapse when she spoke of my feelings for K.C.

Hagger repeated his question. "Kat, I'm sorry, but can you tell us what happened next?"

"Yes. I sat on the couch next to his brother, and when they turned on the flashlight, I saw that his whole jaw area, well …" She brushed over her own jaw and down her neck area to indicate what she was talking about. "It was terribly swollen. His face was red, and he was dripping with sweat. From my own experience as a mother, his temperature was probably close to 102. My fear left, and I was angry. I wanted to talk to their dad, the man that lived there. But when I said to Tyler, 'Go get your father,' he froze and took a step back. I'll never forget the fear in his eyes; it took my breath away. And all he said was, 'But we thought you could help us make him better.' He may have said his brother's name, I can't remember."

"K.C.?"

"Yes, that might be it. Anyway, I just remember looking around at what I could see inside the bungalow. The filth and smell and then these two sweet boys, and I made my decision, maybe the wrong decision, I don't know. I think about it all the time now. Like I should have done more or called the child protective services right away … but my late husband, he would always tell me to stay out of people's business. I just did what I thought was okay to do then."

"And what was that? What did you do?"

"I had the boy, you know Tyler there, come back to my apartment. I gave him all the Tylenol I had at my place and showed him how to make a hot pack, you know, a hot compress. My assumption was that his brother had a toothache, a bad toothache. I told Tyler that's what I thought the problem was and that his dad had to take him to the doctor right away, but that the Tylenol and hot packs should help the pain and maybe would get him through the night."

"And did you see Tyler, his brother, or Robert Starker the next day?"

"I didn't see anybody. They were gone. They had lived there for a long time, before I was the manager, and the next evening, before I went to sleep, that next night, I walked back there, to their bungalow, and they were gone. The front door was open and most of the furniture was there, but their clothes, the boxes and stuff had disappeared. It looked like they left in a hurry. No one ever came back. Today is the first time I've seen Tyler since that night."

"Thank you, Mrs. Katood—ah, Mrs. Katoundsky. Your Honor, I have no further questions."

The manager lady went to stand, but the judge stopped her. "Hold on, Mrs. Katoundsky. Mr. Braide may have some questions for you." She sat back down.

My attorney stood, grabbed his yellow pad and pen, and started walking over to the podium where the attorneys stand to ask their questions. "Mrs. Katoundsky, my name is Randall Braide. I'm the attorney for Tyler Roberts. Just a few questions. Did you know Tyler's name when you saw him at the bungalow?"

"No, I don't think so. I think I remember knowing that the man's name was Robert Starker, you know, because I was the manager and he paid his rent to me."

"So the name Landon doesn't sound familiar to you?"

"You know, that could be it. That sounds more familiar than Tyler, but honestly I don't remember."

"That's fine. Now, you mentioned something about a truancy officer in response to a question that Mr. Hagger posed to you. Can you elaborate on that for us?"

"Oh sure. This was quite a few months before the middle of the night incident, but I was noticing the boy wasn't in school, and I asked the father, Robert, why he wasn't in school, and all he would say was, 'He's going, but he needs special help.' I mean, I didn't see anything wrong with the young boy, and I knew that he was probably home alone during the day when the father went to work, so I called the school district to have a truancy officer come out."

"And did they?"

"I don't know. I assume they did, because a month later or so, the father made some comment to me about me getting my way and that his son was in school. I think I remember the conversation happened when he came to pay his rent one time, or something."

"Did you ever see Robert Starker, the father, physically abuse the boy, Tyler?"

"No, not in front of me. But … well …" She had a confused tone to her voice, and she hesitated. Braide didn't let her answer end there. "Please, go ahead. What were you going to say?"

"When I reached out to hug him, that night when he came over to my place … I mean, I'm a mother, and … well, when he jerked away from my arms, I knew what it was about. It's the jerk of an abused child."

Hagger jumped up from his chair. "Objection. Speculation."

Immediately the judge leaned forward into her microphone. "Sustained. Mr. Braide, move on."

"I have no further questions." Braide took his seat.

The witness slowly stepped down from the witness stand. I saw a young woman in the audience area rise. I figured it had to be her daughter, the one who drove her. Both my attorney and the D.A. stood and bowed a little when she walked by. She ignored them. Her eyes landed on me and then glided over to my dad sitting to my right and came back to me. She smiled, and it conveyed the message that she was happy to see me sitting next to my real father.

(39)

I don't think I would ever want to live in a town where I couldn't see the mountains. And I doubted any place in the world compared to waking up to Pike's Peak, the centerpiece of Colorado Springs. It was spring and the snowcaps were still on. There was nothing in Nebraska that compared. There's also something about the Colorado air that expands my lungs and gives me this light feeling. Maybe that's because I lived on that cow-shit farm for so long. I mean, the cows and the dairy farm were gone, but the smell stayed, and it always freaked me out to take in a deep breath, knowing that I filled my lungs up with the crap I smelled.

I took my Saturday morning break at the grocery store standing at the magazine rack checking out the new *National Geographic*. My mom bought me a subscription, but because we were in Nebraska for the trial, I wasn't home when it came in. Every other page somehow reminded me that I had to go back to the trial on Monday. The bungalow manager lady really bothered me. I still didn't recall anything about the night she talked about. But when she talked about the bungalows, the "Cordia" sign came to life in my mind. And the bungalow we lived in? All I could recall is being able to look outside the window by the front door and see the parking spot where Bob would park his van.

It was the apartment before the Cordia Bungalows that I remember the best. That's where the tuna-fish sandwiches and the pillow tents were made. It's when K.C. and I were Bob's brave soldiers. In the last year since leaving the trailer, I was learning to hate Bob, but I still didn't know what to do with the fun memories like that. Do I try to ruin them? Do I try to think about them without seeing Bob in my memory? Do I have fun thinking about them, about when Bob was nice, but then remind myself after the thought leaves that I hate Bob?

"Hey, what's up?" It was the girl from the deli. She was my age and had to wear a hairnet because she worked with the food.

"Hey." I put the magazine back in its place.

"The manager wants you to cover me at the deli so I can go on break."

I looked over at the cash registers. There was Kirsten, tying her smock, starting her shift. Damn it! I didn't want to be sent to the deli. I wanted to bag groceries. I wanted to do price-checks for Kirsten. I answered without taking my eyes away from the cash register area. "Are you going on break right now?"

"Duh." She walked away.

I followed.

The deli chick took her break in the deli. I didn't get it. She sat on the counter, in the corner, which was stupid, because if a customer came up and I was in the back, they'd think she was on duty talking on her cell phone about stupid stuff and laughing out loud instead of helping them. When she finished her call, she hopped off the counter and came over to where I was slicing the low-sodium turkey breast for my first customer. "What school do you go to?" she asked.

I didn't answer. I didn't want to answer. I focused on slicing.

"I go to Mitchell."

"Cool." I wrapped up the turkey, gave it to the guy. When I turned around, she was putting the turkey breast back in the refrigerator case. When she looked over to me, I asked, "Are you done with your break?"

"No. I'm gonna go smoke a cigarette."

"Why? That's stupid." I sounded like one of the nerds from my English class. I didn't know why I said it. I hadn't had a cigarette since the atrium at the York center, but that's only because I didn't think about it.

"You don't smoke?" She slid the refrigerator door shut.

"No. I had to quit." I liked the tone of my words.

"Cool." She nodded.

I wiped down the slicer, cleaned it up. She stirred the potato salad. She didn't have her hairnet on. "I thought you have to wear your hair in a net, or something."

"Not on breaks."

"Oh. Cool."

There was this weird silence. I tried to find crap to clean, you know, but I couldn't. I only worked the deli one other time, and it was really busy. I washed my hands. She was sitting back on the counter, staring at me kind of weird. "Hey, Jacob Styles, our first baseman, is having a kickback tonight. He's gonna have a keg. Five-dollar cover. You wanna go?"

Her cell phone on the counter where she was sitting vibrated. "Your cell phone is vibrating."

"Oh, cool. Thanks." She flipped it open.

I looked up at the clock. Her break was over. I took off the white apron you have to wear in the deli and almost forgot about the hair net I had on. As I was walking out, I looked over at her. "Later."

She had pretty brown hair. Kind of too much makeup, though. She pulled the phone away from her mouth. "Bye. See ya tonight." She had a nice-enough smile. Straight teeth.

I gave her a nod. "Cool."

I didn't know what anyone at my work knew about me. I'd been working at the store almost four months, and no one who worked there had ever said anything. My dad's engineering firm did some work for the manager's parents, and that's how I got my interview. The manager asked right then and there when I wanted to start. Getting the job was easy, but an eight-hour day was a long ass time. I learned that six hours into my first day on the job.

The manager only scheduled me Saturday and Sunday shifts while the trial was happening. He said I could take the whole time off, but I told him no, I needed the cash because I wanted to buy a car. Henry Schlick, my psych guy, came up with this idea, and my parents went along with it. However much money I spent on research or education stuff, they agreed to put the same amount into a savings account. That money that my parents matched in the savings account would be for me to get a car when I turned eighteen. I could put my own money in the savings account, too, but the education stuff was important. Not in a college way, though. It was for educating me about who I was and where I wanted to be headed. I was no longer that loner kid that swirled around in black bouts of anger, spitting at the thought of tomorrow. The weight of the world on my shoulders had gotten lighter and bouncier. I wanted to be someone.

My first step in educating myself was to take a photography class at the community college. My GED tutor recommended the teacher. I spent seventy-five dollars to register for the class, so my parents opened my savings account with seventy-five dollars. I bought my own digital camera, which totally wiped out my paycheck, but my parents matched it, and the deposit bumped up my car bank account to just over three hundred dollars.

The biggest expense, though, was going to be a summer adventure that my photography teacher and the geology nerd from the community college were putting together. It was a weekend exploration trip up to Pike's Peak. Only about eight of us would be going, but all in, I was going to end up spending nearly seven hundred dollars for stuff like hiking shoes, camping equipment, plus the new photography stuff I'd already bought.

And I learned that when my dad was involved in stuff like that, it was never one trip to Target or something. He would research the best and then buy the second or third best. It seemed so stupid when we were doing it because it took forever, but when I looked at all the stuff that I got, I knew a lot about each thing I bought and why I got the one I bought.

"Hey." It was the deli chick again, coming up from behind. I was bringing in the stray shopping carts left in the parking lot.

"Hey," I said back.

"Here." It was a piece of paper with an address. "It's where the kickback is tonight."

"Cool." I took it. I looked at her name tag: "Emmie."

"See ya later." She skipped off. I tucked the piece of paper in my shirt pocket, not really thinking about whether I would go or not. I had two hours before my shift would be over.

When I came back into the store, I saw that in Kirsten's line was the pharmacy assistant from the drugstore next door. He was always coming in and saying stupid stuff to Kirsten, trying to get her to laugh. His smile made him look dumb, but I wasn't going to tell him that. He never bought enough for me to bag. It was always a soda, Red Bull or a piece of fruit. I called it "excuse crap," something small that gave him an excuse to go through her line. And if he didn't have anything for me to bag, I was supposed to move on to the next register, which made it hard for me to hang out and listen to his bullshit. But on a Saturday night, the store was dead. So when he made it through the line to check out, I was standing there, organizing the paper bags.

"Hi there, Kristen. You're working late tonight." The pharmacy guy was so lame, I couldn't help but laugh. He didn't even get her name right. She didn't respond. I knew she was smarter than that. He didn't know when to shut up either. "Yeah, I have the late shift at the pharmacy." He was looking for exact change, probably to take longer. Kirsten was making small talk like she does with all the customers. He kept rambling on like a fool, though. "Hold on, let me find that quarter … you know, my cousin's name is Kristen. It's a great name."

I couldn't help myself. "Her name's *Kirsten*." They both looked at me kind of shocked. I surprised myself. I didn't really think before I blurted it out. The pharmacy guy picked his jaw off the floor and looked Kirsten's way. "Oh, wow. I feel so stupid. I've been calling you 'Kristen' for months now. I'm so sorry."

Yeah, dude, you should be.

"Oh that's fine. I get it all the time." She flashed him her signature smile—the one where you forget what you were saying because it makes you smile too.

When I bagged the groceries at her register, I usually only saw her profile, you know, because she was looking at the customers. I would always get a little jealous of the customer standing straight in front of Kirsten because I never got to see her smile straight on. I had to settle for a profile half-smile.

But the pharmacy jerk's smile, that, I saw. A real dumb looking one, too. He looked at me and winked, like he was thanking me that I helped him out somehow. "So, *Kir-sten*," he said, making it like it was two words, I guess trying to correct all the stupid ass times he said it wrong, "please, let me take you to lunch to make up for the *name calling*." It was a lame joke and … she fell for it. Their smiles linked and they broke out into laughter. She ended her giggle halfway through and said to him, "I'd really like that …"

"Peter. My name's Peter."

"I'd really like that, Peter." She threw a small nervous laugh on the end of his name, and that's when she finally looked my way. And there it was: her smile, head on, face to face … it wasn't as pretty as I thought actually, but maybe that's because it wasn't for me. I reached into my shirt pocket, pulled out the deli chick's piece of paper and put it into my pant pocket. That little voice in my head said to make sure it didn't fall out.

The last two hours of my shift went by quickly, mostly because Kirsten and I had something in common to talk about: Peter, the pharmacy assistant.

(40)

My mom picked me up from work that night. During my weekday shifts I took her car, but because it was a weekend, she needed it for errands. Five minutes before closing, I saw her driving by in the parking lot. She had on what I called her hunting smile, where she'd go like three miles an hour right along the storefront windows, rubbernecking with a huge smile on her face, looking for me in action. She loved to see me working, but I wanted to save my dignity. Anytime a set of headlights came into the parking lot right before closing, everyone looked worried that it was a customer with a long grocery list. I couldn't bear the thought of yelling out, "Don't worry, guys. It's my mom." So I bolted for the frozen food section to put back a bag of string beans that a coupon-crazed customer refused to buy. When I made my way back up to the front of the store, the manager was standing at the exit letting out the employees but prepared to send away unwanted customers. I hung out organizing the grocery bagger's station until I heard the "Bye, Tyler," from Kirsten.

"Later."

When Kirsten's headlights went on, I untied my apron and gave the manager a nod. He unlocked the door and before I got my foot over the threshold, my mom dropped the car into drive and swung up to the front of the store, valet style. The passenger window was down so she could start talking to me before I even got in. "Hi, honey. How was your day? Was it busy?"

"Hey." I shut the car door, reached over, and pressed the FM button. That reminded me that I needed to get new headphones for my iPod. Her questions kept coming at me. "Did you have a nice day? Did you have any big orders to bag? Do you like working Saturdays? It's supposed to be hot tomorrow. Evan missed you at his baseball game."

"Did they win?"

"No, he was so upset. I think that's why he missed you so much."

"Oh, I'll talk to him when I get home. I need you to go get me new headphones for my iPod."

"Okay. Where do I get that?"

"At the mall. But you have to go tomorrow because I need them before we go back to the trial on Monday."

"Okay." The funny thing about her was as soon as I gave her a "mom chore," it's like she would drift off into daydream land and this la-la smile would occupy her face. Thinking about what, I don't know.

"Mom."

She popped out of her thoughts. "Yeah."

"I have to go hang out with some friends tonight." I learned that that's how I had to ask for things from her. If I made it sound like that's what I needed and had to do, it wasn't a problem. It's when I asked, "What should I do?" or, "Is it okay?" that she didn't know how to answer. My dad was different.

"Was it busy today? I would think Saturdays are so much busier than the weekdays. Are they?"

That wasn't a good sign. That meant I'd have to ask my dad. I tried again, though. "My friends are having a kickback, just like a little get-together thing. I'm only going for a little while. I won't be late. I have to work early tomorrow." I also knew that if I threw in a responsible-kid comment, she was quicker to say it was fine.

Didn't happen that time, though.

"You'll have to ask your dad about going out, honey."

"Why? It's no big deal. Just to hang out and then come home."

"Well, what friends?"

"The girl from the deli, at the store." I forgot her name.

"Well, let's just see what your dad says, okay?"

I didn't say anything else on the way home. I leaned my elbow against the window, rested my head on my knuckles, and stared off into space. I wasn't mad. It's just that my mom was easy to figure out. She wanted me to be happy so bad that if she thought I was upset, she'd be on my side when we went to talk to my dad.

"No, it's already ten o'clock, Tyler. You can't go out this late."

"Dale, maybe it's a good thing for him to get to know some people his age." She knew how to work him better than I did, so I took her lead.

"Yeah, I wanna meet some people my age. I'm only around you guys and Evan, and my tutor and stuff. And ten o'clock isn't late. That's what time everyone meets up. If all of our stuff hadn't happened, you guys would see that this is what teenagers do. But it's like I'm back here in Colorado, and I'm almost seventeen, and you guys don't know what it's like to have a teenager."

"No, I don't buy that, Tyler." He shut me down. "We have too much going on right now. With the trial and everything, no, I can't let you risk anything."

"That's not cool. I do everything you guys ask. Everything."

"Don't raise your voice, Tyler." He raised his, though.

"But it's not cool. I've been working at the store for months now and this is the first time that someone asked me to do something. Come on. I just want to do something for myself."

"Everything your mother and I do is for you. Our whole life is consumed by the trial."

"No, I know, okay, but I mean, I just want to hang with people my age. I'm sick of everything being so serious. I'm almost seventeen, and, well, what if the trial doesn't turn out like you say it will?"

"It will, Tyler." It was my dad's normal matter-of-fact jerk voice.

"Then let me go tonight."

"No. I don't know these people or whose house it's at. What if it gets out of control, the police come, and then we'll have a whole new set of issues?"

"Why can't you guys learn to trust me? You think I would let myself get into a situation like that? Don't you think I'm learning anything?" I looked at them both. My mom was sitting at the kitchen table, baffled, not knowing who made more sense: my dad or me. My dad just stood there, his normal tensed-up self. There was like seven seconds of silence. I thought I might get my way. I kept looking back and forth between them. More silence. Then my dad's shoulder twitched slightly and he gave me a light nod. "No, Tyler, you're not going."

"This is so damn stupid! I can't believe it." I stormed out of the kitchen and slammed the door behind me. Went to my room, which still had some of the guest-room furniture in it even though I got the other crap out. I kicked the door shut and knocked my desk chair over. I reached for my iPod but remembered the earplugs were broken. I threw my iPod on the floor. I started pacing. "Fuck!"

The pacing didn't help. I wanted my old attitude back, and it wasn't there. I wanted to be angry enough to throw shit around, pull down pictures, kick crap over. But I looked at my iPod on the floor. *Palmer gave me that.*

I was still mad at my parents, but Tracie's words echoed: "If you get your act together, you can be on your own in a couple of years." I sat on my bed and ran my hands through my hair. Next to me was my *National Geographic* magazine. I picked it up and leaned back on my bed. My heart started to slow. I wanted to be angry because it felt like the right thing to do, but I felt the rage inside me leaving and this "whatever" feeling replacing it. *I just needed to save to get my own car, that's all.* I flipped the pages of the magazine.

There was a knock at the door. I knew it was my dad because as soon as the knock came, the door started to open. My mom would have followed up with another knock and asked, "Honey?"

"Tyler." He said it in his lecture-type voice.

I pulled the magazine away. "Yeah, what?"

He stood halfway in and out of my room, with his body sandwiched between the door frame and the door. I saw him look over at the desk chair that was turned over. He cleared his throat. "You didn't have to leave the kitchen like that. You're almost seventeen, and that kind of behavior won't help you in life."

"Okay." I picked the magazine back up to read, flipped the page. He cleared his throat again. I looked up. "Well, your mother and I have been talking, and we think that you brought up a good point in the kitchen."

Weird. "Whatta you mean?"

"You're right. If we hadn't lost you for that time, we would have grown into accepting what normal sixteen- or seventeen-year-olds do. We're figuring out things as we go. This has been a trying time for us, too. But your mother and I agree that the number one message to send to you, at your age, is that this is your life, and if you think you can handle things on your own then …"

I couldn't grasp the meaning of his sentences. I recognized the individual words, but what they meant when they were strung together stirred a fear inside me that halted all voluntary muscles. The words "my life" and "my responsibility" in one sentence sounded like they were getting rid of me, wanting to send me out, away, "on my own." I wanted to utter the words, "I'm sorry," but my little voice inside humiliated me, telling me, *Sorry won't be good enough. You've screwed it all up.* What usually was a small insecure dot in my chest expanded to a huge abyss, threatening to swallow me whole.

"Tyler. Are you listening to me?"

"Yeah, what?"

"Why don't you come into the living room, and we'll talk about the consequences of your going tonight and what you expect will happen. And if we can all come to an agreement about how you think the night will play out, I'll—well, either your mother or I will give you a ride."

"What do you mean?"

"Do you still want to go tonight?"

I nodded. "Yeah, for sure."

Maybe it was how the lighting in my room fell on his face, softening his forehead lines, or how his hand gently rested on the doorknob and his shoulder slouched forward, toward me, but I saw the other side of him. Although his chest, where he housed his heart, was blocked from my view, I knew he was trying to send me a caring message. I got it.

He started to back out of the doorway. "But we'll also have to pick you up."

"Can you guys drop me off down the street, like not in front of the house?"

"Sure." He spoke out as he headed down the hall. "I'll see you in the living room."

I sat there kind of stunned. I picked up my iPod. It still turned on, looked like it worked. I was relieved that my anger hadn't caused too much damage.

(41)

I regretted going to the kickback as soon as I saw the front of the house. Everything looked way too clean, way too rich, way too perfect. I followed a group of guys up to the front door, and I would have turned around, but I'd forked out the five dollars for the security guy. Paying to leave didn't make sense, you know.

The entryway had marble flooring, a big crystal chandelier, and this huge, wide circular staircase that I'm sure led up to perfectly furnished rooms. Within two steps of entering, on an expensive polished antique table, there was the Styles's perfect family photo: one son, one daughter, mother and father. All four in coordinated clothes and fake smiles.

A group of kids were coming down the stairs with plastic cups and beers in hand. One of them was Emmie. "Hey, bag boy." She broke away from the group. "Wanna beer?"

"Sure." I was going to hold it but not drink it. It was part of the deal with my parents.

"Do you get high?" she asked.

"I used to."

"Cool. Me, too. I'm afraid they'll test us at work so I don't do it anymore. Come on. The keg's out back, and I'll introduce you to Jacob." When Emmie said "Jacob," I looked back at the family photo and was afraid I'd hate him as soon as my eyes landed on him. I walked behind her. She knew a lot of people, and different kinds of people, which I thought was cool about her. She wasn't as obnoxious as I thought she was when we were behind the deli counter.

We stood at the keg for a while talking about the people at work and how stupid we thought some of them were. I liked laughing with her, knowing that we found the same stupid stuff funny. Then she asked, "Do you like working with Kirsten?" At first I thought it was a trap, you know, like she wanted to find out if I had a crush on Kirsten or something. "She's all right."

"Yeah, I think she's pretty cool. I hope when I'm her age I have my act together like she does." *I liked that answer.*

I looked to the left and saw the Jacob from the family photo coming toward us, his beer swooshing the sides of his cup and a bottle of whiskey in his other hand. He bounced off people's shoulders, and when he got within jumping range, he stretched his arms out wide and yelled, "Emmmmmieeee." Emmie tried to plant her feet and had enough time to roll her eyes at me just before the collision took place. I think it was the football team standing behind Emmie that softened the blow and brought Jacob back on balance. His eyelids were heavy, his speech slurred. Emmie made the introduction. "Hey, Jacob. Pretty wicked party. This is Tyler from my work."

He looked at me, but his eyes immediately traveled over my shoulders to a group of guys who were walking through the sliding glass door from the house. He took off toward them, almost on all fours, incoherently yelling something about being happy to see them.

Emmie leaned into me to say something just between us. "Jacob's crazy. Want to know something wild?"

"What?" I followed her eyes over to Jacob, leaning on someone, his knees wobbling, the whiskey bottle flying in the air like a conductor's wand.

"His dad is a spokesman for AA."

"Alcoholics Anonymous?" I knew of NA from Sam's mom. She brought the brochures home one day when I was at Sam's house after some court hearing she had.

"Yeah, that's why they're out of town, at some convention."

That family photo in the entryway popped into my head. I wondered who in Jacob's family still smiled when they saw that photo, you know … probably only strangers who had the same family photo in their entryway.

I kept looking at my watch. I settled in with a group of kids by the pool, and met a guy who is the teacher's assistant for the photo class at Mitchell High where Emmie goes to school. He knew about the trip I was taking up to Pike's Peak. I lost like thirty minutes talking to him and his girlfriend about different lens filters and exposure times.

Not everyone was drinking or getting high. I might have thought for like a split-second about getting high, but there was no way I was going to ruin things with my parents. When they passed the blunt around the group and I said no, it went to the guy next to me without hesitation, and then the two girls next to him said no also, and passed it on.

When it came time to leave, I knew I had made friends. They weren't like Sam, you know, but they made me feel the same way Sam did. The party was breaking up and the security guard was double-checking designated drivers. I walked out and headed down the street, walking as fast as I could. If my dad was picking me up, he'd be where he dropped me off. But if it was my mom, I knew there was a chance she'd see me coming and instead of staying parked, she'd drive up to me, thinking she was helping out.

"Hey, Tyler, wait up." I stopped. Turned around. It was Emmie, and she yelled out to me, "I'm walking, too." We picked up where we left off talking about work. She said she wasn't working tomorrow because she's on the robotics club at school, and they were having some kind of competition. At one point when she was talking, I thought about the kids at my old high school that I hated and how they were probably like Emmie. Like, you could have mixed them up with the people I met that night at Jacob's party, and I wouldn't have known the difference.

There was a set of headlights creeping up the street toward us. I went to cuss under my breath, hoping that some kind of pissed-off attitude would soften the embarrassment. "See you later, Tyler." Emmie hoped off the curb and ran up to the car coming our way. It was her mom, not mine. My mom was parked right where my dad dropped me off.

"How was it, Honey? Did you have fun? Are you glad you went?"

"Yeah." I pressed the FM button on the radio as we drove off. I liked the song that was playing. It was the first song I downloaded onto my iPod. Palmer's advice played over in my mind: "Only download the music ya like." The song didn't have any meaning for my mom, though. She stared straight ahead, the same la-la smile, the same hand position on the steering wheel. For me, though, everything started to have more meaning.

(42)

I was smiling when we walked up to the courthouse Monday morning. It's not that I forgot what I heard on Friday from the bungalow manager, but like my parents and my attorney said, whatever happened to K.C., as much as I cared about him, was out of my control. And whatever was erased from my memory was a blessing. I started to believe them.

We met with Braide before the day started, and he felt confident things were on track. He and my parents started talking about whether I would testify. I didn't have to, but they said they'd wait to see what Bob had to say, you know, whether it would be my word against his.

Braide pulled me aside before we walked into the courtroom. We took a seat on one of the hallway benches. "Tyler, I want you to be prepared for this week's testimony."

"What do you mean?"

"When I've talked to you before about K.C. and what happened to him, you use the word 'hurt' a lot." I had no idea that I did that, but I kept listening to what he had to say. "And of course you know this is a murder trial that we're defending, and that's what the testimony is going to focus on from now on."

"What do you mean?"

"The witnesses are going to be giving details about K.C.'s killing, and I want you to be ready for that, I want you to be ready to hear that, okay?"

I nodded. To hear the words "killing" and "K.C." at the same time hurt, and I knew at some deep level, Braide was right. I was trying to deny that reality.

Braide leaned over toward me. "Are you all right?"

"I think so."

He stood. Waited for me to stand. And then we headed for the courtroom.

"Do you recognize the young man seated at the defense table?" Hagger, the district attorney, lifted his arm to indicate our table.

"Yes, that's Landon Starker."

Whoa, that sounded weird, I thought. I wasn't Landon Starker even in my own mind anymore. At times I hesitated calling myself Tyler Roberts, but for sure I wasn't Landon Starker. Landon Starker was Bob Starker's son, and that wasn't me. But the lady on the witness stand didn't know any better. It was Evelyn Barker, the old lady up at the main house from the trailer. Her black hair was grayer, but she looked the same: sun-beaten skin and harsh wrinkles. Hagger's next question came right away. "And do you remember the first time you met the person you call Landon?"

"Yeah, when I rented the trailer out to Bob Starker. I saw the boy there movin' stuff in, you know, the boxes."

"And that was close to five years ago, that Landon and Bob moved into the trailer?"

"Yeah, about that. And during the summer months, when I still had the dairy farm, I'd see the boy with Jandro, the ranch hand, helpin' out. And then sometimes I'd see him here or there walkin' to the bus or home from the bus, and up at the main house emptyin' their trash from the trailer." She didn't look my way, which didn't surprise me. In the four, almost five years that we were at the trailer, I couldn't recall too many conversations with her. That's not to say, though, that she didn't yell at me plenty of times to do this or that. She just never *talked* to me.

"And Ms. Barker, I want to keep your recollection on the first few days of Robert Starker moving into the trailer. Did there come a time when you had an opportunity to see someone else you thought was moving into the trailer with Robert and the young man you've identified as Landon?"

"Yeah."

I think it was the way Hagger phrased the question, but I couldn't follow it with my own memory. I felt my eyebrows lock together. I'd told Drysdale that K.C. didn't move into the trailer with—I caught myself before I finished the thought. It had been almost a year since I tried to explore that memory of walking up to the trailer and Bob wanting to know what happened to K.C. My attention stayed on the witness stand, wanting to know what hints she might offer that recollection.

"Ms. Barker, please describe to the court who you saw on the first days of when Robert Starker moved into the trailer."

"Well, I had hired Robert Starker to be the ranch supervisor for the dairy farm, you know, to help me with the workers and keep stuff repaired, all workin' right. And so when he first moved in, I was takin' over the equipment rules—not the rules, but you know, the guidelines that tell you how to run the different dairy equipment. Anyway, I was bringin' one of those papers that I had down to the trailer there, and Bob wasn't there. Landon answered the door, and I saw in the livin' room there on the small couch that is built into the trailer there—the trailer came furnished, you know, I rented it furnished. But anyway, I saw someone on the couch when the trailer door opened and he, the kid on the couch was moanin', like almost cryin'. I asked Landon what was wrong, and he said his teeth were hurtin'. He had some bandages or kind of wraps around his chin."

I could see in my mind the couch in the trailer, the one I slept on, but I couldn't place K.C. on the couch in my memories. I took in a deep breath and listened to Hagger's next question. "And did Landon tell you who the person on the couch was?"

"I remember for sure he told me that that was his brother. I know that for sure, because I was surprised that there was more than one kid movin' in. But then it just left my mind. I was more focused on gettin' Bob up and runnin' on takin' care of the farm."

"Yes, of course. Let me ask you this: did you ever have an opportunity to talk to Robert Starker about the boy that you saw on the couch in the trailer?"

"Yeah, I remember the next day or the day after that, you know, a couple days after they moved into the trailer, I asked him how his other son was doin'. And I kind of caught him off guard because he said, 'What do you mean?' And I said, 'When I was over at the trailer, I saw your son, your other son, when he was sick with the toothache.' I mean, I didn't care how many kids moved into the trailer, I just wanted good help, and Bob was workin' out just fine for me."

"And do you remember what Robert Starker said in response."

"Yes."

"What was that?"

"He said that that kid wasn't his son. That it was Landon's friend visitin', and that he was gone, went back home, and I wouldn't see him around again."

"Did you think that was strange?"

"What was?"

"That Landon said the boy was his brother and Robert said it wasn't, that the boy was actually Landon's friend?"

"Nah. I just figured that the boys were close friends, you know how kids say stuff like they're related when they really aren't."

"And did you ever see that boy again?"

There was a pause in the courtroom. For the first time since Evelyn Barker took the stand, she looked my way and gave her answer directly to me. "Never … I never saw that boy again, until the police started diggin' around out there on my property last year." Her glare was meant to push me off a cliff where apparently she thought I deserved to be. I understood at that moment what Braide was telling me in the hallway. It was time to start bracing for reality.

(43)

I hadn't seen Braide and Hagger talk to one another since we turned down the plea deal. I don't think it was because Hagger was a jerk, or because it's the case that two attorneys sitting opposite sides automatically become enemies. I saw it as courtroom behavior. After lunch, before the judge came out, though, Hagger came up to our table asking if I'd look over some pictures of Evelyn Barker's farm and the trailer because he wanted them for evidence.

Braide told him it wasn't a problem, and he pushed the stack over to me like they were baseball cards, and he needed me to label the teams. It wasn't like that, though. I looked over and saw my mom and dad talking to some random courtroom visitor. I didn't want to look at the photos without one of them sitting next to me, because I knew the pictures held the power to suck me in and transport me to the past. I didn't want to go back in time, so I needed someone to sit beside me and anchor me to the here and now.

I looked around once more, hoping they would read the concern in my eyes. No one heard me and the little voice in my head kept taunting me, *C'mon, Tyler. Don't be a wuss.* I dropped my head and looked at the first picture.

It was of the trailer kitchen, and I could tell it was taken the night the FBI took me. My eyes refused to scan the photo. Instead, I crept over every detail, making sense of why things were the way they were that night. The half-empty Jack Daniel's bottle sat on the counter, still capped, waiting for Bob to break his vow to only be half-drunk. The empty TV dinner boxes were stacked by the microwave, and the trays with the food scraps were still on the counter where I tossed them.

The next photo was the living room: dingy and dark. Cluttered with papers and gun-cleaning supplies, just as I remembered it. There was Bob's TV remote control on the floor. I saw the couch pillow, flat and filthy, that

I used for so many years to ease my neck cramps. My tennis shoes ... one flat-footed, the other tilted on its side, stood together, on the floor by the couch.

My tennis shoes ... mine.

Every detail in the pictures talked about Bob and me ... us.

A world I now knew I hated.

I pushed myself out of the living room by forcing in the memory of the FBI busting into the trailer, grabbing me. How the light beams from outside pierced the window blinds, crisscrossing in the darkness of the living room. How the agents gripped me by my arms and led me out under the helicopter blades in my socks and sweats.

I revisited the haunting curiosity that had been plaguing me. Why was the television off when the FBI showed up? Where was Bob? Where was his nine millimeter, the gun that never left his side? I abandoned that question to look more intently at the pictures in my hand, looking for what other items were missing that I didn't notice that night. Bob's work boots that he always took off at the front door and set next to the refrigerator: not there. His wallet and keys on the counter: not there.

"Tyler." Braide's whisper jolted my mind back into the courtroom. "Hagger only needs to know if you can verify whether those pictures are of the trailer and Evelyn Barker's farm. That's it. Nothing more."

I looked around. My dad was seated back at the table next to me, my mom in her chair behind Braide. Hagger had his next witness on the stand, already sworn in. I quickly ran through the stack of photos and pushed them back toward Braide. He took them and reached across the aisle, putting the stack on Hagger's table. In response, Hagger nodded our way as a sign of thanks and didn't miss a beat in his questioning. "Investigator Yarman, could you please tell the court how you became familiar with the Evelyn Barker property and the trailer that was placed on that property?"

"Yes, of course. My office had been notified earlier in the day by FBI Agent Drysdale to say that they were planning a recovery operation of Tyler Roberts, a fifteen-year-old who had been abducted several years previously out of Colorado Springs. Drysdale requested of me at that time to remain on standby, not knowing what he might find upon entering the property."

"Did Drysdale share with you how the FBI came to learn the whereabouts of Tyler Roberts?"

Braide gently stood from his chair and inclined his head toward the judge, saying "Your Honor …" The witness froze at the microphone, holding his answer. The judge leaned forward and responded to Braide, "Counsel, do you have an objection?"

"No, not exactly, Your Honor. But I wanted to put on the record a stipulation that Mr. Hagger and I have agreed upon."

The judge glanced over at Hagger, who nodded in response. She looked back over at Braide. "What's the agreement?"

"I've consented to the hearsay of this witness with regard to what Drysdale told him happened. I do believe, based on the FBI reports, that if Drysdale were to testify, it would only support the hearsay. And considering the relationship my client had with Drysdale upon the initial investigation while he was at the York center, calling Drysdale to the stand may do more emotional harm than judiciary justice. So for the purposes of Investigator Yarman's testimony, I'm willing to stipulate that the hearsay can be considered."

The judge looked my way, offered a gentle smile. I didn't really understand what the agreement was, but then I guess I didn't need to. The judge looked back to Braide and responded by saying, "I see the value in the stipulation. Very good." She looked down at the witness. "Investigator Yarman, you may answer Mr. Hagger's question. Did Drysdale tell you how they found Tyler Roberts?"

"Yes, he did. He said that the abducted individual had been using an alias name of Landon Starker, and that this Landon Starker was arrested the night before and booked into the state jail. And that because the individual, Landon Starker, did not hold a driver's license or a legal form of identification, as a precaution, even though the individual was released to a man who purported to be his father, a Robert Starker, the state police department submitted his prints as a background check, more than likely checking to see if this Landon Starker had a possible criminal record. When the prints went out into the data system, in simple terms, the Department of Missing and Exploited Children reported that the fingerprints were a match for a child in their database. That individual was named Tyler Roberts. It was the case that upon Tyler Roberts being abducted, his fingerprints were obtained from a company named Ameritek ID, which offered to parents a fingerprint service of their children for later identification purposes, such as the situation at hand."

"Thank you for that explanation." It was Hagger speaking.

I still had the Ameritek ID card that Drysdale gave me that first night. As the witness was describing the events and how they all linked up in one day, I was going over in my mind how, when Sam and I were busted, all I could worry about was Bob's reaction. I thought about how Drysdale must have gotten the call from the missing children place at the same time that Bob was holding the gun to my temple, or I was on the couch and Bob was telling me to go to bed when Drysdale was probably calling my parents. How strange it was to think about what was going on in the world behind my back.

"And Investigator, at what point were you notified that they would need your investigation work at the Barker property?"

"I received a call from Drysdale pretty close to five AM. I knew that the recovery of Tyler Roberts was scheduled to take place at a little past midnight. Drysdale notified me that the recovery was successful, and that they had Tyler Roberts in custody at their Omaha office, but that Robert Starker, the perpetrator, was missing. In addition, Drysdale notified me that based upon their initial intake of the crime scene, they believed that a possible killing had taken place in the spare bedroom of the trailer."

My heart rattled. My lungs froze. All I could think of was how I walked up to the trailer that first day after we moved in and I didn't have an answer for Bob about what happened to K.C.

"And did you arrive at the crime scene? Is that an appropriate way to refer to the trailer and the Barker property?"

"Absolutely. As soon as I arrived at the property and assessed the area in the spare bedroom, based on the few blood splatters that still remained on the wood paneling in the room, there was no doubt that a crime had occurred. It was also apparent that someone had attempted to clean the blood from the wood paneling, but because there were grooves in the paneling, the blood traces remained. The carpet as well had been pulled up from the spare room, and the flooring in that room was the bare aluminum of the trailer foundation."

I never looked at the flooring in the spare bedroom. I mean, I had used that weird hatch that was in the room there, but I had never really thought about why the carpet was gone; I just accepted it.

Hagger grabbed the stack of photos that Braide placed on his table and turned back around to the witness. "I'd like to show you some pictures, Investigator Yarman, and have you tell me whether you recognize them." Hagger passed him the pictures that I had looked through.

"Yes. Yes, this one here is of the spare bedroom." He flipped it around to show Hagger. It was of the spare room, with all the moving boxes and random items on the floor. Bob had kept his cleaning and refurbishing stuff for guns in there, and also his random plumbing tools. It was always a mess, but Bob never told me to clean the room. We kept the door closed and ignored the area, just like we tried to ignore that K.C. was ever with us.

"Investigator, your specialty in the world of crime scenes is what your profession calls forensic archaeology?"

"That's correct. My focus of study in the forensic world has been on identifying potential gravesites, or what we call in the forensic world, 'human remains retrievals.'"

"And could you please explain to us how your expertise came to be used at this crime scene?"

"Most certainly. Our first job was to secure the property. All individuals were removed from the area, which I believe included only a Ms. Evelyn Barker, who lived up at the main house. We do that to ensure there is no evidence contamination. Based on my opinion of what I saw in the spare room of the trailer, I proceeded on the assumption that we might find the human remains on the property."

"And were you correct in that assumption?"

"Yes, I was."

I didn't want the questioning to move on. I was afraid that the witness would say K.C.'s name and force me to face a reality that I was hiding from. The more he spoke about the trailer, the closer I felt to Bob, in a sick and disgusting way. Like there was a string that intertwined and attached us to one another so our secrets stayed close. I knew on a deep level that whatever happened to K.C., Bob and I put it behind us at the same time, trying to forget about K.C. at the same pace.

(44)

.My palms were sweating. I gripped my knees so hard, my knuckles turned white. Braide noticed and put a hand on the back of my chair, "Tyler, don't worry. I know everything this investigator is going to say. It helps prove that Bob is responsible for the killing."

Braide was right. I hate the word "killing." But even so, his words calmed me and loosened the string that tied me to Bob. I tried to slow my breathing and inhaled more deeply, opening my ears to the sadness that was calling out to me from the witness stand as Investigator Yarman proceeded to answer Hagger's questions about where K.C.'s body was found. "Yes, my assumption was correct, the human remains were on the Barker property. By midday, once we had the property secured, an assistant investigator from my office approached me to say they had found what they believed looked like a potential gravesite."

Hagger stood at the podium and led the witness through his testimony. "Where was that located? Before you answer that, we have an aerial map that I'd like to put up for viewing, that may help identify for everyone in the courtroom that location about which you are speaking." Hagger propped up a huge map of the Barker property.

It was interesting to see the world I lived in at a glance, you know. Like the dirt road to and from the highway that when I walked alone on it everything was fine, but when I drove on it with Bob, I had to be on the lookout whether he was angry or not. And then there was our trailer, sitting crooked on a square plot of land, almost hidden from the world by trees. My eyes scanned over the empty cow corrals, the yellow cornfields, the main house ... all of it, you could see it all at a glimpse.

The investigator picked up a thing that looked like a pen, but it lit up at the end and sent a red laser dot onto the blown-up picture that Hagger put on the tripod. The dot swirled like the eye of a tornado along the surface of the photo. I held my breath, fearful that wherever it landed, a recollection of where K.C.'s body was located would be unleashed in my mind. "Here, this is the area my assistant summoned me to." The red dot came to rest. "It's along a line of trees on the far north side of the property."

I vaguely knew of the area. I'd seen it from a distance when I used to help Jandro, the dairy farm worker. Feelings of relief flooded in, and I felt a mild sense of surprise. I had never been in that area. I knew I didn't know that area. I mean, I knew *of* the area from living on the property so long, but I didn't even know for sure what the area looked like. I listened intently, knowing that the investigator wasn't describing my actions.

"Go on, Investigator Yarman." It was Hagger's voice.

"Yes, thank you. What brought the area to my assistant's attention was a large hole that someone had started to dig out, but it appeared that the individual had abandoned the task." When the investigator spoke, he moved the red laser dot over the area.

Hagger approached the witness with a small photo. "And Mr. Yarman, can you take a look at this photo and tell us whether this is of the area you are describing?" I could see from my chair the photo wasn't of the same stack that they had me look at.

"Yes. This is a photo taken of the large hole to which I referred. You'll see in the photo, under the tree to the right, there's a shovel on the ground, and next to the shovel, that's the hole that I referenced. The space was approximately four feet deep, fairly narrow, and almost four feet in length."

"Based on your expertise, what were your initial assumptions as to why someone would be digging such a large hole?"

"Before I forensically examined the area, the assumption was either that someone was in the process of looking for something or, more likely, the individual who brought the shovel to the location was preparing a grave."

"And why do you say 'more likely'?"

"The size and configuration of the hole indicates a burial. If the person had been attempting a retrieval, it would more likely be that we would see small holes, sporadically placed, trying to locate the item underground."

"And if it were the site of a retrieval of some item as you are describing, based on the evidence that was taken from the trailer on the property, what did you think that item would be?"

"The remains of a human body. The individual who was killed in the spare bedroom."

"Please explain to the court what you did next."

"We secured the specific hole that you see in the picture to ensure there was no evidentiary contamination, and once that was completed, we proceeded to investigate the surrounding area looking for a potential gravesite."

"And what were your findings?"

"At approximately four AM the following night, we discovered what we immediately believed to be human remains."

"And where in relation to the hole that your investigator initially found was this grave where the human remains were retrieved?"

"From a position facing due north and standing directly before the large, newly dug hole, the grave was approximately seven feet to the left, or due west."

"And other than the remains of a body, were any other items retrieved?"

"Yes. Under the remains, we found what appeared to be a package. The item inside was wrapped in several layers of polyurethane, which most people identify as black trash bags, and then within the layers of polyurethane was a towel and wrapped within that towel, a gun."

"Anything else found?"

"We also found, resting within the bone remains, a bullet. Both the bullet and the package as we found them were sent to the ballistics lab for testing."

"And Investigator Yarman, based on your expertise, for how long had the remains been buried in that location?"

"Years."

"Would it be safe to estimate at least four years?"

"Most certainly."

The courtroom was silent, as if we were there at the burial site paying our last respects. If they had known the K.C. I knew, they would have been crying. My own mind was quiet, though, thankfully celebrating that the details of the witness's testimony were completely foreign to any reality I had ever experienced. I felt a sense of relief, knowing the truth was that I didn't have anything to do with what the witness was describing.

(45)

When Hagger finished his questioning and before the judge could ask whether there would be any cross-examination, Braide had in hand his yellow writing pad and a separate notebook that had the witness's name written on the spine. He was prepared for battle, and his questions started immediately. "Investigator Yarman, my name is Randall Braide. I'm the attorney for Tyler Roberts, the individual being charged with the murder of Kennedy Charles Nelson, whom we have been referring to as K.C. Thank you for coming today." The witness flashed Braide this relaxed smile, but at the same time he straightened his tie and corrected his posture. Braide didn't hesitate in his speech. "I have just a few questions, Investigator Yarman. The remains that were discovered, were they intact?"

"What do you mean?"

"Did it appear that the body that was buried was placed in the grave still intact?"

"Do you mean that when the individual was initially put into the grave, was he—"

"All in one piece, yes."

"Yes, the remains we found, although decomposed, indicated the body was intact, as you say, when it was buried."

"Very well. Next, your expertise extends to forensic anthropology; is that correct?"

"Yes, it does."

"That means that you can study the remains of an individual, such as we have here, and be able to determine with sufficient probability the age and stature of the remains at the time of death; is that correct?"

"Correct."

"What were your findings with regard to the burial remains retrieved at the Barker property?"

"It was a male. Approximate height of five feet. Age range between twelve and thirteen, possibly fourteen, but having said that, we sent the dentals in for a precise age determination."

"And based on an average body mass index for a thirteen-year-old male being the height that you have described, five feet tall, what would you place his weight at?"

"The average would be between the 105 to 115 pound range."

"Very well. Let's call it 110. And Investigator Yarman, 110 pounds of dead weight, is it plausible to assume that an eleven-year-old weighing approximately eighty pounds could have dug this grave and transported the remains from that trailer to that location?"

"Objection." Hagger's chair threw back. "Your Honor, this witness's expertise is in the area of forensic science, not weightlifting."

"Overruled. I'll allow it." Hagger's objection and the judge's statement went back and forth like a ping-pong ball, too fast to comprehend. I just kept my face on Braide to see if he agreed with what the judge said. He responded with a, "Thank you, Your Honor. Investigator Yarman, you may answer."

The investigator picked up the picture that he was looking at earlier. "You can see from this photo, there's quite a significant increase to the topography of the landscape leading up to the burial location."

Braide clarified. "A small hill?"

"Yes, in layman terms. And the soil as well is very soft, making it unlikely that the body was transported by any form of machinery, like a wheelbarrow or something of that nature."

"So to answer my question, it is highly unlikely that an eleven-year-old boy weighing no more than eighty pounds could have placed the body in that burial site, and in fact, more likely to be the case that it was a forty-five-year-old man towering over six feet tall?"

"Objection, Your Honor!" Hagger's voice was approaching a yell.

"Sustained." The judge looked to the witness. "Don't answer that, sir." She looked over to Braide, and in her calm voice said, "I get the point, Mr. Braide. Move on."

"Thank you, Your Honor." Braide looked my way and winked, then moved back over to the podium, reviewed his notes, and looked up at the witness. "Investigator Yarman, I'd like to turn your attention back to the gravesite that was being dug next to the area where you found the human remains of K.C. Nelson."

Once again, Hagger rose. "Objection, Your Honor. That's a misrepresentation. The witness used the word 'hole' to describe the area, not 'gravesite'; Mr. Braide should do the same."

The judge leaned forward toward the microphone, "Mr. Hagger, it is my job to tell Mr. Braide what he should do, not yours. The witness—*your* witness, Mr. Hagger—did testify that in his expertise the 'hole' that they found was a potential gravesite. I'll let it stand." She sat back in her chair, and indicated with her hand for Braide to continue.

I looked over to Hagger. He was seated, put back in place by the judge's words. When the judge finished her statement, Braide followed his "thank you" with a small bow of his head, and then turned back to the witness. "The shovel, that's what I want to talk about, Investigator Yarman. What happened to the shovel that you found at the site?"

"We sent it in for fingerprinting identification."

"Very well. And based on your expertise of being a forensic archaeologist, when do you think that gravesite was dug?"

"Hours before our arrival, not even a full day before."

"Really? Please explain for the court."

"The soil removed from the ground was off to the side, and it hadn't started to settle yet. The tip of the shovel, from penetrating the moisture in the ground, still had clots of mud sticking to it. Again, the digging was taking place, in my opinion, the previous night, when Drysdale's agents converged on the property."

"So that would explain where Robert Starker was when the FBI came to the Barker property. By sheer luck and coincidence, Robert Starker was digging my client's grave side-by-side to K.C. Nelson's."

"Objection! Complete speculation!" Hagger's face was red. His hand slammed the table.

"Sustained." The judge's voice ushered order into the room. "Mr. Braide, you know better than that."

"Sorry, Your Honor. I have no further questions."

I felt my jaw drop. Saliva started to puddle against the back of my teeth. In a single moment, the curiosity that lived in the back of my mind, starving to know how Bob got away from the FBI invasion, was satisfied.

My eyes scanned the courtroom, but my mind drifted to the memory of Bob in his recliner, his gun on his lap, telling me, "Landon, go to bed." I had thought at the time he was trying to be a sober father. I had stood up from the couch trying to be his good son. Now I sat in my courtroom chair, completely still and lifeless.

The first sign of life was my head moving up and down, telling myself how Bob was wrong that morning in the van when he told me no one gets a second chance. A cold, tingling feeling started creeping up from my feet. I looked over at the picture on the tripod: the open grave, the shovel on the ground, the loose dirt ready to be pushed back into the hole.

Seconds went by. I kept staring.

I shattered my frozen nerves by pinching my index finger. I was in the here and now, not in that picture on the tripod. My lungs expanded. My eardrums relaxed, letting in my mother's voice. My body quaked with a violent shiver; then the shock settled, and I processed the reality. Bob wasn't sending me to sleep that night. He was sending me to my death bed.

(46)

My parents didn't talk about the tripod picture. During our whole dinner at the hotel, no one made a single comment about the past, whether one minute ago when the waiter served my dad the wrong drink, or two years ago when my parents and I lived in separate worlds. It was my dad's doing. His mind lived two steps in front him, never in the moment and never repeating the past. I studied him for a minute. He was scanning the restaurant for our waiter, calling him over with a hand wave. Before the waiter arrived, my dad looked my way. "Tyler, are you going to want dessert?"

I shrugged and looked down at my plate. I hadn't eaten half of my steak yet. "I don't know. Maybe." I looked up to the waiter coming our way and kept the eye contact so that when he arrived at our table, I had his attention. "When you get a chance, no rush, but can you bring a dessert menu?"

"Absolutely." The waiter refilled our water glasses and stepped away.

There was a quick look from my dad to me. He cleared his throat and picked up his fork. Didn't say anything, just watched the waiter walk away. After a long pause, my dad spoke up, but not about desserts. "There's only one witness on the stand tomorrow, so I'm working on getting an earlier flight back into Colorado Springs. Tyler, you know what's happening Monday in court, right?"

"Yeah." And I did know. Bob was testifying. My mom knew, too. I looked her way but she kept her head focused on her food. That was the sign that she was worried for me, for us, for Monday to come. I tried to relieve the fear the best way I knew how. "I'm gonna talk to the manager to see about not working my shift this weekend. I think I'll try to go talk to Henry Schlick if we get back early enough tomorrow, you know."

217

"That's smart, honey." My mom flashed me the best smile she had for the moment. The concern in her eyes betrayed the curve of her lips, though. I gave her back a stronger smile.

My dad tossed a piece of salad around with his fork and started his words without looking up. "Well, Braide asked me to check in with you about tomorrow's testimony. It's the forensic doctor who examined K.C.'s teeth for the identification."

"Yeah, okay." I needed the smile that I sent to my mom back. It didn't come my way though. All three of us sat there, silent, except for a fork or knife tapping against our dinner plates.

"Tyler." It was my mom. Her hand rested on mine. "We'll just get through tomorrow and focus on a fun weekend. Remember, Evan has a game on Sunday. Maybe we'll all do a movie or something afterward, okay?"

"Sure. Sounds good," I responded. Sometimes she surprised me. I took her words and created a picture of what the weekend would look like: a crowded park with families wandering around, the busy mall where the movie theaters were. I got what she was trying to say. Keep thinking about how you can move forward, you know, no matter how heavy the reality of tomorrow was or Monday would be.

"Dr. Daniels, we haven't met in person before, but we've spoken on the phone. My name is Keith Hagger. I'm a deputy D.A. for the State of Nebraska. Thank you for coming to court this morning."

The witness was business-like, but not in a nerdy way. She crossed her legs, sat up straight, and had this quiet look about her when she listened. Like, there was no expression whether what Hagger was saying was right or wrong, stupid or smart. She just nodded gently as he rambled on. "And Dr. Daniels, we had on the stand the other day Investigator Yarman. Did you have an opportunity to come into contact with him regarding this case?"

"Yes. Investigator Lee Yarman contacted my office to arrange for the transportation of the dental remains that were excavated from the Evelyn Barker property. I was retained initially to provide an age estimate. At the early stages of the investigation, you see, the FBI lacked an identity for the John Doe."

"Meaning that they found the remains but didn't know who the person was?"

"Correct. We were awaiting word from Agent Drysdale of the FBI who had a witness that he thought might be able to provide an identity through the Missing Children database."

Hagger looked my way. Dr. Daniels was unaware that the person who identified K.C. by the database picture was me. Her brown eyes followed Hagger's gaze, and when she put two and two together, she sent me a compassionate nod. She was smart, in a silent, non-flashy way. She didn't use big vocabulary words but instead spoke plainly and to the point. And when she'd finish speaking, Hagger would always thank her for her explanation—probably because he couldn't have said it as precisely as she did. She had silky brown skin that glowed under the courtroom lights, and her black hair was pulled back into a tight ponytail. She looked like what I imagined Drysdale's grown daughter, if he had a daughter, would look like. She would have been his pride.

I still missed Drysdale, but I understood what Tracie explained to me. He had to be loyal to his job in order to be loyal to his own family—he had three sons, I found out. Tracie was saying that it was nothing personal that he couldn't talk to me while all the court stuff was going on. Everyone has their role to play in the working world. Anyway, it didn't stop me from thinking about how one day maybe I'd go back to the York center for a visit and see Drysdale in the conference room and Palmer in the hallway.

I remembered my dad's warning the night before, about the witness, so I brought my focus back to Hagger's words. "And Dr. Daniels, can you tell us what the next step was with regard to the remains found at the Barker property?"

"The next step came from Agent Drysdale's office. Once they had what they believed was the name of the individual whose remains were found at the property, Drysdale's office notified the next of kin in the hopes of obtaining dental records. Fortunately, those dental records did exist and Drysdale's office was able to subpoena the records. Once my office had a copy of the dental records, I was able to proceed with an identification of the human remains."

"In other words, you were able to give the John Doe a name?"

"Correct. He was positively identified as Kennedy Charles Nelson. The investigation file refers to him as K.C."

"And how old at the time of death did you determine K.C. to be?"

"Based on the Demirjian standard, which is the norm within our industry, I determined K.C. to be in the range of thirteen years of age at the time of death. I've brought my report with me. Would you like me to elaborate on how I determined that in a forensic capacity?"

The judge leaned forward into her microphone. "No thank you, Dr. Daniels. I'm familiar with the Demirjian standard. And if the report is going to be submitted for evidence, I'll make use of it. Unless, of course, Mr. Braide, you'd like the testimony on the record?"

Braide stood, gave his small bow. "No, that will be fine, Your Honor. The doctor is quite accomplished based on the resume that has been submitted into evidence, and there's no need to waste the court's time." The judge smiled. That meant that Braide said the right thing. And I understood why Braide made his little bow toward the judge. She was the driver of my destiny. Braide didn't care what she thought about him personally. It was his words being an extension of me that mattered.

Hagger walked over to his table and pulled out a large binder from one of the cardboard boxes. "Dr. Daniels, what I'm holding up, is this the report that you prepared in terms of the identification and age estimate of K.C.?"

"A.K.A. Kennedy Charles Nelson, yes, that's correct. That's my report in its entirety."

Hagger walked toward the judge "Your Honor, if there's no objection from defense attorney Mr. Braide, I'd like to ask that Dr. Daniels's report be admitted as evidence and with that, I have no further questions."

Braide once again rose to his feet, "Your Honor, there's no objection to the report being admitted. I do have a few questions for the doctor, though."

"Very well, Mr. Braide, the witness is yours." The judge motioned with her hand for Braide to step forward to the podium.

Braide grabbed his notebook, and before he headed over to do his questioning, he did his signature hand-on-the-back-of-my-chair move, leaned in, and whispered, "Tyler, remember the conversation I had in the hallway on the first day of trial. If you're not prepared to hear this testimony, you can step out of the courtroom at any time, okay? It's not meant to be disturbing for you."

I murmured, "Yeah, okay," but at the same time I thought to myself, *Weird*. I mean, in a way, he caught me off guard. Like what could a dental doctor say that could bother me any more than all the other things I've had to deal with? I followed up with a nod to get his hand off my chair and get the judge's stare off our conversation. "I'll be fine."

(47)

"Good afternoon, Dr. Daniels. My name is Randall Braide. I'm the defense attorney for Tyler Roberts. We've met in person before, haven't we?"

"Yes, we have."

"Do you have your report in front of you?"

"Yes, I do."

"I'd like to direct your attention to page twelve. What is that?"

"This is a photo-generated copy of K.C.'s x-rays that were given to my office by his dentist, Dr. Rafferty. It was taken of the outside surface of the mandible on the left side."

"Excuse me, the mandible is the jawbone, yes?"

"Correct, yes. The x-rays were taken at Dr. Rafferty's office when K.C. was five years old and in the custodial care of his grandmother, Ruth Nelson."

"Very well. Now please turn to page twenty-four. Can you tell us what this is?"

"It's another photo-generated x-ray of the same jawbone, but taken once the jaw was excavated from the Barker property."

"What was the purpose of placing those two x-rays in your report?"

"If you take note of the x-ray on page twenty-four, which is of the jaw at the time of death, you'll see in the middle of the jaw a hairline fracture. To the layman's eyes—"

"You mean people such as me not trained in the world of dentistry, as we say?"

"Correct. To the layperson, the burial jawbone shows a hairline fracture. The best way to describe it is to say it looks like a hair strand accidentally landed on the jawbone when the x-ray was taken."

"And now, Dr. Daniels, going back to page twelve, the x-ray from when K.C. was five years old, is there any indication that at that time K.C. suffered from a hairline fracture to the jawbone?"

"No, absolutely not. And upon further examination, the hairline fracture that is indicated on page twenty-four, in the excavated jawbone, that x-ray indicates that the fracture hadn't healed completely at the time of death."

"Doctor, does that indicate that K.C. experienced a significant blow to the jawbone at some period before his death?"

"Yes, very shortly before his death. I couldn't determine for you the exact amount of time before his death, but yes, he was struck in the jaw at some point within days leading up to his death."

"Was it likely that that blow was the cause of K.C.'s death?"

"No."

"And how do you arrive at that opinion?"

"I called Investigator Yarman regarding this finding, and he reported to me that there were no blunt signs of force to the skull. It's very unlikely that a single blow to the jaw would be the cause of death. The jaw fracture could have only contributed to the cause of death. Meaning, there was a blow to the jaw, which caused K.C. to fall and strike his head, and it would have been that blunt trauma to the head that would have led to his death. But again, Investigator Yarman reported to me that there were no signs of blunt trauma to the skull. In addition, he confirmed that the ballistics lab verified K.C.'s DNA on the bullet that was recovered from the gravesite, which confirmed that K.C.'s cause of death was by a shooting."

"Very well. Does a hairline fracture, in your opinion, indicate abuse?"

Hagger's chair flew back. "Objection. Speculation."

No matter how quick Hagger flew out of his chair, the judge's reaction was always calm. "I'll allow it." The judge looked at the witness and added, "Dr. Daniels, please answer, in your opinion, what does a finding such as this indicate?"

"Yes, Your Honor. When I took into consideration the level of malnourishment that was indicated by K.C.'s bone density and the lack of oral hygiene that was apparent from his teeth, I would place a high probability on the fact that this child suffered from abuse, or, at the very least, severe neglect."

The witness's answer clicked on a memory in my mind. It was of seeing Bob beat K.C. I had the recollection in my mind before, but never in detail. I had never known the reason for Bob's rage, had never known why I couldn't run to K.C. and help him. But now the details came to life. I was living in my memory more vividly than the reality of the courtroom.

I was at the bungalow. It was the morning after the manager lady came to our place. The morning sun was peeking through a closed window, and the Tylenol bottle was sitting on the coffee table. The red label symbolized help for K.C. when it was dark the night before, but to Bob in the morning hours, it represented betrayal.

I was sitting on the floor watching it all unfold. I wanted to rescue K.C., be near to K.C. but I couldn't, I couldn't help. The memory froze in my mind so I could replay it all and take in the details. I sat propped against a wall, opposite the couch where K.C. was lying. Bob was pacing between us in the living room. I tried to push away from the wall and stand but I stumbled to the ground. My hands were tied, silver duct tape wrapped around both wrists.

Bob lunged toward me, seeing me stumble, yelling, his spit spewing, landing on my forehead. "Is that how I have to send you to bed every night? Your hands tied? Is that the only way to trust you, you piece of shit? Is it!?"

I shook my head wildly, crying out. "I'm sorry, I'm sorry. I thought she would help." And when I said the word "she," I stared at the Tylenol bottle, the red label yelling out to me what a mistake I made.

Bob gripped at his hair, returned to his pacing. His work boots pounded the carpet, ripping at the fabric strands. "Why did you guys fucking let her in!? How could you be so stupid?" He leaned over and yelled at K.C., "And you, you coward, you know better!"

I steadied myself against the wall again. My eyes bolted back and forth between Bob, the Tylenol bottle on the coffee table, and K.C., who was sweating, trying to rock his pain away on the couch with his knees tucked into his chest. I wanted to yell at the Tylenol bottle, how I hated it, how it hurt us.

"How fucking stupid you both are!" Bob's pacing got faster and faster, his face redder and redder. "Why in the hell would you let someone in our apartment? You both are so damn stupid!"

K.C. started crying. The stress of Bob's mood was breaking him. I knew the pain from his toothache was throbbing and aching, getting stronger and stronger. But with every cry K.C. let escape from his mouth, I shook my head, praying for him to silence the tears. Bob's anger was rising. I kept whispering in my mind for K.C. to … *Stop. Don't cry out loud. Don't even murmur a moan.* The silence of surrendering was the only way to slow Bob's anger, which was violently swirling around the room.

"We have to leave. That's what we have to do. We have to go. Leave. Now." Bob's eyes scanned the messy living room. "We have to take only what we can. We have to go. Now."

Confusion. I tried to follow his eyes around the room. *What does 'leave' mean?*

He looked at me, at K.C., at the Tylenol bottle. His fists started clenching. I knew what that meant. My body tensed. K.C. wasn't watching. I peered at K.C. with every ounce of intensity I had, hoping he would somehow sense my stare, but his eyes were closed. I begged in my mind for K.C. to open his eyes, *Look. Please look, K.C. Bob's fists are clenching.*

"It's all your fault." Bob lunged toward me with a closed fist. "All your goddamn fault!" I shuddered, hoping his rage would land on me, that he'd let me absorb the anger.

But he stepped back.

He turned to K.C. Looked at the bottle of Tylenol, evidence of a trespasser. He threw the bottle across the room. Feeling his own strength fueled his rage. He was launching into the realm of uncontrollable anger; I knew the signs. There was no pulling him back. He couldn't even help himself get out of it, and it was our fault, K.C.'s and mine.

Bob started spinning around, looking to send his rage somewhere. I wanted his fist to come my way. "We didn't mean to! It was my fault. My fault." He wouldn't listen. He swung at the glass table lamp. It flew across the room, right in front of my face, hit the wall. Shattered.

I cried out, my words falling on top of each other, "My fault. My fault. I did it. I did it. Please."

Bob's eyes weren't leaving K.C. though.

I yelled out again and again. "No. Don't. Please don't hurt K.C. It was me, my idea. I did it. Please." I knew what was going to happen. He took his last lunge forward …

… not toward me.

His closed fist pummeled right onto the left side of K.C.'s jaw. I heard the crack. Bob pulled away, stepped back. He had released enough rage to act with reason. His voice modulated, slowed. "We're leaving." He grabbed some clothes off the floor and stormed out of the bungalow. I could see he was headed for the van.

K.C. turned his head into the couch pillow, muffling his screams and cries.

I tried to loosen the duct tape tearing at my skin, but I was too weak—not in strength but in courage. Bob's rage was still in the realm of the unknown. It was smarter to stop my movements and stare at the front door, waiting for Bob to come back from the van. When he did, he slammed the front door behind him and stood in the middle of the room, towering over my frame, small for an eleven-year-old. He looked around to see what we were taking with us. He started his footsteps toward me. I tried to hide my coward tears, whispering, "I'm sorry. Please forgive us. We're sorry. Please."

"Are you sorry?" He leaned over me, his breath hot, his skin red, his dull gray eyes glossed over. "Are you sorry, Landon?" He grabbed my wrists, ripped the duct tape away. I swallowed the cries of pain as I looked at my skin, small beads of blood meeting up with one another to form a blood bracelet.

Bob's open hand slapped against the back of my head, "Get your coward crying brother in the van. *Now.* Or we're leaving him behind. Use the sleeping bags." I shook my head wildly. There was no leaving K.C. behind. He was a part of me. I jumped up and did as I was told.

I chased that memory with curiosity and what flooded in was the long van ride into Leigh, Nebraska. It was the recollection that Drysdale was looking for in the interview room asking if I remembered moving into the trailer with K.C. The van ride seemed like days. I was in the front seat, Bob's silent passenger. K.C. was in the back on a stack of sleeping bags, drowned in his fever sweat and trying to rock the pain away. We didn't look at each other, but we were together in trying to right the wrongs we created for ourselves by knocking on the manager's door.

"Tyler," my father whispered. I didn't jump. When I looked back up at the witness, I felt as numb then as I was when Bob pulled up to the gas stations and, instead of crying out for help to the cars at the gas pumps next to us, I started hating the world. I hated the fact that the rest of the world got their freedom while K.C. and I were stuck in ours.

"Tyler." My dad's hand landed on my knee. "Are you okay?"

I looked away from the witness to my dad. I couldn't give an expression. I whispered back, "I'm okay."

I lied. I really wasn't. I was rattled by the memory that surfaced, and I was fearful that there might be more forgotten thoughts that still existed. My father, Braide, everyone remained so confident that I had nothing to do with K.C. being hurt. But if that were so and they were right, why did this fear of the unknown exist inside me? I took a deep breath and pushed away the concern by telling myself that nothing I heard from the witness stand indicated that I was the one who had hurt my brother … the one who killed him.

Braide was still questioning the witness. "Dr. Daniels, we've had two eyewitnesses on the stand testify that they saw K.C. in pain. One witness testified that in her opinion K.C. was suffering from a painful toothache, and the other witness saw K.C. with a compress on his jaw and moaning in pain; again, the assumption being a toothache. Based on your examination of the dental remains taken from the Barker property, could you shed any light on the testimony to which I just referred?"

"Yes, I can. The diagnosis of a toothache is not accurate. If we can all turn to page thirty-two of my report, there's a picture of the dental remains."

The judge, Braide, Hagger, and the witness simultaneously turned the binders in front of them to page thirty-two. I was glad that I didn't have a binder in front of me. I wanted to put K.C.'s pain further and further away from my mind.

Braide took note of the judge's nod, indicating that everyone had arrived on the same page. He turned his attention back to the witness. "And Dr. Daniels, what does this picture on page thirty-two of your report indicate?"

"If you look at the lower jaw, along the exterior side of the teeth, you can see what appear to be holes. Those holes would have been right above the gum line, the soft tissue line in the mouth, where the teeth butt up to the gum area. The holes are not from any deterioration from having been buried for four years. Actually, these holes would have been in K.C.'s teeth when he was alive, no doubt causing severe pain, far beyond the level of discomfort that any toothache causes. And without the intervention of medical assistance, it's hard to imagine that the pain was able to be lessened or alleviated with any over-the-counter products."

"Thank you for that opinion." Braide kept his eye on the judge, making sure she followed along. When he got the indicator he wanted, he continued, "And can you tell the court what caused those holes, based on your expertise?"

"K.C. suffered from a chronic case of dental caries, a disease created by bacteria that eat away the protective enamel of the teeth. The caries, the holes I've indicated that we see at K.C.'s level would indicate that he had lived with the disease for many years. And because of the hygiene issues and lack of medical intervention, it clearly progressed to a chronic level.

I've been a forensic dental examiner for many years, and I have to say this is most certainly the worst case of dental caries I've come across."

There was a pause in the courtroom. Braide stood at the podium reviewing his notes. The judge had her head down, her hair pulled behind her ears, reading the report. The same with Hagger; he was silently sitting with his face buried in the doctor's binder.

I glanced over at the witness. She was looking at me. She leaned into the witness stand microphone. "I think that it would have been devastating for a loved one to have witnessed K.C. in the pain that he must have been in at the time."

Everyone in the courtroom looked my way: the court, Hagger, Braide, the bailiff, my dad. I felt the eyes of the people behind me boring into the back of my head. I didn't look around. I didn't even want to look at myself. Instead, I closed my eyes on the memory of driving in the van and looking back to see K.C. lying on the sleeping bags, rocking back and forth, trying not to cry because he knew that every tear he shed, I shared.

(48)

When we got back Friday afternoon to Colorado Springs, I was drained. I didn't share with my dad or Braide the memory about driving through Nebraska with K.C. in the back of the van on a stack of sleeping bags. The reason why was that neither of them understood how you could have missing links in your recollection that just popped back into place, and I didn't want my memories tainted and discredited. Braide had told me so many times that I was remembering things wrong. The thing he didn't get, though, is that memories come attached to feelings, and feelings don't lie.

But he was doing his job. And like he and my dad said, they were convinced that it's not that I didn't remember the day K.C. left; instead, it's that I wasn't there. Bob killed K.C., and it's Bob who was trying to escape a life in prison sentence. In a weird way, the memory I had in the courtroom while Dr. Daniels was testifying confirmed what my dad and Braide were saying. I wasn't responsible for K.C.'s jaw getting broken. No part of me ever hated K.C., and every memory that lives on inside me confirms what my heart already knew. There was never a day when I wanted to hurt my brother.

I got out of working my weekend shift. I didn't want to smile at strangers. I didn't want to ask people how they were doing when I was too tired to really care. I wanted to sit on my bed with my *National Geographic* magazine. I wanted to download music, listen to my iPod, and get lost in the Saturday morning hours. I wanted to spend my time doing things that had nothing to do with the past, the future, or the witness who was taking the stand on Monday morning, forty-six hours away in another state. I needed to stop questioning what life is about ... what my life *was* about. I thought about calling Tracie. But I left it at that: just a thought.

If I could talk to Palmer, though, I would have. That's the truth. I missed the Palmer talks more than anything or anyone.

With my iPod earplugs in, I didn't hear the knock at my door, just saw my mom. I hit the pause button and looked over at her standing at the threshold. She wasn't her normal jolly self. The reality was that she hadn't been since about two days after the trial started. The courtroom was sucking our positive energy away. At times, I wondered if my parents blamed me, but I dismissed it. I was too tired of wondering, worrying, and trying to think beyond the words and actions of those around me. I had to continually tell myself, *Life is what it is.* I gave my mom a nod, wanting to know what was up, why she was at my door.

"Honey, there's someone on the phone for you."

"For me?"

"Yeah."

"Who is it?"

"I don't know."

"That's weird." I hopped off my bed. My mom knew everyone who called for me, not because I told her but because she prided herself in knowing my business. Whether it was Henry Schlick, the grocery store manager, my tutor, that photography teacher I was taking the trip up to Pike's Peak with—everyone. She knew their voices, so for her not to know who was on the other end of the phone call was weird for us both.

I picked up the phone from the dining room table. "Hello?" My mom stood next to me, leaning in, staring at my face while I stared at the wall trying to figure out the voice on the phone.

"Hey," the person on the other end said. It was a girl. I didn't know who, though. My first thought was wrong number, but then I remembered they asked for me by name.

I said, "Hey" back, and then jerked my head, trying to nudge my mom away. It worked. She pulled back, but only as far as a cop standing at your window asking for your license and registration.

"Why aren't you at work?" The way the girl on the phone asked it, I knew she knew me, and it would be stupid if all of a sudden I said, "Hey, who is this?" Instead, I responded with, "I don't know. I'm just kicking back over the weekend, you know."

I tried to run through my mind who it might be while still listening to what she said. "I got your number from the work directory. I have to work 'til seven tonight. It's really slow. Kinda sucks, you know." The light bulb in my head turned on. It was Emmie from the deli. I responded, "That's cool. I mean, that way you can keep the deli counter clean and stuff, right?"

"Yeah, I don't know though. It's going by really slow."

"Cool."

My mom moved her head in front of me and mouthed, "Who is it?" Her eyes widened, and she gave me that excited nod that I hadn't seen in almost a month. If she were wearing her jewelry store, the symphony would have gone off. I looked over at her long enough to see she was mouthing, "I know it's a girl. Who is it?" I squinted and shook my head, trying to get her off my back. That's when I thought I heard Emmie ask if I wanted to meet up later. But I wasn't sure that's what I heard, and I didn't want to ask, because, like, maybe she was nervous and wouldn't repeat it. I turned my back to my mom and waved my hand behind me for her to go away.

Didn't work.

She was acting stupid and couldn't wipe her own smile away. I put my head down but heard the towel drawer open and close, and I knew she was making herself busy cleaning the kitchen counter that was already clean so she could eavesdrop. I lowered my voice into the phone. "Sounds cool. What's going on?" I tried to make it a random question in case I heard her wrong so I wouldn't look dumb.

"Some friends are meeting up at Billy Blake's, you know, the pizza place at the Springs mall. Or like if you want to hang out and see a movie, that's cool too."

"Yeah, that's cool. Maybe. I don't know if I can meet up, though. I'll let you know."

That's when my mom chirped up like a canary. "It's fine, honey, if you want to meet up, you know, go out."

So not cool. I rolled my eyes, clenched my jaw, and waved at her again … and again … hoping she'd leave the room. Didn't happen. Instead, she moved over to the kitchen sink.

Emmie was silent, and the only response I could think of was, "I'll call you back before you get off work and let you know."

"Cool. Later." She hung up.

I put the phone back on the hook and stared at the wall for a second. I knew when I turned around I'd have to deal with my mom's excitement. I shrugged my shoulders and dropped my eyelids halfway, hoping the nonchalant look would calm her down; it didn't. She ignored my body language and asked, "Who was it, honey?"

"Emmie, the chick who works at the deli."

"Oh, I know who she is. She's so cute. I knew she liked you. She asks me questions about you when I'm in the store."

My shoulders moved back, my eyebrows lifted. "Just great. Why are you in everyone's business?" I wanted to be mad, you know, to try to deflect the embarrassment that my mom walked around town advertising that she knew me, but she piqued my curiosity. "How'd she know you're my mom?"

"I told her."

That wasn't what I wanted to hear. Irritation crept forward to the tip of my tongue. I was trying to put the reins on a smart-ass comment that would punish her for being the nosy, always-in-my-business mom that she was, but she reacted quickly and saved herself. "She saw me talking to you, honey, and she asked if I was your mom. That's all."

I snapped back without a pause. "Whatever, Mom. Just don't talk to her anymore, okay?"

The phone call reminded me that I liked Emmie. I mean, like, I was still thinking about her after the night we left the kickback. Yeah, I kinda forgot about her because of the trial and stuff, but when I did think about her, I liked her.

"Okay. I won't say anything to her." There was no hesitation from my mom. No wondering why. No questioning why. Just complete agreement. Meaning she got what I was saying, which was that she wasn't going to be invited into my world if she didn't clue into my boundaries. The embarrassing feeling left. I told myself that whatever Emmie and my mom had talked about, it couldn't have hurt, because Emmie called me.

My irritation was calming down as the excitement of hanging out with Emmie took over. I stood by the phone with my hands in my pockets, watching my mom line up the jars she kept the coffee, sugar, and flour in. Her lips were shut tight, her eyes still wide. I knew she was fighting back a smile and wanted to explode with some nosy question about where Emmie and I might go. I laughed inside, knowing that she was trying, in her way, to behave. I decided to have a little fun with her by using a tone in my voice that said it was no big deal, almost as if I wasn't interested in going to see Emmie. "Yeah, Emmie invited me to the movies, but I dunno. I gotta see what's going on tonight." I kept a steady eye on her. She wouldn't look over at me, but from the side, I could see that her lips were quivering. She was dying to open up and give me some kind of convincing advice, pleading that I should go. Instead, she moved to the dishwasher and started pulling out clean plates. I wished I had a stopwatch so I could bet myself how long she would stay silent. Maybe it was fifteen seconds, probably more like five or six before her first comment came. "Well, think about going, honey. You might have a nice time. You never know."

"I doubt it." I dug my hands deeper into my pockets and locked away my smile. She dropped her head lower and moved on to the silverware, separating the forks and knives. Everything about my mom when I'm in the right mood made me laugh. I had to keep the game going. "Or I don't know, maybe I should go to the movies with her. I gotta think about it."

I knew that it was taking every ounce of her extra pounds around the waist to keep her from bouncing off the walls with excitement. Her voice was as dull as she could make it when she replied, "Well, why don't you grab some cash from my purse, and the keys are in the car."

"Okay. Thanks, Mom."

I knew that she thought I left the kitchen because when she put the last fork away and turned around with that huge, beaming smile, I caught her by surprise. I had walked up behind her and when our eyes met, I said, "Wanna hug, mom?"

She nodded, wrapped her arms around me, and her tears started streaming in a good way. "I love you, Tyler. Everything will be okay, you know that, right? I know that. I love you so much. Your dad, too, he loves you. I just want to be here, be a part of your life, sweetie, that's all."

"I know, Mom." I let her body relax in my arms. And in between her sobs of joy, I understood the meaning of her words. She was happy that she didn't miss out on everything: car borrowing, cash begging, curfew breaking. She was all mixed up, you know. Her sobs were coming not only from the stored-up fear that she had missed all my teenage stuff but also from the joy of knowing that she hadn't.

(49)

The movie Emmie and I went to was stupid. We left early. The theater was in this huge mall in our area that everyone called Springs mall. When Emmie told me where the movie was playing, I felt stupid thinking about how I had only been to the theaters there with Mom, Dad, and Evan on Friday nights. I didn't tell her that, though. It sounded way too much like a loser, loner thing—but a different kind of loner than I was when my only friends were Sam and my John Deere hoodie.

After we left the movie, we walked through the closed mall. They locked up all the stores at night, but at the other end of the mall was Billy Blake's, the pizza place Emmie was talking about. There was a group that saw Emmie coming in. They all turned around to say "hey" to her. Two girls broke away and ran toward us. I started trailing behind so if I got word that I didn't belong I could in some way act like I wasn't really trying to—you know, just playing it cool. Then I heard my name. I turned around. It was the boyfriend and girlfriend I was talking to at the kickback about my Pike's Peak trip. For the next five minutes it was names and handshakes. And when it all settled, I was part of the crowd.

Then one real girly chick asked what school I went to. I tried to ignore her because even though I was a part of the group, there was this cautious feeling that at any moment the music would turn off and the crowd would get quiet and separate, leaving me alone in the middle. Then someone would unmistakably point at me and with an authority that everyone listened to would tell me that I didn't belong.

The chick asked again what school I went to.

I acted like I didn't hear her.

She asked again.

Emmie leaned over and said it like it was no big deal, that I was "home-schooled." I had told Emmie I was being tutored for my GED. I didn't use the word "home-schooled," but I guess you could call it that. I just nodded at the girl, hoping Emmie's answer was enough and the chick would get off my back. She didn't. She wanted to know more. "That's so intense, dude. Do you, like, have to sit there one-on-one with your teacher?"

"Yeah."

"Do you get to sleep in?"

"No, I tried at first, but the tutor guy was sitting at my desk when I woke up. Freaked me out." She started laughing. Someone else asked me a question. Then a friend of that guy knew someone else who was homeschooled. The crowd didn't part. Instead, I moved closer to the center. And before Emmie and I left, I found out that my GED tutor had been a science teacher at Mitchell, where Emmie goes to school, and that everyone thought he was cool but they heard that he quit teaching there because the principal was a real dick.

When Emmie and I left Billy Blake's, we went out into the parking lot instead of walking back through the closed mall. The front of the restaurant that you saw from the parking lot had all these windows so you could see everything that was going on inside the pizza place.

I looked back as we were walking away, and I saw the group of friends that we had just left. The corners of the restaurant were empty, the tables dead, but in the one area where Emmie and I were hanging out, it was like an invisible circle that clustered everyone together. I was in that circle. I still felt weird, like I didn't belong, but I knew for sure I was accepted, if that made sense.

Emmie was already talking about something: the movie, work, I'm not sure. She did kind of talk a lot, but I liked it. It told me what her mood was about, and I liked hearing how she saw the world.

I gave the front of the restaurant one more scan, one more look over at the empty tables. A year ago, I would have stood where I was in the parking lot hating on the people inside, convinced that my world was way too different from theirs.

I looked over at Emmie. She hadn't stopped talking, and honestly, I hadn't started listening. But she was my link to a world that I could join, and I really liked her. I wanted her to like me. I wanted the friends I left at Billy Blake's to like me. I wanted the world to like me. For the first time, I liked the world.

We hung out in my mom's car in front of Emmie's house for close to an hour. Her house isn't as perfect as the kickback house that I went to the weekend before. It's in a nice neighborhood, and it's bigger than our house, but my mom's flowers in the front yard are nicer than the ones at Emmie's house. And they should be because I'm always wheelbarrowing the cow shit for my mom on Sunday mornings. I caught myself thinking that way. I stopped it. How can the house someone lives in or the car they drive tell me anything about the person they are?

When Emmie asked what I was thinking, I told her. She knew what I was saying. But the thing about Emmie is she doesn't just say, "Yeah, that's how I feel, too." Instead, she would tell me a real-life story that proved that that's how she felt. She was telling me that her sister's friend's parents bought this thousand-dollar wallet or something for their kid. And when the rich friend would come to pick up Emmie's sister, all she did was talk crap about her friends.

I asked her, "She hates on her friends?"

"Yeah, I'm serious. I'm always like, to my sister, you know, 'Don't you think she talks shit about you when you're not around?' But I feel like just because she has this expensive wallet and nice car, my sister thinks that her friend is better than everyone else, you know. It bothers me."

"What's your sister say?"

"She's always telling me that I don't understand her life because she's so much older than me. I mean, we're only two years apart. It's stupid."

"Yeah, that sounds pretty messed up. She should listen to you."

Emmie's eyes lit up. "Really?"

"Yeah, I mean, you make sense, the way you see the world. I think that's cool. And you're serious about your future, like what you're gonna do with yourself."

"Really? My sister seems perfect, you know, and all her friends act like they're so much better than everyone else … I don't know, I don't want to be like that, and I don't like it when my sister's being like that."

"But I mean you get stuff, you're not like the girls I knew back at my old school. You know what's up. You've got high school dialed in."

"Really? Thanks. That means a lot coming from you." She looked down at her hands. I think she was blushing because she didn't know how to take a compliment. I could hear that her cell was buzzing in her purse, text messages coming through, but she ignored them and sat crossed-legged in the passenger seat. She started playing with the buckle on her shoe and her voice was soft. "I like hanging out with you, Tyler. I feel like I can be myself." Her head tilted to the side and her smile made all her words come alive. I realized then that I actually really liked Emmie. She gave me this feeling like I was meant to be in the world, in that place and at that time. She reminded me of Palmer in that way, and it made me not want to be away from her because I knew I'd miss her like I do Palmer. And I wanted her to know about me like I wanted to know about her. I didn't share everything, though. I decided I would start from the end and work backwards, so I wouldn't say anything too weird too soon. "At my old school, I got high all the time, you know. Like going to class was stupid. I didn't get what school was about it. And I got kicked out."

"You got kicked out of high school?"

"Yeah."

"But you're so smart. Why?"

"I had so much anger in me that I didn't care anymore. It was like I walked around and I wanted to explode and hate on the world around me every chance I got. And getting high in a weird way was helping me, you know. But then I had to ask myself, what am I doing? I mean, not right away. I had a lot counselors and people involved, but in the end it was me. Like, I had to keep asking myself, what am I about, you know? And most of the time I couldn't answer myself. I had to get used to this feeling like I was in space, not attached to anything that was valuable to me. That's what's cool about you."

"What?"

"Like, you're just Emmie, not trying to be somebody else. You know who you are, and I feel like I'm almost there, too. I'm working on some goals and stuff."

She opened up to me. "I had to go to a counselor last year and tell her about my feelings with my sister and stuff."

"Did it help?"

"Yeah, totally." She looked over at me, smiling, but not a laughing smile. Her eyes had this happy gloss in them. I was hoping she recognized the same about me. I leaned over toward her to see myself in her eyes. She tilted her head to make it easier.

I kissed her.

Her hand gently rested on my cheek. I felt her shoulder moving closer to me. Her lips, so soft and smaller than mine. I slowly pulled back, making sure it was okay, and I wasn't taking something I didn't deserve.

She took out her cell to check her text messages. I put my hands on the steering wheel to slouch my shoulders forward. I wanted my T-shirt to loosen around my chest so she wouldn't see my heart racing, begging for her touch.

A light in one of the bedrooms of her house went on. She knew she needed to go. I knew it, too. She put her cell back in her purse, not responding to any of the messages, and looked over at me. "Wanna hang out tomorrow?"

"Yeah." I didn't hesitate. "My brother has a Little League game that I gotta go to."

"Where at? Over at Sydley? I used to play soccer there."

"Yeah, wanna meet up there?" My mom's overly happy face flashed in front of me with Evan's Little League game as a backdrop. Her nosy questions bombarded my brain, as I imagined Emmie walking toward us as we sat on the bleachers. I wanted to take back my offer about meeting up at Sydley, but I didn't because I didn't want Emmie to get confused about why I would be changing things up.

She responded right away with, "Yeah, cool. I'll text you."

"Cool." I saw her hand reaching for the door handle. I wanted to touch her lips before the night air flooded the car. I reached over and whispered, "Hey." She responded with her head turned and her body leaning toward me. I read the sign. *We kissed again.*

(50)

On Monday, everything started out wrong. My dad locked the keys in the car when we parked at the Colorado Springs airport. He tried to blame my mom, but it didn't work. She fought back. Their argument in the middle of the parking lot made us run late for our flight. Then, after we checked in at the airline kiosk and got through security, the monitors flashed that our plane was delayed two hours. That meant we couldn't go to the hotel first, and when we landed in Omaha, we had to grab our luggage and change into our courtroom clothes at the airport.

We got stuck in bumper-to-bumper traffic getting into downtown from the airport. My dad couldn't sit still and kept trying to rush the taxi driver to go faster, tailgate if he had to. I sensed he just needed to talk to someone, and the taxi driver was an interim friend. He didn't want to irritate me, and my mom was giving him the silent treatment because of the sarcastic comments he made about her losing everything she owned and how that somehow accounted for him locking the keys in the car.

When we turned the corner to the front of the courthouse, Braide stepped to the curb and welcomed us with a wave. I saw my dad's shoulders drop and heard a sigh of relief. Braide's assistant was standing behind him, and as soon as the taxi driver popped the trunk and we started climbing out of the sedan, Braide's assistant stepped forward to help unload our luggage. My dad went to lend a hand, still staying clear of my mom, but the assistant told him that Braide had him come by to grab the luggage and take it over to the hotel. By the look on my dad's face, I doubted I'd ever hear another complaint about how much Braide's legal services had cost us.

Meanwhile, Braide walked over to my mom and handed her a plastic shopping bag. She opened it and pulled out a new cell phone charger. She let out a little chuckle and said, "Thanks, Randy." My mom never charged her phone overnight—no surprise—but to make things worse, she couldn't find her phone charger before we left for the airport. She lost that, too, as my dad said. And right before she boarded the plane, her phone went dead when she was talking to Ronnie, who was giving her an update on Evan. He was home sick, throwing up with some kind of stomach flu thing.

Braide walked over to my dad, shaking one hand while gripping his shoulder with the other one. "Don't worry, Dale. I told the judge and Hagger you guys were running late. Court is in recess until eleven o'clock. No more rushing. Just relax. Everything is in order." Braide looked at me over my dad's shoulder, nodded, and then returned his attention to my dad. The words might have been meant for only my dad to hear, but everything about me was on hypersensitive mode. I didn't have to lean closer to hear Braide loud and clear. "They transported him over already. He's in a holding cell on the bottom floor. They'll bring him up right before he's ready to testify."

My stomach dropped. Braide was talking about Bob. All the crap that went wrong that morning from the time we woke up, I knew right then it was a blessing in disguise. Made to happen so I wouldn't think about what I didn't have the courage to think about. Bob and I would be in the same building, sharing the same four walls, breathing the same air. I lost my ability to focus on Braide's words.

My mom and dad were calming down, the taxi driver was leaving, but I wasn't escaping. Survival mode was kicking in so that all five of my senses were trying to shut down. It was as if the brain part of me was going to leave, just take off, and the shell that was my body would drop to the ground. I looked over at my mom. She was talking to Braide's assistant. I wanted to warn someone that if I fell because my legs collapsed under me, it's not that I was sick. It was because I left.

My eyes drifted away from my mom and traced the concrete sidewalk, thinking about what it would feel like to hit the ground as dead weight. Then I heard Tracie's voice in my ear, coming over my shoulder, guiding me by repeating all the advice she pumped into me at the center. I scanned my body, searching out where the anxiety was living. My lungs felt like cold steel. The anxiety had lodged itself in there and wasn't coming out, only delving deeper into my blood system, trying to get distributed over every inch of my flesh. Through my nose, I took in a slow, deep breath. I exhaled. I filled my mind with thoughts about Emmie. The kiss on Saturday night, the stupid movie we left early from, Billy Blake's pizza, talking to her in the deli ... the anxiety was diluting. I was staying. Every thought of Emmie brought with it a good feeling, and I used those sensations as a glue to keep my mind in my body and create the desire to fight for my stability.

Braide's hand landed on my back. "Tyler, are you ready?"

"I guess."

"Good answer." He opened the door to the courthouse and ushered me in. My parents walked behind us. I only heard about every other word, but I got the gist of what he was saying. Bob would be kept in handcuffs and ankle shackles. He'd be wearing an orange jumpsuit. He was not to intimidate me. It would be better if I could stay in the courtroom. I would be testifying. On the every other word I didn't hear, I was breathing in through my nose, out through my mouth, and running through my mind like a photo album Emmie's kiss, the movie we saw, Billy Blake's pizza, and the two of us at the deli.

(51)

There was a door behind the witness stand, across the room from our table. The knob turned. The door swung out. A bailiff stepped through the threshold and put his foot against the door to keep it propped open. One hand was resting on his gun and the other was giving a "come on" signal to someone. *That someone was Bob.*

No beard.

His face down.

Long messy hair. Gray.

His feet shackles clanked.

His walk was a shuffle.

Taller than anyone else.

Bigger than I remembered.

I looked away.

There was a bailiff behind him and two more in the courtroom, one of those behind my dad. The clerk swore Bob in. When he said in his low voice, "I do," the bailiff pulled the witness chair out. Bob sat. He held his hands at his chest, handcuffed and chained around his waist. The bailiff pushed his chair in. Poured him a glass of water. Bob looked up at the bailiff and lifted his manacled hands, but the chain around his belly yanked them back down. "How in the fuck will I drink that? You gotta straw?" He chuckled.

No one laughed back. The bailiff looked up at the judge. The judge looked at Bob. "Mr. Starker, you will respond in my courtroom when asked to respond. You will not volunteer remarks, and you will not use foul language."

I stared at the chains that linked his hands. I didn't think there was anything in the world that could hold back Bob's rage. I was hoping that I was wrong, but my sweaty palms were telling me I was right: *Nothing stops him.* He grumbled at the judge's comment. The long gray hairs around his face stuck to his sweaty forehead.

He found me in the courtroom and didn't move his eyes away. I felt his anger. And I wasn't deflecting it. Instead, my first thought was to allow him to unleash it on me, to sacrifice myself like I had for so many years. I was supposed to be his release, the place to store his anger. I was merely the flesh that lay in its path, praying his aggressions would leave quickly.

Chains and handcuffs.

Bailiffs with guns.

I looked away.

The judge leaned into her microphone. "Mr. Hagger, it's your witness. You may proceed."

"Thank you, Your Honor."

My mind started arguing with me, saying that I deserved Bob's anger. I tried to yell back and defend myself. I looked at my clasped hands resting in my lap. I looked at how my fingers interlocked and brought my wrists side by side. *My wrists.* I stared at my wrists. Like two puzzle pieces fitting together, there was the blood bracelet scar from the duct tape binding during K.C.'s beating. I used that evidence as fuel. I took my mind back to the memory of Bob punching K.C. in the jaw. I replayed the memory over and over, until my heart rate increased, my hatred toward Bob swelled, and the defenseless voice in my head died down.

(52)

"Robert Bernard Starker, my name is Keith Hagger. Please tell the court what federal prison institution you are housed in."

Bob's dull eyes slowly scanned the courtroom, making their way toward the judge. The stare was lifeless, devoid of emotion. His eyes went across my face with no acknowledgement. A strand of his long, disheveled gray hair fell in front of his left eye as he leaned forward into the microphone, looking up at the judge. His words were slow and the syllables clearly pronounced. "Leavenworth, Kansas. Great place." He chuckled. The judge had no response. She motioned with her hand for Hagger to continue with his questioning.

"Mr. Starker, is it true that you were taken into custody sometime last year around this time?"

"I surrendered."

"You surrendered yourself to the FBI; is that correct?"

"That's what I said." Bob leaned back in the chair. His handcuffed wrists rested on his belly. I thought he would have been thinner from prison, you know, with no beer or frozen TV dinners. Or maybe it was the orange jumpsuit that made him look bigger. Whatever it was, he still looked larger than life in an ass-kicking way. He tilted his head to the side, and the unruly strand of hair blocking his eye moved away. The intent of his gaze was to study Hagger. I knew the look.

Bob hated educated people. His favorite saying was, "Big words don't give people big power." He lived by the principle that the angrier the man, the bigger his presence. And nothing inflated his sense of self more than his guns: holding them, touching them, talking about them. He'd pet them and talk about the ways he owned the world when he held a bullet between his fingers. I wondered if Hagger knew what Bob's stare was about; I doubted it. No one in the courtroom knew Bob like I did. Head tilts; lazy eyelids; small, slow nods … all were signs of pending doom.

Hagger's voice wasn't rattled, though. "And Mr. Starker, what prompted you to surrender to the FBI?"

Bob sat there, staring. No answer.

"Mr. Starker, did you hear my question?"

Bob dropped his head down slightly, leaned forward, and looked up. The bottom half of his eyes remained barely visible behind his drooped lids. "What do you mean, what prompted me to surrender?"

"Excuse me? What do I mean? I'm asking you why it was that you turned yourself in to the FBI."

"Why didn't you ask it like that?" Bob glared at Hagger.

The judge interjected, "Answer the question, Mr. Starker."

Bob leaned back in his chair. Paused. Stared at Hagger. "I had to clear things up."

Hagger sighed. "What things, Mr. Starker?"

"I knew the Roberts kid would be lying to the FBI."

He didn't call me Landon? I cried out in my mind. He wouldn't look my way. My body swayed back and forth. My eyes jumped away, looking at things around me. I didn't know how to process the feeling. I felt hurt in a twisted way. He made me feel like an outsider, an outsider to his world. *But why do I care? I hate myself for caring.*

My own reasoning, within seconds, snapped away my confusion. I cared because *Landon* wanted to unleash his anger on Bob. I wanted my rage toward him to radiate out of me and for him to absorb it. How do I do that when my existence was denied, erased? When he referred to me as someone who was never part of his world? I let it be, calming myself down, trying not to care.

Hagger's next question came on quick. "And Mr. Starker, what did you think that Tyler Roberts would be lying to the FBI about?"

"About killing my son."

"*What?*" It slipped out under my breath. "He was my brother before he was your son," my voice raised. It was Bob who forced me to forget about K.C. Bob was the one who sent K.C.'s memories away. "Why are you saying it like that?" My words spoke out before the thought formed. Braide's hand slapped against the front of my chest. The judge leaned forward, her attention on me. Bob didn't flinch. Didn't look my way. The bailiff behind my dad took a step toward us. Braide stood. "I apologize for my client's outburst, Your Honor."

The judge gave me a polite smile, nodded. "Mr. Roberts, please contain yourself. There's a process as to how the information has to get onto the record. Okay?"

I nodded to the judge but stared at Bob. He wasn't hearing me. His stare remained off in the distance. He was looking toward Hagger, but his eyes were cold and deserted, detached and unreachable to me. Hagger continued. "Mr. Starker, when you say 'my son,' who are you referring to?"

"K.C."

"Kennedy Charles Nelson?"

"K.C."

"But K.C. wasn't your biological child, was he?"

"His mother gave him to me. Deborah Nelson. She didn't know who his real father was, but she wasn't fit to take care of him, and so she gave him to me."

Hagger gave the judge a quick glance, a lifted eyebrow. "Mr. Starker, we had Deborah Nelson on the stand. She testified that she and K.C. were living with you but that she never gave permission for you to take K.C. Instead, she assumed that when she was arrested, you would return K.C. to his grandmother."

There was no answer and Bob wasn't indicating there would be.

Seconds went by. A full minute.

Bob leaned forward into the microphone. "Is that a question?"

Hagger responded, "I'm trying to clarify the record, sir."

When Bob was in control of his anger and thinking straight, his eyelids rested halfway closed and his facial muscles would relax, dropping any hint of how the abuse would come at you. I had to stand tall in front of that body language so many times. Bob would challenge me to look away when he stared at me like that. That's kinda the wrong word, actually. It was more like his body language announced, "See what happens to you, kid, if you turn your back on me." That's actually the best advice I can give someone: never turn your back on an angry man.

Hagger didn't read Bob's reaction the same, though. "Can you clarify your answer, Mr. Starker?"

"She left her kid in the middle of the night. I gave him a home."

"And Tyler Roberts, how did he come to live with you?"

No answer.

"Mr. Starker, did you hear the question?"

"Yeah, I heard it."

"Could you please answer? How did Tyler Roberts come to live with you?"

A pause.

The first sign that he was answering was a huffing sound through his nose. The microphone picked it up and spread his breath out like a filthy blanket covering us all. The answer finally came. "It was a mistake."

Hagger jerked his head back. "A mistake?"

My mom gasped.

My dad cleared his throat.

Bob chuckled.

Hagger asked, "Can you tell us what you mean by 'a mistake'?"

Bob leaned forward again and towered over the microphone. The courtroom stood still, ready to hear his explanation. His heavy breathing echoed off the courtroom walls. I felt his presence all over me; nausea coated my senses.

Hagger repeated the question. "Mr. Starker, can you explain your answer?"

The seconds spread into a minute. Bob's voice lowered. His speech pattern slowed. "I said, it was a mistake."

"But sir, what do you mean by saying it was a mistake?"

Bob answered right away. "You don't know what a mistake is?"

"It's not that. It's that I have your plea agreement with the FBI. And it's my understanding that you pled guilty to abducting Tyler Roberts."

"So what's your question?"

"I asked you how Tyler Roberts came to live with you and your answer was that it was a mistake."

No answer.

Hagger looked over at the judge. He needed help. He took a quick back and forth pace behind the podium. "Mr. Starker, are you serving a sentence at Leavenworth federal penitentiary for the kidnapping of Tyler Roberts?"

"You're the one with the plea deal in front of him."

The judge didn't miss a beat. "Mr. Starker, answer the question."

He responded with a long, single syllable, "Yeah." He looked around and then added, "Yeah, I pled to that mistake."

Hagger shook his head. "And why did you enter that plea deal if the abduction of Tyler Roberts was a mistake?"

The courtroom fell silent.

Bob wasn't answering.

Hagger ended the awkwardness. "I'll withdraw that question and get at it this way. Mr. Starker, why did you accept a plea deal for the kidnapping of Tyler Roberts?"

"I told you, I knew the Roberts kid would lie about killing my son. I wasn't gonna be framed for the murder, so I told that Drysdale guy at the FBI everything that happened. I turned myself in so I could tell the truth."

Hagger looked relieved, like he was back on track with his questioning. He turned over a page in his notes and took a few seconds to read his handwriting. Bob leaned back in his chair with the same detached eyes. His stare stayed on Hagger as the next question came his way. "Mr. Starker, I'd like to direct your attention to the days leading up to the killing of K.C. Nelson. In the days before K.C. was killed, where were you living?"

"Leigh, Nebraska."

"In the trailer on the property owned by Evelyn Barker?"

"Yeah, that's the one."

"And how long had you been living there before K.C.'s killing?"

"Not long."

"Do you know how long?"

"No. Don't remember."

I started to calm down. His testimony was linking up with my recollections, and the rhythm of the questions and answers, quick and precise, kept me in the courtroom and out of the stirring chaos of unresolved emotions.

"And Mr. Starker, were you living in Coleridge, Nebraska, before moving to the trailer in Leigh?"

"Yeah."

"And was the name of that place the Cordia Bungalows?"

"I think so. Could've been."

"We've heard testimony from the manager at the time that you and the boys lived at the Cordia Bungalows. Her testimony was that Tyler Roberts came to her house in the middle of the night because he, Tyler, was concerned about his brother who appeared to be in pain from a toothache."

Bob bolted forward. "They weren't brothers." His voice rumbled over the microphone.

"Excuse me?" Hagger looked up from his notes.

"The Roberts kid and K.C., they never got along. Don't call 'em brothers."

"What?" I tried to keep it a whisper. Braide heard me. *How could Bob say that?* My mind pulsated with memories: wrestling matches and pillow tents in the living room, tuna sandwiches, TV shows, the two of us helping Bob refurbish guns. I couldn't keep my anger in. The words spewed out. "No, you called us brothers. How can you say that!" Bob wouldn't look my way. His mouth hovered over the microphone. Breathing in and out, in and out.

Braide's hand rested on my back. "Tyler, please."

I looked around the courtroom. A surge of anger shot up through my spinal cord. I hadn't told Braide or my dad about the van ride and K.C. lying on the sleeping bags, but the memories told the truth. The feelings that came with them didn't lie. Bob needed to acknowledge the reality that he created, that he was responsible for. My heart started pounding, thriving, fighting.

Braide's voice came again, saying, "Tyler, calm yourself down. His lies don't matter."

But they did matter.

I stared with anger at Bob. My palms perspired. My eyes tried to pierce into Bob and make him feel the rage I had toward him for beating K.C., for hurting K.C. My jaw was clenching. Nostrils flaring. I stared at him like I should have every time he took a part of me away, every time he crushed me, humiliated me. How I had to become Tyler Roberts with screwed-up remnants of Landon Starker inside me. He needed to pay for it, and now—now he was denying me my brother?

While Hagger's questioning continued, my rage was building, swelling, festering. I barely focused on Hagger's words. "Mr. Starker, why did you move out of the bungalow in Coleridge?"

"I found out that there was a job at a dairy farm. I headed out to Leigh with what I could take in the van. It didn't have anything to do with that manager lady."

"That's not the truth." I shook my head back and forth wildly. I couldn't let Bob's lies sit out there in the world. "We left with sleeping bags in the van. With K.C. lying on the van floor in his fever sweat. You're not telling the truth! You were yelling at me to shut K.C. up or he wasn't going to go with us. You were going to leave him."

Braide grabbed my shoulder. "Stop, Tyler."

"No, I can't stop! K.C. was sick and you punched him in the jaw. You were mad that the manager came to our place."

Bob sat with a blank look, staring into the distance. No words. No expression. No eye movement.

The judge's tone was stern. "Mr. Braide, control your client. Mr. Roberts, you cannot speak out like this."

I tried to bolt up out of my seat. "But this isn't how it was. K.C. was my brother." The bailiff's firm hand landed on my shoulder. Didn't matter. I wasn't going to be held back. No one was going to take my voice from me.

I yelled out.

I hollered.

I wanted to be heard for all the times Bob's abuses made me silent. "You even called us brothers!" I shouted out every detail. I didn't care if the words were landing on courtroom ears. It was all directed at Bob. My sentences were broken but the rage in my words was understood. The duct-taped hands, scarred wrists, bedroom abuses, the Tylenol bottle, the crack of K.C.'s jaw, the clicking sound of guns at my temple … *I said it all*, and I repeated it *all* over and over, louder and louder, shoving my anger into Bob's ears.

Bob's head started slowly turning toward me.

I froze.

I was eleven years old again. Punishment was coming. I had to brace myself.

His words didn't escape his mouth until his eyes locked onto mine. And in the time it took for his head to turn toward me, every person, sound, thing, and detail in the courtroom moved to the outer limits of my view. It was just Bob and me, face to face. I leaned forward, my body tensed. I was under his control. Everything about me, my breath, my beating heart, *everything* hinged on hearing his response. When he spoke, he said his words directly to my soul. "If K.C. was your brother, why did you kill him?"

(53)

"Let's step in here." Braide opened the door to the conference room down the hall. It had the same feel as Drysdale's FBI room on the night I was taken from the trailer. Cold linoleum flooring, one table, six chairs, and a metal trashcan in the corner. Braide pulled out a chair for me, one for himself, and sat across from me. My parents stood off to the side, silently. "Tyler, we can't have outbursts in the courtroom. You're giving Robert Starker way too much energy."

"What do you mean? He's lying." My voice was still raised from my courtroom rage.

"What did you think he would do?" Braide's question caught me off guard.

"I don't know. I just—it's like when he talks, his words aren't matching up with how I know things went."

"He's a mentally sick man, and I'm saying that politely."

"But still, it's ... I dunno, it's like—" I stopped myself. Looked at my parents. I felt so in between, so conflicted between Landon and Tyler. I mean, I was Tyler Roberts, who worked at the grocery store, daydreamed about Emmie, and loved photography. But I still had parts of Landon inside me that needed to be acknowledged, that needed to be expressed.

Braide learned forward and lowered his voice. "What? Get it out. I need you to be strong when we go back into the courtroom."

"It's nothing. I just need a couple of minutes."

Braide bolted up. The momentum of his stand threw the chair legs screeching against the flooring. He turned around, looked over at my parents. "Dale, Cathy, I need a few minutes alone with Tyler."

My dad barked back, "No way, we're not leaving the room." My mom's response was louder. "Of course, Randy. We'll be right outside." She looked over at me and smiled, letting a tear freely roll out the corner of her eye. My dad followed behind her. I looked away, stared at the ground. I was

250

trying to look inside myself, but I couldn't get past this feeling of disgust. I couldn't explain why I cared about how Bob felt, why what Bob said on the witness stand affected me. I felt disgusted that I kept myself linked to him. As soon as the door closed behind my parents, Braide took his seat across from me. "Tyler, we've got about ten minutes to get you back on track. What's going on?"

"No, I'm cool. I just—I dunno. I'm being stupid, I guess."

"Tell me what you're thinking about."

"I don't know."

"Yes, you do know. Tell me. Now. We've got nine minutes, and I'm not losing control of the case when we're this close to victory."

"I just, it's that, it's just that I loved K.C. like my brother and the way Bob called me the Roberts kid, it hurt me. I mean, I want to be with my parents, I want the life I have in Colorado Springs, but it's like in a way it hurt when Bob was talking about me like I wasn't a part of that world, you know."

I hated myself for talking that way. I looked up at the clock. Any normal person would turn their back and write me off as too screwed up to care about. I kept watching the second's hand go from second to second without stopping. I was never going to be fixed. I was never going to be completely detached from Bob. *What's done is done*, I thought. At that point, I just wanted Braide off my back. "I'm being stupid. I just have to stop caring about how Bob makes me feel, you know? I'll be fine."

Braide put a heavy hand on my shoulder, making sure I didn't try to stand up and leave. "But you're not fine. I see it in your eyes."

I double checked to make sure my parents weren't around. It was only Braide and me in the room when I said, "I know what you're saying about Bob being a sick person, you know. I mean, the memories explain all that, and my brain gets it. But you don't really see that stuff when you're around the person, you know, and when you live with them … I dunno, when Bob was up there talking, I felt like I was back in the trailer. It's like I feel sick that I care about how Bob feels or how I react to his words. Why do I care at all about any of that? It's stupid. It shows how messed up I am, you know."

Braide sat and stared. Didn't say a word. Within seconds, more of what I felt spilled out. "Look, it's … it's like I spent so much time trying to make him happy, you know, make Bob happy. Sometimes I was able to, and I remember how he would be happy, which meant K.C. and I were happy. Like all I would ever think about was how Bob was thinking about things, how Bob would react. That makes me think I really cared about him. And then he gets on the stand, and he doesn't—he doesn't look at me and the way he talks about me … jeez, I hate myself. I'm so stupid."

"Why? Tell me why you think you're stupid?"

"It hurt me when he wouldn't even call me Landon." I couldn't hold back the sobs, but in my heart I knew they were black tears expressing a sadness that I shouldn't have. "I tried to be there for him, and he just sits there, and he hates me. That's it. He hates me and I don't know why … or I know why, you know, because the cops got him, but it hurts me. And I'm mad at myself that it hurts me. It's stupid. I wasn't ever trying to hurt anyone, you know."

"I believe you." Braide's voice was sincere. I pulled my shirt sleeve over my hand to wipe the tears. I took in a deep breath.

"Tyler, look at me." He nodded at me when our eyes met and paused, like he was about to say something that he wanted to make sure I understood. "Bob gave you life."

I froze. My stare iced over. "What do you mean?"

"Just that. He allowed you to live, and for that, you feel a deep sense of obligation to him. Maybe you define that as love or caring. I define it as an obligation."

"I don't get it."

"Because Bob could have killed you at any moment, but he didn't, he let you live—in a weird way, he saved you from death. He gave you life. You understand? But the flawed logic here is that all those years he was only saving you from himself."

I let his words sink in. Tracie and I had had similar talks when I described how I felt that Bob was still a part of me. I started to calm down. The part of me that was still Landon wasn't totally healed yet, and that's what was going on, I guess. Not that I had a double personality thing going on, but the Tyler I was growing into needed to help Landon through it, be the stronger part of myself.

Braide looked at his watch. "We have about four minutes. The best advice I can give you, Tyler, is that you were never supposed to be with Bob. Put aside the brother feelings for K.C., take that out of the equation, and when you look at Bob and the feelings come up, just tell yourself that if Bob hadn't kidnapped you, abused you, tormented you, you wouldn't be here today, and the reality is you *shouldn't* be here today. You don't deserve this. Your family doesn't deserve this. You shouldn't have the feelings you have, but Bob's abuse rewired you." He looked at his watch again. "Got it? He's a sick man. And I want you ready for my questioning of him. I'm not going easy on the bastard."

I smiled. Not a laughing smile, you know, but a smile that said to Braide, "I got it."

Braide stood and started for the door. "Oh, one other thing, we got the fingerprint report back. The shovel that was at the gravesite … you remember that, right, your gravesite? That's another thing to think about when you look at Bob on the stand. Anyway, we got the report and the prints on the shovel, just as I suspected, are Bob's. That will allow me to argue in closing that that alone shows that Bob has the intent to kill. Be ready to hear that, okay?"

"All right." I sat there with my shoulders slouched, tired from the outpouring of my emotions. Braide had his hand on the doorknob and his eyes on me. "We're all on track here, Tyler. And also, the gun that was found buried with K.C., your fingerprints are on that."

My heart skipped a beat. "What's that mean?"

"Bob's prints are on it as well. It means that you touched Bob's gun. It doesn't show anything or mean anything."

The gun that Bob kept on the nightstand and on his lap when he watched TV flashed before my eyes. I never touched Bob's guns. Bob's guns were off limits. Like that ranch worker who picked up the rifle and Bob shot at him for it, the same would have happened to me. No one touched Bob's guns. Braide didn't recognize my look of confusion. I barely got the sentence out: "But I never touched Bob's guns."

"Of course you did. You told me about how you helped him refurbish guns and that he had guns all over the trailer, right?"

I nodded. That was the truth. But a bigger truth was that Bob didn't let anyone touch his guns.

(54)

The courtroom was back in order. The bailiffs stood in their designated areas. The audience sat, silenced. I glanced over at Bob. Immediately, my eyes jumped over to the judge, who was giving a direction to Hagger: "Continue with your questioning, Counsel."

"Thank you, Your Honor." Hagger settled in at the podium. "Mr. Starker, I'd like to draw your attention to the moment you learned of K.C.'s death. Do you remember that day?"

Bob leaned into the microphone. "Of course. Like it was yesterday."

"Where were you?"

"At the trailer."

"Are you referring to the trailer on the Evelyn Barker property?"

"Yeah."

"What time of day was this?"

"Mid morning, almost lunchtime."

"Walk us through what you remember occurring that day."

"Okay." Bob flashed a look my way. It caught me off guard. My reaction was to lean forward, toward him, like he was a magnet sucking me out of my world and into his. Braide saw it happening and a quick hand against my chest planted me in my seat. I pushed my back against the chair and repeated Braide's advice. I needed to detach myself from Bob. I should have never been a part of his world. I was never supposed to be Landon Starker. The louder in my mind I repeated Braide's advice, the less meaning Bob's words took on. I kept my grounding.

Bob's glare turned to Hagger. He leaned into the microphone to deliver his answer. Unlike minutes before the break, his breathing was now in check and his voice normal, like he was having a conversation. It was the Bob I recognized from grocery trips and gun show conventions, the Bob who, on the outside, was only strange enough that people didn't care who he was behind closed doors. They just felt relieved when he'd walk away, and I'm sure they gave no concern as to why I stood behind him. At the time, with my John Deere hoodie and no eye contact, I could see how the outside world saw that I wasn't worth the community energy to save. I was a rotten teenager with dead morals. But whatever, with Braide's advice playing over and over, I sat and listened as a courtroom bystander. I sat and listened as Tyler Roberts.

"It was the first or second day when I started my job as the ranch hand at the diary farm. I was hired to be a supervisor, you know, to keep the equipment up, supervise the Mexicans. I left the boys at the trailer that morning, and I was coming back around lunchtime because I had to take … him—" Bob nodded toward me but kept his eyes on Hagger, "—to register at the school. I couldn't go earlier in the morning because I had to make sure the ranch was in order and that the workers—"

"Excuse me, Mr. Starker." Hagger put his hand up to stop Bob's word flow. "When you say 'him,' who are you referring to?"

No response.

Hagger went at it again. "Are you referring to Tyler Roberts?"

Bob gave a heavy exhale into the microphone. "Yeah."

"Okay. Please go on. You came back to the trailer. Was that during your lunch break?"

"Yeah, you could call it that. And when I opened the door, the front door of the trailer …" Bob's words drifted into silence as though behind his cold eyes there were detailed thoughts robbing his here-and-now attention.

"Mr. Starker?"

Bob didn't respond to his name. He only uttered a statement that described his senses. "I smelled it."

"You smelled what?"

"Blood. And I knew right away things were wrong."

"You could smell what?" Hagger's voice was raised.

Bob didn't repeat himself. "We still had moving boxes stacked in the living room, and the one box was open, except I hadn't opened it yet to unpack it. When I was still at the front door coming in, I called out to see who was there." Bob's eyes shifted side to side. He went to adjust his body in the chair but the chains dictated his movement. The shackles fell silent at Hagger's next question. "Who did you think would answer when you called out?"

"One of the boys. K.C. for sure."

"Okay. What did you do next?"

"The trailer had two bedrooms and—well, I'm sure you guys have pictures of it here, but I ran to the back bedroom. It was a small trailer. Fifteen, twenty steps for me to get across the living room to the hallway, and then down the hallway to the back bedroom. But the smell, it got stronger in the back of the trailer. I didn't see anything wrong in the back bedroom so I turned to come back into the living room. That's when I saw that the door to the spare room was shut. We hadn't moved anything into the room yet. I called out again for K.C. and Landon, but no one answered me."

He called me Landon. A shiver went through my body. The way he said "K.C. and Landon," it confirmed we were the unit I remembered: we were brothers, his brave soldiers. I let out an emotional sigh. I went to lean toward Bob's words, looking for more validation, but I caught myself. I planted my feet on the ground and pressed my back against the chair. I had to be stronger than that and refuse to acknowledge that dysfunctional part of myself that felt drawn to Bob.

"Mr. Starker, can you please continue?" It was Hagger's voice. "Did you open the door to the spare room?"

Bob nodded.

"Is that a yes?"

"Yeah." Bob leaned forward. *"And there K.C. was."*

The courtroom fell silent. It was a vague response, but in it were thousands of details. For the first time, emotions seemed to flood into Bob's eyes. Braide called it acting; I was afraid to say it, but I saw it as sincerity. Braide leaned over to me and whispered, "Don't buy into it, Tyler." I couldn't help it, though. Bob's word choices didn't sound like fiction.

"Go on, Mr. Starker." It was Hagger's voice.

"I opened the door and K.C. was there lying on a sleeping bag, dead. The blood, it was everywhere." Bob tried to raise an open hand to indicate how the blood splattering landed on the wall, but the chain yanked his arm back to his chest. It didn't break his concentration, though. It didn't send him into the realm of frustration. His words continued to flow out. "I knew right away he had been shot. His chest, the sleeping bag, it was all drenched in blood. So much that you couldn't tell where the bullet hit him." His words trailed off.

"And Mr. Starker, what did you—"

Bob didn't need Hagger's guidance. "I dropped to my knees. I was confused. The carpet was soaked with his blood. My jeans around my knee area, soaked."

My mind linked up with Bob's words. I remembered when he yanked me through the front door and I crawled into the kitchen to hide behind a cabinet door. When Bob lunged toward me, the first sign I had that K.C. was hurt was the blood on Bob's jeans, the circles of blood on each kneecap. An epiphany struck me about the recollection: Bob had K.C.'s blood on him; I didn't.

For the first time, I embraced my innocence the way Braide and my dad had done. Maybe it was true that the day K.C. was hurt, I wasn't at the trailer but instead came home in the midst of Bob's killing. The first thought when I came into the trailer that day was how Bob's rage was unleashed, and I wanted to link that up with the sight of blood on Bob's jeans. Maybe the rage came from his own actions just minutes before I came home. I started scrambling through my mind, flipping over memories, asking what I had been doing minutes before coming into the trailer.

The microphone picked up a swallow of emotions from Bob.

Braide smirked at the gesture.

I was consumed with my own thoughts, but I saw Bob look around the courtroom. His eyes weren't searching anything out. His expression was blank. His head was moving but his mind's eye was seeing the past. His speech slowed. "At first, I thought for sure it had to be one of the immigrant workers at the ranch, you know. I couldn't think straight. I started panicking, wondering where Landon was."

I was seeing in my mind what Bob was describing. I wanted to answer for myself where I was on the dairy farm when Bob was searching for me. He continued to detail the moment. "I ran through the trailer again, then outside, looking for Landon, calling out for Landon. I was thinking maybe the killer took him. I ran back into the trailer, toward the spare room. I knew that I was panicking, and I wanted to look around to see if I could figure out what happened. When I got back into the spare room, that's when I saw my gun, my Taurus nine millimeter lying on the ground close to the closet area, not far away from where K.C.'s dead body was." He gulped. He paused. "Then it all clicked into place."

Hagger didn't lose a beat. "What clicked into place, Mr. Starker?"

"It was Landon. Landon killed him."

The words escaped my mouth: *"No."* That burdening sadness that lived in my heart when I thought about what happened to K.C. weighed down my jaw. *"Don't say that, please,"* I whispered out loud.

Braide ignored me.

Hagger didn't hear me. "How did you conclude that, Mr. Starker?"

"I hadn't unpacked my handguns yet. The nine millimeter that he used to shoot K.C. was in that box that I saw was unpacked when I came in the trailer at lunchtime. Earlier that morning, I hung my gun rack and took the rifles from the van, but I didn't know where I was going to put the handguns, so I just left the box there, unopened."

I was listening to every word, but I couldn't stop my head from shaking side to side, nor did I share the same recollection knowing that the nine millimeter gun was in that moving box. I was backpedaling desperately through my memories, begging for disclosure.

Bob continued, unfazed by any courtroom expression. "And Landon was the one who helped me pack the handguns, so he knew where they were."

I didn't remember any of what Bob said. Braide whispered it was all lies, so not to worry because I wasn't going to find any of it in my memory.

Bob went on, "I realized then that no one else could have come in and killed K.C., because they wouldn't have known where my handguns were. The trailer would have been ransacked if they looked in the boxes and stuff. Or they would have brought their own gun."

Braide bolted up from his chair. "Your Honor, motion to strike. The witness is speculating about what the trailer would have looked like had he not been the one that killed K.C. Nelson."

The judge barked into the microphone. "Don't be cute, Mr. Braide. However, it is speculation. The objection is sustained. Next question, Mr. Hagger."

"Yes, Your Honor. Mr. Starker, did you confront Tyler Roberts about K.C.'s killing?"

"Of course."

"What happened?"

"I didn't know where he had been, but pretty soon after I figured out what happened, I saw Landon out of the living room window walking up to the trailer."

Bob's words went straight to my brain. Every detail he spoke, my memory confirmed. It was as he said. I just couldn't bring to surface the minutes before, the hour before I walked up to the trailer that day. I remembered walking up and seeing that Bob was looking out the trailer window toward me. As I replayed my memories, I listened intently to Bob's testimony. "As soon as I saw Landon turning the doorknob, I grabbed him and pulled him inside and started asking him what he did to K.C. I could tell that he was lying, though. He was trying to hide behind one of the kitchen cabinet doors."

I leaned over to Braide and whispered, "No, I wasn't lying ... I was confused. I remember being confused." Braide gave me a nod and mouthed to me, "I know. Don't worry." I turned my attention back to Bob's words. "Landon kept saying he didn't know, but I knew by the look on his face he was lying. I kept yelling for him to tell me, and the more he denied it or was acting stupid, the angrier I got. I was losing it. I couldn't believe he did that."

The last part of Bob's statement, where he said he was losing it, was his vague way of describing how he grabbed his rifle and thrust the butt of it into my ribcage. I remembered every detail of that. Not because of the pain, but because of the mixed emotions of how I felt when I passed out, looking at K.C.'s name written on the moving boxes, and knowing that K.C. somehow got to escape the hell I was still stuck in.

At that moment in the courtroom, my hatred for Bob started rising up in my throat. I wanted again to yell out in the courtroom, force Bob to speak of the details, admit the abuse. Braide leaned into me, "Are you listening to the testimony?" I nodded, barely coming back to the moment in time to hear Hagger's words. "And what did you do next, Mr. Starker?"

"I made the decision not to call the police because I wanted to help the kid out, the Roberts kid. And I knew the cops wouldn't get it right, so I started figuring out how to get rid of the body."

"I'd like to show you an aerial photo of the Barker property." Hagger put the tripod photo back up. "Is this the area where you disposed of the body?"

"Yeah, and the gun. I wrapped the gun up to make sure the Roberts kid's prints were on it because ..." Bob's dead eyes looked my way and found me. I tried to challenge the look with my own anger and rage, but he was taller, bigger, louder, and angrier than me. I looked away but heard his words. "I made sure I kept the prints on the gun so I wouldn't go to jail for a crime I didn't commit." Bob's eyes stayed on me until Hagger's question took his glare away. "And did Tyler Roberts ever admit to the killing?"

"No. He lied about it and kept lying about it, just like he's doing right now sitting there at that table."

Braide flew up from his seat. "Objection, Your Honor."

The judge responded, "We don't need your opinions, Mr. Starker."

It was an opinion, and Bob was wrong. I wasn't lying to him in the trailer that day. I was confused. I wanted to know what happened to K.C., too. I was confused by his rage because I walked in on it instead of anticipating it. I was eleven years old, and I remember begging for the truth. My confusion was looking to Bob for explanations, just like when I was seven years old, sitting on the coffee table, wondering why my parents didn't want me. When I walked into the trailer that day and ran into Bob's rage, it was still that time in my life when I thought Bob held all the truths ... *but no longer.* I looked over at my dad; I sat taller than him. My mom, I no longer stood at her belt buckle. I wasn't seven years old anymore. I wasn't eleven anymore. I told myself that I was almost a man, and I needed to confront my truths like one. I brought my stare back to Bob.

(55)

Hagger had about another forty-five minutes of questioning. When he was done, Braide made ready to get up and ask his own questions. Before stepping away from our table, though, he made me promise to sit there with my head down and my lips silenced. Like he said, we were too close to victory to have misunderstandings.

When Braide made his way to the podium, he went with no notes, no pen, and no pieces of paper. It was just himself but not empty-handed. He had months and months of preparation he was bringing to the podium and his confidence showed it. The content of his first question came as a surprise. The tone of his voice friendly. "Mr. Starker, it's my understanding we have something in common." Bob's eyebrows lifted. Braide gently smiled. "It's my understanding that you refurbish guns ... revolvers, rifles."

Bob shrugged.

Braide took to a slow pace back and forth behind the podium. "Is that true?"

Bob's eyes followed him. "I don't know what your hobbies are. But yeah, I refurbish firearms."

"My client, Tyler Roberts, whom you refer to as Landon, spoke of a Burnside rifle from the Civil War that he helped you refurbish; is that correct?"

Bob started to look my way but stopped. Looked back. "Yeah, that's correct." Quizzical.

"Did my client help quite often refurbish the guns?"

"Sometimes."

"And the times he did help, that would involve him handling the guns, correct?"

"Yeah."

"And the guns you had in your possession, the ones you owned, whether the rifles in the gun rack above the television ..." Braide paused in his pacing, looked directly at Bob, letting him know that I told of every abuse *in every room*. "… or the nine millimeter that you kept on the nightstand, did my client have opportunities to handle those guns?"

"No one touched my guns."

"But that wasn't your testimony just a minute ago, was it?"

"What do you mean?" Bob raised his tone. His voice boomed into the microphone. My fight-or-flight sensors kicked in. With my head looking down into my lap, I scanned what I could see of Bob's body, making sure the chains and shackles were keeping him in place.

"I'm the one asking the questions, Mr. Starker. But in this instance, I'll be happy to clarify. You testified, when describing how you knew my client was responsible for the killing, that, and I quote, 'Landon was the one that helped me pack the handguns,' implying that he handled the guns."

"Well, that was different. We were trying to pack things in—"

Braide cleared his throat. Bob stopped midsentence. Braide finished, "I haven't asked the question yet, Mr. Starker. That's how it works in a courtroom. I ask questions. You answer." Bob leaned into the microphone, his heavy breathing a backdrop to Braide's words. Braide kept his cool, though. Crossed his arms. Paused. Stood still and stared at Bob. "It's true, isn't it, that my client did help you pack the handgun that was used in this killing?"

"He went and got it and brought the gun to me. That's all I meant. He didn't handle it like you say when we packed the guns from the bungalow. He just went and got it for me when I told him to."

"You've answered the question, Mr. Starker. We're moving on." Braide took his signature slow pace back and forth. Bob's breathing was getting louder and louder. His neck muscles started twitching, his jaw clenching. Braide remained unfazed. "So, Mr. Starker, you didn't call the police when you found K.C. dead, did you?"

No response.

"And the reason you didn't call the police was that you, Mr. Starker, were the one with the blood on your clothing, true?"

No response.

"Or was it because it was your gun, with your prints on it as well, registered to you, that was used in the killing?"

No response.

"Or was it because you had broken K.C.'s jaw days before, and you just knew the police wouldn't quite understand?"

I looked over at Hagger. He sat there, expressionless, back hunched over, waiting with suspense for Bob's response. No one in the courtroom was Bob's friend, and I didn't feel like I had to be either. I brought to the forefront all the therapy and support sessions I had had. I straightened my back, inhaled slowly. I looked up. There was no more convincing myself. I knew I was entitled to hate Bob for all the things he did to me. I looked back over to Braide. He sensed my look, gave me a confident nod, and returned his attention to Bob. "Mr. Starker, I'm going to want a response for that question. Aside from having an abducted child in your possession, was the reason you didn't call the police because you had broken K.C.'s jaw in a fit of rage in the days before, and you just knew the police wouldn't quite understand?"

Bob leaned into the microphone. His steely eyes didn't waver from Braide. He huffed. Paused. "Fuck you."

Braide liked the response. He smiled back and said, "That answer says a lot. Thank you, Mr. Starker. I'll be moving on to another subject now." He took another few steps left and right. Stopped. Stared at Bob. "Instead of calling the police, you took matters into your hands; is that correct?"

No response.

"And it's true, isn't it, that you did that by knocking my client unconscious, which you forgot to mention in response to Mr. Hagger's question, correct?"

Silence.

Braide stopped his pacing. "Again, Mr. Starker, no response?" Bob didn't answer with words. Instead, he sent a lethal stare, but his chains rendered it meaningless, futile. Braide continued. "And it is true, isn't it, that once my client was knocked unconscious, you locked him in the back bedroom? The back bedroom where you forced my client to sleep with you?"

No answer.

I felt my father's body twitch, tense, and sway away from me. I didn't feel ugly hearing Braide's words, yet I understood my father's reaction. He was afraid to learn how the bedroom abuses affected me. Braide threw his shoulders back, his stature unwavering, and asked another question. "And then you waited until the evening hours and took K.C.'s body to the outskirts of the property and dug him a grave; is that correct?"

Bob hovered over the microphone, breathing through his nose. "You seem to know everything. I was helping the kid out."

"Oh. You were helping my client out, I see. Is it that, or is it that the abduction of my client wasn't a mistake, as you say, and you knew if anyone found out about the killing of K.C., you wouldn't just be charged with murder, but you'd be facing kidnapping charges as well?"

Bob stared at Braide; his deep breathing pounded into the microphone.

Braide didn't flinch. He moved around the courtroom with confidence, picking up the tripod picture of the gravesites and putting it in front of Bob. "Mr. Starker, if we fast forward four years, give or take, after the night you buried K.C.'s body to the morning you picked my client up from the police station, would I be accurate in saying that you felt things were unraveling, that the police might be closing in, and so you set out to dispose of my client just like you conveniently disposed of K.C.?"

Bob didn't respond.

"Let me rephrase it another way." Braide used a red laser dot to point to that area of the Barker property where the new grave was dug. "Mr. Starker, this shovel on the ground next to the tree has your fingerprints on it. There's been testimony that that excavated soil was so freshly dug that when the FBI located this area, the dirt was still unsettled." The red laser dot wiggled around the area Braide referred to. "This area here is where you buried K.C. That's true, isn't it, given that you testified to as much for Mr. Hagger, correct?"

No answer.

"That's fine. We have that testimony on the record. But to bring this line of questioning to a close, on the night that the FBI converged on the property, you were in this location digging a grave to dispose of Tyler Robert's body; Tyler, whom you were planning to kill, knowing that his contact with the police the night before was too close for comfort. Am I correct?"

No answer.

The judge leaned into the microphone. "Mr. Braide, would you like me to instruct the witness to answer?"

"No thank you, Your Honor. His silence speaks louder than his lies." Braide looked over at me. I caught his eye, letting him know I was fine. He nodded toward Bob. "And Mr. Starker, wasn't that the same motivation behind K.C.'s killing? That when—"

Bob broke off Braide's rhythm by blasting out a response. "Ask your client about the motivation."

The tone of Braide's voice didn't change. "But I'm questioning you, Mr. Starker."

Bob's eyelids dropped, his piercing stare intensified, and he started to rise out of his seat. The bailiffs leaned forward in their chairs. Bob settled. The courtroom settled.

"Mr. Starker, isn't it true that when you learned that the manager of the Cordia Bungalows had been in your apartment, had met K.C., met my client, that again, the police might be called and learn of your illegal activity, that that's exactly why you fled Coleridge?"

Bob's voice was lowered by the rage he was holding in. His vocal cords rattled. "I told you. I got myself a new job. That's why we left."

"And when you got to the trailer in Leigh, the stress of K.C.'s illness, the broken jaw that he suffered at your hands, and the fact that you knew Deborah Nelson never intended for you to keep K.C., all those things combined with knowing that if you got K.C. medical help, things might unravel further, *all of that* is what led to your decision to take K.C.'s life; isn't it, Mr. Starker?"

Bob's eyes scanned the courtroom. Our table. My father. Me. Behind us to my mom. To the back of the courtroom. The audience. Back over to Hagger. The bailiffs. I followed his stare, curious to see what he saw. His eyes came back to me. He was done. No more responses. And he sat there staring at me until the judge sent him away.

(56)

The next hour went by in fifteen seconds. Bob shuffled away, and I was put on the witness stand. The room looked different from the truth chair, and I didn't want to be there. I wanted to be in Colorado. I wanted to be with Emmie. I wanted to be doing a frozen-food section go-back. I wanted to be at my brother's baseball game. Or maybe more than anything, I wanted to know for sure I'd be going to his next one. Everything I wanted was miles away, almost another lifetime.

The witness chair sat on a platform above everyone except the judge, and when I looked around the courtroom, every glance I took I made eye contact with someone I didn't know but knew me. They were there for judging. They knew me through Bob's words and the words of every other person who had been sworn to tell the truth.

Braide's questions about my helping Bob refurbish guns seemed endless, but I understood why. Explaining how my fingerprints got onto the gun found with K.C.'s bones was the crux of my case. The only thing was that I kept wanting to follow up my answers with, "But no one touched Bob's guns." I started to worry that possibly leaving that out was lying or somehow preventing the truth from forming.

Before I took the stand, I had told Braide once more about how no one touched Bob's guns, but he bluntly believed that that fear was a remnant of Bob's abuses. He instructed me not to forget that Bob himself had testified that I packed the handguns when we left the bungalow. I took a few breaths and bought into that explanation. If not for me, then for my dad, for Braide, and for all the daydreams of what I thought tomorrow would bring. Every time the urge to clarify came up, I pumped my fist trying to reroute the compulsion to volunteer information. So I sat there with my fists hidden and repeated over and over in my head, *Just answer the question that Braide asks.*

I thought I would feel relief, you know, when Braide moved on to the next subject, but instead his words opened the door to a world that I had, until that day, been describing from the outside looking in. His words pulled me, pushed me, sucked me into Landon's world. I felt jolted. The questions kept coming in such a way that soon I was answering from the past, from Landon's perspective, and not the detached present of Tyler Roberts looking back.

Braide's voice was monotone and calm. "And Tyler, have you ever been known by any other name?"

"Yes."

"And what name was that?"

"Landon Starker."

"And do you remember how it came about that you used the name Landon Starker?"

I looked at my dad, at my mom. I wanted them there, but I didn't. The first day in Tracie's office popped into my head, how my dad refused to call me Landon, and how angered I was toward him because he wouldn't accept my world with Bob.

"Tyler?" It was Braide's calm way of demanding I stay in the moment.

"Yeah."

"Do you remember how it came about that you used the name Landon Starker?"

"Yeah. Yeah, I do."

"Please tell us in your words how that came about."

The judge's hand lifted toward me, palm open. I knew she wanted me to wait. She leaned into the microphone and asked, "Mr. Hagger, I assume you have no objection to the narrative?" Hagger slowly rose. His chair didn't fly back. "No, not at all, Your Honor. Mr. Braide and I spoke about this. It's apparent how Tyler feels on the stand, and I think a narrative format where Tyler can speak freely will help move the testimony along."

I was surprised. Hagger had hurled objection after objection when Braide asked his questions about how my fingerprints could have gotten on the gun, but his comment to the judge just then made it sound like he was helping me. My gaze stayed on Hagger after he finished speaking. He was giving me space to tell my story.

My heartbeat slowed even as it pounded harder.

My eyes trailed to the left toward my father. He sat at the defense table, scribbling notes and jiggling his foot up and down. If there was a way to shape the world by force of will, he was the kind of guy who could do it. When he set out to do something, whether it was to prove my innocence or to help me pack for my photography trip, he plotted out the path and stayed the course. He was an intense person who was always trying to push his intelligence. I had my mom's traits in that regard. I wanted to wait for destiny to unveil my purpose, fearing that forcing life's hand might set me off in the wrong direction.

While the judge, Hagger, and Braide discussed the court process, I replayed in my mind the telephone call to my father after the Drysdale interview night, and how from that night on, my dad and everyone had been so careful not to trigger unwanted memories for me. I felt grateful that his advice allowed me to shape my future and not dwell in the past, but the closer I started feeling to Landon Starker, the more pangs of regret started popping up like a Geiger counter reading radiation. I regretted not knowing the truth of my experiences, and it was shaking my sense of self, all the way at my core.

I forced my mind to jump from memory to memory, kind of like a teaser, you know, to prove I still remembered Landon's world. The thoughts were superficial though: walking on the dirt road to the school bus, emptying the trash at the trailer, TV dinner trays, empty Jack Daniel's bottles, Bob's boots by the front door, dried leaves outside the trailer, Jandro the ranch hand. There were hundreds of random thoughts about inconsequential things that came with empty emotions. The judge's voice swept the mental pictures away. I instinctively turned toward her, knowing that she was talking to me. "Mr. Roberts."

"Yeah?"

"Do you remember Mr. Braide's question?"

I shook my head.

She repeated it. "How did it come about that you used the name Landon Starker?"

"Oh, right." I looked back to Braide. I took in a deep breath, but like the reins on a wild horse, my pounding chest wouldn't hold back. I tried to make the words come out smoothly. "Not now, not today, you know, but when I was younger, eight or nine years old—" I heard my own sentences as disconnected and jumbled words strung together. I knew what I wanted to say and formed the words, but once they left my mouth, the microphone seemed to twist them. I couldn't think before I spoke, and the way my words bounced off the courtroom walls and came back to me, it was as if someone else were speaking. I forced another deep breath and pushed the microphone away, hoping the extra couple of inches would let me hear myself talk. I softened my fists and grounded my feet.

One more try.

It was Braide's voice. "The question is, how did you start using the name Landon Starker?"

"Right, I'm sorry." I paused. "Bob used to tell me how sad he was that my parents didn't want me, you know. He even would say that he tried to go see them and ask them to take me back, but that they refused. And, I mean, at my age now I know that sounds stupid, but when you're young, it's different. You don't figure things out the same way as you do when you're older."

The memory of sitting under the dining room table, hoping my mom was going to walk in behind Bob, slithered into my mind uninvited. I tried to fight the thoughts off with more recent memories of my mom, like her picking me up from the grocery store or eavesdropping on my phone calls with Emmie. I was unsuccessful. I wasn't getting back to the here and now. I had to accept I was in Landon's world.

A noise in the courtroom broke my train of thought. I looked around to locate where the noise came from. Braide was tapping his pen on the podium ledge. He was staring at me, waiting for me to finish my answer. I shook my head, lifted my shoulders. He recognized the body language and repeated his question. "And Tyler, when did using the name Landon Starker come up?"

"The lady that testified, you know, the manager of the Cordia Bungalows, she called a truancy officer because I was supposed to be in school. And when they came out to talk to Bob, everything was fine, but they wanted to make sure I would be going to school. I think Bob said we had just moved there or something, I dunno. But anyway, I was excited about going to school and Bob said if I went to school as Tyler Roberts, they would find out that I was a kid whose parents didn't want him, and instead of letting me stay with Bob and K.C., they would put me into foster care."

I wanted to search out my mom in the courtroom. I wanted to smile at her and have her smile back. I wanted something in her eyes to tell me she always wanted me. But before I could make it happen, Braide saw my eyes drift and, with his words, he stopped me. "Go on, Tyler. You had been with Bob about a year or more at that point?"

"Right. And K.C. and I, we wanted to make sure we all stayed together, so Bob said he'd get the paperwork that said I was his son, Landon Starker."

My voice dropped, and I don't know why I added the next comment, but I did: "And that felt good because they were my family then, you know."

Braide didn't expand on my answer. Instead, he moved forward with the questions he had typed out in his notes. "And did Bob get the same paperwork for K.C. so he could go to school?"

"No. K.C. had never been to school. His mom never put him in school, so Bob didn't either. And because he was older, you know, Bob said it would be too hard for K.C., and that the school would turn him into foster care for being so far behind in learning. And also, the bungalow manager lady that you had testify was right about K.C.'s teeth. Bob said—"

"Did you just remember that?" Braide's voice picked up, and I knew why. I couldn't count how many times Braide went over my testimony with me. How many times he checked and double-checked with me what my answers would be. He didn't like new information. He didn't want new information.

"Yeah, I remember now that K.C.'s teeth bothered him a lot."

Braide scribbled something down in his notepad. I didn't wait for him to finish. I wanted the chance to say more. "And Bob said the school would wonder about K.C.'s teeth, and why his mom didn't take him to a doctor. And if all that happened, his mom and my parents would get in more trouble. K.C. and I, you know, just wanted to make things right for everyone, and we believed Bob."

Braide moved away from the subject quickly. "And Tyler, did Bob abuse you and K.C.?"

I nodded.

"Is that a yes?"

"Yeah. I grew up thinking I deserved his beatings because I was so bad, you know. Everything clicked into place once I accepted my parents didn't want me. I mean, you have to be a pretty bad kid if your parents don't want you. I don't think that now, of course, because I know better. But then, that's how I looked at it. And Bob had this rage in him that once he snapped, he couldn't bring himself back. Like the jaw incident. I remember when that happened."

"You remember when K.C.'s jaw was broken?" It was a quick-reaction question from Braide, concerned again that I was taking us off course from the scripted question and answers. And I guess I was. I didn't have an answer why except that I wanted the truth out in the universe.

I answered from my memory. "Yeah, Bob didn't know how to handle that we had the manager come into our bungalow. That was always a rule, you know: don't bring anyone into our place. And Bob found out because I left the Tylenol bottle on the coffee table. At first, he was just kind of upset and his morning was starting out normal. Then he started asking over and over again why we did it, why we let her in. Like he was starting to obsess over it, and every time he asked us why, you could tell he was getting angrier and angrier. And I didn't have the right answers, and K.C. was in so much pain that he kept moaning, which was making Bob mad too. I had never seen K.C.'s teeth hurt him that bad. Then Bob started in on what a failure K.C. was. How he was a disappointment. He was yelling about how his mom didn't want him. And I just—"

Braide went to interrupt me, move me to our next rehearsed question, but Hagger stood and spoke out. "Your Honor, I stipulated to a narrative. I'm entitled to it. I'd like for Mr. Roberts to finish his answer."

The judge leaned toward me and in a soft voice told me to continue. When I looked away from her, I knew not to look toward Braide. I was nervous his glare would shut me up. Instead, I locked my eyes on the Kleenex box in front of me and tried to give the details that described the memory. The words flowed out with no effort.

"When I saw that Bob was getting angrier, I tried to take the blame so he wouldn't take his rage out on K.C. but it wasn't working. Bob wouldn't stop his focus on K.C. It's like he was mad that K.C. was sick and his anger started focusing on that part of K.C.'s body that was causing the problem. I just remember K.C. rocking back and forth with his eyes closed, holding the wet towel to his mouth, moaning and not answering. And Bob started pacing and pumping his fists harder and harder, and that's when he lunged forward, fist back"—without even meaning to, I drew my fist back, imitating the image I could see in my head—"and with all his weight he punched K.C. in the mouth. I heard the jaw break but I couldn't run to K.C. I tried to get up and go to him, but I stumbled because Bob had duct-taped my hands together, you know, with silver duct tape, to teach me a lesson about leaving the bungalow. And when I stumbled, the coffee table was in my way and kept me from seeing K.C., but I heard him cry out at first and then his screams became a muffled sound like he had buried his head into the pillow. I wanted to run to him so bad."

The court allowed me a pause. I wondered if we all had the same vision and were taking the time to feel K.C.'s pain. I looked around. I had more to say. I didn't hold the words back. "That's how close we were, K.C. and I. When Bob would do whatever he had to do to one of us, it didn't matter because the other one was waiting nearby to make us whole again. But when Bob broke K.C.'s jaw, I couldn't get over to K.C. to put him back together, and I felt like I was letting him down, you know. I kind of feel that way right now ..." I took in a deep breath. Looked up to Braide. He wasn't mad, but he clearly was ready to move on to the next subject. Not me, though. I wanted to stay with K.C.

(57)

Hagger didn't recognize how Braide jumped in on the next pause I had in my testimony. I knew his intent was to bring my thoughts back to our scripted question and answers. "Tyler, I'd like to jump ahead now to when the FBI found you at the trailer." He was successful. I knew exactly where Braide was in our plotted out testimony. "Tell us, based on your knowledge and understanding, what happened that night."

I knew what answer he was waiting for. "Well, my best friend at the time was Sam Ricksen. We both went to Clarkson High. It was our junior year. And the night before all this started, Sam came out to our trailer because he wanted me to take Bob's van and give him a ride to this drug dealer's house. It was his mom's boyfriend who knew the dealer, some guy who would take prescription pills and do basically a swap for weed. Anyway, on the way back, we got arrested. I was fingerprinted and booked under the name of Landon Starker. I didn't have an ID or anything. I just gave them my name. And in a weird way, that's who I was, you know, Landon Starker. I mean, I wasn't pretending to be Landon Starker. It's just that, like, over time, I became Bob's son and started living in the moment as Landon."

"And so you were released from jail, what, early that morning?"

"Yeah. They released me to Bob, who they thought was my dad, and gave me a date to come back to juvenile court. And the police, when we checked out, were giving Bob a hard time for not having the right paperwork for me. I wasn't really listening, but they did tell Bob that I was fingerprinted and would be checked for other crimes. I remember thinking that Bob was calmer than I thought he would be. And besides, I didn't really care about them checking me for other crimes because I didn't have any."

"And Tyler, fast-forward for us to that night. When did you first learn that the FBI was on the property?"

"Well, I was really tired from everything that happened with Sam and the cops, so I went to bed early, which I hated to do—early, like, I mean, before Bob." Out of the corner of my eye, I saw my dad toss his pen down on the desk next to his writing pad and look away. My instinct was to yell out in frustration how I hated when people didn't want to hear the ugly parts. Beating abuses were talkable stuff, you know. But bedroom abuses, when people asked what they were like, they didn't really want an answer. They wanted to hear vague words like "uncomfortable" or "you have to learn how to survive." I wanted to react to my father, but Braide chimed in, trying to keep us on track. "Go on, Tyler. What else do you remember? When did you learn the FBI was on site?"

"I woke up like two hours later because I heard something outside, but by the time I stood up, the doors were busted open and the FBI agents were everywhere. I didn't know what was going on, and I didn't see Bob anywhere. I was dazed at first, kinda still half-asleep, and I remember looking around thinking how weird it was that the gun that Bob kept on our nightstand was gone and that the TV was off. I was asking stuff but no one was telling me anything. I was really confused. And, I mean, I know that may sound strange to people. Like, I've been asked before, how could I not know what's going on. It would be obvious that the FBI was there because I was kidnapped, but that's not how the mind works … or my mind, I guess. After years of being Landon, that's who I became. That's the only way I can explain it."

"I think you're doing perfectly well." Braide flashed me his confident attorney smile and then moved on to the next question. "So you got to the FBI offices here in Omaha, and what did you learn?"

"I was in the room forever, not knowing what was going on. I thought honestly it had something to do with Sam Ricksen and a handgun that the cops found in his backpack. Then Drysdale came in, the FBI agent, and one of the first things he started asking about was who lived in the trailer and what did I know about the spare bedroom. At first, I was confused, you know, because in a way I had totally ignored the spare bedroom in the trailer. I mean, if someone asked me how many bedrooms we had, I'd almost say 'one' because I forgot about the spare bedroom. And then Drysdale wouldn't let up asking about who else lived in the trailer with us, and it's like I didn't have control over what I was saying. K.C.'s name escaped my mouth. But the problem was that I didn't have a recollection of K.C. moving into the trailer with us or ever living there. I just knew that I came home to the trailer on the first day, and I didn't know what happened to K.C."

Braide followed up with a question right away. "And did you learn at that time, on the first day of living in the trailer, whatever happened to K.C.?"

"No. I mean, I remember things just like Bob testified. It was the first day of moving into the trailer and I was walking up to the front door, and when I started to turn the doorknob, Bob yanked it open and pulled me inside. I could tell he was mad. I remember crawling away, trying to hide from him. And he kept yelling, 'What happened to K.C.?' But I didn't have an answer. I was confused, actually. And I do remember seeing the blood on Bob's pants. But the scariest thing was seeing that Bob was getting angrier, like his rage was already at the uncontrollable level. He was yelling with so much force that I couldn't make sense of his words. He was angrier than he was when we left the bungalow. And my nerves were paralyzing me because I didn't know how to handle it."

"And do you remember anything else about that day?"

"Yeah. Like I said, I didn't know what I could say to Bob because he was so mad. But I was standing against the refrigerator, holding my hands up, kind of like, you know, saying to him, 'I surrender.' And that's when he turned and grabbed a rifle from the gun rack that he hung that morning and …"

It seemed like my pause after the word "and" lasted forever.

Braide didn't catch it, though.

During that pause, I saw in my mind Bob hanging the gun rack earlier that morning. I wasn't repeating Bob's testimony. I was testifying to a new memory. I put myself on autopilot, spewing out the answer Braide was expecting from me, but behind my eyes, memories were rewinding, replaying. I remembered being there when Bob hung the gun rack that morning. My skinny eleven-year-old self was sitting on the floor, cross-legged, trying to be happy for Bob, glad that he was unpacking his rifles. When Bob would turn away to hammer a nail into the wall, I'd look over at K.C., who was on the couch drenched in his fever sweat. K.C.'s stare was blank. His pain was beyond expression.

If I had been able to jump into my mind, I would have been able to touch the moving boxes stacked near me, the one on the bottom with K.C.'s name written on it, another one off to the left where Bob's handguns and cleaning supplies were packed.

"Tyler?" It was Braide's voice, paying no attention to the fact that my mind had drifted.

"Yeah."

"Please tell us what happened after Bob grabbed the rifle from the gun rack."

Part of me wanted Braide to catch what he and my dad would call a mistake in my testimony. He didn't, though. Instead, he waited there behind the podium for me to rattle off the words he was expecting. I did just that. "What happened after that was that I passed out from the pain of having the butt of the rifle shoved into my ribs."

"And Tyler, before I move onto my next topic, I'd like to ask if you can identify these exhibits." Braide walked over to a stack of documents. He hadn't shown me the documents before, but I knew what they related to. In our courthouse meetings talking about how Braide's questioning would go, he said he was going to show me some papers that would indicate how close K.C. and I were. With so much going on, my curious mind didn't catch on, and I never questioned what documents they would be. But when Braide walked toward me with the papers in his hands, an element of surprise arrested me. They were crayon-colored pictures, and they carried with them more details than any still photo.

"Tyler, these were recovered from the boxes in the spare room that had K.C.'s name written on them. Do you recognize them?"

I nodded. I reached my hands out slowly and brought the colored pictures before me. I lost my breath. It was the first time I had touched something that came from the trailer.

I kept nodding.

"Can you tell us who created these drawings?" It was Braide's voice.

In a whisper, I said, "I did. I colored these. I remember drawing these." I pulled out of the stack the one that meant the most. It had an orange sunshine in the top right corner because K.C. and I lost the yellow crayon. There were two stick figures riding bikes. It was my way of drawing K.C. and me. There were black-and-white spotted cows in the background with "Moo" written in the cartoon balloons to give the picture life. I drew the cows because I wanted to take K.C. outside and give him hope to make it through his pain. And in big letters on the front, in forest green crayon, I had written, "Get Well."

I kept running my index finger over the waxy texture of the orange sun.

I gulped.

I was in my own world, even though I remained surrounded by everyone in the courtroom. "Yeah, we lost the yellow crayon."

"What's that, Tyler?"

I looked up slowly to Braide. "Huh?"

"What did you just say?"

"Oh, yeah, I remember these pictures." I looked down again at the grass sprigs all along the bottom of the paper. I remembered mixing the dark greens with the light ones, trying to give K.C. a reality of what it was like outside the trailer, outside our new home. I wanted him to walk around and see, breathe the fresh air. I let the picture transport me. I dropped back in time to a point when the crayon picture was only half finished. I was coloring it on the floor in the trailer next to K.C., who was on the couch. I was so nervous for K.C. He hadn't been talking, only soft moans, not loud enough to catch Bob's ears. I was scared and couldn't stop the tears. I had slept all night on the floor with my eleven-year-old hand reached up and resting on K.C.'s forearm.

With my mind back in the courtroom, I looked closer at the picture, at the wheel on one of the bicycles, and there they were …

… *dried tear stains.* I remembered smearing the droplets away from the picture and how the crayon lines didn't smear, but the paper warped and discolored.

It was Braide talking to me. "Tyler, just set the colored picture off to the side there." His request wasn't that simple, though. I couldn't let go. I pushed the picture into the corner of the witness stand desk, but I kept my hand on it. I couldn't leave it.

"I just have a few more questions, Tyler. When you came to after passing out from the pain of the rifle hitting you, where were you?"

I looked up from the crayon drawing. No one noticed that my mind was still focusing on it. My mouth answered but I was staying in the past. "Oh. Yes. I was in the back bedroom of the trailer, but the door was locked from the outside. I couldn't get out. And I could hear that Bob was moving stuff around in the spare bedroom."

"How long did Bob lock you in the bedroom for?"

"All night."

"And the spare bedroom, was there anything different about it the next day, when Bob let you out of the back bedroom?"

I looked down at the crayon picture, my open hand still resting on it. I lifted my head toward Braide. "Yeah, the carpet had been ripped out and the moving boxes that were in the living room with K.C.'s name on them, they were stacked in the spare room."

"Last question, Tyler. When Bob let you out of the room, did he ever tell you what happened to K.C.?"

"No, we never talked about it. He refused to ever mention K.C.'s name after that."

I ran my index finger over the tear smearing. It told me something. It confirmed that I loved K.C., he was my brother. The feeling of the warped paper told me I felt what he felt. We cared for each other, trying to be one another's savior. My body jolted from a bolt of emotions that flooded in.

"Those are all the questions I have, Tyler. Thank you." Braide closed his notebook and made his walk back to the table where my father was sitting. The courtroom activity went into slow motion. I pulled the crayon picture closer to me. I stared at the wax lines, at the colorful letters. I begged for the drawing to speak to me.

Hagger stood. Stepped to the podium.

I lifted my head. The courtroom sounds weren't coming into focus. People's movements were blurring. And to everyone in the courtroom, it appeared as if my eyes were fixed on Hagger. *But they weren't.* I was looking at the progression of lost memories that flooded into my mind. I was full of emotions: saddened by the reality of what was being disclosed yet mixed with relief that the truth was speaking.

Hagger's lips moved, and although his voice remained a million miles away, when it hit the mark, I answered immediately.

"Tyler, did you kill Kennedy Charles Nelson?"

"Yes, I believe I did."

(58)

Before the last word escaped my mouth, chaos broke out. My dad yelled my name. Slammed his hand down on the table. Stood.

I looked away and murmured, "K.C. kept telling me he wanted to leave."

Braide's chair flew back. His booming voice drowned out the stunned shufflings that came from the courtroom audience. "Your Honor! Your Honor!"

My mother gasped for air and screamed, "No, Tyler, you don't know what you're talking about." Her face turned to my dad. "Dale, stop him!" Then she whipped around to Braide, clasped her hands. She was pleading. Crying. Braide's hand went to her shoulder as he yelled out to the judge, "Objection, Your Honor!"

I brought my stare to Hagger's eyes. I focused on his lips moving. "Tyler, what did you just say?" I didn't answer, but I created a glass tunnel between him and me. I needed the silent space to contemplate the consequences of the truth that pressed against my lips.

Hagger repeated his question again. "Tyler, please, what did you say a second ago?"

My jaw remained clenched. My upper and lower teeth locked together so as to trap my words. Braide's yelling jolted my body. "Your Honor! Objection. I move to strike the witness's utterance!"

I increased my concentration. Leaned my head forward, trying to shorten the distance between Hagger and myself. I wanted to obscure my peripheral vision so as to ignore the emotions I saw my parents and Braide wearing. The judge moved toward the microphone. "Mr. Braide, you better have a valid objection, and I certainly can't think what it would be. Otherwise, be seated—now!"

The noises settled. I felt my shoulders drop, my chest relax. But my vocal cords remained taut. I inhaled, exhaled, tried to relax my jaw. Then

I cleared my throat, proving that I could control my words, proving that ... *I have a voice.*

"Tyler, you said something just a minute ago. Could you repeat that for us?" Hagger pressed.

I heard the exhales of others. I saw, in the distance, scrunched-up tissues reaching for wet eyes. The squeaks of chairs died down. The courtroom fell into silence. I was being given time to think. My mind pulsed with snippets from the last year of my life: FBI car rides, Drysdale, linoleum floors, trashcans, Tracie's office, elevator panics, bathroom anxieties. Bob living inside me.

Hagger's lips moved again, but my mind was talking too loud. The voice in my head asked me, *Do I stay where I am, who I am? Tyler Roberts, Little League big brother, grocery store clerk with Palmer talk memories,* National Geographic *subscriptions, Emmie and Billy Blake's Pizza memories? A son?* I could stay. I could freeze in time and not say another word.

The judge's voice demanded I make a decision. "Tyler, can you tell us what you remember of the day Kennedy Charles Nelson was killed?"

I nodded. The self-worth that I had been nurturing for the last year imbued me with confidence. I sat tall. I wanted to tell them. I wanted to be free. *Speak loud. Be heard.* And I wanted K.C. to be heard through me.

It was the judge again asking for an answer. She had been waiting long enough. Everyone had. I started to speak. "I didn't really sleep the night before, you know, the first night in the trailer. I was worried about K.C. being okay because he was in so much pain. I kept myself sitting up, like leaning against the couch where K.C. was lying. And Bob was still mad at K.C. from the manager coming into the bungalow. It's like he wouldn't look at K.C. or talk to him. K.C. didn't exist to Bob, which—like, Bob did that to us sometimes. He'd put us away, out of sight, out of mind, until he was ready to deal with us. But I recall how I just wanted to make sure I was right there next to K.C. that night in case he asked for anything.

"I remember I'd start to fall asleep sitting up, but then I'd hear something, and when I opened my eyes and looked at K.C., I realized it was him, crying in his sleep, like a moaning sound. I just sat there in the dark because that's all I knew how to do, just looking at him, wishing I could change things. But at the same time, I was afraid of Bob, like if I tried to help K.C. again, you know, find the Tylenol bottle that was packed in one of the boxes, Bob might make K.C. suffer even more. All I could do was sit there. And then by morning things started to get weird."

I realized that my testimony had stopped and my face fell into a blank stare. My glance traveled the room. The faces of my mother, my father, the bailiff, all the strangers … everyone seemed to have this blank stare looking back at me. I let my head drop down and my mouth hover over the microphone. "And then when the sun started coming up, that's when K.C. really started talking about it and telling me it was the right thing to do. Every time I asked if he was okay, he just kept saying he wanted to leave and that it would be the right thing … you know, to help him leave. I knew what he was talking about because he had said that stuff before.

"I mean, sometimes when we got into trouble with Bob and he would yell at us with the gun, waving it at us, afterward K.C. would tell me it would have been better if Bob just ended everything right then and there. And I would always say, 'But what if Bob didn't get rid of us both, you know, not use the gun on us at the same time? Then one of us would be alone with Bob.' And that's what I started saying that morning when he would talk about wanting to go. I told him, 'You can't leave me alone with Bob. Everything's going to get better. Just wait.'

"But all he was doing was shaking his head at my words, like I was wrong, that things weren't going to get better. And when he kept saying that and I would see his jaw so swollen and red, it was hard to tell him he was wrong. I was only eleven but I felt deep down things weren't going to get better, you know. I really didn't think they would."

"Tyler?" It was Hagger bringing me back to the moment. "What's going through your mind?"

I couldn't say the words while keeping eye contact with him. Instead, I focused on the crayon picture still in front of me. "There was something about K.C.'s eyes that was different that morning. It was like K.C. wasn't inside himself anymore. That might not make sense, but he looked empty. And I remember I was so worried about it that I started talking about memories, you know, like setting up our tents in the living room or making tuna-fish sandwiches. I was trying to see if hearing the memories would somehow prove that he was still inside himself. But he wouldn't, he wouldn't talk about anything. He just kept moving his head back and forth slowly, saying, 'No, I'm not that way anymore. I don't want to be here. I have to go.' And the way his eyes looked at me, I saw that a part of him was already gone. It was … it was like his body just wanted to catch up with that piece of him that had already left."

"And Tyler," added Hagger, calm and collected, utterly devoid of emotion, "do you remember when Bob woke up that morning?"

"Yeah. He wouldn't help."

"Help with what?"

"He was ignoring K.C., acting like he wasn't there. He wouldn't even look at him. And I remember when Bob came into the living room, after he woke up, I was already drawing the 'get well' picture, the crayon picture, and Bob stepped on it when he walked by. All he would talk about is where to hang his gun rack, and I was too afraid I would make him mad if I talked about K.C. I remember looking back and forth between Bob and K.C. and trying to act happy when Bob looked my way because that's what it was like with him, you know. As long as your mood was his mood, you had a better chance of things going okay. But deep down, I was nervous about K.C., and every time Bob turned his back to me to hang the gun rack, I looked over at K.C."

I reached down and grabbed the crayon picture still in front of me on the witness desk. I brought it closer to me. With it in my hand, I traced over the area where the paper warped from my streaming tears that morning. I remembered how the tears fell when Bob's back faced me and how my hand immediately reached down to wipe the wetness away, trying to erase the evidence of sadness, fearful of what would come our way if Bob turned to see my true attention was focused on K.C. and not him.

"Tyler?"

I gasped for air. "Yeah?"

"What else do you remember?"

"Well, Bob had to leave to check on the workers. He was going to be coming back soon, because he wanted to do the school thing for me. And when Bob left the trailer, I was showing K.C. the drawing, this one, the crayon one, and I was trying to say things like maybe Bob would let us have bikes like the ones I drew. But K.C. wouldn't listen, and he'd just shake his head.

"Then I thought maybe having the TV on would help, you know, to get his mind off all the things he was saying. So I started trying to get that to work, and that's when Evelyn Barker came into the trailer looking for Bob. She knocked first but then just walked in and stood in the living room. When I saw her standing there, all these worried feelings came back, like I screwed things up again and I let the manager at the Cordia Bungalows in our place. My heart started racing. I couldn't hear anything she said. I just wanted her to get out of the trailer because all I could think about was Bob's rage at the bungalow and how if he saw Evelyn in the trailer, he would lose it again.

"And when she left, I couldn't calm myself down. I kept saying out loud, 'What are we going to do? What are we going to do?' Every sound in the trailer made my heart jump like Bob was walking into the trailer, and he was going to be furious, and I didn't know what he would do to us knowing that someone was in our trailer.

"And the other thing was that I knew Evelyn Barker saw K.C. when she came in, and Bob told me when I met her the day before not to tell her about K.C., you know, because she wouldn't want a sick kid in the trailer. So I was panicking, trying to think how I could explain everything to Bob so he wouldn't go crazy like he did at the bungalow, because she might go and say something to Bob about being in the trailer, and then he would know, even if I didn't tell him.

"The only thing I could think of doing was to put K.C. in the spare bedroom so when Bob came home and asked why I let Evelyn in there, I could be like, 'But she didn't see K.C. because he was in the other room,' and maybe that would be okay and Bob would stay calm.

"I tried to get K.C. worried about Bob getting angry too, but he didn't care anymore. He just didn't care about what Bob would do. And he didn't have the strength to walk into the spare bedroom because he was so sick."

At that point, I wanted my mind to hit a brick wall. I wanted the tunnel of memories I was standing in to close in on me, to block me off from the past and future. I wanted to be able to stop talking because I was afraid of reliving what I felt was about to come. I was searching for a way to detach and tell of the memory without seeing it ... hearing it ... feeling it. But it doesn't work that way—at least not for me—*when you live it, you relive it.*

"Tyler, can you go on? How did you get K.C. to the spare bedroom?"

"The sleeping bag. I dragged it. And when I pulled him off the couch, I was trying to be gentle, you know, but I caused him so much pain. I can hear his cries in my mind right now. When he hit the floor, he didn't have control over his cries. He was howling. But I kept staring at the front door like Bob was going to come in any second. I was trying to save us from Bob, that's all.

"And when I got him into the spare bedroom, K.C. stopped the crying but I kept hearing it, and I felt so bad like I was the one who hurt him. I remember squatting down and I was leaning against the wall next to K.C., and every muscle in my body was tense, and I kept rocking back and forth trying not to hear K.C.'s words play over in my mind, telling me that he wanted to leave, that he wanted to leave right then, right there. And at the same time, I was begging into the empty air, 'Please don't let Bob know that Evelyn saw K.C.' And then I don't know how it happened or why it happened but K.C. started making sense."

It was my first chest heave I had on the witness stand. A piece of the emotional pain that had been living in me since that day escaped my body. It was a moan, a black cloud of sadness that crept up my throat and out my mouth. No tears, although I knew there was a sloshing ocean of them buried deep inside me.

Hagger asked the question. "What do you mean, Tyler, that K.C. started making sense?"

"K.C. kept saying … begging, 'Just go get it. I can't be here anymore. Help me get out of here.' And sometimes his words slurred because of the pain. And I tried to say that I couldn't. I tried over and over again to say, 'No, let's not leave each other,' but then it got confusing."

"What got confusing?"

"K.C. and I were like brothers. We cared so much for each other. And it got confusing because if you love someone so much and they trust you, it seemed like the right thing to do, you know, to give them what they wanted, help them get out of their pain."

I tried to calm the emotional turbulence stirring and expanding within my chest. I froze my lungs, refused to exhale, trying to contain the sadness until I could anticipate the depths of it. But my body tricked me. Silent tears sneaked into my eyes. I looked around the courtroom, not at anyone in particular. I just wanted to take in the reality, tell myself where I was and why I was there. And besides, if I were looking for anyone, it would have been K.C. because I still missed him.

"And Tyler, did you go get the handgun that you packed when you moved from the bungalow?"

I moved my head.

"Is that a yes, Tyler?"

"Yes, I went and got it. And it was his look when he saw the gun that told me it was the right thing to do. All of a sudden, he had life in his eyes, and he reached up to motion for me to come over to him with the gun. I kept trying to say to myself, *It's okay. He wants to leave because he's going to another place.* And he kept using the words 'Please, please,' and 'Thank you'; he was saying them over and over because he wouldn't be able to say them later, after I helped him. And I don't know why for sure ... *but I did it."*

"You fired the gun?"

"Yeah. And the last thing I remember was looking at him and the emptiness in his eyes was back, and I knew right away that he was really gone." I started to sob. "I was trying to make him happier, in a weird way." My words were scrambled. "I was trying to help him get to another place. He wanted to leave so bad. I thought I was helping him." My chest heaved. My shoulders shuddered. My sobs echoed off the courtroom walls. "He was my brother and I loved him ... *I love him now."*

Those were the last words I spoke on the witness stand.

Moments later, maybe seconds, I felt a hand on the back of my neck. I looked over with an expression of exhaustion. I saw my mother, my father. They took me in their arms, held me until my sobbing quieted. It was just the three of us. Their only words to me were that they loved me. That day, right then and there, they loved me, Tyler Roberts, who was almost seventeen. They loved the Tyler who went missing at seven. They loved the Landon Starker who was eleven and was trying to help his brother get to a better place. And most importantly, to my shattered self, they told me that they loved the man I was becoming. A person who, when he remembered the truth, he spoke it.

EPILOGUE

I made it to Pike's Peak for the photography trip that summer.

When the courtroom settled down and I was sitting back at Braide's side, the judge retired to her chamber, telling us she'd be out shortly with my sentencing. It took her less than two hours. She released me to my parents and ordered me to remain on probation until I was twenty-one. I was to undergo a battery of psychological tests, much like the ones Dr. Williams gave me, and remain in counseling while on probation, which I did, and voluntarily stayed in for two years beyond the court-ordered time.

I was on track with my life when the trial started, but it's true that the repressed memory of K.C.'s killing took me back a few steps. For months, I had to remind myself that at the time I fired the gun, I was looking at my abused world through eleven-year-old eyes. At that time, in that moment, I was trying to do the right thing. As a man, I didn't think I would ever fully forgive myself for it, but I understood it and moved on from it.

I passed my GED test a month after the trial and spent two-and-a-half years enrolled in all the photography, geology, geography, and cultural history classes that Colorado Springs Community College offered. I didn't care about the math and English requirements to be able to transfer to the university as my dad hoped I would one day do. Instead, I took the classes that developed me and my interests.

When I turned eighteen, I didn't buy the car that I was saving for. Instead, I continued to save so I could afford taking unpaid intern jobs for the National Geographic Society, which finally happened after applying eight times. My first unpaid internship was about six years ago. It was an office job helping to organize the gear for an in-the-field photo shoot. I stayed in touch with one of the photography assistants that I met, Mark Faus. After many unpaid intern jobs for the Society, which eroded my savings, Faus got me in on my first in-the-field photo shoot. I was an assistant to an assistant on his crew, which researched and photographed endangered species. I got paid. I got a passport. And I fell in love with the giant armadillos of Uruguay.

When I made it out of the country, my first postcard went to Palmer. I asked him to say "Hi" to Tracie for me, who calls me at least twice a year. I mentioned also that if he saw Drysdale to give him a wink and a friendly smile from me. Thoughts of Palmer and our talks entered my mind often. I still had the world map that he gave me. When I started traveling regularly with Faus and the crew, I'd keep the map with me and marked the places I had been. But fearful it was becoming too worn and tattered, I put it back in the top drawer of my nightstand.

Right after my twenty-seventh birthday, Faus told me he got a better job and recommended me for his old position as lead photography assistant. I got the job. It paid well. And now I have a mortgage and live on my own. I still don't have a car, though, but not because I couldn't afford it. It's that I'm usually only in town for a few weeks before I go out again on the next photo shoot. And when I am in town, my mom loves to help me out with rides. It's her way to visit with me.

My dad is still the intense guy who had my life planned out for me, but when he saw my first published illustration with my name under it in print, he framed it and hung it in his office.

I never heard again from my best friend Sam Ricksen. At times, I wanted to reach out and know what happened to him, but I was painfully afraid I'd find him where I left him: with no dad and a non-existent mother.

And Emmie. She still made me feel like I did on that night sitting in the car outside her parents' house. She stayed with her interest in robotics and went to work for a design company in Colorado Springs that developed the machinery pharmacists use to count out prescription drugs. She still talks a lot and loves to talk a lot with my mom. That's how the question of marriage and kids always comes up way too often. I'm not sure that either of those adventures would work for me.

I've been out of counseling for several years, and honestly, I would have to say that I reached a point where I wanted to be done with therapy for good. I liked my life just as it was, even though I knew there was a part of me that still feared the trust it takes to have a wife. When the day comes and Emmie says that the status quo isn't working for her, I guess I'll have a decision to make. I hope I have the courage to make the right choice. She'll make a beautiful bride.

Evan. He graduated high school and was accepted to a university in Boston. When I was at his graduation, I was so proud to see him walk across the stage. I looked over at my mom and dad, parental pride beaming from their faces. When the ceremony came to an end, the seniors threw their hats in the air, the crowd broke out into a cheer, and I yelled out Evan's name as loud as I could. He turned around, hearing his older brother, and gave me a thumbs-up.

The thought occurred to me in that moment that I was acting like one of those parents from that eighth grade Back to School Night, and I liked it. I sacrificed a photo shoot of the endangered Rodrigues fruit bat in Ireland, and I'm glad I did. I liked being surrounded by the other parents and family members, knowing that we were all there to show we cared.

After the graduation ceremony, family and friends headed over to my parents' house for a barbecue. I had planned on only staying for an hour or two, because Emmie and I were taking a road trip into Kansas. The two hours turned into four, and I was still having fun. I was where I belonged.

I glanced over and saw Emmie coming my way. The sight of her prolonged my smile. "Tyler, your mom wants us to wait until the morning to take off because it's getting late." Any time Emmie told me what my mom wanted us to do, I never knew if she wanted it too or if she was simply relaying the message.

I reached for her hand and asked, "What about you? Do you still want to leave tonight? Leavenworth is a nine-hour drive. I'd like to make it into Kansas, get a motel, and get back on the road early tomorrow. The visiting hours are only 8:00 to 3:00."

She sat on my lap and threw her arm over my shoulder. "Yeah, I agree, babe. But we should probably head out soon so your mom doesn't worry that we're on the road too late." She had a good point.

I looked around for Evan. He was off in the corner with his buddies, laughing over what they called "an epic senior prank." He sensed my eyes on him, looked up and waved, knowing he'd see me in a few days.

I gave Emmie a gentle kiss on the cheek. I was glad that she was keeping me on track. The road trip was something I needed for myself. I broke away from the group I was talking to about my upcoming assignment in the Sahara Desert and looked around for my mom. Goodbyes weren't easy when it came to her or her friends, and she was surrounded by a lot of them. One consequence of having a mom who gabbed a lot was that she had friends who gabbed, too.

About an hour later, Emmie and I were in the car, and my dad waved us off with a simple, "See you guys when you get back."

If you didn't know that Leavenworth was a federal prison, you'd think you were walking up to a pretentious building on Pennsylvania Avenue in Washington DC. At least from a distance, that was my first impression. The doom on the walls became apparent the closer I got, though. I parked as far away as I could. I wanted the extra walking time to clear my mind and understand exactly why I was going to see Bob.

Emmie stayed back at the hotel in Kansas City. It wasn't her choice not to come with me. It was more that I didn't want her innocence contaminated by Bob's presence. And besides, she knew everything I had been through, and could recite the same details that lived in my mind.

The visiting room was like a larger FBI interview room, with more tables and chairs and the addition of vending machines along the back wall. The first sight I had as the guard buzzed me into the room was children: some happy and skipping around the tables, their fathers in khaki prison outfits, smiling; others sat in isolation off to the side while their mothers whispered who knows what to their husbands.

The room was full.

The guard who kept order in the visitor's room looked my way as soon as the door shut behind me. He gave me a casual lift of the hand that was meant to guide my way. I turned in the direction he indicated, but my focus was to make sure I didn't run into any of the children, who were darting back and forth from the vending machines to their family visiting tables.

One little girl in cute blonde pigtails ran into my leg. She looked up at me, scared to confront my reaction. I leaned down, braced her shoulder, and gave her a smile that hopefully said she didn't bother me. I looked up with the smile still on my face, and by accident I locked eyes with Bob.

Thin.

Old.

I quickly calculated his age in my mind. He was nearing sixty. His skin coloring had a grayish hue to it. But there he was, sitting with his back to the corner, alone at a round table. I dropped my smile, slightly irritated with myself that he possibly may have thought the smile was for him.

I pulled out a chair and sat.

Silence.

He leaned back in his plastic chair. No more beer belly. No beard or mustache. Still the long hair, but thinned out and in a ponytail. He said the first words. "Nice collared, preppy shirt." He chuckled with sarcasm.

I looked down, pinched the fabric between my fingers. "Just a polo shirt." I caught myself. I didn't like it that my reaction was to defend myself. I leaned forward, clasped my hands, and rested my elbows on my knees.

Silence.

He lowered his eyelids, removed any sign of emotion from his face. But the look no longer carried with it the threat of an unknown, impending punishment. He broke the silence again. "I didn't have to let you come visit, you know. I could have denied your request."

I didn't twitch a muscle when I responded, "I understand that. Do you want a thank you?"

He shifted in his seat subtly. I just stared at him. He was no longer the Bob that I had to kick out of my mind so many times for so many years. I compared our differences. I was taller than him now. I had more strength. I sat quietly, relishing the reality that he was no longer a part of me.

I felt something soft brush against my left arm. I turned my head in reaction to the feeling. It was the little blonde girl who'd run into me by accident. She smiled. I smiled back. Her father commanded that she get back to their table. She was probably seven or eight—the age that I was when Bob named me Landon Starker. Like that little girl, I was small and vulnerable then. The epiphany didn't stir in me any unresolved rage. I took it as a sign that I didn't have any. The little girl ran off. I wiped the smile away and brought my eyes back to Bob. That's when he asked, "So what did you come here for, kid?"

I shrugged. "It wasn't to see you."

"What do you mean?" He crossed his arms.

"That's it." I inhaled, fully expanded my lungs. Exhaled. My body was relaxed. "I wanted to know if you had any control over me still." I looked over at a window in the room, the metal bars on the outside, then brought my eyes back to Bob, and in a conversational tone said, "And you don't."

He leaned forward, resting his elbows on the table. He rocked his head back and forth slowly. "Is that right?" He had this thing about him where he'd take his saliva and suck it through the crack of his two front teeth, making a smacking sound. When he did it, my mind rushed with an image of him in his recliner at the trailer, finishing a TV dinner, and barking at me to come get the tray so he didn't have to get up. The memory had details but no emotions attached it.

"You know, *Landon,* I've been thinking, and I've gotta question for you." His voice dropped and his cold-blooded eyes tried to instill fear and arouse insecurities in me. "Don't you think the brave thing would've been to kill me and save K.C., if he was the true brother you said he was?"

I went to correct him and say, "My name is Tyler," but the urge left immediately. He had a valid question, actually. I had wondered many times in the past why it was I didn't use the gun on Bob. The answer came easily, though: *I'm not a killer.*

He didn't like my silence. He sat up straight and leaned away from the table. "You don't have an answer, huh?" He chuckled softly. "I know the answer. It's because you were never strong enough like me or K.C. You were the coward."

Our eyes locked. I didn't move or shuffle my body around. I kept his stare, kept my attention on him. I wanted to hear whatever he said, to prove to myself he had no hold on me. His voice rose as he added, "Yeah, that's right, I knew from the day I got you, you were a coward. You think you're so much better than everyone, don't you, with your collared shirt, and your church-going mommy and daddy." He slammed his open hand on the table.

My body didn't move.

I heard the footsteps of a guard coming our way. "Inmate Starker …"

Bob leaned into me, yelling, "Answer me, damn it! You're a coward, aren't you? Aren't you!" The guard went to reach for him, but Bob reacted quickly with a nod of the head. He stood, ready to leave. The guard backed away and gave him some space, I guess to walk away with dignity, but in my eyes, he didn't have any. He took his first step, turned around, and spat on the table in front of me. "You were a nothing the day you were born. I saw it in your eyes when I took you."

He left.

I sat there with my back turned away from him. I didn't feel the need to turn around and confront him or yell out words in my defense. *He wasn't worth the energy.*

Emmie texted me the address of a pizza place near our hotel and said she'd meet me there. She said the place reminded her of Billy Blake's, our old hangout as teenagers. I walked through the door and saw her immediately. Took a seat across from her. She knew not to bombard me with questions.

We sat there. The waiter brought menus. My mind drifted to thinking about which pizza toppings would be a good combo for us. That's when I felt Emmie's hand caress mine. I lowered the menu from my face, looked over at her. She looked at me. "I love you, Tyler."

My eyes drifted. The pizza place was crowded. It did look a little like Billy Blake's.

The judge's last words before we left the courthouse rang in my ear. "Mr. Roberts, I would like to commend you for speaking the truth at a time when it appeared to be an option."

That thought left, and I focused again on what Emmie and I should order.

Then a piece of advice from Tracie ran through my mind. It was right before I met my parents, and I was asking her why it felt so weird to call them "Mom" and "Dad." Her explanation stuck with me. She said I was probably afraid to call them that because it would indicate that I wanted a close relationship, which involved trusting them to offer it back to me.

It made me ask myself, *How do you ever fully trust another human being to give back the love you put in?* I think because of my experiences, I just can't ever know that for sure. There's always going to be some risk of rejection, unless I chose not to love my one and only.

"Emmie?"

"Yeah." She looked at me right away, smiling her pretty smile.

"I love you, too."

Afterword

As a psychologist and specialist in the aftermath of traumatic experiences, the author has allowed me to comment on the emotional and psychological components touched upon in this book. At the outset I want to say that Dayna Hester has done a good job in this novel to introduce the reader to the world of the abducted individual. She would be the first to say that the story required that she make some accommodations in order for the reader to understand some of the complex themes that such an experience would bring up including: mental confusion, memory loss, loyalty binds, emotional conflicts, and auto-biographical chaos (trying to figure out who you are).

The main character in *Speaking Truths* is not presented as a typical trauma survivor or typical victim of abduction because if he were the story would be nearly impossible to follow or understand. The reason for this is the aftermath of severe trauma, such as those experienced by Landon/Tyler, often leaves the victim in a hopelessly confusing state of not understanding what has happened, who is responsible, and not trusting either his or her perceptions, facts, or feelings about oneself, or the experience. From such a position, the ability to tell a cohesive story of the events outside and inside the individual would be next to impossible. To address this difficulty the author had to accommodate the reader by bringing some level of cohesiveness to the narrative of the protagonist. In essence the reader receives the insights of the author projected onto the abducted individual. This was not only necessary but it was a very good way to invite the reader into the inner world of a person who experienced much more than his ability to cope, and enter the experience of trauma that would be expected to seriously impact the brain and mental and emotional processes.

Everyone is different and traumatic experience is uniquely felt by the individual involved. It is not impossible that Landon/Tyler in the story could have the level of personal insight, self reflection, openness to question what was going on, and sufficient trust to let others into his chaotic inner world. While not impossible, the level of mental functioning and his rapid development of trust in those reaching out to help him portrayed in the book are not typical from my experience. I say this not to be critical of the author or story, but to take the story another step in the process of educating the reader to the profound impacts on the brain of individuals who have experiences like those in this story. Is it typical to forget whole parts of one's life due to a traumatic event? Yes, it is not only typical but nearly universal. Is it possible to cause someone's death, as in the story, as well as experience abduction, sexual abuse, profound neglect and other far too frequent traumatic events in our society and not have any recollections of the details? Once again, this is not only possible but the rule rather than the exception, and the reason is how the brain processes traumatic events.

I will not go into a detailed description of the impact of trauma on the brain here. For someone interested in more detail there are many informative resources and websites including my own www.jaspermountain. org. However I believe a brief description can complement the educational component of *Speaking Truths*.

The brain's primary job is to promote survival. It has amazing capacities to do its job that we are still discovering. The brain will adapt to the environment it finds itself in regardless of how negative or painful. It does this by changing reality, turning off emotional pain, forgetting the most stressful events, altering perceptions, and adapting to situations that never cease to impress trauma specialists. An example that immediately comes to mind are the thousands of young children in Haiti whose parents died in the earthquake, whose schools are destroyed, who do not know where to find food and water from one day to the next, and some of whom are now *restoviches*, or indentured servants or even sex slaves. And yet as I write this, rescue workers find these same children laughing and playing in the midst of destroyed buildings and a crumbling society with little safety, stability, or reason to hope for the future. The human brain can adapt to such overwhelming circumstances as catastrophes, war zones, and the very personal hell of traumatic events.

Adapting to trauma does not come without a price the individual pays. It is not unusual for the memory of whole childhoods to be lost to victims of serious abuse and trauma. While explicit memories can be lost, traumatic memories are never lost, nor do they decrease in intensity over time. The individual may not be aware this is happening either before, during or even after the memory arises. Because these memories are located in the emotional center of the brain, they often cause fear, dread, rage and a host of very strong and very negative feelings that come up whenever and wherever the brain is reminded of traumatic events, or what is called a trigger to a traumatic memory. Unfortunately trauma memories expand to a broad range of triggers, such as a child who has been sexually touched by a male relative may be triggered by being in the proximity of all males. The number of similar issues the traumatized individual must live with or heal from has filled whole books. Some of these impacts are: loss of trust, self-loathing, depression, self-harm, loss of self-regulation, anti-social behavior, aggression, substance abuse, mental disorders, loss of a sense of self, not able to trust perceptions and feelings, along with a profound inability to get close to people or what is referred to as difficulty with attachment to others. The list of impacts goes far beyond this list but suffice it to say they are pervasive and very long lasting. If each of these expected consequences were reflected in *Speaking Truths*, the narrative would have been scattered, negative, chaotic, and I would expect most readers would put the book down in short order. While the author could and needed to make some accommodations to readers for the sake of this story, many traumatized individuals cannot alter their experience on their own to escape the pervasive impacts on their brain. The only path out of this condition is the right type of help, such as the help generally reflected in this book.

There is good news along with the bad news caused by traumatic events. The brain not only is capable of adapting but it wants to survive and thrive. One of the most profound messages coming out of brain research is the capacity of the human brain to heal given the right help and circumstances. Such help may not be universally available but it can be found and must be found to give traumatized individuals not only their lives back, but also the chance at a positive future. *Speaking Truths* reflects a positive improvement overtime with the support and help of not only a supportive although flawed family, a trained therapist, and even a caring janitor. The positive ending of the story is that it is very possible for the victim of an abduction or traumatizing experience to heal and move forward in a positive way, but the brain needs help to do this.

For my part I would like to thank Dayna Hester for her contribution to understand what it is like for a child to go through the events in this story. This book also is an opportunity to communicate events that happen every day in our society and how difficult it is to cope and to live with the results. The number of stranger abductions in the United States is fortunately low, but one is too many. The number of parent abductions is not low, and when the full range of traumatic experiences are included there are millions of children who need understanding, support and the help to heal as reflected in this story. If we do not help these children when they are young, the possibility of an isolated, fearful and painful life is all too predictable. Thanks to decades of research and new information on the human brain, there is help and hope available for the victims of any traumatic experiences. Unless we help these children, not only will they pay the price of a life cut short, but we are all diminished because they are our friends, partners, family members and members of our community. *Speaking Truths* may be a fictional novel but for those who have lived through this or a similar trauma, there is nothing fictional about the aftermath. As in this book, despite the level of the traumatic events or how profound the resulting impact is on the individual, we must reach out to every trauma survivor and give them hope.

Dave Ziegler, Ph.D., L.M.F.T., Psychologist author of *Traumatic Experience and the Brain* and *Beyond Healing, the Path to Personal Contentment after Trauma*.